THE HUMAN COMEDY, VOL. IV:
A Second Home and Other Works
by Honoré de Balzac

Translated from the French
by Clara Bell and George Burnham Ives

Revised and annotated by R.J. Allinson

with Illustrations by Tony Johannot,
Eugène Lampsonius, G. Staal, & Others

Noumena Press
Whately, Massachusetts
www.noumenapress.com

Noumena Classics are published by Noumena Press
Printed by Lightning Source on acid-free paper
Distributed worldwide by Ingram

Version 1.0
ISBN-13: 9780976706267 (paperback)
LCCN: 2008943784 (v.4)

Cover: altered detail of *Une Double Famille* by Tony Johannot
Cover design & interior layout: Rachel Thern

NOUMENA CLASSICS
THE HUMAN COMEDY, VOL. IV:
A Second Home and Other Works
by Honoré de Balzac

A Second Home

Day after day, a poor but beautiful young seamstress toils away by her window, waiting for the mysterious *Monsieur Noir*: a gentleman she hopes will be the answer to all her prayers . . .

Domestic Peace

A ball given at the height of Napoléon's power is the scene of a wager between army comrades to see who will be the first to dance with an unknown lady in blue . . .

Madame Firmiani

Who is Madame Firmiani? Is she a beautiful society lady? A dangerous woman, a siren? Or is she perhaps nothing more than an innocent and charming hostess who gives delightful tea parties? The rich uncle of a young man who has come under her sway is determined to find out . . .

Also included in this volume are *A Study of Woman*, *The Imaginary Mistress*, and *A Daughter of Eve*. Taken together, the six works presented in this volume could be said to share adultery and suspicion as their primary themes.

La Comédie Humaine, left unfinished at the time of Balzac's death, is a vast literary work comprising nearly one hundred short stories, novellas, and novels set in the shadow of the Napoleonic Wars during the Bourbon Restoration and the July Monarchy. Throughout, Balzac utilizes nineteenth century French society to examine humanity and the human experience with all its attendant virtues, vices, and peculiarities.

Honoré de Balzac (1799-1850) was one of France's most prolific and influential writers, and is generally considered to be one of the first and greatest of the literary realists. In his lifetime, he tried and failed at a number of professions, including that of legal clerk, printer, publisher, and as a businessman who engaged in a number of abortive ventures. These experiences, as well as numerous affairs with admiring ladies—many of them from the nobility—and an unsuccessful run for public office, provided him with a wealth of material for his writing, in which he was able to create some of the most memorable characters in French literature.

De Balzac

Table of Contents

The Human Comedy
Studies of Manners
Scenes From Private Life

Addenda that follow each story provide cross-references to character appearances in other works of *The Human Comedy*.

Appendices

List of Plates

The frontispiece and plates I, V, VIII, and XI are taken from the 1842 Furne edition of Balzac's works; most, if not all of these, also appear in the 1851 Marescq et Cie edition of *Oeuvres illustrées de Balzac,* as do plates II-IV, VI-VII, IX-X, and XII-XVIII.

A Second Home
(*Une double famille*)
February 1830-January 1842

Translated by Clara Bell

*To Madame la Comtesse Louise de Turheim**
as a token of remembrance and affectionate respect

A toute heure du jour les passants apercevaient cette jeune
ouvrière.....

Sa mère, Madame Crochard.....

UNE DOUBLE FAMILLE.

Plate I

The Rue du Tourniquet-Saint-Jean, formerly one of the darkest and most tortuous streets of the old quarter surrounding the Hôtel-de-Ville, wound its way round the little gardens of the Paris Prefecture and ended at the Rue du Martroi,* exactly at the angle of an old wall now pulled down. Here stood the turnstile to which the street owed its name; it was not removed till 1823, when the municipality built a ballroom on the garden plot adjoining the Hôtel-de-Ville for the fête given in honour of the Duc d'Angoulême* on his return from Spain. The widest part of the Rue du Tourniquet was the end opening into the Rue de la Tixéranderie,* and even there it was less than six feet across. Hence in rainy weather the gutter water was soon deep at the foot of the old houses, sweeping down with it the dust and refuse deposited at the cornerstones by the residents. As the dust carts could not pass through, the inhabitants trusted to storms to wash their always miry alley, for how could it be clean? When the summer sun shed its perpendicular rays on Paris like a sheet of gold, but as piercing as the point of a sword, it lighted up the blackness of this street for a few minutes without drying the permanent damp that rose from the ground floor to the first story of these dark and silent tenements. The residents, who lighted their lamps at five o'clock in the month of June, in winter never put them out. To this day the enterprising wayfarer who should approach the Marais* along the quays, past the end of the Rue du Chaume, the Rues de l'Homme-Armé, des Billettes, and des Deux-Portes*, all

3

leading to the Rue du Tourniquet, might think he had passed through cellars all the way. Almost all the streets of old Paris, of which ancient chronicles laud the magnificence, were like this damp and gloomy labyrinth where antiquaries still find historical curiosities to admire. For instance, on the house then forming the corner where the Rue du Tourniquet joined the Rue de la Tixéranderie, the clamps might still be seen of two strong iron rings fixed to the wall, the relics of the chains put up every night by the watch to secure public safety. This house, remarkable for its antiquity, had been constructed in a way that bore witness to the unhealthiness of these old dwellings, for, to preserve the ground floor from damp, the arches of the cellars rose about two feet above the soil, and the house was entered up three outside steps. The door was crowned by a closed arch, of which the keystone bore a female head and some time-eaten arabesques. Three windows, their sills about five feet from the ground, belonged to a small set of rooms looking out on the Rue du Tourniquet, whence they derived their light. These windows were protected by strong iron bars, very wide apart, and ending below in an outward curve like the bars of a baker's window. If any passerby during the day were curious enough to peep into the two rooms forming this little dwelling he would see nothing, for only under the sun of July could he discern, in the second room, two beds hung with green serge placed side by side under the panelling of an old-fashioned alcove; but in the afternoon by about three o'clock when the candles were lighted, through the pane of the first room, an old woman might be seen sitting on a stool by the fireplace where she nursed the fire in a brazier to simmer a stew, such as porters' wives are expert in. A few kitchen utensils, hung up against the wall, were visible in the twilight. At that hour an old table on trestles, but bare of linen, was laid with pewter spoons and the dish concocted by the old woman. Three wretched chairs were all the furniture of this room, which was at once the kitchen and the dining room. Over the chimney shelf were a piece of looking glass, a tinderbox, three glasses, some matches, and a large, cracked, white jug. Still, the floor, the utensils, the fireplace, all gave a pleasant sense of the perfect cleanliness and thrift that pervaded the dull and gloomy home. The old woman's pale, withered face was quite in harmony with the darkness of the street and the mustiness of the place. As she sat there, motionless, in her chair, it might have been thought that she was as inseparable from the house as a snail from its brown shell; her face, alert with a vague expression of mischief, was framed in a flat cap made of net which barely covered her white hair; her fine, grey eyes were as quiet as the street, and the many wrinkles in her face might be compared to the cracks in the walls. Whether she had been born to poverty or had fallen from some past splendour, she now seemed to have been long resigned to her melancholy existence. From sunrise till dark, unless she was getting a meal ready, or, with a basket on her arm, was out purchasing provisions, the old woman sat in the adjoining room by the further window, opposite a young girl. At any hour of the day the passerby could see the needlewoman seated in an old, red velvet chair bending over an embroidery frame, and stitching indefatigably. Her mother had a green pillow on her knee, and busied herself with handmade net, but her fingers could move the bobbins but slowly; her sight was feeble, for on her nose there rested a pair of those antiquated spectacles which keep their place on the nostrils by the grip of a spring. By night these two hardworking women set a lamp between them, and the light, concentrated by two globe-shaped bottles of water, showed the elder the fine network made by the threads on her pillow, and the younger the most delicate details of the pattern she was embroidering. The outward bend of the window bars had allowed the girl to rest a box of earth on the window sill, in which grew some sweet peas, nasturtiums, a sickly little honeysuckle, and some convolvulus that twined its frail stems up the iron bars. These etiolated plants produced a few pale flowers and added a touch of indescribable sadness and sweetness to the picture offered by this window, in which the two figures were appropriately framed. The most selfish soul who chanced to see this domestic scene would carry away with him a perfect image of the life led in Paris by the working class of women, for the embroideress evidently lived by her needle. Many, as they passed through the turnstile, found themselves wondering how a girl could preserve her colour, living in such a cellar. A student of lively imagination, going that way to cross to the Quartier-Latin,* would compare this obscure and vegetative life to that of the ivy that clung to these chill walls, or to that of the peasants doomed to labour who are born, toil, and die unknown to the world they have helped to feed. A house owner, after studying the house with the eye of a valuer, would have said, "What will become of those two women if embroidery should go out of fashion?" Among the men who, having some appointment at the Hôtel-de-Ville or the Palais de Justice,* were obliged to go through this street at fixed hours, either on their way to business or on their return home, there may have been some charitable soul. Some widower or Adonis of forty, brought so often into the secrets of these sad lives, may perhaps have reckoned on the poverty of this mother and daughter, and have hoped to become the master at no great cost of the innocent seamstress whose nimble and dimpled fingers, youthful figure, and white skin—a charm due, no doubt, to living in this sunless street—had excited his admiration. Perhaps, again, some honest clerk, with twelve hundred francs a year, seeing every day the diligence the girl gave to her needle, and appreciating the purity of her life, was only waiting for improved prospects to unite one humble life with another, one form of toil to another, and to bring at any rate a man's arm and a calm affection, pale-hued like the flowers in the window, to uphold this home. Vague hope certainly gave life to the mother's dim, grey eyes. Every morning, after the most frugal breakfast, she took up her pillow, though chiefly for the look of the thing, for she would lay her spectacles on a little mahogany worktable as old as herself, and look out of window from about half-past eight till ten at the regular passersby in the street; she caught their glances, remarked on their gait, their dress, their countenance, and almost seemed to be offering her daughter; her gossiping eyes so evidently tried to attract some magnetic sympathy by manoeuvres worthy of the stage. It was evident that this little review was as good as a play to her, and perhaps her single amusement. The daughter rarely looked up. Modesty, or a painful consciousness of poverty, seemed to keep her eyes riveted to the work frame, and only some exclamation of surprise from her mother moved her to show her small features. Then a clerk in a new coat, or who unexpectedly appeared with a woman on his arm, might catch sight of the girl's slightly upturned nose, her rosy mouth, and grey eyes, always bright and lively in spite of her fatiguing toil. Her late hours were only betrayed, ever so slightly, by a circle, more or less white, drawn beneath each of her eyes upon the fresh skin of her cheeks. The poor child looked as if she were made for love and gaiety: for love because of the two perfect arcs which had been painted above her slanting eyelids and her ample forest of chestnut hair which she might have hidden herself beneath as under a tent, impenetrable to a lover's eye; for gaiety because of the quivering animation of her nostrils which formed two dimples in her rosy cheeks and made her quick to forget her troubles—it was gaiety, this flower of hope, that gave her the strength to look upon the barren path of her life without shuddering. The girl's hair was always carefully dressed. After the manner of Paris needlewomen, her toilette seemed to her quite complete when she had brushed her hair smooth and tucked up the little short curls that played on each temple in contrast with the whiteness of her skin. The growth of it on the back of her neck was so pretty, and the brown line, so clearly traced, gave such a pleasing idea of her youth and charm, that the observer, seeing her bent over her work, and unmoved by any sound, was inclined to think of her as a coquette. Such inviting promise had excited the interest of more than one young man, who turned round in the vain hope of seeing that modest countenance.

"Caroline, it would seem we have a new visitor, one who is far handsomer than all the rest."

These words, spoken in a low voice by her mother one August morning in 1815, had vanquished the young needlewoman's indifference, and she looked out on the street, but in vain; the stranger was gone.

"Where has he flown to?" said she.

"He will come back no doubt at four; I shall see him coming and will touch your foot with mine. I am sure he will come back; he has been through the street regularly for the last three days, but his hours vary. The first day he came by at six o'clock, the day before yesterday it was four, yesterday as early as three. I remember seeing him occasionally some time ago. He is some clerk in the prefect's office who has moved to the Marais. Why!" she exclaimed, after glancing down the street, "our gentleman in the brown coat has taken to wearing a wig; how much it alters him!"

The gentleman in the brown coat was, it would seem, one of the regulars at the end of the daily procession, for the old woman put on her spectacles and took up her work with a sigh, glancing at her daughter with so strange a look that Lavater* himself would have found it difficult to interpret. Admiration, gratitude, and a sort of hope for better days were mingled with pride at having such a pretty daughter. At about four in the afternoon the old lady pushed her foot against Caroline's, and the girl looked up quickly enough to see the new actor, whose regular advent would thenceforth lend variety to the scene. Tall, thin, pale, and dressed in black, the man appeared to be about forty, and his gait had something rather solemn about it; as his piercing hazel eyes met the old woman's dull gaze, he made her quake, for she felt as though he had the gift of reading hearts, or much practice in it, and his presence must surely be as icy as the air of this dank street. Was the dull, sallow complexion of that ominous face due to excess of work, or the result of delicate health? The old woman supplied twenty different answers to this question, but Caroline, the next day, discerned the lines of long mental suffering on that brow that was so prompt to frown. The rather hollow cheeks of the unknown bore the stamp of the seal which sorrow sets on its victims as if to grant them the consolation of common recognition and brotherly union for resistance. Though the girl's expression was at first one of lively but innocent curiosity, it assumed a look of gentle sympathy as the stranger receded from view, like the last relation following in a funeral train. The heat of the weather was so great, and the gentleman was so absent-minded, that he had taken off his hat and forgotten to put it on again as he went down the squalid street. Caroline could see the stern look given to his countenance by the way the hair was brushed up from his forehead. The strong impression, devoid of charm, made on the girl by this man's appearance was totally unlike any sensation produced by the other passengers who used the street; for the first time in her life she was moved to pity for someone else than herself and her mother; she made no reply to the absurd conjectures that supplied material for the old woman's provoking volubility, and drew her long needle in silence through the web of stretched net; she only regretted not having seen the stranger more closely, and looked forward to the morrow to form a definite opinion of him. It was the first time, indeed, that a man passing down the street had ever given rise to much thought in her mind. She generally had nothing but a smile in response to her mother's hypotheses, for the old woman looked on every passerby as a possible protector for her daughter. And if such suggestions, so crudely presented, gave rise to no evil thoughts in Caroline's mind, her indifference must be ascribed to the persistent and unfortunately inevitable toil in which the energies of her sweet youth were being spent, and which would infallibly mar the clearness of her eyes or steal from her fresh cheeks the bloom that still coloured them. For two months or more *Monsieur Noir*—the name they had given him—was erratic in his movements; he did not always come down the Rue du Tourniquet; the old woman sometimes saw him in the evening when he had not passed in the morning, and he did not come by at such regular hours as the clerks who served Madame Crochard instead of a clock; moreover, except on the first occasion when his look had given the old mother a sense of alarm, his eyes had never once dwelt on the weird picture of these two female gnomes. With the exception of two carriage gates and a dark ironmonger's shop, there were in the Rue du Tourniquet only barred windows giving light to the staircases of the neighbouring houses; thus the stranger's lack of curiosity was not to be accounted for by the presence of dangerous rivals, and Madame Crochard was greatly piqued to see her Monsieur Noir always lost in thought, his eyes fixed on the ground or straight before him, as though he hoped to read the future in the fog of the Rue du Tourniquet. However, one morning, about the middle of September, Caroline Crochard's roguish face stood out so brightly against the dark background of the room, looking so fresh among the belated flowers and faded leaves that twined round the window bars, the daily scene was so gay with such contrasts of light and shade, of pink and white blending with the light material on which the pretty needlewoman was working, and with the red and brown hues of the chairs, that the stranger gazed very attentively at the effects of this living picture. In point of fact, the old woman, provoked by Monsieur Noir's indifference, had made such a clatter with her bobbins that the gloomy and pensive passerby was perhaps prompted to look up by the unusual noise. The stranger merely exchanged glances with Caroline, swift indeed, but enough to effect a certain contact between their souls, and both were aware that they would think of each other. When the stranger came by again at four in the afternoon, Caroline recognised the sound of his step on the echoing pavement; they looked steadily at each other, and with evident purpose; his eyes had an expression of kindliness which made him smile, and Caroline coloured; the old mother noted them both with satisfaction. Ever after that memorable afternoon, Monsieur Noir went by twice a day, with rare exceptions, which both the women observed. They concluded from the irregularity of the hours of his homecoming that he was neither promptly as free, nor strictly as punctual as a subordinate official. All through the first three winter months, twice a day, Caroline and the stranger thus saw each other for so long as it took him to traverse the piece of road that lay along the length of the door and three windows of the house. Day after day this brief interview had a hue of friendly sympathy which at last had acquired a sort of fraternal kindness. Caroline and the stranger seemed to understand each other from the first, and then, by dint of scrutinising each other's faces, they learned to know them well. Before long it came to be, as it were, a visit that the unknown owed to Caroline;

11

if by any chance Monsieur Noir went by without be-
stowing on her the half-smile of his expressive lips or
the cordial glance of his brown eyes, something was
missing to her all day. She resembled one of those old
men for whom the daily study of their newspaper has
become such an indispensable pleasure that, the day
after any solemn holiday, they wander about quite lost,
as much from inadvertence as from impatience, seeking
the sheet by which they cheat for a moment the empti-
ness of their existence. But these fleeting appearances
had the charm of an intimate conversation, quite as
much for the stranger as for Caroline. The girl could no
more hide a vexation, a grief, or some slight ailment
from the keen eye of her appreciative friend than he
could conceal anxiety from hers. "He must have had
some trouble yesterday," was the thought that constantly arose in the embroideress's mind as she saw some
change in the features of Monsieur Noir. "Oh, he has
been working too hard!" was a reflection due to another
shade of expression which Caroline could discern. The
stranger, on his part, could guess when the girl had
spent Sunday in finishing a dress, and he felt an interest in the pattern. As the day that the rent was due
approached, he could see that her pretty face was clouded by anxiety, and he could guess when Caroline had
sat up late at work, but, above all, he noted how the
gloomy thoughts that dimmed the cheerful and delicate
features of her young face gradually vanished by degrees as their acquaintance ripened. When winter had
killed the climbers and plants of her window garden,
and the window was kept closed, it was not without a
smile of gentle amusement that the stranger observed
the concentration of the light within, just at the level of
Caroline's head. The very small fire and the frosty red
of the two women's faces betrayed the poverty of their
home, but if ever his own countenance expressed re-
gretful compassion, the girl proudly met it with assumed

cheerfulness. Meanwhile the feelings that had arisen in their hearts remained buried there, no incident occurring to reveal to either of them how deep and strong they were in the other; they had never even heard the sound of each other's voice. These mute friends were even on their guard against any nearer acquaintance, as though it meant disaster. Each seemed to fear lest it should bring on the other some grief more serious than those they felt tempted to share. Was it shyness or friendship that checked them? Was it a dread of meeting with selfishness, or the odious distrust which sunders all the residents within the walls of a populous city? Did the voice of conscience warn them of approaching danger? It would be impossible to explain the instinct which made them as much enemies as friends, at once indifferent and attached, drawn to each other by impulse, and severed by circumstance. Each perhaps hoped to preserve a cherished illusion. It might almost have been thought that the stranger feared lest he should hear some vulgar word from those lips as fresh and pure as a flower, and that Caroline felt herself unworthy of the mysterious personage who was evidently possessed of power and wealth. As to Madame Crochard, that tender mother, almost angry at her daughter's persistent lack of decisiveness, she now showed a sulky face to Monsieur Noir, on whom she had hitherto smiled with a sort of benevolent servility. Never before had she complained so bitterly of being compelled, at her age, to do the cooking; never had her catarrh and her rheumatism wrung so many groans from her; finally, she could not, this winter, promise so many ells of net as Caroline had hitherto been able to count on. Under these circumstances, and towards the end of December, at the time when bread was dearest, and that dearth of grain* was beginning to be felt which made the year 1816 so hard on the poor, the stranger observed on the features of the girl, whose name was still unknown to him, the painful traces

13

of a secret sorrow which his kindest smiles could not dispel. Before long he saw in Caroline's eyes the dimness attributable to long hours at night. One night, towards the end of the month, Monsieur Noir passed down the Rue du Tourniquet-Saint-Jean at the quite unwonted hour of one in the morning. The silence of the night allowed him to hear from a distance, before he had even arrived at the house, the lachrymose voice of the old mother and Caroline's even sadder tones, mingling with the swish of a shower of sleet. He crept along as slowly as he could, and then, at the risk of being taken up by the police, he stood still below the window to hear the mother and daughter while watching them through the largest of the holes in the yellow muslin curtains, which were eaten away by wear as a cabbage leaf is riddled with caterpillars. The inquisitive stranger saw a sheet of paper on the table that stood between the two work frames, and on which stood the lamp and the globes filled with water. He at once identified it as a writ. Madame Crochard was weeping, and Caroline's voice was thick and had lost its sweet, caressing tone.

"Why be so heartbroken, mother? Monsieur Molineux will not sell our furniture or turn us out before I have finished this dress; only two nights more and I shall take it home to Madame Roguin."

"And supposing she keeps you waiting as usual? And will the money for the gown pay the baker too?"

The spectator of this scene had long practice in reading faces; he fancied he could discern that the mother's grief was as false as the daughter's was genuine; he turned away, and presently came back. When he next peeped through the hole in the curtain, Madame Crochard was in bed. The young needlewoman, bending over her frame, was embroidering with indefatigable diligence; on the table, with the writ, lay a triangular piece of bread, placed there, no doubt, to sustain her in the night and to remind her of the reward of her industry. The stranger was tremulous with pity and sympathy; he threw his purse in through a cracked pane so that it should fall at the girl's feet, and then, without waiting to enjoy her surprise, he escaped, his cheeks tingling. Next morning the shy and melancholy stranger went past with a look of deep preoccupation, but he could not escape Caroline's gratitude; she had opened her window and affected to be digging in the square window box buried in snow, a pretext of which the clumsy ingenuity plainly told her benefactor that she had been resolved not to see him only through the pane. Her eyes were full of tears as she bowed her head, as much as to say to her benefactor,

Il jeta sa bourse à travers une vitre fêlée, de manière à la faire tomber...

Plate II

15

"I can only repay you from my heart." But the stranger affected not to understand the meaning of this sincere gratitude. In the evening, as he came by, Caroline was busy mending the window with a sheet of paper, and she smiled at him, showing her row of pearly teeth like a promise. Thenceforth Monsieur Noir went another way, and was no more seen in the Rue du Tourniquet.

One Saturday morning in the early days of the following May, Caroline caught sight of a small portion of cloudless sky between the black lines of two houses as she was watering the roots of a honeysuckle from a glass, and she said to her mother—"Mamma, we must go tomorrow for a trip to Montmorency!"* She had scarcely uttered these words, in a tone of glee, when Monsieur Noir came by, sadder and more dejected than ever. Caroline's innocent and ingratiating glance might have been taken for an invitation. And, in fact, on the following day, when Madame Crochard, dressed in a frock coat of russet-coloured merino wool, a silk bonnet, and a widely-striped shawl of imitation cashmere, came out to choose seats in a chaise at the corner of the Rue du Faubourg-Saint-Denis and the Rue d'Enghien,* she found her stranger standing like a man waiting for his wife. A smile of pleasure lit up the stranger's face when his eye fell on Caroline: her neat feet shod in puce-coloured prunelle gaiters; her white dress tossed by a breeze that would have been fatal to an ill-made woman, but which displayed her graceful form; her face, shaded by a rice straw hat lined with pink satin, was illuminated like a celestial reflection; her broad, plum-coloured belt set off a waist he could have spanned; and her hair, parted in two brown bands over a forehead as white as snow, gave her an expression of innocence which no other feature contradicted. Enjoyment seemed to have made Caroline as light as the straw of her hat, but when she saw Monsieur Noir, radiant hope suddenly eclipsed her bright dress and her beauty. The stranger, who appeared to be in doubt, had not perhaps made up his mind to be the girl's escort for the day till this revelation of the delight she felt on seeing him. He at once hired a cabriolet with a fairly good horse to drive to Saint-Leu-Taverny, and he offered Madame Crochard and her daughter seats by his side; the mother accepted without ado, but presently, when they were already on the way to Saint-Denis,* she realised that she should have some scruples, and hazarded a few pleasantries as to the possible inconvenience two women might cause their companion.

"Perhaps, Monsieur, you wished to drive alone to Saint-Leu?" said she, with affected simplicity. Before long she complained of the heat, and especially of her catarrh, which, she said, had hindered her from closing her eyes all night, and by the time the carriage had reached Saint-Denis, Madame Crochard seemed to be fast asleep. Her snores, indeed, seemed to the stranger rather doubtfully genuine, and he frowned as he looked at the old woman with a very suspicious eye.

"Oh, she is fast asleep," said Caroline guilelessly; "she never ceased coughing all night. She must be very tired."

Her companion made no reply, but he looked at the girl with a smile that seemed to say—"Poor child, you little know your mother!" However, in spite of his distrust, as the chaise made its way down the long avenue of poplars leading to Eaubonne,* the stranger thought that Madame Crochard was really asleep; perhaps he did not care to inquire how far her slumbers were genuine or feigned. Whether it were that the brilliant sky, the pure country air, the heady fragrance of the first green shoots of the poplars, the catkins of willow, and the flowers of the blackthorn had inclined his heart to open like all the nature around him, or that any longer restraint was too oppressive while Caroline's sparkling eyes responded to his own, the stranger entered on a conversation with his young companion, as aimless as the swaying of the branches in the wind, as devious as the flitting of the butterflies in the azure air, as illogical as the melodious murmur of the fields, and, like it, full of mysterious love. At that season is not the rural country as tremulous as a bride that has donned her marriage robe; does it not invite the coldest soul to be happy? What heart could remain unthawed, and what lips could keep its secret, on leaving the gloomy streets of the Marais for the first time since the previous autumn and entering the smiling and picturesque valley of Montmorency—on seeing it in the morning light, its endless horizons receding from view, and then lifting a charmed gaze to eyes which expressed no less infinitude mingled with love? The stranger discovered that Caroline was sprightly rather than witty, affectionate rather than educated; but while her laugh was giddy, her words promised genuine feeling. When, in response to her companion's shrewd questioning, the girl spoke with the heartfelt effusiveness of which the lower classes are lavish, not guarding it with reticence like people of the world, Monsieur Noir's face brightened, and seemed to renew its youth. His countenance by degrees lost the sadness that lent sternness to his features, and little by little they gained a look of handsome youthfulness which made Caroline proud and happy. The pretty needlewoman guessed that her new friend had been long weaned from tenderness and love, and no longer believed in the devotion of woman. Finally, some unexpected sally in Caroline's light prattle lifted the last veil that concealed the real youth and genuine character of the stranger's physiognomy; he seemed to bid farewell forever to the ideas that haunted him, and showed the natural liveliness that lay beneath the solemnity of his expression. Their conversation had insensibly become so intimate, that by the time when the carriage stopped at the first houses of the village of Saint-Leu, Caroline was calling the gentleman Monsieur Roger. Then for the first time the old mother awoke.

"Caroline, she has heard everything!" said Roger suspiciously in the girl's ear.

Caroline's reply was an exquisite smile of disbelief which dissipated the dark cloud that his fear of some plot on the old woman's part had brought to this suspicious mortal's brow. Madame Crochard was amazed at nothing, approved of everything, and followed her daughter and Monsieur Roger into the park of Saint-Leu, where the two young people had agreed to wander through the smiling meadows and fragrant copses made famous by the taste of Queen Hortense.*

"*Mon Dieu*, how lovely it is!" exclaimed Caroline. Standing on the green ridge where the forest of Montmorency begins, she saw lying at her feet the immense valley and its many windings that sheltered scattered villages, its horizon of blue hills, its church towers, its meadows and fields, from whence a murmur came up, to die on her ear like the swell of the ocean. The three wanderers made their way by the bank of an artificial stream and came to the Swiss valley, where stands a chalet that had more than once given shelter to Hortense and Napoléon. When Caroline had seated herself with pious reverence on the mossy wooden bench where kings and princesses and the Emperor had rested, Madame Crochard expressed a wish to have a nearer view of a bridge that hung across between two rocks at some little distance, and bent her steps towards that rural curiosity, leaving her daughter in Monsieur Roger's care, though telling them that she would not go out of sight.

"What, poor child!" cried Roger, "have you never longed for wealth and the pleasures of luxury? Have you never wished that you might wear the beautiful dresses you embroider?"

"It would not be the truth, Monsieur Roger, if I were

to tell you that I never think how happy people must be who are rich. Oh yes! I often fancy, especially when I am going to sleep, how glad I should be to see my poor mother at her age no longer compelled to go out, whatever the weather, to buy our little provisions. I should like her to have a servant who, every morning before she was up, would bring her up her coffee, nicely sweetened with white sugar. And she loves reading novels, poor dear soul! Well, and I would rather see her wearing out her eyes over her favourite books than over twisting her bobbins from morning till night. And again, she ought to have a little good wine. In short, I should like to see her comfortable—she is so good."

"Then she has shown you great kindness?"

"Oh yes," said the girl, in a tone of conviction. Then, after a short pause, during which the two young people stood watching Madame Crochard, who had got to the middle of the rustic bridge and was shaking her finger at them, Caroline went on—"Oh yes, she has been so good to me. What care she took of me when I was little! She sold her last silver forks to apprentice me to the old maid who taught me to embroider. And my poor father! What did she not go through to make him end his days in happiness!" The girl shivered at the remembrance, and hid her face in her hands. "Oh, but let us forget past sorrows!" she added, trying to rally her high spirits. She blushed as she saw that Roger too was moved, but she dared not look at him.

"Who was your father?" he asked.

"He was a dancer at the Opéra, before the Revolution," said she, with an air of perfect simplicity, "and my mother sang in the chorus. My father, who was in charge of stage direction, happened to be present at the siege of the Bastille. He was recognised by some of the assailants, who asked him whether he could not direct a real attack, since he was used to leading such enterprises on the stage. My father was brave; he accepted the post, led the insurgents, and was rewarded by the nomination to the rank of captain in the army of Sambre-et-Meuse,* where he distinguished himself so far as to rise rapidly to be a colonel. But at Lutzen he was so badly wounded that, after a year's sufferings, he died in Paris. The Bourbons returned;* my mother could obtain no pension, and we fell into such abject misery that we were compelled to work for our living. For some time she has been ailing, poor dear, and I have never known her so little resigned; she complains a good deal, and, indeed, I cannot wonder, for she has known the pleasures of an easy life. For my part, as I cannot pine for delights I have never known, I have but one thing to wish for."

Mon père était brave, il accepta, conduisit les insurgés...

Plate III

"And that is?" said Roger eagerly, as if roused from a dream.

"That women may long continue to wear embroidered net dresses, so that I may never lack work."

The frankness of this confession interested the young man, who looked with less hostile eyes on Madame Crochard as she slowly made her way back to them.

"Well, children, have you had a long talk?" said she, with a half-laughing, half-indulgent air. "When I think, Monsieur Roger, that the *little Corporal* has sat where you are sitting . . ."* she continued after a moment of silence. "Poor man! How my husband worshipped him! Ah! Crochard did well to die, for he could not have borne to think of him where *they* have sent him!"

Roger put his finger to his lips, and the good old woman, nodding her head, said in a more serious tone— "All right, mouth shut and tongue still. But," added she, unhooking a bit of her bodice and showing a ribbon and cross tied round her neck by a piece of black ribbon, "*they* shall never hinder me from wearing what *l'autre** gave to my poor Crochard, and I will have it buried with me . . ."

On hearing this speech, which at that time was regarded as seditious, Roger interrupted the old lady by rising suddenly, and they returned to the village by way of the park. The young man left them for a few minutes while he went to order a meal at the best restaurant in Taverny; then, returning to fetch them, he led the way along the paths in the forest. The dinner was cheerful. Roger was no longer the melancholy shade that was wont to pass along the Rue du Tourniquet; he was not *Monsieur Noir*, but rather a confiding young man ready to take life as it came, like the two hard-working women who, on the morrow, might lack bread; he seemed alive to all the joys of youth, his smile was quite affectionate and childlike. When, at five o'clock, this happy meal was ended with a few glasses of champagne, Roger was the first to propose that they should join the village ball under the chestnuts, where he and Caroline danced together. Their hands met with sympathetic pressure, their hearts beat with the same hopes, and under the blue sky and the slanting, rosy beams of sunset, their eyes sparkled with fires which, to them, made the glory of the heavens pale. How strange is the power of an idea, of a desire! To these two nothing seemed impossible. In such magic moments, when enjoyment sheds its reflections on the future, the soul foresees nothing but happiness. This sweet day had created memories for these two to which nothing could be compared in all their past existence. Would the source prove to be more beautiful than the river, the desire more enchanting than its gratification, the thing hoped for more delightful than the thing possessed?

"So the day is already at an end!" On hearing this exclamation from her unknown friend when the dance was over, Caroline looked at him compassionately, as his face assumed once more a faint shade of sadness.

"Why should you not be as happy in Paris as you are here?" she asked. "Is happiness to be found only at Saint-Leu? It seems to me that I can henceforth never be unhappy anywhere."

Roger was struck by these words, spoken with the glad unrestraint that always carries a woman further than she intended, just as prudery often lends her greater cruelty than she feels. For the first time since that glance, which had, in a way, been the beginning of their friendship, Caroline and Roger had the same idea; though they did not express it, they felt it at the same instant, as a result of a common impression like that of a comforting fire cheering both under the frost of winter; then, as if frightened by each other's silence, they made their way to the spot where the carriage was waiting. But before getting into it, they playfully took hands and ran on together down the dark avenue in front of Madame Crochard.

When they could no longer see the white net cap, which showed as a speck through the leaves where the old woman was—"Caroline!" said Roger in a tremulous voice, and with a beating heart. The girl was startled and drew back a few steps, understanding the invitation this question conveyed; however, she held out her hand, which was passionately kissed, but which she hastily withdrew, for by standing on tiptoe she could see her mother. Madame Crochard pretended to see nothing, as if, in memory of her former roles, she should appear there only as an *aside*.

The adventures of these two young people were not continued in the Rue du Tourniquet. To see Roger and Caroline once more, we must leap into the heart of modern Paris, where, in some of the newly-built houses, there are apartments that seem made on purpose for newly-married couples to spend their honeymoon in. There the paper and paint are as fresh as the bride and bridegroom, and the decorations are in blossom like their love; everything is in harmony with youthful notions and ardent wishes. Halfway down the Rue Taitbout,* in a house whose stone walls were still white, where the columns of the hall and the doorway were as yet spotless, and the inner walls shone with the neat painting which our recent intimacy with English ways had brought into fashion, there was, on the second floor, a small set of rooms fitted by the architect as though he had known what their use would be. A simple airy anteroom, with a stucco wainscot, formed an entrance into a salon and a small dining room. Out of the salon opened a pretty bedroom, with a bathroom beyond. Every chimney shelf had over it a fine mirror elegantly framed. The doors were crowned with arabesques in good taste, and the cornices were in the best style. Any amateur would have discerned there the sense of distinction and decorative fitness which mark the work of modem French architects. For about a month Caroline

had been at home in this apartment, furnished by an upholsterer who submitted to an artist's guidance. A short
description of the principal room will suffice to give an
idea of the wonders it offered to Caroline's delighted
eyes when Roger installed her there. Hangings of grey
stuff trimmed with green silk adorned the walls of her
bedroom; the seats, covered with light-coloured wool-
len sateen, were of easy and comfortable shapes, and
in the latest fashion; a chest of drawers of some simple
wood, inlaid with lines of a darker hue, contained the
treasures of the toilette; a matching desk served for the
writing of love letters on scented paper; the bed, with
antique draperies, could not fail to suggest thoughts of
love by its soft hangings of elegant muslin; the window
curtains, of drab silk with green fringe, were always
half drawn to subdue the light; a bronze clock represented Love crowning Psyche; finally, a carpet of Gothic
design printed onto a reddish background set off the
other accessories of this delightful retreat. There was a
small dressing table in front of a long glass, and here
the ex-needlewoman sat, out of patience, with Plaisir,
the famous hairdresser.

"Do you think you will have it done today?" said
she.

"Your hair is so long and so thick, Madame," replied
Plaisir.

Caroline could not help smiling. The man's flattery
had no doubt revived in her mind the memory of the
passionate praises lavished by her lover on the beauty
of her hair, which he delighted in. The hairdresser having done, a maid came and held counsel with her as to
the dress in which Roger would like best to see her. It
was in the beginning of September 1816, and the weather was cold; she chose a green grenadine trimmed with
chinchilla. As soon as she was dressed, Caroline flew
into the salon and opened a window, out of which she
stepped on to the elegant balcony that adorned the front

of the house; there she stood with her arms crossed, in a charming attitude, not to show herself to the admiration of the passersby and see them turn to gaze at her, but to be able to look out on the Boulevard at the bottom of the Rue Taitbout. This side view, really very comparable to the peephole made by actors in the drop scene of a theatre, enabled her to catch a glimpse of numbers of elegant carriages, and a crowd of people swept past with the rapidity of *Ombres Chinoises*.* Not knowing whether Roger would arrive in a carriage or on foot, the needlewoman from the Rue du Tourniquet looked by turns at the foot passengers and at the tilburies—light cabs introduced into Paris by the English. Expressions of refractoriness and of love passed by turns over her youthful face when, after waiting for a quarter of an hour, neither her keen eye nor her heart had announced the arrival of him whom she knew to be due. What disdain, what indifference were shown in her beautiful features for all the other creatures who were bustling like ants below her feet! Her grey eyes, sparkling with mischief, now positively flamed. Given over to her passion, she avoided admiration with as much care as the proudest devote to encouraging it when they drive about Paris, certainly feeling no care as to whether her fair countenance leaning over the balcony, her little foot between the bars, and the picture of her bright eyes and delicious turned-up nose would be effaced or not from the minds of the passersby who admired them; she saw but one face, and had but one idea. When the spotted head of a certain bay horse happened to cross the narrow strip between the two rows of houses, Caroline gave a little shiver and stood on tiptoe in hope of recognising the white traces and the colour of the tilbury. It was *him!* Roger turned the corner of the street, saw the balcony, whipped the horse, which came up at a gallop, and stopped at the bronze-green door that he knew as well as his master did. The door of the apartment was opened at once by the maid, who had heard her mistress's exclamation of delight. Roger rushed up to the salon, clasped Caroline in his arms, and embraced her with the effusive feeling that is natural when two beings who love each other rarely meet. He led her, or rather they went by a common impulse, their arms about each other, into the quiet and fragrant bedroom; a settee stood ready for them to sit by the fire, and for a moment they looked at each other in silence, expressing their happiness only by their clasped hands and communicating their thoughts in a fond gaze.

"Yes, it is he!" she said at last. "Yes, it is you. Do you know, I have not seen you for three long days, an age! But what is the matter? You are unhappy."

"My poor Caroline——"

"There, you see! 'Poor Caroline——'"

"No, no, do not laugh, my darling; we cannot go to the Feydeau Theatre* together this evening."

Caroline put on a little pout, but it vanished immediately.

"How absurd I am! How can I think of going to the play when I see you? Is not the sight of you the only spectacle I care for?" she cried, pushing her fingers through Roger's hair.

"I am obliged to go to the public prosecutor's house, for we have a difficult case in hand. He met me in the great hall at the Palais, and as I am to plead, he asked me to dine with him. But, my dearest, you can go to the theatre with your mother, and I will join you if the meeting breaks up early."

"To the theatre without you!" cried she in a tone of amazement; "enjoy any pleasure you do not share! Oh my Roger! You do not deserve a kiss," she added, throwing her arms round his neck with an artless and impassioned impulse.

"Caroline, I must go home and dress. The Marais is some way off, and I still have some business to finish."

"Take care what you are saying, Monsieur," said she, interrupting him. "My mother says that when a man begins to talk about his business, he is ceasing to love."

"Caroline! Am I not here? Have I not stolen this hour from my pitiless——"

"Hush!" said she, laying a finger on his mouth. "Don't you see that I am in jest?"

They had now come back to the salon, and Roger's eye fell on an object brought home that morning by the cabinetmaker. Caroline's old rosewood embroidery frame, by which she and her mother had earned their bread when they lived in the Rue du Tourniquet-Saint-Jean, had been refitted and polished, and a net dress of elaborate design was already stretched upon it.

"Well, then, my dear, I shall do some work this evening. As I stitch, I shall fancy myself gone back to those early days when you used to pass by me without a word, but not without a glance; the days when the remembrance of your look kept me awake all night. Oh my dear old frame—the best piece of furniture in my room, though you did not give it to me! You have no idea . . . " said she, seating herself on Roger's knees, for he, overcome by irresistible feelings, had dropped into a chair. "Listen. All I can earn by my work I mean to give to the poor. You have made me rich. How I love that pretty home at Bellefeuille, less because of what it is than because you gave it to me! But tell me, Roger, I should like to call myself Caroline de Bellefeuille—can I? You must know: is it legal or permissible?"

As she saw a little affirmative grimace—for Roger hated the name of Crochard—Caroline jumped for glee, and clapped her hands.

"I feel," said she, "as if I should more especially belong to you. Usually a woman gives up her own name and takes her husband's——"An idea forced itself upon her and made her blush. She took Roger's hand and led him to the open piano. "Listen," said she, "I can play my sonata now like an angel!" and her fingers were already running over the ivory keys, when she felt herself seized round the waist.

"Caroline, I ought to be far away from here."

"You insist on going? Well, go," said she, with a pretty pout, but she smiled as she looked at the clock and exclaimed joyfully, "At any rate, I have detained you a quarter of an hour!"

"Adieu, Mademoiselle de Bellefeuille," said he, with the gentle irony of love.

She kissed him and saw her lover to the door; when the sound of his steps had died away on the stairs, she ran out on to the balcony to see him get into the tilbury, to see him gather up the reins, to catch a parting look, hear the crack of his whip and the sound of his wheels on the stones, watch the handsome horse, the master's hat, the tiger's gold lace,* and at last to stand gazing long after the dark corner of the street had eclipsed this vision.

Five years after Mademoiselle Caroline de Bellefeuille had taken up her abode in the pretty house in the Rue Taitbout, we again look in on one of those home scenes which tighten the bonds of affection between two persons who truly love. In the middle of the blue salon, in front of the window opening to the balcony, a little boy of four was making a tremendous noise as he whipped the rocking horse, whose two curved supports for the legs did not move fast enough to please him; his pretty face, framed in fair curls that fell over his white collar, smiled up like a cherub's at his mother when she said to him from the depths of an easy chair, "Not so much noise, Charles; you will wake your little sister." The inquisitive boy suddenly got off his horse, and treading on tiptoe as if he were afraid of the sound of his feet on the carpet, came up with one finger between his little teeth, and standing in one of those childish attitudes that are so graceful because they are so perfectly natural, raised the muslin veil that hid the rosy face of a little girl sleeping on her mother's knee.

"Is Eugénie asleep, then?" said he, quite astonished. "Why is she asleep when we are awake?" he added, looking up with large, liquid black eyes.

"That only God can know," replied Caroline with a smile.

The mother and boy gazed at the infant, only that morning baptized. Caroline, now about twenty-four, showed the ripe beauty which had expanded under the influence of cloudless happiness and constant enjoyment. In her the woman was complete. Delighted to obey her dear Roger's every wish, she had acquired the accomplishments she had lacked; she played the piano fairly well and sang sweetly. Ignorant of the customs of a world that would have treated her as an outcast, and which she would not have cared for even if it had welcomed her—for a happy woman does not care for the world—she had not caught the elegance of manner or learned the art of conversation, abounding in words and devoid of ideas, which is current in fashionable salons; on the other hand, she worked hard to gain the knowledge indispensable to a mother whose chief ambition is to bring up her children well. Never to lose sight of her boy, to give him from the cradle that training of every minute which impresses on the young a love of all that is good and beautiful, to shelter him from every evil influence and fulfil both the painful duties of a nurse and the tender offices of a mother—these were her chief pleasures. This discrete and gentle creature had from the first day so fully resigned herself never to step beyond the enchanted sphere where she found all her happiness, that, after six years of the tenderest intimacy, she still knew her lover only by the name of Roger. A print of the picture of Psyche lighting her lamp to gaze on Love in spite of his prohibition hung in her room and constantly reminded her of the conditions of her happiness. Through all these six years her humble pleasures had never importuned Roger by a single indiscreet ambition, and his heart was a treasure house of kindness. Never had she longed for diamonds or fine clothes, and had again and again refused the luxury of a carriage which he had offered her. To look out from her balcony for Roger's cab, to go with him to the play or make excursions with him on fine days in the environs of Paris, to long for him, to see him, and then to long again—these made up the history of her life, poor in incidents but rich in happiness. As she rocked the infant, now a few months old, on her knee, singing all the while, she allowed herself to recall the memories of the past. She lingered more especially on the months of September, when Roger was accustomed to take her to Bellefeuille and spend the delightful days which seem to combine the charms of every season. Nature is equally prodigal of flowers and fruit, the evenings are mild, the mornings bright, and a blaze of summer often returns after a spell of autumn gloom. During the early days of their love, Caroline had ascribed the even mind and gentle temper, of which Roger gave her so many proofs, to the rarity of their always longed-for meetings, and to their mode of life, which did not compel them to be constantly together, as a husband and wife must be. But now she could remember with rapture that, tortured by foolish fears, she had watched him with trembling during their first stay on this little estate in the Gatinais.* Vain suspiciousness of love! Each of these months of happiness had passed like a dream in the midst of joys which never rang false. She had always seen that kind creature with a tender smile on his lips, a smile that seemed to mirror her own. As she called up these vivid pictures, her eyes filled with tears; she thought she could not love him enough, and was tempted to regard her ambiguous position as a sort of tax levied by Fate on her love. Finally, invincible curiosity led her to wonder for the thousandth time what events they could be that had led so tender a heart as Roger's to find his pleasure in clandestine and illicit happiness. She invented a thousand romances on purpose really to avoid recognising the true reason, which she had long suspected but tried not to believe in. She rose, and carrying the baby in her arms, went into the dining room to oversee the preparations for dinner. It was the 6th of May 1822, the anniversary of the excursion to the Park of Saint-Leu, which had been the turning point of her life; each year it had been marked by heartfelt rejoicing. Caroline chose the linen to be used, and arranged the dessert. Having attended with joy to these details, which touched Roger, she placed the infant in her pretty cot and went out on to the balcony, whence she presently saw the carriage which her friend, as he grew to riper years, now used instead of the smart tilbury of his youth. After submitting to the first fire of Caroline's embraces and the kisses of the little rogue who addressed him as papa, Roger went to the cradle, looked at his little sleeping daughter, kissed her forehead, and then took out of his pocket a document covered with black writing.

"Caroline," said he, "here is the marriage portion of Mademoiselle Eugénie de Bellefeuille."

The mother gratefully took the paper, a deed of gift of securities in the State funds.

"But why," said she, "have you given Eugénie three thousand francs a year, and Charles no more than fifteen hundred?"

"Charles, my love, will be a man," replied he. "Fifteen hundred francs are enough for him. With so much for certain, a man of courage is above poverty. And if by chance your son should turn out a nonentity, I do not wish him to be able to play the fool. If he is ambitious, this small income will give him a taste for work. Eugénie is a girl; she must have a little fortune."

The father then turned to play with his boy, whose

effusive affection showed the independence and freedom in which he was brought up. No sort of shyness
between the father and child interfered with the charm
which rewards a parent for his devotion, and the cheerfulness of the little family was as sweet as it was genuine.
In the evening a magic lantern displayed its illusions
and mysterious pictures on a white sheet, to Charles's
great surprise, and more than once the innocent child's
heavenly rapture made Caroline and Roger laugh heartily. Later, when the little boy was in bed, the baby woke
and craved its liquid nourishment. By the light of a lamp
in the chimney corner, Roger enjoyed the scene of peace
and comfort, and gave himself up to the happiness of
contemplating the sweet picture of the child clinging to
Caroline's white bosom as she sat, as fresh as a newly
opened lily, while her hair fell in long brown curls that
almost hid her neck. The lamplight enhanced the grace
of the young mother, shedding over her, her dress, and
the infant, the picturesque effects of strong light and
shadow. The calm and silent woman's face struck Roger
as a thousand times sweeter than ever, and he gazed
tenderly at the rosy, pouting lips from which no harsh
word had ever been heard. The very same thought was
legible in Caroline's eyes as she gave a sidelong look at
Roger, either to enjoy the effect she was producing on
him, or to see what the end of the evening was to be.

He, understanding the meaning of this cunning
glance, said with assumed regret, "I must be going. I
have a serious case to be finished, and I am expected at
home. Duty before all things—don't you think so, my
darling?"

Caroline looked him in the face with an expression
at once sad and sweet, with the resignation which does
not, however, disguise the pangs of a sacrifice. "Good-
bye, then," said she. "Go, for if you stay an hour longer
I cannot so lightly bear to set you free."

"My dearest," he said with a smile, "I have three days'

holiday and am supposed to be twenty leagues away from Paris."

A few days after this anniversary of the 6th of May, Mademoiselle de Bellefeuille hurried off one morning to the Rue Saint-Louis, in the Marais,* only hoping she might not arrive too late at a house where she commonly went once a week. An express messenger had just come to inform her that her mother, Madame Crochard, was sinking under a complication of disorders produced by constant catarrh and rheumatism. While the hackney coach driver was flogging up his horses at Caroline's urgent request, fortified by the promise of a handsome tip, the timid old women, who had been Madame Crochard's friends during her later years, had brought a priest into the neat and comfortable second floor rooms occupied by the old widow. Madame Crochard's maid did not know that the pretty lady at whose house her mistress so often dined was her daughter, and she was one of the first to suggest the services of a confessor, in the hope that this priest might be at least as useful to herself as to the sick woman. Between two games of boston, or out walking in the Jardin Turc,* the old beldames with whom the widow gossiped all day had succeeded in rousing in their friend's stony heart some scruples as to her former life, some visions of the future, some fears of hell, and some hopes of forgiveness if she should return in sincerity to a religious life. So on this solemn morning, three ancient women had settled themselves in the salon where Madame Crochard received them every Tuesday. Each in turn left her armchair to go to the poor old woman's bedside and sit with her, giving her the false hopes with which people delude the dying. At the same time, when the end was drawing near, when the physician called in the day before would no longer answer for her life, the three dames took counsel together as to whether it would not be well to send word to Mademoiselle de Bellefeuille. Françoise having been duly informed, it was decided that a messenger should go to the Rue Taitbout to inform the young relation whose influence was so disquieting to the four women; still, they hoped that the Auvergnat* would be too late in bringing back the person who so certainly held the first place in the widow Crochard's affections. The widow, evidently in the enjoyment of a thousand crowns a year, would not have been so fondly cherished by this feminine trio, but that neither of them, nor Françoise herself, knew of her having any heir. The opulence enjoyed by Mademoiselle de Bellefeuille, whose gentle maiden name Madame Crochard refrained from mentioning due to the *customs* of the old Opéra, almost justified the plan formed by these four women to divide up the dying woman's estate.

Presently one of these three sibyls who kept watch over the sick woman shook her head at the other two, and said—"It is time we should be sending for the Abbé Fontanon. In another two hours she will neither have the wit nor the strength to write a line."

Thereupon the toothless old cook went off and returned with a man wearing a black gown. A low forehead showed a small mind in this priest, whose features were mean; his flabby, fat cheeks and double chin betrayed the easygoing egotist; his powdered hair gave him a pleasant look, till he raised his small, brown eyes, prominent under a flat forehead, and not unworthy to glitter under the brows of a Tartar.

"Monsieur l'Abbé," said Françoise, "thank you for all your advice, but believe me, I have taken the greatest care of this dear soul."

But the servant, with her dragging step and woebegone look, was silent when she saw that the door of the apartment was open, and that the most insinuating of the three dowagers was standing on the landing to be the first to speak with the confessor. When the priest had politely faced the honeyed and bigoted broadside of words fired off from the widow's three friends, he went into the sickroom to sit by Madame Crochard. Decency, and some sense of reserve, compelled the three women and old Françoise to remain in the sitting room, and to make such grimaces of grief as are possible in perfection only to such wrinkled faces.

"Oh, is it not ill luck!" cried Françoise, heaving a sigh. "This is the fourth mistress I have buried. The first left me a hundred francs a year, the second a sum of fifty crowns, and the third a thousand crowns down. After thirty years' service, that is all I have to call my own."

The woman took advantage of her freedom to come and go to slip into a cupboard, whence she could hear the priest.

"I see with pleasure, daughter," said Fontanon, "that you have pious sentiments; you have a sacred relic round your neck."

Madame Crochard, with a feeble vagueness which seemed to show that she had not all her wits about her, pulled out the Imperial Cross of the Legion of Honour. The priest started back at seeing the Emperor's head; he went up to the penitent again, and she spoke to him, but in such a low tone that for some minutes Françoise could hear nothing.

"Woe upon me!" cried the old woman suddenly, "Do not desert me. What, Monsieur l'Abbé, do you think I shall be called to account for my daughter's soul?"

The Abbé spoke too low, and the partition was too thick for Françoise to hear the reply.

"Alas!" sobbed the woman, "the wretch has left me nothing that I can bequeath. When he robbed me of my dear Caroline, he parted us, and only allowed me three thousand francs a year, of which the capital belongs to my daughter."

"Madame has a daughter, and nothing to live on but an annuity!" shrieked Françoise, bursting into the salon.

The three old crones looked at each other in dismay.

One of them, whose nose and chin nearly met with an expression that betrayed a superior type of hypocrisy and cunning, winked her eyes, and as soon as Françoise's back was turned, she gave her friends a nod, as much as to say, "That girl is a sly one; her name has figured in three wills already." So the three old dames sat on. However, the Abbé presently came out, and at a word from him the witches scuttered down the stairs at his heels, leaving Françoise alone with her mistress. Madame Crochard, whose sufferings had increased in severity, rang, but in vain, for this woman, who only called out, "Coming, coming—in a minute!" The doors of cupboards and wardrobes were slamming as though Françoise were hunting high and low for a lost lottery ticket. Just as this crisis was at a climax, Mademoiselle de Bellefeuille came to stand by her mother's bed, lavishing tender words on her.

"Oh my dear mother, how criminal I have been! You are ill, and I did not know it; my heart did not warn me. However, here I am——"

"Caroline——"

"What is it?"

"They fetched a priest——"

"But send for a doctor, bless me!" cried Mademoiselle de Bellefeuille. "Françoise, a doctor! How is it that those ladies never sent for a doctor?"

"They sent for a priest——" repeated the old woman, with a gasp.

"She is so ill! And no soothing draught, nothing on her table!"

The mother made a vague sign, which Caroline's watchful eye understood, for she was silent to let her mother speak.

"They brought a priest—to hear my confession, as they said. Beware, Caroline!" cried the old woman with an effort, "the priest made me tell him your benefactor's name."

"But who can have told you, poor mother?"

With a mischievous look the old woman expired. If Mademoiselle de Bellefeuille had noted her mother's face, she might have seen what no one will ever see—Death laughing.

To understand the relevance that lies beneath the introduction to this scene, we must for a moment forget the actors in it, and look back at certain previous incidents, of which the last was closely concerned with the death of Madame Crochard. The two parts will then form a whole—a story which, by a law peculiar to life in Paris, was made up of two distinct sets of actions.

Towards the close of the month of November 1805, at about three o'clock one morning, a young attorney, aged about six-and-twenty, was going down the stairs of the hotel where the High Chancellor of the Empire resided. Having reached the courtyard in full evening dress under a keen frost, he could not help giving vent to an exclamation of dismay—qualified, however, by the spirit which rarely deserts a Frenchman—at seeing no hackney coach waiting outside the gates, and hearing no noises such as arise from the wooden shoes or harsh voices of the hackney coachmen of Paris. The occasional pawing of the horses of the Chief Justice's carriage—the young man having left him still playing *bouillotte** with Cambacérès—alone rang out in the paved court, which was scarcely lit by the carriage lamps. Suddenly the young lawyer felt a friendly hand on his shoulder, and turning round, found himself face to face with the Judge, to whom he bowed. As the footman let down the steps of his carriage, the old gentleman, who had served the National Convention, suspected the junior's dilemma. "All cats are grey in the dark," said he good-humouredly. "The Chief Justice cannot compromise himself by putting a pleader in the right way! Especially," he went on, "when that pleader is the nephew of an old colleague, one of the lights of the great Council of State which gave to France the Code Napoléon." At a gesture from the Chief Magistrate of France under the Empire, the young man got into the carriage. "Where do you live?" asked the Minister, before the footman who awaited his orders had closed the door. "Quai des Augustins,* Monseigneur." The horses started, and the young man found himself alone with the Minister, to whom he had vainly tried to speak before and after the sumptuous dinner given by Cambacérès; in fact, the great man had evidently avoided him throughout the evening. "Well, Monsieur *de* Granville, you are on the high road!"

"So long as I sit by your Excellency's side——"

"Nay, I am not jesting," said the Minister. "You were called two years since, and your defence in the case of Ximeuse and Hauteserre has raised you high in your profession."

"I had supposed that my interest in those unfortunate émigrés had done me no good."

"You are still very young," said the Minister gravely. "But the High Chancellor," he went on, after a pause, "was greatly pleased with you this evening. Get a judgeship in the lower courts; we want men. The nephew of a man in whom Cambacérès and I take great interest must not remain in the background for lack of encouragement. Your uncle helped us to tide over a very stormy season, and services of that kind are not to be forgotten." The Minister sat silent for a few minutes. "Before long," he went on, "I shall have three vacancies open in the lower courts and in the Imperial Court in Paris. Come to see me, and take the place you prefer. Till then work hard, but do not be seen at my receptions. In the first place, I am overwhelmed with work, and besides that, your rivals may suspect your purpose and do you harm with the patron. Cambacérès and I, by not speaking a word to you this evening, have averted the accusation of favouritism."

As the Minister ceased speaking, the carriage drew up on the Quai des Augustins; the young lawyer thanked his generous patron for the two lifts he had conferred on him, and then began knocking loudly at the door, for the bitter wind blew cold about his calves. At last the old lodge keeper pulled up the latch, and as the young man passed his window, called out in a hoarse voice, "Monsieur Granville, here is a letter for you." The young man took the letter, and in spite of the cold, tried to identify the writing by the gleam of a dull lamp fast dying out. "From my father!" he exclaimed, as he took his candle, which the porter at last had lighted. And he ran up to his room to read the following epistle:

Set off by the next mail, and if you can get here soon enough, your fortune is made. Mademoiselle Angélique Bontems has lost her sister; she is now an only child, and, as we know, she does not hate you. Madame Bontems can now leave her about forty thousand francs a year, besides whatever she may give her when she marries. I have prepared the way. Our friends will wonder to see a family of old nobility allying itself with the Bontems. Old Bontems was a red republican of the deepest dye, owning large quantities of the nationalised land that he bought for a mere song. But he held nothing but convent lands, and the monks will not come back, and then, as you have already so far derogated as to become a lawyer, I cannot see why we should shrink from a further concession to the prevalent ideas. The girl will have three hundred thousand francs; I can give you a hundred thousand; your mother's property must be worth fifty thousand crowns, more or less; so if you choose to take a judgeship, my dear son, you are quite in a position to become a senator as much as any other man. My brother-in-law, the Councillor of State,* will not indeed lend you a helping hand; still, as he is not married, his property will some day be yours, and if you are not senator by your own efforts, you will get it through him. Then you will be perched high enough to look on at events. Farewell. Yours affectionately.

So young Granville went to bed full of schemes, each more wondrous than the last. Under the powerful protection of the High Chancellor, the Chief Justice, and his mother's brother—one of the originators of the Code—he was about to make a start in a coveted position before the highest court of the Empire, and he already saw himself a member of the bench whence Napoléon selected the chief functionaries of the realm. He could also promise himself a fortune handsome enough to keep up his rank, for which the slender income of five thousand francs from an estate left him by his mother would be quite insufficient. To crown his ambitious dreams with a vision of happiness, he called up the guileless face of Mademoiselle Angélique Bontems, the companion of his childhood. Until he came to boyhood, his father and mother had made no objection to his intimacy with their neighbour's pretty little daughter, but when, during his brief holiday visits to Bayeux, his parents, who prided themselves on their good birth, became aware of his close friendship with the young lady, they forbade him to think of her. Thus for ten years past, Granville had only had occasional glimpses of the girl, whom he still sometimes thought of as *his little wife*. And in those brief moments when they met free from the active watchfulness of their families, they had scarcely exchanged a few vague civilities at the church door or in the street. Their happiest days had been those when, brought together by one of those country festivities known in Normandy as *assemblées*, they could steal a glance at each other from afar. In the course of the last vacation, Granville had twice seen Angélique, and the downcast eyes and sad manner of his little wife had led him to suppose that she was crushed by some unknown despotism. He was off by seven next morning to the coach office in the Rue Notre-Dame-des-Victoires,* and was so lucky as to find a vacant seat in the diligence then starting for Caen. It was not without deep emotion that the young lawyer saw once more the spires of the cathedral at Bayeux. As yet no hope of his life had been cheated, and his heart swelled with the generous feelings that expand in the youthful soul. After the too lengthy feast of welcome prepared by his father, who awaited him with some friends, the impatient youth was conducted to a house, long familiar to him, standing in the Rue Teinture.* His heart beat high when his father—still known in the town of Bayeux as the Comte de Granville—knocked loudly at a carriage gate off which the green paint was dropping in scales. It was about four in the afternoon. A young maid-servant, in a cotton cap, dropped a short curtsy to the two gentlemen, and said that the ladies would soon be home from vespers. The Comte and his son were shown into a low room used as a salon, but more like a convent parlour. The polished walnut panelling darkened the room, around which a few upholstered chairs and antique armchairs were symmetrically arranged. The stone chimney shelf had no ornament but a discoloured mirror, and on each side of it were the twisted branches of a pair of candle brackets, such as were made at the time of the Peace of Utrecht.* Against a panel opposite, young Granville saw an enormous crucifix of ebony and ivory surrounded by a wreath of boxwood that had been blessed. Though there were three windows to the room looking out on a country town garden, laid out in formal square beds edged with boxwood, the room was so dark that it was difficult to discern, on the wall opposite the windows, three pictures of sacred subjects painted by a skilled hand, and purchased, no doubt, during the Revolution by old Bontems, who, as governor of the district, had never neglected his opportunities. From the carefully polished floor to the green checked holland curtains, everything shone with a monastic cleanliness. The young man's heart felt an involuntary chill in this silent retreat where Angélique dwelt. The habit of frequenting the glittering Paris salons, and the constant whirl of society, had effaced from his memory the dull and peaceful surroundings of a country life, and the contrast was so startling as to give him a sort of internal shiver. To have just left a party at the house of Cambacérès, where life was so large, where minds could expand, where the splendour of the Imperial Court was so vividly reflected, and to be dropped suddenly into a sphere of squalidly narrow ideas—was it not like a leap from Italy into Greenland? "Living here is not life!" said he to himself, as he looked round the Methodistical room. The old Comte, seeing his son's dismay, went up to him, and taking his hand led him to a window, where there was still a gleam of daylight, and while the maid was lighting the yellow tapers in the candle branches he tried to clear away the clouds that the dreary place had brought to his brow.

"Listen, my boy," said he, "Old Bontems's widow is a frenzied bigot. 'When the devil is old——' you know! I see that the place goes against the grain. Well, this is the whole truth; the old woman is priest-ridden; they have persuaded her that it was high time to make sure of heaven, and the better to secure Saint Peter and his keys she pays beforehand. She goes to Mass every day, attends every service, takes the Communion every Sunday God has made, and amuses herself by restoring chapels. She has given so many ornaments, and albs, and chasubles, she has crowned the canopy with so many feathers, that on the occasion of the last Corpus Christi as great a crowd came together as to see a man hanged, just to stare at the priests in their splendid vestments and all their gilded implements. This house too is a sort of Holy Land. It was I who hindered the old fool from giving those three pictures to the Church—a Dominiquin,* a Correggio, and an André del Sarto—worth a good deal of money."

"But Angélique?" asked the young man.

"If you do not marry her, Angélique is done for," said

43

the Comte. "Our holy apostles counsel her to live a virgin martyr. I have had the utmost difficulty in stirring up her little heart, since she has been the only child, by talking to her of you—but, as you will easily understand, as soon as she is married you will carry her off to Paris. There, festivities, married life, the theatres, and the rush of Parisian society, will soon make her forget confessionals, and fasting, and hair shirts, and Masses, which are the exclusive nourishment of such creatures."

"But the fifty thousand francs a year derived from Church property? Will not all that return——?"

"That is the point!" exclaimed the Comte, with a cunning glance. "In consideration of this marriage—for Madame Bontems's vanity is not a little flattered by the notion of grafting the Bontems on to the genealogical tree of the Granvilles—the aforenamed mother agrees to settle her fortune absolutely on the girl, reserving only a life interest. The priesthood, therefore, are set against the marriage, but I have had the banns published, everything is ready, and in a week you will be out of the clutches of the mother and her abbés. You will have the prettiest girl in Bayeux, a good little soul who will give you no trouble, because she has sound principles. She has been mortified, as they say in their jargon, by fasting and prayer—and," he added in a low voice, "by her mother."

A modest tap at the door silenced the Comte, who expected to see the two ladies appear. A little page came in, evidently in a great hurry, but, abashed by the presence of the two gentlemen, he beckoned to a housekeeper, who followed him. Dressed in a blue cloth jacket with short tails and blue-and-white striped trousers, his hair cut short all round, the boy's expression was that of a chorister, so strongly was it stamped with the compulsory propriety that marks every member of a sanctimonious household.

"Mademoiselle Gatienne," said he, "do you know where the books are for the offices of the Virgin? The ladies of the congregation of the Sacré-Cœur are going in procession this evening round the church."

Gatienne went in search of the books.

"Will they go on much longer, my little man?" asked the Comte.

"Oh, half an hour at most."

"Let us go to look on," said the father to his son. "There will be some pretty women there, and a visit to the cathedral can do us no harm."

The young lawyer followed him with a doubtful expression.

"What is the matter?" said the Comte.

"The matter, father, is that I am sure I am right."

"But you have said nothing."

"No, but I have been thinking that you have still ten thousand francs a year left of your original fortune. You will leave them to me—as long a time hence as possible, I hope. But if you are ready to give me a hundred thousand francs to make a foolish match, you will surely allow me to ask you for only fifty thousand to save me from such a misfortune, and enjoy as a bachelor a fortune equal to what your Mademoiselle Bontems would bring me."

"Are you mad?"

"No, father. These are the facts. The Chief Justice promised me yesterday that I should have a seat on the bench. Fifty thousand francs added to what I have, and to the pay of my appointment, will give me an income of twelve thousand francs a year. And I then shall most certainly have a chance of marrying a fortune, better than this alliance, which will be poor in happiness if rich in goods."

"It is very clear," said his father, "that you were not brought up under the old regime. Does a man of our rank ever allow his wife to be in his way?"

"But, my dear father, in these days marriage is——"

"*Ah çà!*" cried the Comte, interrupting his son, "then what my old émigré friends tell me is true, I suppose. The Revolution has left us habits devoid of pleasure, and has infected all the young men with vulgar principles. You, like my Jacobin brother-in-law, will harangue me, I suppose, on the nation, public morals, and disinterestedness! *O mon Dieu!* But for the Emperor's sisters, where should we be?"

The still hale old man, whom the peasants on the estate persisted in calling the Seigneur de Granville, ended his speech as they entered the cathedral porch. In spite of the sanctity of the place, and even as he dipped his fingers in the holy water, he hummed an air from the opera of *Rose et Colas** and then led the way down the side aisles, stopping by each pillar to survey the rows of heads, all in lines like ranks of soldiers on parade. The special service of the Sacré-Cœur was about to begin. The ladies affiliated to that congregation were in front near the choir, so the Comte and his son made their way to that part of the nave and stood leaning against one of the columns where it was darkest, whence they could command a view of this mass of faces, looking like a meadow full of flowers. All at once, close to young Granville, a voice sweeter than it seemed possible for a human being to possess broke into song like the first nightingale when winter is past. Though it mingled with the voices of a thousand other women and the notes of the organ, the voice stirred his nerves as though they had been assaulted by the overly full and piercing sounds of a harmonium. The Parisian turned round and saw a young figure, and although her head was inclined so that her face was entirely concealed by a large white bonnet, he concluded that she alone could have made that clear melody; he fancied that he recognised Angélique in spite of a brown merino pelisse that covered her, and he nudged his father's elbow.

"Yes, there she is," said the Comte, after looking where his son pointed. And then, by an expressive glance, he directed his attention to the pale face of an elderly woman who had already detected the strangers, though her false eyes, deep set in dark circles, did not seem to have strayed from the prayer book she held. Angélique raised her face, gazing at the altar as if to inhale the heavy scent of the incense that came wafting in clouds over the two women. And then, in the doubtful light that the tapers shed down the nave, with that of a central lamp and of some lights round the pillars, the young man beheld a face which shook his determination. A white watered silk bonnet closely framed features of perfect regularity, the oval being completed by the satin ribbon tie that fastened it under her dimpled chin. Above a narrow but quite lovely forehead, hair of a pale gold colour parted in two bands and fell over her cheeks, like the shadow of a leaf upon a bunch of flowers. The arches of her eyebrows were drawn with the accuracy we admire in the best Chinese paintings. Her nose, almost aquiline, possessed a rare firmness in its contours, and her lips were like two rosy lines lovingly traced with a delicate brush. Her eyes, of a light blue, were expressive of innocence. Though Granville discerned a sort of rigid reserve in this girlish face, he could ascribe it to the devotion in which Angélique was rapt. The solemn words of prayer, visible in the cold, came from between rows of pearls like a fragrant mist, as it were. The young man involuntarily bent over her a little to breathe this diviner air. This movement attracted the girl's notice; her gaze, raised to the altar, was diverted to Granville, whom she could see but dimly in the gloom, but she recognised him as the companion of her youth, and a memory more vivid than prayer brought a supernatural glow to her face; she blushed. The young lawyer trembled with joy at seeing the expectations of another life overpowered by the expectations of love, and the glory

47

of the sanctuary eclipsed by earthly reminiscences, but his triumph was brief: Angélique dropped her veil, assumed a calm demeanour, and went on singing without letting her voice betray the least emotion. Granville was a prey to one single wish, and every thought of prudence vanished. By the time the service was ended, his impatience was so great that he could not leave the ladies to go home alone, but came at once to make his bow to "his little wife." They bashfully greeted each other on the cathedral porch in the presence of the congregation. Madame Bontems was tremulous with pride as she took the Comte de Granville's arm, though he, forced to offer it in the presence of all the world, was vexed enough with his son for his ill-advised impatience. For about a fortnight, between the official announcement of the intended marriage of the young Vicomte de Granville to Mademoiselle Bontems and the solemn day of the wedding, he came assiduously to visit his ladylove in the dismal salon, to which he became accustomed. His long calls were devoted to watching Angélique's character, for his prudence, happily, had made itself heard again the day after their first meeting. He always found her seated at a little table of some West Indian wood, and engaged in marking the linen of her trousseau. Angélique never spoke first on the subject of religion. If the young lawyer amused himself with fingering the handsome rosary that she kept in a little green velvet bag, if he laughed as he looked at the relic that always accompanies this instrument of devotion, Angélique would gently take the rosary out of his hands and replace it in the bag without a word, putting it away at once. When, now and then, Granville was so bold as to make mischievous remarks as to certain religions practices, the pretty girl listened to him with the obstinate smile of assurance. "You must either believe nothing, or believe everything the Church teaches," she would say. "Would you wish to have a woman without religion as the mother of your children? No. What man may dare judge as between disbelievers and God? And how can I then blame what the Church allows?" Angélique appeared to be animated by such fervent charity, and the young man saw her look at him with such perfect conviction, that he sometimes felt tempted to embrace her religious views; her firm belief that she was on the only right road aroused doubts in his mind, which she tried to turn to account. But then Granville committed the fatal blunder of mistaking the enchantment of desire for that of love. Angélique was so happy in reconciling the voice of her heart with that of duty, by giving way to a liking that had grown up with her from childhood, that the deluded man could not discern which of the two spoke the louder. Are not all young men ready to trust the promise of a pretty face and to infer beauty of soul from beauty of feature? An indefinable impulse leads them to believe that moral perfection must coexist with physical perfection. If Angélique had not been at liberty to give vent to her sentiments, they would soon have dried up in her heart like a plant watered with some deadly acid. How should a lover be aware of a fanaticism so well hidden? Such was the course of young Granville's feelings during that fortnight, which was sped through like a book which promises an absorbing conclusion. Angélique, carefully watched by him, seemed the gentlest of creatures, and he even caught himself feeling grateful to Madame Bontems, who, by implanting so deeply the principles of religion, had in some degree inured her to meet the troubles of life. On the day named for signing the inevitable contract, Madame Bontems made her son-in-law pledge himself solemnly to respect her daughter's religious practices, to allow her entire liberty of conscience, to permit her to go to communion, to church, to confession as often as she pleased, and never to control her choice of priestly advisers. At this critical moment Angélique looked at her future husband with such pure and innocent eyes that Granville did not hesitate to give his word. A smile puckered the lips of the Abbé Fontanon, a pale man who directed the consciences of this household. Mademoiselle Bontems, by a slight nod, seemed to promise that she would never take an unfair advantage of this freedom. As to the old Comte, he gently whistled the tune of an old song, *Va-t-en voir s'ils viennent!**

A few days after the *retours de noce,** of which so much is thought in the provinces, Granville and his wife went to Paris, where the young man was recalled by his appointment as Public Prosecutor to the Imperial Court of the Seine. When the young couple set out to find a residence, Angélique used the influence that the honeymoon gives to every wife in persuading her husband to take a large apartment in the ground floor of a house at the corner of the Vieille-Rue-du-Temple and the Rue Neuve-Saint-François.* Her chief reason for this choice was that the house was close to the Rue d'Orléans,* where there was a church, and not far from a small chapel in the Rue Saint-Louis. "A good housewife provides for everything," said her husband, laughing. Angélique pointed out to him that this part of Paris, known as the Marais, was within easy reach of the Palais de Justice, and that the lawyers they knew lived in the neighbourhood. A fairly large garden made the apartment particularly advantageous to a young couple; the children, *if Heaven should send them any*, could play in the open air; the courtyard was spacious, and there were good stables. The lawyer wished to live in the Chaussée-d'Antin,* where everything is fresh and bright, where the fashions may be seen while still new, where a well-dressed crowd throngs the boulevards, and the distance is less to the theatres or places of amusement; but he was obliged to give way to the coaxing ways of a young wife, who asked this as his first favour; so, to please her, he settled in the Marais. Granville's duties required him to work hard—all the more, because they were new to him—so he devoted himself in the first place to furnishing his private study and arranging his books. He was soon established in a room crammed with papers, and left the decoration of the house to his wife. He was all the more willing to plunge Angélique into the bustle of buying the initial furniture and fittings of their household, the source of so much pleasure and of so many memories to most young women, because he was rather ashamed of depriving her of his company more than the rules of the honeymoon would allow. As soon as his work was fairly under way, the Public Prosecutor allowed his wife to tempt him out of his study to consider the effect of the furnishings and the decorations, which before he had only seen piecemeal or unfinished. If the old adage is true that says a woman may be judged by her front door, her rooms must express her mind with even greater fidelity. Whether Madame de Granville had put her trust in decorators with no taste, or whether she had imposed her own stainless character onto a world of things that she had arranged, the young magistrate was surprised by the lack of charm and the cold solemnity that reigned in these rooms: he beheld nothing that was graceful; everything there was discordant, nothing was there that might please the eye. The spirit of uprightness and pettiness stamped into the sitting room at Bayeux lived on in his home beneath the broad panels that were hollowed in circles and decorated with those arabesques of which the long, monotonous mouldings are in such bad taste. Anxious to find excuses for his wife, the young husband began again, looking first at the long and lofty anteroom through which the apartment was entered. The colour of the panels, as ordered by his wife, was too heavy, and the very dark green velvet used to cover the benches added to the gloom of this entrance—not, to be sure, an important room, but giving a first impression—just as we measure a man's intelligence by his first words. An anteroom is a kind of preface which announces what is to follow, but promises nothing. The young husband wondered whether his wife could really have chosen the lamp of an antique pattern which hung in the centre of this bare hall, the pavement of black and white marble, and the paper in imitation of blocks of stone, with green moss on them in places. A handsome, but not new, barometer hung on the middle of one of the walls, as if to accentuate the void. At the sight of it all, he looked round at his wife; he saw her so much pleased by the red braid binding to the cotton curtains, so satisfied with the barometer and the strictly decent statue that ornamented a large Gothic stove, that he had not the barbarous courage to overthrow such deep convictions. Instead of blaming his wife, Granville blamed himself, accusing himself of having failed in his duty of guiding the first steps in Paris of a girl brought up at Bayeux. From this specimen, what might not be expected of the other rooms? What was to be looked for from a woman who took fright at the bare legs of a caryatid, and who would not look at a chandelier or a candlestick if she saw on it the nude outlines of an Egyptian bust? At this date the school of David was at the height of its glory; all the art of France bore the stamp of his correct design and his love of antique types, which indeed gave his pictures the character of coloured sculpture. But none of these devices of Imperial luxury found civic rights under Madame de Granville's roof. The spacious, square salon remained as it had been left from the time of Louis XV, in white and tarnished gold, lavishly adorned by the architect with chequered latticework and the hideous garlands due to the uninventive designers of the time. Still, if harmony at least had prevailed, if the furniture of modem mahogany had but assumed the twisted forms of which Boucher's corrupt taste first set the fashion, Angélique's room would only have suggested the fantastic contrast of a young couple in the nineteenth

century living as though they were in the eighteenth, but
a number of details were in ridiculous discord. The consoles, the clocks, and the candelabra were decorated with
the military trophies which the wars of the Empire commended to the affections of the Parisians, and the Greek
helmets, the Roman crossed daggers, and the shields so
dear to military enthusiasm that they were introduced
on furniture of the most peaceful uses, were hardly in
accord with the delicate and profuse arabesques that delighted Madame de Pompadour. Devoutness tends to
an indescribably tiresome kind of humility which does
not exclude pride. Whether from modesty or by choice,
Madame de Granville seemed to have a horror of light
and cheerful colours; perhaps, too, she imagined that
brown and purple was becoming to the dignity of a magistrate. How could a girl accustomed to an austere life
have admitted the luxurious divans that may suggest
evil thoughts, the elegant and perfidious boudoirs where
sin begins to take shape? The poor magistrate was in
despair. From the tone in which he approved, only sec-
onding the praises she bestowed on herself, Angélique
understood that nothing really pleased him, and she
expressed so much regret at her want of success, that
Granville, who was very much in love, regarded her
disappointment as a proof of her affection instead of
resentment for an offence to her self-conceit. After all,
could he expect a girl just snatched from the mediocrity of provincial notions, unfamiliar with the style and
the elegance of Parisian life, to know or do any better?
The magistrate preferred to believe that his wife's choice
had been overruled by the tradesmen rather than admit to himself the truth. If he had been less in love, he
would have understood that the dealers, always quick
to discern their customers' ideas, had blessed Heaven
for sending them a tasteless little bigot, who would take
their old-fashioned goods off their hands. So he comforted the pretty young *Normande*.*

"Happiness, dear Angélique, does not depend on a more or less elegant piece of furniture; it depends on the wife's sweetness, gentleness, and love."

"Why, it is my duty to love you," said Angélique mildly, "and I can have no more delightful duty to carry out."

Nature has implanted in the heart of woman so great a desire to please, so deep a craving for love, that, even in a sanctimonious young woman, the ideas of salvation and a future existence must give way to the happiness of early married life. And, in fact, from the month of April, when they were married, till the beginning of winter, the husband and wife lived in perfect union. Love and hard work have the grace of making a man tolerably indifferent to external matters. Being obliged to spend half the day in court fighting for the gravest interests of men's lives or fortunes, Granville was less alive than another might have been to certain facts in his household. If, on a Friday, he found none but Lenten fare, and by chance asked for a dish of meat without getting it, his wife, forbidden by the Gospel to tell a lie, could still, by such subterfuges as are permissible in the interests of religion, cloak what was premeditated purpose under some pretext of her own carelessness or the scarcity in the market. She would often exculpate herself at the expense of the cook, and even go so far as to scold him. At that time young magistrates did not, as they do now, keep the fasts of the Church, the four rogation seasons, and the vigils of festivals; so Granville was not at first aware of the regular recurrence of these meager meals, which his wife took perfidious care should be made palatable by the addition of teal, moorhen, and fish pies, that their amphibious meat or high seasoning might cheat his palate. Thus the magistrate unconsciously lived in strict orthodoxy, and worked out his salvation without knowing it. On weekdays he did not know whether or not his wife went to Mass; on Sundays, with a kind of natural condescension, he accompanied her to church to make up to her, as it were, for sometimes giving up vespers in favour of his company; he could not at first fully enter into the strictness of his wife's religious views. The theatres being intolerable in summer by reason of the heat, Granville had not even the opportunity of a successful play to propose to take his wife to the theatre. So the serious question of the theatre was not discussed. And, in short, at the early stage of a union to which a man has been led by a young girl's beauty, he can hardly be exacting as to his amusements. Youth is eager rather than refined, and possession has a charm in itself. How should he be keen to note coldness, dignity, and reserve in the woman to whom he ascribes the excitement he himself feels, and lends the glow of the fire that burns within him? It is necessary to attain a certain degree of conjugal tranquility to see that a sanctimonious woman sits waiting for love with her arms crossed. Granville, therefore, believed himself happy till a fatal event brought its influence to bear on his married life. In the month of November 1808, the Canon of Bayeux Cathedral, who had been the keeper of Madame Bontems's conscience and her daughter's, came to Paris, spurred by the ambition to be at the head of a church in the capital—a position which he regarded perhaps as the stepping stone to a bishopric. On resuming his former control of this wandering lamb, he was horrified to find her already much deteriorated by the air of Paris, and strove to reclaim her to his chilly fold. Frightened by the exhortations of this priest, a man of about thirty-eight, who brought with him, into the circle of the enlightened and tolerant Paris clergy, the bitter provincial Catholicism and the inflexible bigotry which fetter timid souls with endless exactions, Madame de Granville did penance and returned from her Jansenist errors. It would be tiresome to describe minutely all the circumstances which insensibly brought disaster on this household; it will be enough to relate the simple facts without giving them in strict order of time. The first misunderstanding between the young couple was, however, a serious one. When Granville took his wife into society she never declined solemn functions, such as dinners, concerts, or parties given by the magistrates above her husband in the judicial hierarchy, but for a long time she constantly excused herself with the plea of a headache when they were invited to a ball. One day Granville, out of patience with these assumed indispositions, destroyed a note of invitation to a ball at the house of a state councillor, and gave his wife only a verbal invitation. Then, on the evening, her health being quite above suspicion, he took her to a magnificent entertainment.

"My dear," said he, on their return home, seeing her wear an offensive air of depression, "your position as a wife, the rank you hold in society, and the fortune you enjoy, impose on you certain duties of which no divine law can relieve you. Are you not your husband's pride? You are required to go to balls when I go, and to appear in a becoming manner."

"And what is there, my love, so disastrous in my dress?"

"It is your manner, my dear. When a young man comes up to speak to you, you look so serious that a spiteful person might believe you doubtful of your own virtue. You seem to fear lest a smile should undo you. You really look as if you were asking forgiveness of God for the sins that may be committed around you. The world, my dearest, is not a convent. But, as you have mentioned your dress, I may confess to you that it is no less a duty to conform to the customs and fashions of Society."

"Do you wish that I should display my shape like those indecent women who wear gowns so low that impudent eyes can stare at their bare shoulders and their——"

"There is a difference, my dear," said her husband, interrupting her, "between uncovering your whole bust and giving some grace to your dress. You wear three rows of net frills that cover your throat up to your chin. You look as if you had desired your dressmaker to destroy the graceful line of your shoulders and bosom with as much care as a coquette would devote to obtaining from hers a bodice that might emphasise her covered form. Your bust is wrapped in so many folds that everyone was laughing at your affectation of prudery. You would be really grieved if I were to repeat the ill-natured remarks made on your appearance."

"Those who admire such obscenity will not have to bear the burden if we sin," said the lady curtly.

"And you did not dance?" asked Granville.

"I shall never dance," she replied.

"If I tell you that you ought to dance!——" said her husband sharply. "Yes, you ought to follow the fashions, wear flowers in your hair, wear diamonds. Remember, my dear, that rich people—and we are rich—are obliged to keep up the luxury of the state! Is it not far better to encourage manufacturers than to distribute money in the form of alms through the medium of the clergy?"

"You talk as a statesman!" said Angélique.

"And you as a priest," he retorted.

The discussion was bitter. Madame de Granville's answers, though spoken very sweetly and in a voice as clear as a church bell, showed an obstinacy that betrayed priestly influence. When she appealed to the rights secured to her by Granville's promise, she added that her confessor specially forbade her going to balls; then her husband pointed out to her that the priest was overstepping the regulations of the Church. This odious theological dispute was renewed with great violence and acerbity on both sides when Granville proposed to take his wife to the play. Finally, the magistrate, whose sole aim was to defeat the pernicious influence exerted over his wife by her old confessor, placed the question on such a footing that Madame de Granville, in a spirit of defiance, referred it by writing to the Court of Rome, asking in so many words whether a woman could wear low gowns and go to the play and to balls without compromising her salvation. The reply of the venerable Pope Pius VII came at once, strongly condemning the wife's recalcitrancy and blaming the priest. This letter, a chapter on conjugal duties, might have been dictated by the spirit of Fénelon, whose grace and tenderness pervaded every line.

A wife is right to go wherever her husband may take her. Even if she sins by his command, she will not be ultimately held answerable.

These two sentences of the Pope's homily only made Madame de Granville and her confessor accuse him of irreligion. But before this letter had arrived, Granville had discovered the strict observance of fast days that his wife forced upon him, and gave his servants orders to serve him with meat every day in the year. However much annoyed his wife might be by these commands, Granville, who cared not a straw for such indulgence or abstinence, persisted with manly determination. Is it not an offence to the weakest creature that can think at all to be compelled to do, by the will of another, anything that he would otherwise have done simply of his own accord? Of all forms of tyranny, the most odious is that which constantly robs the soul of the merit of its thoughts and deeds. It has to abdicate without having reigned. The word we are readiest to speak, the feelings we most love to express, die when we are commanded to utter them. Before long, the young magistrate ceased to invite his friends, to give parties or dinners; the house might have been shrouded in crape. A house where the mistress is a bigot has an atmosphere of its own. The

servants, who are, of course, under her immediate control, are chosen among a class who call themselves
pious, and who have an unmistakable physiognomy.
Just as the jolliest fellow alive, when he joins the gen-
darmerie, has the countenance of a gendarme, so those
who give themselves over to the practices of devotion
acquire a uniform expression; the habit of lowering their
eyes and preserving a sanctimonious mien clothes them
in a livery of hypocrisy which rogues can affect to perfection. And besides, sanctimonious women constitute
a sort of republic; they all know each other; the servants
they recommend and hand on from one to another are
a race apart and preserved by them, as horse breeders
will admit no animal into their stables that has not a
pedigree. The more the impious—as they are thought—
come to understand a household of bigots, the more
they perceive that everything is stamped with an indescribable squalor; they find there, at the same time, an
appearance of avarice and mystery, as in a usurer's
home, and the dank scent of cold incense which gives
a chill to the stale atmosphere of a chapel. This methodi-
cal meanness, this narrowness of thought, which is
visible in every detail, can only be expressed by one
word—*sanctimoniousness*. In these sinister and pitiless
houses, sanctimoniousness is written on the furniture,
the prints, the pictures; speech is sanctimonious, the
silence is sanctimonious, the faces are those of sanctimonious people. The transformation of men and things
into a state of sanctimoniousness is an inexplicable mystery, but the fact is evident. Everybody can see that the
sanctimonious do not walk, do not sit, do not speak as
men of the world walk, sit, and speak. Under their roof
everyone is ill at ease, no one laughs, stiffness and for-
mality infect everything, from the mistress's cap down
to her pin cushion; eyes are not honest, the people there
seem like shadows, and the lady of the house seems
perched on a throne of ice. One morning, poor Granville

discerned with grief and pain that all the symptoms of sanctimoniousness had invaded his home. There are in the world different spheres in which the same effects are seen, though produced by dissimilar causes. Dulness hedges such miserable homes round with walls of brass, enclosing the horrors of the desert and the infinite void. The home is not so much a tomb as that far worse thing—a convent. In the centre of this icy sphere the lawyer could study his wife dispassionately. He observed, not without keen regret, the narrow-mindedness that stood confessed in the very way that her hair grew, low on the forehead, which was slightly depressed; he discovered in the perfect regularity of her features a certain set rigidity which before long made him hate the assumed sweetness that had bewitched him. Intuition told him that one day of disaster those thin lips might say, "My dear, it is for your own good!" Madame de Granville's complexion was acquiring a dull pallor and an austere expression that put an end to the good humour of all who came near her. Was this change wrought by the ascetic habits of a Pharisaism which is not piety any more than avarice is economy? It would be hard to say. Beauty without expression is perhaps an imposture. The imperturbable set smile that the young wife always wore when she looked at Granville seemed to be a sort of Jesuitical formula of happiness, by which she thought to satisfy all the requirements of married life. Her charity was an offence, her soulless beauty was monstrous to those who knew her; the mildness of her speech was an irritation: she acted, not on feeling, but on duty. There are faults which may yield in a wife to the stern lessons of experience, or to a husband's warnings, but nothing can counteract false ideas of religion. An eternity of happiness to be won, set in the scale against worldly enjoyment, triumphs over everything and makes every pang endurable. Is it not the apotheosis of egotism, of *self* beyond the grave? Thus even the Pope was censured at the tribunal of the priest and the young devotee. To be always in the right is a feeling which absorbs every other in these tyrannous souls. For some time past, a secret struggle had been going on between the ideas of the husband and wife, and the young magistrate was soon weary of a battle to which there could be no end. What man, what temper, can endure the sight of a hypocritically affectionate face and categorical resistance to his slightest wishes? What is to be done with a wife who takes advantage of his passion to protect her coldness, who seems determined on being blandly inexorable, prepares herself ecstatically to play the martyr, and looks on her husband as a scourge from God, a means of flagellation that may spare her the fires of purgatory? What picture can give an idea of these women who make virtue hateful by defying the gentle precepts of that faith which Saint John epitomised in the words, "Love one another?" If there was a bonnet to be found in a milliner's shop that was condemned to remain in the window, or to be packed off to the colonies, Granville was certain to see it on his wife's head; if a material of bad colour or hideous design were to be found, she would select it. These hapless bigots are heartbreaking in their notions of dress. Want of taste is a defect inseparable from false pietism. And so, in this intimate life that needs the fullest sympathy, Granville had no true companionship. He went out alone to parties and the theatres. Nothing in his house appealed to him. A huge crucifix that hung between his bed and Angélique's seemed figurative of his destiny. Does it not represent a murdered divinity, a man-god, done to death in all the prime of life and beauty? The ivory of that cross was less cold than Angélique crucifying her husband under the plea of virtue. This it was that lay at the root of their woes; the young wife saw nothing but duty where she should have given love. Here, one Ash Wednesday, rose the pale and spectral form of fasting in Lent, of total abstinence, commanded in a severe tone—and Granville did not deem it advisable to write in his turn to the Pope and take the opinion of the consistory on the proper way of observing Lent, the Ember days, and the eve of great festivals. His misfortune was too great! He could not even complain, for what could he say? He had a pretty young wife attached to her duties, virtuous—nay, a model of all the virtues. She had a child every year, nursed them herself, and brought them up in the highest principles. Being charitable, Angélique was promoted to rank as an angel. The old women who constituted the circle in which she moved—for at that time young women were still advised not to be religious as a matter of fashion—all admired Madame de Granville's piety, and regarded her, not indeed as a virgin, but as a martyr. They blamed not the wife's scruples, but the procreative barbarity of the husband. By degrees, Granville, overwhelmed with work, deprived of conjugal pleasures, and weary of a world in which he wandered alone, had sunk into the most dreadful stagnation by the time he was thirty-two. He hated life. Having too lofty a notion of the responsibilities imposed on him by his position to set the example of a dissipated life, he tried to deaden feeling by hard study, and began writing a major work on the law. But he was not allowed to enjoy the monastic peace he had hoped for. When the divine Angélique saw him desert worldly society to work at home with such regularity, she tried to convert him. It had been a real sorrow for her to know that her husband's opinions were not strictly Christian, and she sometimes wept as she reflected that if her husband should die it would be in a state of final impenitence, so that she could not hope to snatch him from the eternal fires of Hell. Thus Granville was the mark for the mean ideas, the vacuous arguments, the narrow views by which his wife—fancying she had achieved the first victory—tried to gain a second by bringing him back within the pale of the Church. This was the last straw. What can be more intolerable than the blind struggle in which the obstinacy of a bigot tries to meet the acumen of a magistrate? What could be more terrible than to endure the acrimonious pinpricks to which a passionate soul prefers a dagger thrust? Granville began to neglect his home where everything was becoming unbearable: his children, broken by their mother's frigid despotism, dared not go with him to the play; indeed, Granville could never give them any pleasure without bringing down punishment from their terrible mother. His loving nature was weaned to indifference, to a selfishness worse than death. His boys, indeed, he saved from this hell by sending them to school at an early age, and insisting on his right to train them. He rarely interfered between his wife and her daughters, but he was resolved that they should marry as soon as they were old enough. Even if he had wished to take violent measures, he could have found no justification; his wife, backed by a formidable army of dowagers, would have had him condemned by the whole world. Thus Granville had no choice but to live in complete isolation; but, crushed under the tyranny of misery, he could not himself bear to see how altered he was by grief and toil. And he dreaded any connection or intimacy with women of the world, having no hope of finding any consolation.

The instructive history of this melancholy household gave rise to no events worthy of record during the fifteen years between 1806 and 1825. Madame de Granville was exactly the same after losing her husband's affection as she had been during the time when she called herself happy. She performed novenas, beseeching God and the saints to enlighten her as to the faults which displeased her husband and how she might lead back the lost sheep, but the more fervent her prayers, the less Granville was seen at home. For about five years now, the Public Prosecutor, to whom the Restoration had given a high position in the judiciary, had been living in the mezzanine of his house to avoid being with the Comtesse de Granville. Every morning a little scene took place, which, if evil tongues are to be believed, is repeated in many households as the result of incompatibility of temper, of moral or physical malady, or of antagonisms leading to such disaster as is recorded in this history. At about eight in the morning a housekeeper, bearing no small resemblance to a nun, rang at the Comte de Granville's door. Admitted to the room next to the magistrate's study, she always repeated the same message to the footman, and always in the same tone—"Madame would be glad to know whether Monsieur le Comte has had a good night, and if she is to have the pleasure of his company at breakfast."

"Monsieur presents his compliments to Madame la Comtesse," the valet would say, after speaking with his master, "and begs her to hold him excused; important business compels him to be in court this morning." A minute later the woman reappeared and asked on Madame's behalf whether she would have the pleasure of seeing Monsieur le Comte before he went out. "He is gone," was always the reply, though often his carriage was still waiting. This little dialogue by proxy became a daily ceremonial. Granville's servant, a favourite with his master, and the cause of more than one quarrel over his irreligious and dissipated conduct, would even go into his master's room, as a matter of form, when the Comte was not there, and come back with the same formula in reply. The aggrieved wife was always on the watch for her husband's return, and standing on the steps so as to meet him like an embodiment of remorse. The petty aggressiveness which lies at the root of the monastic temper was the foundation of Madame de Granville's; she was now thirty-five but looked forty. When the Comte was compelled by decency to speak to his wife or to dine at home, she was only too well pleased

to inflict her company upon him, with her acid-sweet remarks and the intolerable dulness of her narrow-minded
circle, and she tried to put him in the wrong before the
servants and her charitable friends. When, at this time,
the presidency of a royal court was offered to the Comte
de Granville, who was in high favour, he begged to be
allowed to remain in Paris. This refusal, of which the
Keeper of the Seals* alone knew the reasons, gave rise to
extraordinary conjectures on the part of the Comtesse's
intimate friends and of her confessor. Granville, a rich
man with a hundred thousand francs a year, belonged to
one of the first families of Normandy; his appointment
to a presidency would have been the stepping stone to
a peerage; from whence this strange lack of ambition?
Why had he given up his great book on Law? What
was the meaning of the dissipation which for nearly six
years had made him a stranger to his home, his family,
his study, to all he ought to hold dear? The Comtesse's
confessor, who based his hopes of a bishopric quite as
much on the families he governed as on the services he
rendered to an association of which he was an ardent
propagator, was much disappointed by Granville's refusal, and tried to insinuate calumnious explanations: "If
Monsieur le Comte had such an objection to provincial
life, it was perhaps because he dreaded finding himself
under the necessity of leading a regular life, compelled
to set an example of moral conduct, and to live with the
Comtesse, from whom nothing could have alienated him
but some illicit connection, for how could a woman so
pure as Madame de Granville ever tolerate the disorderly
life into which her husband had drifted?" The sanctimonious women accepted as facts these hints, which
unluckily were not merely hypothetical, and Madame
de Granville was stricken as by a thunderbolt. Knowing
nothing of the ways of the world, ignorant of love and
its follies, Angélique was so far from conceiving of any
conditions of married life unlike those that had alienated

her husband, that she believed him to be incapable of the errors which are crimes in the eyes of any wife. When the Comte ceased to demand anything of her, she imagined that the tranquillity he now seemed to enjoy was in the course of nature, and, as she had really given to him all the love which her heart was capable of feeling for a man, while the priest's conjectures were the utter destruction of the illusions she had hitherto cherished, she defended her husband; at the same time, she could not eradicate the suspicion that had been so ingeniously sown in her soul. These alarms wrought such havoc in her feeble brain that they made her ill; she was worn by low fever. These incidents took place during Lent 1822; she would not agree to cease her austerities, and fell into a decline that put her life in danger. Granville's indifference was added torture; his care and attention were such as a nephew feels himself bound to give to some old uncle. Though the Comtesse had given up her persistent nagging and remonstrances and tried to receive her husband with affectionate words, the sharpness of the bigot showed through, and one speech would often undo the work of a week. Towards the end of May, the warm breath of spring and a more nourishing diet than her Lenten fare restored Madame de Granville to a little strength. One morning, on coming home from Mass, she sat down on a stone bench in the little garden, where the sun's kisses reminded her of the early days of her married life, and she looked back across the years to see wherein she might have failed in her duty as a wife and mother. She was broken in upon by the Abbé Fontanon in an almost indescribable state of excitement.

"Has any misfortune befallen you, Father?" she asked with filial solicitude.

"Ah! I only wish," cried the Normandy priest, "that the woes inflicted on you by the hand of God were dealt out to me; but, my admirable friend, there are trials to which you can but bow."

"Can any worse punishments await me than those with which Providence crushes me by making my husband the instrument of His wrath?"

"You must prepare yourself, daughter, to yet worse mischief than we and your pious friends had ever conceived of."

"Then I may thank God," said the Comtesse, "for vouchsafing to use you as the messenger of His will, and thus, as ever, setting the treasures of mercy by the side of the scourges of His wrath, just as in bygone days He showed a spring to Hagar when He had driven her into the desert."*

"He measures your sufferings by the strength of your resignation and the weight of your sins."

"Speak—I am ready to hear!" As she said it she cast her eyes up to heaven. "Speak, Monsieur Fontanon."

"For seven years Monsieur Granville has lived in sin with a concubine by whom he has two children, and on this adulterous connection he has spent more than five hundred thousand francs, which ought to have been the property of his legitimate family."

"I must see it to believe it!" cried the Comtesse.

"Far be it from you!" exclaimed the Abbé. "You must forgive, my daughter, and wait in patience and prayer till God enlightens your husband; unless, indeed, you choose to adopt against him the means offered you by human laws."

The long conversation that ensued between the priest and his penitent resulted in an extraordinary change in the Comtesse; she abruptly dismissed him and called her servants, who were alarmed at her flushed face and crazed energy. She ordered her carriage—countermanded it—changed her mind twenty times in the hour, but at last, at about three o'clock, as if she had come to some great determination, she went out, leaving the whole household in amazement at such a sudden transformation.

"Is the Comte coming home to dinner?" she asked of his servant, to whom she never would speak.

"No, Madame."

"Did you go with him to the courts this morning?"

"Yes, Madame."

"And today is Monday?"

"Yes, Madame."

"Then do the courts sit on Mondays nowadays?"

"The devil take you!" cried the valet, as his mistress drove off after saying to the coachman—"Rue Taitbout."

Mademoiselle de Bellefeuille was weeping; Roger, sitting by her side, held one of her hands between his own. He was silent, looking by turns at little Charles—who, not understanding his mother's grief, stood speechless at the sight of her tears—at the cot where Eugénie lay sleeping, and Caroline's face, on which grief had the effect of rain falling across the beams of cheerful sunshine.

"Yes, my darling," said Roger, after a long silence, "that is the great secret: I am married. But some day I hope we may form but one family. My wife has been in a desperate state ever since last March. I do not wish her dead; still, if it should please God to take her to Himself, I believe she will be happier in Paradise than in a world to whose griefs and pleasures she is equally indifferent."

"How I hate that woman! How could she bear to make you unhappy? And yet it is to that unhappiness that I owe my happiness!"

Her tears suddenly ceased.

"Caroline, let us hope," cried Roger. "Do not be frightened by anything that priest may have said to you. Though my wife's confessor is a man to be feared for his power in the congregation, if he should try to blight our happiness I would find means——"

"What could you do?"

"We would go to Italy; I would fly——"

A shriek that rang out from the adjoining room made Roger start and Mademoiselle de Bellefeuille quake, but she rushed into the salon, and there found Madame de Granville in a dead faint. When the Comtesse recovered her senses, she sighed deeply on finding herself supported by the Comte and her rival, whom she instinctively pushed away with a gesture of contempt.

Mademoiselle de Bellefeuille rose to withdraw.

"You are at home, Madame," said Granville, taking Caroline by the arm. "Stay."

The magistrate took up his wife in his arms, carried her to the carriage, and got into it with her.

"Who is it that has brought you to the point of wishing me dead, of resolving to flee from me?" asked the Comtesse, looking at her husband with grief mingled with indignation. "Was I not young? You thought me pretty—what fault have you to find with me? Have I been false to you? Have I not been a virtuous and well-behaved wife? My heart has cherished no image but yours, my ears have listened to no other voice. What duty have I failed in? What have I ever denied you?"

"Happiness, Madame," said the Comte severely. "You know, Madame, that there are two ways of serving God. Some Christians imagine that by going to church at fixed hours to say a *Paternoster*, by attending Mass regularly and avoiding sin, they may win heaven—but they, Madame, will go to hell; they have not loved God for Himself, they have not worshipped Him as He chooses to be worshipped, they have made no sacrifice. Though mild in seeming, they are hard on their neighbours; they see the law, the letter, not the spirit. This is how you have treated me, your earthly husband; you have sacrificed my happiness to your salvation; you were always absorbed in prayer when I came to you in gladness of heart; you wept when you should have cheered my toil; you have never tried to satisfy any demands I have made on you."

"And if they were wicked," cried the Comtesse hotly, "was I to lose my soul to please you?"

"It is a sacrifice which another, a more loving woman, has dared to make," said Granville coldly.

"*O mon Dieu!*" she cried, bursting into tears, "Thou hearest! Has he been worthy of the prayers and penance I have lived in, wearing myself out to atone for his sins and my own? Of what avail is virtue?"

"To win Heaven, my dear. A woman cannot be at the same time the wife of a man and the spouse of Christ. That would be bigamy; she must choose between a husband and a nunnery. For the sake of future advantage you have stripped your soul of all the love, all the devotion, which God commands that you should have for me, you have cherished no feeling but hatred——"

"Have I not loved you?" she put in.

"No, Madame."

"Then what is love?" the Comtesse involuntarily inquired.

"Love, my dear," replied Granville, with a sort of ironical surprise, "you are incapable of understanding it. The cold sky of Normandy is not that of Spain. This difference of climate is no doubt the secret of our disaster. To yield to our caprices, to guess them, to find pleasure in pain, to sacrifice the world's opinion, your pride, your religion even, and still regard these offerings as mere grains of incense burnt in honour of the idol—that is love——"

"The love of ballet girls!" cried the Comtesse in horror. "Such flames cannot last, and must soon leave nothing but ashes and cinders, regret or despair. A wife, Monsieur, ought, in my opinion, to bring you true friendship, equable warmth——"

"You speak of warmth as negroes speak of ice," retorted the Comte, with a sardonic smile. "Consider that the humblest daisy has more charms than the proudest and most gorgeous of the red hawthorns that attract us in spring by their strong scent and brilliant colour. At the same time," he went on, "I will do you justice. You have kept so precisely in the strait path of imaginary duty prescribed by law, that only to make you understand wherein you have failed towards me, I should be obliged to enter into details which would offend your dignity and instruct you in matters which would seem to you to undermine all morality."

"And you dare to speak of morality when you have but just left the house where you have dissipated your children's fortune in debaucheries?" cried the Comtesse, maddened by her husband's reticence.

"There, Madame, I must correct you," said the Comte, coolly interrupting his wife. "Though Mademoiselle de Bellefeuille is rich, it is at nobody's expense. My uncle was master of his fortune, and had several heirs. In his lifetime, and out of pure friendship, regarding her as his niece, he gave her the little estate of Bellefeuille. As for anything else, I owe it to his liberality——"

"Such conduct is only worthy of a Jacobin!" said the sanctimonious Angélique.

"Madame, you are forgetting that your own father was one of the Jacobins whom you scorn so uncharitably," said the Comte severely. "Citizen Bontems was signing death warrants at a time when my uncle was doing France good service."

Madame de Granville was silenced. But after a short pause, the remembrance of what she had just seen reawakened in her soul the jealousy which nothing can kill in a woman's heart, and she murmured, as if to herself—"How can a woman thus destroy her own soul and that of others?"

"Madame," replied the Comte, tired of this dialogue, "you yourself may some day have to answer that question." The Comtesse was scared. "You perhaps will be held excused by the merciful Judge, who will weigh our sins," he went on, "in consideration of the conviction with which you have worked out my misery. I do not hate you—I hate those who have perverted your heart and your reason. You have prayed for me, just as Mademoiselle de Bellefeuille has given me her heart and crowned my life with love. You should have been my mistress and the prayerful saint by turns. Do me the justice to confess that I am no reprobate, no debauchee. The life I lead is pure. Alas! After seven years of wretchedness, the craving for happiness led me by an imperceptible descent to love another woman and make a second home. And do not imagine that I am singular; there are in this city thousands of husbands, all led by various causes to live this twofold life."

"*Grand Dieu!*" cried the Comtesse. "How heavy is the cross Thou hast laid on me to bear! If the husband Thou hast given me here below in Thy wrath can only be made happy through my death, take me to Thyself!"

"If you had always breathed such admirable sentiments and such devotion, we should be happy yet," said the Comte coldly.

"Indeed," cried Angélique, melting into a flood of tears, "forgive me if I have done any wrong. Yes, Monsieur, I am ready to obey you in all things, feeling sure that you will desire nothing but what is just and natural; henceforth I will be all you can wish your wife to be."

"If your purpose, Madame, is to compel me to say that I no longer love you, I shall find the cruel courage to tell you so. Can I command my heart? Can I wipe out in an instant the traces of fifteen years of suffering? I have ceased to love. These words contain a mystery as deep as lies in the words *I love*. Esteem, respect, friendship may be won, lost, regained; but as to love—I might school myself for a thousand years, and it would not blossom again, especially for a woman too old to respond to it."

"I hope, Monsieur le Comte, I sincerely hope, that such words may not be spoken to you some day by the woman you love, and in such a tone and accent——"

"Will you put on a dress *à la Grecque** this evening, and come to the Opera?"

The shudder with which the Comtesse received the suggestion was a mute reply.

Early in December 1833, a man, whose perfectly white hair and worn features seemed to show that he was aged by grief rather than by years, was walking at midnight along the Rue Gaillon.* Having reached a house of modest appearance, and only two stories high, he paused to look up at one of the attic windows that pierced the roof at regular intervals. A dim light scarcely showed through the humble panes, some of which had been repaired with paper. The man below was watching the wavering glimmer with the vague curiosity of a Paris idler, when a young man came out of the house. As the pale rays of the streetlamp fell upon the curious face, it will not seem surprising that, in spite of the darkness, this young man went towards the passerby, though with the hesitancy that is usual when we have any fear of making a mistake in recognising an acquaintance.

"What, is it you," cried he, "Monsieur le Président? Alone at this hour, and so far from the Rue Saint-Lazare. *Allow me to have the honour of giving you my arm. The pavement is so treacherous this morning, that if we do not hold each other up," he added, to soothe the elder man's susceptibilities, "we shall find it hard to escape a tumble."

"But, my dear Monsieur, I am no more than fifty-five, unfortunately for me," replied the Comte de Granville. "A physician of your celebrity must know that at that age a man is still hale and strong."

"Then you are in waiting on a lady, I suppose," replied Horace Bianchon. "You are not, I imagine, in the habit of going about Paris on foot. When a man keeps such fine horses——"

"Most of the time, when I am not out and about, I commonly return from the Palais-Royal or the Cercle des Étrangers* on foot," replied the Comte.

"And with large sums of money about you, perhaps!" cried the doctor. "It is a positive invitation to the assassin's knife."

"I am not afraid of that," said Granville, with melancholy indifference.

"But, at least, do not stand about," said the doctor, leading the Comte towards the boulevard. "A little more and I shall believe that you are bent on robbing me of your last illness, and dying by some other hand than mine."

"You caught me playing the spy," said the Comte. "Whether on foot or in a carriage, and at whatever hour of the night I may come by, I have for some time past observed at a window on the third floor of your house the shadow of a person who seems to work with heroic constancy." The Comte paused as if he felt some sudden pain. "And I take as great an interest in that garret," he went on, "as a citizen of Paris must feel in the finishing of the Palais-Royal."

"Well," said Horace Bianchon eagerly, "I can tell you——"

"Tell me nothing," replied Granville, cutting the doctor short. "I would not give a centime to know whether the shadow that moves across that shabby blind is that of a man or a woman, nor whether the inhabitant of that attic is happy or miserable. Though I was surprised to see no one at work there this evening, and though I stopped to look, it was solely for the pleasure of indulging in conjectures as numerous and as idiotic as those of idlers who see a building left half finished. For nine years, my young——" the Comte hesitated to use a word; then he waved his hand, exclaiming—"No, I will not say friend—I hate everything that savours of sentiment. Well, for nine years past I have ceased to wonder that old men amuse themselves with growing flowers and planting trees; the events of life have taught them disbelief in all human affection, and I grew old within a few days. I will no longer attach myself to any creature but to unreasoning animals, or plants, or superficial things. I think more of Taglioni's grace* than of all human feeling. I abhor life and the world in which I live alone. Nothing, nothing," he went on, in a tone that startled the younger man, "no, nothing can move or interest me."

"But you have children?"

"My children!" he repeated bitterly. "Yes—well, is not my eldest daughter the Comtesse de Vandenesse? The other will, through her sister's connections, make some good match. As to my sons, have they not succeeded? The Vicomte was public prosecutor at Limoges, and is now First President of the Court at Orléans; the younger is public prosecutor here in Paris. My children have their own cares, their own anxieties and business to attend to. If of all those hearts one had been devoted to me, if one had tried by entire affection to fill up the void I have here," and he struck his breast, "well, that one would have failed in life, have sacrificed it to me. And why should he? Why? To bring sunshine into my few remaining years—and would he have succeeded? Might I not have accepted such generosity as a debt? But, Doctor," and the Comte smiled with deep irony, "it is not for nothing that we teach them arithmetic and how to count. At this moment perhaps they are waiting for my money."

"Oh Monsieur le Comte, how could such an idea enter your head—you who are kind, friendly, and humane! Indeed, if I were not myself a living proof of the benevolence you exercise so liberally and so nobly——"

"To please myself," replied the Comte. "I pay for a sensation as I would tomorrow pay a pile of gold to recover the most childish illusion that would but make my heart glow. I help my fellow creatures for my own sake, just as I gamble, and I look for gratitude from none. I should see you die without blinking, and I beg of you to feel the same with regard to me. I tell you, young man, the events of life have swept over my heart like the lavas of Vesuvius over Herculaneum. The city is there—dead."

"Those who have brought a soul as warm and as living as yours was to such a pitch of indifference are indeed guilty!"

"Say no more," said the Comte, with a shudder of aversion.

"You have a malady which you ought to allow me to treat," said Bianchon in a tone of deep emotion.

"What, do you know of a cure for death?" cried the Comte irritably.

"I undertake, Monsieur le Comte, to revive the heart you believe to be frozen."

"Are you a match for Talma,* then?" asked the Comte satirically.

"No, Monsieur le Comte. But Nature is as far above Talma as Talma is superior to me. Listen—the garret you are interested in is inhabited by a woman of about thirty, and in her, love is carried to fanaticism. The object of her adoration is a young man of pleasing appearance, but endowed by some malignant spirit with every conceivable vice. This fellow is a gambler, and it is hard to say which he is most addicted to—wine or women; he has, to my knowledge, committed acts deserving punishment by law. Well, and to him this unhappy woman sacrificed a life of ease, a man who worshipped her, and the father of her children. But what is wrong, Monsieur le Comte?"

"Nothing. Go on."

"She has allowed him to squander a perfect fortune; she would, I believe, give him the world if she had it; she works night and day, and many a time she has, without a murmur, seen the wretch she adores rob her even of the money saved to buy the clothes the children need, and their food for the morrow. Only three days ago she sold her hair, the finest hair I ever saw; he came in, she could not hide the gold piece quickly enough, and he asked her for it. For a smile, for a kiss, she gave up the price of a fortnight's life and peace. Is it not dreadful, and yet sublime? But work is wearing her cheeks hollow. Her children's crying has broken her heart; she is ill, and at this moment moaning on her wretched bed. This evening they had nothing to eat; the children have not the strength to cry; they were silent when I went up."

Horace Bianchon stood still. Just then the Comte de Granville, in spite of himself, as it were, had put his hand into his waistcoat pocket.

"I can guess, my young friend, how it is that she is yet alive if you attend her," said the elder man.

"Oh poor soul!" cried the Doctor, "who could refuse to help her? I only wish I were richer, for I hope to cure her of her passion."

"But," exclaimed the Comte, taking his hand out of his pocket empty of the notes which Bianchon had supposed his patron to be feeling for, "how can you expect me to feel pity for a form of misery whose pleasures would seem to me cheaply purchased with my entire fortune! That woman feels, she is alive! Would not Louis XV have given his kingdom to rise from the grave and have three days of youth and life! And is not that the history of thousands of dead men, thousands of sick men, thousands of old men?"

"Poor Caroline!" cried Bianchon.

As he heard the name, the Comte de Granville shuddered and grasped the doctor's arm with the grip of an iron vice.

"Her name is Caroline Crochard?" asked the President, in a voice that was evidently broken.

"Then you know her?" said the doctor, astonished.

"And the wretch's name is Solvet. Ay, you have kept your word!" exclaimed Granville; "you have roused my heart to the most terrible pain it can suffer till it is dust. That emotion, too, is a gift from hell, and I always know how to pay those debts."

By this time the Comte and the doctor had reached the corner of the Rue de la Chaussée-d'Antin.* One of those children of the night who wander round with a wicker basket on their back and crook in hand, and were, during the Revolution, facetiously called members of the Committee of Research,* was standing by the curbstone where the two men now stopped. This scavenger had a shrivelled face worthy of those immortalised by Charlet in his caricatures of the sweepers of Paris.*

"Do you ever pick up a thousand-franc note?" asked the Comte.

"Now and then, Monsieur."

"And you return them?"

"It depends on the reward offered."

"You are the man for me!" cried the Comte, giving the man a thousand-franc note. "Take this, but remember, I give it to you on condition of your spending it at the wineshop, of your getting drunk, fighting, beating your wife, blacking your friends' eyes. That will give work to the watch, the surgeon, the druggist—perhaps to the police, the public prosecutor, the judge, and the prison warders. Do not try to do anything else, or the devil will be revenged on you sooner or later."

A draughtsman would need at once the pencil of Charlet and of Callot, the brush of Teniers and of Rembrandt, to give a true notion of this night scene.

"Now I have squared accounts with hell, and had some pleasure for my money," said the Comte in a deep voice, pointing out the indescribable physiognomy of the gaping scavenger to the doctor, who stood stupefied. "As for Caroline Crochard! She may die of hunger and thirst, hearing the heartrending shrieks of her starving children, and convinced of the baseness of the man she loves. I will not give a sou to rescue her, and because you have helped her, I will see you no more——"

The Comte left Bianchon standing like a statue, and walked as briskly as a young man to the Rue Saint-Lazare, soon reaching the little house where he resided, and where, to his surprise, he found a carriage waiting at the door.

Un membre du comité des recherches

Plate IV

"Monsieur, your son, the public prosecutor, came about an hour since," said the manservant, "and is waiting for you in your bedroom."

Granville signed to the man to leave him.

"What motive can be strong enough to require you to infringe the order I have given my children never to come to me unless I send for them?" asked the Comte of his son as he went into the room.

"Father," replied the younger man in a tremulous voice, and with great respect, "I venture to hope that you will forgive me when you have heard me."

"Your reply is proper," said the Comte. "Sit down," and he pointed to a chair. "But whether I walk up and down, or take a seat, speak without heeding me."

"Father," the son went on, "this afternoon, at four o'clock, a very young man who was arrested in the house of a friend of mine, whom he had robbed to a considerable extent, appealed to you. He says he is your son."

"His name?" asked the Comte hoarsely.

"Charles Crochard."

"That will do," said the father, with an imperious wave of the hand. Granville paced the room in solemn silence, and his son took care not to break it. "My son," he began, and the words were pronounced in a voice so mild and fatherly, that the young lawyer started, "Charles Crochard spoke the truth. I am glad you came to me tonight, my good Eugène," he added, "Here is a considerable sum of money"—and he gave him a bundle of bank notes—"you can make any use of them you think proper in this matter. I trust you implicitly, and approve beforehand whatever arrangements you may make, either in the present or for the future. Eugène, my dear son, kiss me. We part perhaps for the last time. I shall tomorrow request my dismissal from the King, and I am going to Italy. Though a father owes no account of his life to his children, he is bound to bequeath to them the experience Fate sells him so dearly—is it not a part of their inheritance? When you marry," the Comte went on, with a little involuntary shiver, "do not undertake it lightly; that act is the most important of all those which society requires of us. Remember to study at your leisure the character of the woman who is to be your partner, but consult me too: I will judge of her myself. A lack of union between husband and wife, from whatever cause, leads to terrible misfortune; sooner or later we are always punished for contravening the social law. But I will write to you on this subject from Florence: a father, especially one who has the honour of presiding over a supreme court of justice, should not have to blush in the presence of his son. Adieu."

Paris, February 1830-January 1842

ADDENDUM TO A SECOND HOME
The following personages appear or are mentioned
in other volumes of *The Human Comedy*:

Beaumesnil, Mademoiselle
XIX: *The Splendors and Miseries of Courtesans*
XXV: *The Petits Bourgeois*

Bianchon, Horace
I: *Letters of Two Brides*
IV: *The Imaginary Mistress*
V: *Honorine*
VIII: *Old Goriot*
IX: *The Atheist's Mass, The Interdiction*
XII: *Pierrette*
XIII: *The Rabouilleuse*
XIV: *The Muse of the Department*
XVI: *Lost Illusions*
XVIII: *César Birotteau*
XIX: *The Splendors and Miseries of Courtesans*
XX: *The Secrets of the Princesse de Cadignan*
XXI: *Cousin Bette*
XXIII: *A Prince of Bohemia*
XXIV: *The Bureaucrats*
XXV: *The Petits Bourgeois*
XXVI: *The Brotherhood of Consolation*
XXXII: *The Village Curé*
XXXIV: *The Magic Skin*
In addition, Monsieur Bianchon narrated the following:
IV: *A Study of Woman*
V: *La Grande Bretèche*
IX: *Another Study of Woman*

Crochard, Caroline (Mademoiselle de Bellefeuille)
XIX: *The Splendors and Miseries of Courtesans*

Crochard, Charles
XXV: *The Petits Bourgeois*

Tillet, Madame Ferdinand du
(née Marie-Eugénie de Granville)

Vandenesse, Comtesse Félix de
(née Marie-Angélique de Granville)

Domestic Peace
(*La Paix du ménage*)
July 1829

Translated by Clara Bell

*Dedicated to my dear niece Valentine Surville**

LE COLONEL DE SOULANGES.

L'affaissement de ses membres et l'immobilité de son front
accusaient toute sa douleur.

LA PAIX DU MÉNAGE.

Plate V

The incident recorded in this Scene took place towards the end of the month of November 1809, the moment when Napoléon's fugitive Empire attained the apogee of its splendour. The trumpet blasts of Wagram were still sounding an echo in the heart of the Austrian monarchy. Peace was being signed between France and the Coalition.* Kings and princes came to perform their orbits, like stars, round Napoléon, who gave himself the pleasure of dragging all Europe in his train—a magnificent experiment in the power he afterwards displayed at Dresden.* Never, as contemporaries tell us, did Paris see entertainments more superb than those which preceded and followed the sovereign's marriage with an Austrian archduchess.* Never, in the most splendid days of the monarchy, had so many crowned heads thronged the shores of the Seine, never had the French aristocracy been so rich or so splendid. The diamonds lavishly scattered over the women's dresses, and the gold and silver embroidery on the uniforms contrasted so strongly with the penury of the Republic, that the wealth of the globe seemed to be rolling through the salons of Paris. Intoxication seemed to have turned the brains of this Empire of a day. All the military, not excepting their chief, revelled like parvenus in the treasure conquered for them by a million men with worsted epaulettes, whose demands were satisfied by a few yards of red ribbon.* At this time most women affected that lightness of conduct and facility of morals which distinguished the reign of Louis XV. Whether in imitation of the tone of the fallen monarchy, or because certain members of the Imperial family had set the example— as certain malcontents of the Faubourg Saint-Germain* chose to say—it is certain that men and women alike flung themselves into a life of pleasure with an intrepidity which seemed to forebode the end of the world. But there was at that time another cause for such licence. The infatuation of women for the military became a frenzy, and was too consonant to the Emperor's views for him to try to check it. The frequent calls to arms, which gave every treaty concluded between Napoléon and the rest of Europe the character of an armistice, left every passion open to a termination as sudden as the decisions of the commander-in-chief of all these busbys, pelisses, and aiguillettes, which so fascinated the fair sex. Hearts were as nomadic as the regiments. Between the first and the fifth bulletin from the *Grande Armée* a woman might be in succession mistress, wife, mother, and widow. Was it the prospect of early widowhood, the hope of a jointure, or that of bearing a name promised to history, which made the soldiers so attractive? Were women drawn to them by the certainty that the secret of their passions would be buried on the field of battle? Or may we find the reason of this gentle fanaticism in the noble charm that courage has for a woman? Perhaps all these reasons, which the future historian of the manners of the Empire will no doubt amuse himself by weighing, counted for something in their facile readiness to abandon themselves to love intrigues. Be that as it may, it must here be confessed that at that time laurels hid many errors; women showed an ardent preference for the brave adventurers, whom they regarded as the true fount of honour, wealth, or pleasure, and in the eyes of young girls, an epaulette—the hieroglyphic of a future—signified happiness and liberty. One feature, and a characteristic one, of this unique period in our history was an unbridled mania for everything glittering.

Never were fireworks so much in vogue, never were diamonds so highly prized. The men, as greedy as the women for these translucent pebbles, displayed them no less lavishly. Possibly the necessity for carrying plunder in the most portable form made gems the fashion in the army. A man was not ridiculous then, as he would be now, if his shirt frill or his fingers blazed with large diamonds. Murat, an Oriental by nature, set the example of preposterous luxury to modern soldiers.

The Comte de Gondreville, formerly known as Citizen Malin, whose elevation had made him famous, having become a Lucullus of the *Sénat Conservateur*,* which "conserved" nothing, had postponed an entertainment in honour of the peace only that he might the better pay his court to Napoléon by his efforts to eclipse those flatterers who had been beforehand with him. The ambassadors from all the powers friendly with France, with an eye to favours to come, the most important personages of the Empire, and even a few princes, were at this hour assembled in the wealthy senator's salons. Dancing flagged; everyone was watching for the Emperor, whose presence the Comte had promised his guests. And Napoléon would have kept his word but for the scene which had broken out that very evening between him and Joséphine—the scene which portended the impending divorce of the august pair.* The report of this incident, at the time kept very secret, but recorded by history, did not reach the ears of the courtiers, and had no effect on the gaiety of Comte de Gondreville's party beyond keeping Napoléon away. The prettiest women in Paris, eager to be at the Comte's on the strength of mere hearsay, at this moment were a besieging force of luxury, coquettishness, elegance, and beauty. The financial world, proud of its riches, challenged the splendour of the generals and high officials of the Empire, so recently gorged with orders, titles, and honours. These grand balls were always an

opportunity seized upon by wealthy families for introducing their heiresses to Napoléon's Praetorian Guard,
in the foolish hope of exchanging their splendid fortunes for uncertain favours. The women who believed
themselves strong enough in their beauty alone came to
test their power. There, as elsewhere, amusement was
but a blind. Calm and smiling faces and placid brows
covered sordid interests, expressions of friendship were
a lie, and more than one man was less distrustful of his
enemies than of his friends. These remarks are necessary
to explain the incidents of the little imbroglio which is
the subject of this Scene, and the picture, softened as it
is, of the tone then dominant in Paris salons.

"Turn your eyes a little towards the pedestal support-
ing that candelabrum—do you see a young lady with
her hair drawn back *à la Chinoise?**—there, in the corner to the left; she has bluebells in the knot of chestnut
curls which fall in clusters on her head. Do not you see
her? She is so pale you might fancy she was ill, deli-
cate-looking, and very small; there—now she is turning
her head this way; her almond-shaped blue eyes, so
delightfully soft, look as if they were made expressly for tears. Look, look! She is bending forward to see
Madame de Vaudremont below the crowd of heads in
constant motion; the high coiffures prevent her having
a clear view."

"I see her now, my dear fellow. You had only to say
that she had the whitest skin of all the women here; I
should have known whom you meant. I had noticed
her before; she has the loveliest complexion I ever admired. From hence I defy you to see against her throat
the pearls between the sapphires of her necklace. But
she is a prude or a coquette, for the tucker of her bodice
scarcely lets one suspect the beauty of her bust. What
shoulders! What lily-whiteness!"

"Who is she?" asked the first speaker.

"Ah! that I do not know."

"Aristocrat! Do you want to keep them all to yourself, Montcornet?"

"You of all men to banter me!" replied Montcornet, with a smile. "Do you think you have a right to insult a poor general like me because, being a happy rival of Soulanges, you cannot even turn on your heel without alarming Madame de Vaudremont? Or is it because I came only a month ago into the Promised Land? How insolent you can be, you men in office, who sit glued to your chairs while we are dodging shot and shell! Come, Monsieur le Maître des Requêtes,* allow us to glean in the field of which you can only have precarious possession from the moment when we evacuate it. The deuce is in it! We have all a right to live! My good friend, if you knew the German women, you would, I believe, do me a good turn with the Parisian you love best."

"Well, General, since you have vouchsafed to turn your attention to that lady, whom I never saw till now, have the charity to tell me if you have seen her dance."

"Why, my dear Martial, where have you dropped from? If you are ever sent with an embassy, I have small hopes of your success. Do not you see a triple rank of the most undaunted coquettes of Paris between her and the swarm of dancing men that buzz under the chandelier? And was it not only by the help of your eyeglass that you were able to discover her at all in the corner by that pillar, where she seems buried in the gloom, in spite of the candles blazing above her head? Between her and us there is such a sparkle of diamonds and glances, so many floating plumes, such a flutter of lace, of flowers and curls, that it would be a real miracle if any dancer could detect her among those stars. Why, Martial, how is it that you have not understood her to be the wife of some subprefect from Lippe or Dyle,* who has come to try to get her husband promoted?"

"Oh, he will be!" exclaimed the Master of Appeals quickly.

"I doubt it," replied the Colonel of Cuirassiers, laughing. "She seems as raw in intrigue as you are in diplomacy. I dare bet, Martial, that you do not know how she got into that place."

The lawyer looked at the Colonel of Cuirassiers with an expression as much of contempt as of curiosity.

"Well," proceeded Montcornet, "she arrived, I have no doubt, punctually at nine, the first of the company perhaps, and probably she greatly embarrassed the Comtesse de Gondreville, who cannot put two ideas together. Repulsed by the mistress of the house, routed from chair to chair by each newcomer, and driven into the darkness of this little corner, she allowed herself to be walled in, the victim of the jealousy of the other ladies, who would gladly have buried that dangerous face. She had, of course, no friend to encourage her to maintain the place she first held in the front rank; then each of those treacherous beauties will have given the order to the men in her circle, under threat of terrible punishment, not to engage with our poor friend. That, my dear fellow, is the way in which those sweet faces, in appearance so tender and so artless, would have formed a coalition against the fair stranger, and that without a word beyond the question, 'Tell me, *ma chère*, do you know that little woman in blue?' Look here, Martial, if you want to run the gauntlet of more flattering glances and inviting questions than you will ever again meet in the whole of your life, just try to get through the triple rampart which defends that Queen of Dyle, or Lippe, or Charente. You will see whether the dullest woman of them all will not be equal to inventing some wile that would hinder the most determined man from bringing the plaintive stranger to the light. Does she not have something like the air of an elegy about her?"

"Do you think so, Montcornet? Then she must be a married woman?"

"Why not a widow?"

"She would be less passive," said the lawyer, laughing.

"She is perhaps the widow of a man who is gambling," replied the handsome Colonel.

"To be sure; since the peace there are so many widows of that class!" said Martial. "But, my dear Montcornet, we are a couple of simpletons. That face is still too ingenuous, there is too much youth and freshness on the brow and temples for her to be married. What a lovely complexion! Nothing has sunk in the modelling of the nose. Lips, chin, everything in her face is as fresh as a white rosebud, though her expression is veiled, as it were, by the clouds of sadness. Who can it be that makes that young creature weep?"

"Women cry for so little," said the Colonel.

"I do not know," replied Martial, "but she does not cry because she is left there without a partner; her grief is not of today. It is evident that she has beautified herself for this evening with intention. I would wager that she is in love already."

"Bah! She is perhaps the daughter of some German princeling; no one talks to her," said Montcornet.

"Ah! How unhappy a poor girl can be!" Martial went on. "Can there be anything more graceful and refined than our little stranger? Certainly not one of those furies surrounding her who consider themselves to be so delicate; not one of them will say a single word to her. If she would but speak, we should see if she has fine teeth."

"Bless me, you boil over like milk at the least increase of temperature!" cried the Colonel, a little nettled at so soon finding a rival in his friend.

"What!" exclaimed the lawyer, without heeding the General's question, "Can nobody here tell us the name of this exotic flower?"

"Some lady companion!" said Montcornet.

"What next? A companion! Wearing sapphires fit for a queen, and a dress of Malines lace? Tell that to the marines, General. You, too, would not shine in diplomacy if, in the course of your conjectures, you jump in a breath from a German princess to a lady companion."

Montcornet stopped a man by taking his arm—a fat little man, whose iron-grey hair and clever eyes were to be seen at the lintel of every doorway, and who mingled unceremoniously with the various groups which welcomed him respectfully.

"Gondreville, my friend," said Montcornet, "who is that quite charming little woman sitting out there under that huge candelabrum?"

"The candelabrum? Ravrio's work; Isabey made the design."*

"Oh, I recognised your lavishness and taste, but the lady?"

"Ah! I do not know. Some friend of my wife's, no doubt."

"Or your mistress, you old rascal."

"No, on my honour. The Comtesse de Gondreville is the only person capable of inviting people whom no one knows."

In spite of this very acrimonious comment, the fat little man's lips did not lose the smile which the Colonel's suggestion had brought to them. Montcornet returned to the lawyer, who had joined a neighbouring group, intent on asking, but in vain, for information as to the fair stranger. He grasped Martial's arm, and said in his ear—"My dear Martial, mind what you are about. Madame de Vaudremont has been watching you for some minutes with ominous attentiveness; she is a woman who can guess by the mere movement of your lips what you say to me; our eyes have already told her too much; she has perceived and followed their direction, and I suspect that at this moment she is thinking even more than we are of the little blue lady."

"That is too old a trick in warfare, my dear Montcornet! However, what do I care? Like the Emperor, when I have made a conquest, I keep it."

"Martial, your fatuity cries out for a lesson. What! You, a civilian, and so lucky as to be the future husband of Madame de Vaudremont, a widow of twenty-two, burdened with four thousand napoleons a year—a woman who slips such a diamond as this on your finger," he added, taking the lawyer's left hand, which the young man complacently allowed, "and, to crown all, you affect the Lovelace,* just as if you were a colonel and obliged to keep up the reputation of the military in the garrisons! *Fi!* Only think of all you may lose."

"At any rate, I shall not lose my liberty," replied Martial, with a forced laugh.

He cast a passionate glance at Madame de Vaudremont, who responded only by a smile of some uneasiness, for she had seen the Colonel examining the lawyer's ring.

"Listen to me, Martial. If you flutter round my young stranger, I shall set to work to win Madame de Vaudremont."

"You have my full permission, my dear cuirassier, but you will not gain this much," and the young Master of Appeals put his polished thumbnail under an upper tooth with a little mocking click.

"Remember that I am unmarried," said the Colonel; "that my sword is my whole fortune, and that such a challenge is setting Tantalus down to a banquet which he will devour."

"Prrr!"

This defiant roll of consonants was the only reply to the General's declaration, as Martial looked him from head to foot before turning away. The fashion of the time required men to wear at a ball white kerseymere breeches and silk stockings. This pretty costume showed to great advantage the perfection of Montcornet's fine shape. He was thirty-five, and attracted attention by his stalwart height, insisted on for the cuirassiers of the Imperial Guard whose handsome uniform enhanced the dignity of his figure, still youthful in spite of the stoutness occasioned by living on horseback. A black moustache emphasised the frank expression of a thoroughly soldierly countenance, with a broad, high forehead, an aquiline nose, and bright red lips. Montcornet's manner, stamped with a certain superiority due to the habit of command, might please a woman sensible enough not to aim at making a slave of her husband. The Colonel smiled as he looked at the lawyer, one of his favourite college friends, whose small figure made it necessary for Montcornet to look down a little as he answered his raillery with a friendly glance.

Baron Martial de la Roche-Hugon was a young Provençal patronised by Napoléon; his fate might probably be some splendid embassy. He had won the Emperor by his Italian suppleness and a genius for intrigue, a salon eloquence, and a knowledge of manners, which are so good a substitute for the higher qualities of a sterling man. Though young and eager, his face had already acquired the rigid brilliancy of tinned iron, one of the indispensable characteristics of diplomatists, which allows them to conceal their emotions and disguise their feelings, unless, indeed, this impassibility indicates an absence of all emotion and the death of every feeling. The heart of a diplomat may be regarded as an insoluble problem, for the three most illustrious ambassadors of the time have been distinguished by their perdurable hatreds and the most romantic of attachments. Martial, however, was one of those men who are capable of reckoning on the future in the midst of their intensest enjoyment; he had already learned to judge the world, and hid his ambition under the fatuity of a lady-killer, cloaking his talent under the commonplace of mediocrity as soon as he observed the rapid advancement of those men who gave the master little umbrage.

The two friends now had to part with a cordial grasp of hands. The introductory tune, warning the ladies to form in squares for a fresh quadrille, cleared the men away from the space they had filled while talking in the middle of the large room. This hurried dialogue had taken place during the usual interval between two dances, in front of the fireplace of the great salon of Gondreville's mansion. The questions and answers of this very ordinary ballroom gossip had been almost whispered by each of the speakers into his neighbour's ear. At the same time, the chandeliers and the flambeaux on the chimney shelf shed such a flood of light on the

E.L.   *RWET*

Le colonel sourit en regardant le maitre des requêtes ..

Plate VI

two friends that their faces, strongly illuminated, failed, in spite of their diplomatic discretion, to conceal the faint expression of their feelings either from the keen-sighted Comtesse or the artless stranger. This espionage of thought is perhaps to idlers one of the pleasures they find in society, while numbers of disappointed simpletons are bored there without daring to admit it.

To fully appreciate the interest of this conversation, it is necessary to relate the event which would presently serve as an invisible bond, drawing together the actors in this little drama, who were at present scattered through the rooms. At about eleven o'clock, just as the dancers were returning to their seats, the company had observed the entrance of the most beautiful woman in Paris, the queen of fashion, the only person missing from this brilliant assembly. She made it a rule never to appear till the moment when a party had reached that pitch of excited movement which does not allow the women to preserve much longer the freshness of their faces or of their dress. This brief hour is, as it were, the springtime of a ball. An hour after, when pleasure falls flat and fatigue is encroaching, everything is spoilt. Madame de Vaudremont never committed the blunder of remaining at a party to be seen with drooping flowers, hair out of curl, tumbled frills, and a face like every other that sleep is courting—not always without success. She took great care not to let her beauty drowse as her rivals did; she was so clever as to keep up her reputation for smartness by always leaving a ballroom in brilliant order, as she had entered it. Women whispered to each other with a feeling of envy that she planned and wore as many different dresses as the parties she went to in one evening. This time, Madame de Vaudremont would not be free to choose when she would leave the salon where she had just arrived in triumph. Pausing for a moment on the threshold, she shot swift but observant glances at the women present, hastily scrutinising their dresses to assure herself that her own eclipsed them all. The illustrious beauty presented herself to the admiration of the crowd at the same moment with one of the bravest colonels of the Guards' Artillery and the Emperor's favourite, the Comte de Soulanges. The transient and fortuitous association of these two had about it a certain air of mystery. On hearing the names of Monsieur de Soulanges and the Comtesse de Vaudremont announced, a few women sitting by the wall rose, and men, hurrying in from the side rooms, pressed forward to the principal doorway. One of the jesters who are always to be found in any large assembly said, as the Comtesse and her escort came in, that "women had quite as much curiosity about seeing a man who was faithful to his passion as men had in studying a woman who was difficult to enthrall." Though the Comte de Soulanges, a young man of about thirty-two, was endowed with the nervous temperament which in a man gives rise to fine qualities, his slender build and pale complexion were not at first sight attractive; his black eyes betrayed great vivacity, but he was taciturn in company, and there was nothing in his appearance to reveal the gift for oratory which subsequently distinguished him, on the Right, in the legislative assembly under the Restoration.* The Comtesse de Vaudremont, a tall woman, somewhat full of figure, with a skin of dazzling whiteness, a small head that she carried well, and the immense advantage of inspiring love by the graciousness of her manner, was one of those creatures who keep all the promise of their beauty. The pair, who for a few minutes were the centre of general observation, did not for long give curiosity an opportunity of exercising itself about them. The Colonel and the Comtesse seemed perfectly to understand that accident had placed them in an awkward position. Martial, as they came forward, had hastened to join the group of men by the fireplace, that he might watch Madame de Vaudremont with the

jealous anxiety of the first flame of passion, from behind the heads which formed a sort of rampart; a secret
voice seemed to warn him that the success on which he
prided himself might perhaps be precarious. But the
coldly polite smile with which the Comtesse thanked
Monsieur de Soulanges, and her little bow of dismissal
as she sat down by Madame de Gondreville, relaxed
the muscles of his face which jealousy had made rigid.
Seeing Soulanges, however, still standing quite near the
sofa on which Madame de Vaudremont was seated, not
apparently having understood the glance by which the
lady had conveyed to him that they were both playing
a ridiculous part, the volcanic Provençal again knit the
black brows that overshadowed his blue eyes, smoothed
his chestnut curls to keep himself in countenance, and
without betraying the agitation which made his heart
beat, watched the faces of the Comtesse and of Monsieur
de Soulanges while still chatting with his neighbours.
He then took the hand of Colonel Montcornet, who had
just renewed their old acquaintance, but he listened to
him without hearing him; his mind was elsewhere.
Soulanges calmly glanced at the women sitting four
ranks deep who framed the Senator's immense ballroom, admiring this border of diamonds, rubies, gold
wreaths, and well-dressed people whose brightness was
almost enough to outshine the light of the candles, the
crystal chandeliers, and the gilding. His rival's stolid
indifference put the lawyer out of countenance. Quite
incapable of controlling his secret transports of impatience, Martial went towards Madame de Vaudremont
with a bow. On seeing the Provençal, Soulanges gave
him a covert glance, and impertinently turned away his
head. Solemn silence now reigned in the room, where
curiosity was at the highest pitch. All the tensed faces
offered up the strangest of expressions; everyone dreaded and waited for one of those outbursts which men of
breeding carefully avoid. Suddenly the Comte's pale

face turned as red as the scarlet facings of his coat, and he fixed his gaze on the floor that the cause of his agitation might not be guessed. On catching sight of the unknown lady humbly seated by the pedestal of the candelabrum, he moved away with a melancholy air, passing in front of the lawyer, and took refuge in one of the cardrooms. Martial and all the company thought that Soulanges had publicly surrendered the post, out of fear of the ridicule which invariably attaches itself to a discarded lover. The lawyer proudly raised his head and looked at the strange lady; then, as he took his seat at his ease near Madame de Vaudremont, he listened to her so inattentively that he did not catch these words spoken behind her fan—"Martial, you will oblige me this evening by not wearing that ring that you snatched from me. I have my reasons, and will explain them to you in a moment when we go away. You must give me your arm to go to the Princesse de Wagram's."*

"Why did you come in with the Colonel?" asked the Baron.

"I met him in the hall," she replied. "But leave me now; everybody is looking at us."

Martial returned to the Colonel of Cuirassiers. Then it was that the little blue lady had become the object of the curiosity which agitated in such various ways the Colonel, Soulanges, Martial, and Madame de Vaudremont. When the friends parted, after the challenge which closed their conversation, the Baron flew to Madame de Vaudremont and led her to a place in the most brilliant quadrille. Favoured by the sort of intoxication which dancing always produces in a woman, and by the turmoil of a ball, where men appear in all the trickery of dress, which adds no less to their attractions than it does to those of women, Martial thought he might yield with impunity to the charm that attracted his gaze to the fair stranger. Though he succeeded in hiding his first glances towards the lady in blue from the anxious activity of the Comtesse's eyes, he was ere long caught in the act, and though he managed to excuse himself once for his absence of mind, he could not justify the unseemly silence with which he presently heard the most insinuating question which a woman can put to a man—"Do you like me very much this evening?" And the more dreamy he became, the more the Comtesse pressed and teased him. While Martial was dancing, the Colonel moved from group to group, seeking information about the unknown lady. After exhausting the good humour of even the most indifferent, he had resolved to take advantage of a moment when the Comtesse de Gondreville seemed to be at liberty, to ask her the name of the mysterious lady, when he perceived a little space between the pedestal of the candelabrum and the two sofas, which ended in that corner. The dance had left several of the chairs vacant, which formed rows of fortifications held by mothers or women of middle age, and the Colonel seized the opportunity to make his way through this palisade hung with shawls and wraps. He began by making himself agreeable to the dowagers, and so from one to another, and from compliment to compliment, he at last reached the empty space next the stranger. At the risk of catching on to the griffins and chimeras of the huge candelabrum, he stood there, braving the glare and drippings of the wax candles, to Martial's extreme annoyance. The Colonel, far too tactful to speak suddenly to the little blue lady on his right, began by saying to a plain woman who was seated on the left—"This is a splendid ball, Madame! What luxury! What life! On my word, every woman here is pretty! If you are not dancing, it is no doubt because you do not care for it."

This vapid conversation was solely intended to induce his right-hand neighbour to speak, but she, silent and absent-minded, paid not the least attention. The officer had in store a number of phrases which he intended should lead up to: "And you, Madame?" a question from which he hoped great things. But he was greatly surprised to see tears in the strange lady's eyes, which seemed wholly absorbed in gazing on Madame de Vaudremont.

"You are married, no doubt, Madame?" he asked her at length, in hesitating tones.

"Yes, Monsieur," replied the lady.

"And your husband is here, of course?"

"Yes, Monsieur."

"And why, Madame, do you remain in this spot? Is it to attract attention?"

The mournful lady smiled sadly.

"Allow me the honour, Madame, of being your partner in the next quadrille, and I will take care not to bring you back here. I see a vacant settee near the fire; come and take it. When so many people are ready to ascend the throne, and royalty is the mania of the day, I cannot imagine that you will refuse the title of Queen of the Ball which your beauty may claim."

"I do not intend to dance, Monsieur."

The curt tone of the lady's replies was so discouraging that the Colonel found himself compelled to raise the siege. Martial, who guessed what the officer's last request had been, and the refusal he had met with, began to smile, and stroked his chin, making the diamond he wore on his finger sparkle.

"What are you laughing at?" said the Comtesse de Vaudremont.

"At the failure of the poor Colonel, who has just put his foot in it——"

"I begged you to take your ring off," said the Comtesse, interrupting him.

"I did not hear you."

"If you can hear nothing this evening, at any rate you see everything, Monsieur le Baron," said Madame de Vaudremont, with an air of vexation.

"That young man is displaying a very fine diamond," the fair stranger remarked to the Colonel.

"Splendid," he replied. "The man is the Baron Martial de la Roche-Hugon, one of my most intimate friends."

"I have to thank you for telling me his name," she went on; "he seems an agreeable man."

"Yes, but he is rather fickle."

"He seems to be on the best terms with the Comtesse de Vaudremont?" said the lady, with an inquiring look at the Colonel.

"On the very best."

The stranger turned pale.

"All right then," thought the soldier, "she is in love with that lucky devil Martial."

"I fancied that Madame de Vaudremont had long been devoted to Monsieur de Soulanges," said the lady, recovering a little from the suppressed grief which had clouded the fairness of her face.

"For a week past the Comtesse has been faithless," replied the Colonel. "But you must have seen poor Soulanges when he came in; he is still trying not to think of his misfortune."

"Yes, I saw him," said the lady. Then she added, "Thank you very much, Monsieur," in a tone which signified a dismissal.

At this moment the quadrille was coming to an end. Montcornet had only time to withdraw, saying to himself by way of consolation, "She is married."

"Well, valiant cuirassier," exclaimed the Baron, drawing the Colonel aside into a window bay to breathe the fresh air from the garden, "how are you getting on?"

"She is a married woman, my dear fellow."

"What does that matter?"

"Oh, deuce take it! I am a decent sort of man," replied the Colonel. "I have no idea of paying my addresses to a woman I cannot marry. Besides, Martial, she expressly told me that she did not intend to dance."

"Colonel, I will bet a hundred napoleons to your grey horse that she will dance with me this evening."

"Done!" said the Colonel, putting his hand in the coxcomb's. "Meanwhile I am going to look for Soulanges; he perhaps knows the lady, as she seems interested in him."

"You have lost, *mon brave*," cried Martial, laughing. "My eyes have met hers, and I know what they mean. My dear friend, you owe me no grudge for dancing with her after she has refused you?"

"No, no. Those who laugh last, laugh longest. But I am an honest gambler and a generous enemy, Martial, and I warn you, she is fond of diamonds."

With these words the friends parted; General Montcornet made his way to the card room, where he saw the Comte de Soulanges sitting at a *bouillotte** table. Though there was no friendship between the two soldiers, beyond the superficial comradeship arising from the perils of war and the duties of the service, the Colonel of Cuirassiers was painfully struck by seeing the Colonel of Artillery, whom he knew to be a prudent man, playing at a game which might bring him to ruin. The heaps of gold and notes piled on the fateful cards showed the frenzy of play. A circle of silent men stood round the players at the table. Now and then a few words were spoken—*pass, play, I stop, a thousand louis, taken*—but, looking at the five motionless men, it seemed as though they talked only with their eyes. As the Colonel, alarmed by Soulanges's pallor, went up to him, the Comte was winning. Field Marshal the Duc d'Isemberg, Keller, and a famous banker rose from the table completely cleaned out of considerable sums. Soulanges looked gloomier than ever as he swept up a quantity of gold and notes; he did not even count it; his lips curled with bitter scorn, he seemed to defy fortune rather than be grateful for her favours.

"Courage," said the Colonel. "Courage, Soulanges!"

Then, believing he would do him a service by dragging him from play, he added: "Come with me. I have some good news for you, but on one condition."

"What is that?" asked Soulanges.

"That you will answer a question I will ask you."

The Comte de Soulanges rose abruptly, placing his winnings with reckless indifference in his handkerchief, which he had been twisting with convulsive nervousness, and his expression was so savage that none of the players took exception to his walking off with their money. Indeed, every face seemed to dilate with relief when his morose and crabbed countenance was no longer to be seen under the circle of light which the shaded lamp cast on the gaming table.

"Those military devils are always as thick as thieves at a fair!" said a diplomat who had been looking on, as he took Soulanges's place.

One single pallid and fatigued face turned to the newcomer, and said with a glance that flashed and died out like the sparkle of a diamond: "When we say military, we do not mean civil, Monsieur le Ministre."

"My dear fellow," said Montcornet to Soulanges, leading him into a corner, "the Emperor spoke warmly in your praise this morning, and your promotion to be field marshal is a certainty."

"The Master does not love the artillery."

"No, but he adores the nobility, and you are an aristocrat. The Master said," added Montcornet, "that the men who had married in Paris during the campaign were not therefore to be considered in disgrace. Well then?"

The Comte de Soulanges looked as if he understood nothing of this speech.

"And now I hope," the Colonel went on, "that you will tell me if you know a charming little woman who is sitting under a huge candelabrum——"

At these words the Comte's face lit up; he violently seized the Colonel's hand: "My dear General," said he, in a perceptibly altered voice, "if any man but you had asked me such a question, I would have cracked his skull with this mass of gold. Leave me, I entreat you. I feel more like blowing out my brains this evening, I assure you, than—I hate everything I see. And, in fact, I am going. This gaiety, this music, these stupid faces, all laughing, are killing me!"

"My poor friend!" replied Montcornet gently, and giving the Comte's hand a friendly pressure, "you are too vehement. What would you say if I told you that Martial is thinking so little of Madame de Vaudremont that he is quite smitten with that little lady?"

"If he says a word to her," cried Soulanges, stammering with rage, "I will thrash him as flat as his own portfolio, even if the coxcomb were in the Emperor's lap!"

And he sank quite overcome on an easy chair to which Montcornet had led him. The Colonel slowly went away, for he perceived that Soulanges was in a state of fury far too violent for the pleasantries or the attentions of superficial friendship to soothe him. When Montcornet returned to the ballroom, Madame de Vaudremont was the first person on whom his eyes fell, and he observed on her face, usually so calm, some symptoms of ill-disguised agitation. A chair was vacant near hers, and the Colonel seated himself.

"I dare wager something has vexed you?" said he.

"A mere trifle, General. I want to be gone, for I have promised to go to a ball at the Grand Duchess of Berg's,* and I must look in first at the Princesse de Wagram's. Monsieur de la Roche-Hugon, who knows this, is amusing himself by flirting with the dowagers."

"That is not the whole secret of your disturbance, and I will bet a hundred louis that you will remain here the whole evening."

"Impertinent man!"

"Then I have hit the truth?"

107

"Well, tell me, what am I thinking of?" said the Comtesse, tapping the Colonel's fingers with her fan. "I might even reward you if you guess rightly."

"I will not accept the challenge; I have too much the advantage of you."

"You are presumptuous."

"You are afraid of seeing Martial at the feet——"

"Of whom?" cried the Comtesse, affecting surprise.

"Of that candelabrum," replied the Colonel, glancing at the fair stranger, and then looking at the Comtesse with embarrassing scrutiny.

"You have guessed it," replied the coquette, hiding her face behind her fan, which she began to play with. "Old Madame de Lansac, who is, you know, as malicious as an old monkey," she went on, after a pause, "has just told me that Monsieur de la Roche-Hugon is running into danger by flirting with that stranger, who sits here this evening like a skeleton at a feast. I would rather see a death's head than that face, so cruelly beautiful, and as pale as a ghost. She is my evil genius. Madame de Lansac," she added, after a flash and gesture of annoyance, "who only goes to a ball to watch everything while pretending to sleep, has made me miserably anxious. Martial shall pay dearly for playing me such a trick. Urge him, meanwhile, since he is your friend, not to make me so unhappy."

"I have just been with a man who promises to blow his brains out, and nothing less, if he speaks to that little lady. And he is the man, Madame, to keep his word. But then I know Martial; such threats are to him an encouragement. And, besides, we have wagered——" Here the Colonel lowered his voice.

"Can it be true?" said the Comtesse.

"On my word of honour."

"Thank you, my dear Colonel," replied Madame de Vaudremont, with a glance full of invitation.

"Will you do me the honour of dancing with me?"

"Yes, but the next quadrille. During this one I want to find out what will come of this little intrigue, and to ascertain who the little blue lady may be; she looks intelligent."

The Colonel, understanding that Madame de Vaudremont wished to be alone, retired, well content to have begun his attack so well.

At most entertainments women are to be met who are there, like Madame de Lansac, as old sailors gather on the seashore to watch younger mariners struggling with the tempest. At this moment Madame de Lansac, who seemed to be interested in the personages of this drama, could easily guess the agitation which the Comtesse was going through. The lady might fan herself gracefully, smile on the young men who bowed to her, and bring into play all the arts by which a woman hides her emotion—the dowager, one of the most clear-sighted and mischief-loving duchesses bequeathed by the eighteenth century to the nineteenth, could read her heart and mind through it all. The old lady seemed to detect the slightest movement that revealed the impressions of the soul. The imperceptible frown that furrowed that calm, pure forehead, the faintest quiver of the cheeks, the curve of the eyebrows, the least curl of the lips, whose living coral could conceal nothing from her, all these were to the Duchesse like the print of a book. From the depths of her large armchair, completely filled by the flow of her dress, the coquette of the past, while talking to a diplomat who had sought her out to hear the anecdotes she told so cleverly, was admiring herself in the younger coquette; she felt kindly to her, seeing how bravely she disguised her annoyance and grief of heart. Madame de Vaudremont, in fact, felt as much sorrow as she feigned cheerfulness; she had believed that she had found in Martial a man of talent on whose support she could count for adorning her life with all the enchantment of power, and at this moment she perceived her mistake, as injurious to her reputation as to her good opinion of herself. In her, as in other women of that time, the suddenness of their passions increased their vehemence. Souls which love much and love often, suffer no less than those which burn themselves out in one affection. Her liking for Martial was but of yesterday, it is true, but the least experienced surgeon knows that the pain caused by the amputation of a healthy limb is more acute than the removal of a diseased one. There was a future before Madame de Vaudremont's passion for Martial, while her previous love had been hopeless, and poisoned by Soulanges's remorse. The old Duchesse, who was watching for an opportunity of speaking to the Comtesse, hastened to dismiss her ambassador, for in comparison with a lovers' quarrel every interest pales, even with an old woman. To engage battle, Madame de Lansac shot at the younger lady a sardonic glance which made the Comtesse fear lest her fate was in the dowager's hands. There are looks between woman and woman which are like the torches brought on at the climax of a tragedy. It is necessary to have known the Duchesse for one to fully appreciate the terror that the play of her expressions inspired in the Comtesse. Madame de Lansac was tall, and her features led people to say, "That must have been a handsome woman!" She coated her cheeks so thickly with rouge that the wrinkles were scarcely visible; but her eyes, far from gaining a factitious brilliancy from this strong carmine, looked all the more dim. She wore a vast quantity of diamonds, and dressed with sufficient taste not to make herself ridiculous. Her sharp nose promised epigram. A well-fitted set of teeth preserved a smile of such irony as recalled that of Voltaire. At the same time, the exquisite politeness of her manners so effectually softened the mischievous twist in her mind, that it was impossible to accuse her of spitefulness. The old woman's eyes lit up, and a triumphant glance, seconded by a smile, which said, "I promised you as much!" shot across the room, and brought a blush of hope to the pale cheeks of the young creature languishing under the great chandelier. This alliance between Madame de Lansac and the stranger could not escape the practised eye of the Comtesse de Vaudremont, who scented a mystery and was determined to penetrate it. At this instant the Baron de la Roche-Hugon, after questioning all the dowagers without success as to the blue lady's name, applied in despair to the Comtesse de Gondreville, from whom he received only this unsatisfactory reply, "A lady whom the *ancient* Duchesse de Lansac introduced to me." Turning by chance towards the armchair occupied by the old lady, the lawyer intercepted the glance of understanding she sent to the stranger, and although he had for some time been on bad terms with her, he determined to speak to her. The ancient Duchesse, seeing the jaunty Baron prowling round her chair, smiled with sardonic irony, and looked at Madame de Vaudremont with an expression that made Montcornet laugh.

"If the old witch affects to be friendly," thought the Baron, "she is certainly going to play me some spiteful trick. Madame," he said, "you have, I am told, undertaken the charge of a very precious treasure."

"Do you take me for a dragon?" said the old lady. "But of whom are you speaking?" she added, with a sweetness which revived Martial's hopes.

"Of that little lady, unknown to all, whom the jealousy of all these coquettes has imprisoned in that corner. You, no doubt, know her family?"

"Yes," said the Duchesse. "But what concern have you with a provincial heiress, married for some time, a woman of good birth whom none of the rest of you know; she goes nowhere."

"Why does not she dance? She is such a pretty creature! May we conclude a treaty of peace? If you will vouchsafe to tell me all I want to know, I promise you that a petition for the restitution of the woods of Navarreins by the Commissioners of Crown Lands shall be strongly urged on the Emperor."

The younger branch of the house of Navarreins bears quarterly with the arms of Navarreins those of Lansac, namely, azure and argent party per pale raguly, between six spearheads in pale,* and the old lady's liaison with Louis XV had earned her husband the title of duke by royal patent. Now, as the Navarreins had not yet resettled in France, it was sheer trickery that the young lawyer thus proposed to the old lady by suggesting to her that she should petition for an estate belonging to the elder branch of the family.

"Monsieur," said the old woman with deceptive gravity, "bring the Comtesse de Vaudremont across to me. I promise you I will reveal to her the mystery that makes our fair stranger so interesting. You see, every man in the room has reached as great a curiosity as your own. All eyes are involuntarily turned towards the corner where my protégée has so modestly placed herself; she is reaping all the homage the women wished to deprive her of. Happy the man she chooses for her partner!" She interrupted herself, fixing her eyes on Madame de Vaudremont with one of those looks which plainly say, "We are talking of you." Then she added, "I imagine you would rather learn the stranger's name from the lips of your handsome Comtesse than from mine?"

There was such marked defiance in the Duchesse's attitude that Madame de Vaudremont rose, came up to her, and took the chair Martial placed for her; then without noticing him she said, "I can guess, Madame, that you are talking of me, but I admit my want of perspicacity; I do not know whether it is for good or evil."

Madame de Lansac pressed the young woman's pretty hand in her own dry and wrinkled fingers, and answered in a low, compassionate tone, "Poor child!"

The women looked at each other. Madame de

Vaudremont understood that Martial was in the way and dismissed him, saying with an imperious expression, "Leave us."

The Baron, ill pleased at seeing the Comtesse under the spell of the dangerous sibyl who had drawn her to her side, gave one of those looks which a man can give— potent over a blinded heart, but simply ridiculous in the eyes of a woman who is beginning to criticise the man who has attracted her.

"Do you think you can play the Emperor?" said Madame de Vaudremont, turning three-quarters of her face to fix an ironical sidelong gaze on the lawyer.

Martial was too much a man of the world, and had too much wit and acumen, to risk breaking with a woman who was in favour at court, and whom the Emperor wished to see married. He counted, too, on the jealousy he intended to provoke in her as the surest means of discovering the secret of her coolness, and withdrew all the more willingly, because at this moment a new quadrille was putting everybody in motion. With an air of making room for the dancing, the Baron leaned back against the marble slab of a console, folded his arms, and stood absorbed in watching the two ladies talking. From time to time he followed the glances which both frequently directed at the fair stranger. Then, comparing the Comtesse with the new beauty, made so attractive by a touch of mystery, the Baron fell prey to the detestable self-interest common to adventurous lady-killers; he hesitated between a fortune within his grasp and the indulgence of his caprice. The blaze of light gave such strong relief to his anxious and sullen face, against the hangings of white silk moreen brushed by his black hair, that he might have been compared to an evil spirit. Even from a distance, more than one observer no doubt said to himself, "There is another poor wretch who seems to be enjoying himself!"

The Colonel, meanwhile, with one shoulder leaning

lightly against the side post of the doorway between the ballroom and the cardroom, could laugh undetected under his ample moustache; it amused him to look on at the turmoil of the dance; he could see a hundred pretty heads turning about in obedience to the figures; he could read in some faces, as in those of the Comtesse and his friend Martial, the secrets of their agitation; and then, looking round, he wondered what connection there could be between the gloomy looks of the Comte de Soulanges, still seated on the sofa, and the plaintive expression of the fair unknown, on whose features the joys of hope and the anguish of involuntary dread were alternately legible. Montcornet stood like the king of the feast. In this moving picture he saw a complete presentment of the world, and he laughed at it as he found himself the object of inviting smiles from a hundred beautiful and elegant women. A Colonel of the Imperial Guard, a position equal to that of a Brigadier General, was undoubtedly one of the best matches in the army. It was now nearly midnight. The conversation, the gambling, the dancing, the flirtations, interests, petty rivalries, and scheming had all reached the pitch of ardour which makes a young man exclaim involuntarily, "What a fine ball!"

"My sweet little angel," said Madame de Lansac to the Comtesse, "you are now at an age when in my day I made many mistakes. Seeing you just now enduring a thousand deaths, it occurred to me that I might give you some charitable advice. To go wrong at twenty-two means spoiling your future; is it not tearing the gown you must wear? My dear, it is not till much later that we learn to go about in it without crumpling it. Go on, *mon cœur*, making clever enemies, and friends who have no sense of conduct, and you will see what a pleasant life you will some day be leading!"

"Oh, Madame, it is very hard for a woman to be happy, is it not?" the Comtesse eagerly exclaimed.

"My child, at your age you must learn to choose between pleasure and happiness. You want to marry Martial, who is not fool enough to make a good husband, nor passionate enough to remain a lover. He is in debt, my dear; he is the man to run through your fortune; still, that would be nothing if he could make you happy. Do not you see how aged he is? The man must have often been ill; he is making the most of what is left him. In three years he will be a wreck. Then he will be ambitious; perhaps he may succeed. I do not think so. What is he? A man of intrigue, who may have the business faculty to perfection, and be able to gossip agreeably, but he is too presumptuous to have any sterling merit; he will not go far. Besides—only look at him. Is it not written on his brow that, at this very moment, what he sees in you is not a young and pretty woman, but the two million francs you possess? He does not love you, my dear; he is reckoning you up as if you were an investment. If you are bent on marrying, find an older man who has an assured position and is half-way on his career. A widow's marriage ought not to be a trivial love affair. Is a mouse to be caught a second time in the same trap? A new alliance ought now to be a good speculation on your part, and in marrying again you ought at least to have a hope of being some day addressed as Madame la Maréchale."

As she spoke both women naturally fixed their eyes on Colonel Montcornet's handsome face.

"If you would rather play the delicate part of a flirt and not marry again," the Duchesse went on, with blunt good nature, "well! my poor child, you, better than any woman, will know how to raise the storm clouds and disperse them again. But, I beseech you, never make it your pleasure to disturb the peace of families, to destroy unions, and ruin the happiness of happy wives. I, my dear, have played that perilous game. Dear heaven! For a triumph of vanity some poor virtuous soul is

115

murdered—for there really are virtuous women, child—and we may make ourselves mortally hated. I learned, a little too late, that, as the Duc d'Albe once said, one salmon is worth a thousand frogs!* A genuine affection certainly brings a thousand times more happiness than the transient passions we may inspire. Well, I came here on purpose to preach to you; yes, you are the cause of my appearance in this house, which stinks of the lower class. Have I not just seen actors here? Formerly, my dear, we received them in our boudoir, but in the salon—never! Why do you look at me with so much amazement? Listen to me. If you want to play with men, do not try to wring the hearts of any but those whose life is not yet settled, who have no duties to fulfil; the others do not forgive us for the errors that have made them happy. Profit by this maxim, founded on my long experience. That luckless Soulanges, for instance, whose head you have turned, whom you have intoxicated for these fifteen months past, God knows how! Do you know at what you have struck? At his whole life. He has been married these two years; he is worshipped by a charming wife, whom he loves, but neglects; she lives in tears and embittered silence. Soulanges has had hours of remorse more terrible than his pleasure has been sweet. And you, you artful little thing, have deserted him. Well, come and see your work."

The old lady took Madame de Vaudremont's hand, and they rose. "There," said Madame de Lansac, and her eyes showed her the stranger sitting pale and tremulous under the glare of the candles, "that is my grand niece, the Comtesse de Soulanges; today she yielded at last to my persuasion, and consented to leave the sorrowful room, where the sight of her child gives her but little consolation. You see her? You think her charming? Then imagine, *chère belle*, what she must have been when happiness and love shed their glory on that face now blighted."

The Comtesse looked away in silence, and seemed lost in sad reflections. The Duchesse led her to the door into the cardroom; then, after looking round the room as if in search of someone—"And there is Soulanges!" she said in deep tones.

The Comtesse shuddered as she saw, in the least brilliantly lighted corner, the pale, set face of Soulanges stretched in an easy chair. The indifference of his attitude and the rigidity of his brow betrayed his suffering. The players passed him to and fro, without paying any more attention to him than if he had been dead. The picture of the wife in tears, and the dejected, morose husband, separated in the midst of this festivity like the two halves of a tree blasted by lightning, had perhaps a prophetic significance for the Comtesse. She dreaded lest she here saw an image of the revenges the future might have in store for her. Her heart was not yet so dried up that feeling and generosity were entirely excluded, and she pressed the Duchesse's hand, while thanking her by one of those smiles which have a certain childlike grace.

"My dear child," the old lady said in her ear, "remember henceforth that we are just as capable of repelling a man's attentions as of attracting them."

"She is yours if you are not a simpleton."

These words were whispered into Colonel Montcornet's ear by Madame de Lansac, while the handsome Comtesse was still absorbed in compassion at the sight of Soulanges, for she still loved him truly enough to wish to restore him to happiness, and was promising herself in her own mind that she would exert the irresistible power her charms still had over him to make him return to his wife.

"Oh! I will talk to him!" said she to Madame de Lansac.

"Do nothing of the kind, my dear!" cried the Duchesse, as she went back to her armchair. "Choose a good husband, and shut your door to my nephew. Believe me, my child, a wife cannot accept her husband's heart as the gift of another woman; she is a hundred times happier in the belief that she has reconquered it. By bringing my niece here I believe I have given her an excellent chance of regaining her husband's affection. All the assistance I need of you is to play the Colonel."

She pointed to the Baron's friend, and the Comtesse smiled.

"Well, Madame, do you at last know the name of our fair stranger?" asked Martial, with an air of pique, to the Comtesse when he saw her alone.

"Yes," said Madame de Vaudremont, looking him in the face.

Her features expressed as much roguery as fun. The smile which gave life to her lips and cheeks, and the liquid brightness of her eyes, were like the will-o'-the-wisp which leads travellers astray. Martial, who believed that she still loved him, assumed the coquetting graces in which a man is so ready to lull himself in the presence of the woman he loves. He said with a fatuous air—"And will you be annoyed with me if I seem to attach great importance to your telling me that name?"

"Will you be annoyed with me," answered Madame de Vaudremont, "if a remnant of affection prevents my telling you, and if I forbid you to make the smallest advances to that young lady? It would be at the risk of your life perhaps."

"To lose your good graces, Madame, would be worse than to lose my life."

"Martial," said the Comtesse severely, "she is Madame de Soulanges. Her husband would blow your brains out—if, indeed, you have any——"

"Ha! ha!" laughed the coxcomb. "What! The Colonel can leave the man in peace who has robbed him of your love, and then would fight for his wife! What a subversion of principles! I beg of you to allow me to dance with the little lady. You will then be able to judge how little love that heart of ice could feel for you; for, if the Colonel disapproves of my dancing with his wife after allowing me to——"

"But she loves her husband."

"A still further obstacle that I shall have the pleasure of conquering."

"But she is married."

"A whimsical objection!"

"Ah!" said the Comtesse, with a bitter smile, "you punish us alike for our faults and our repentance!"

"Do not be angry!" exclaimed Martial eagerly. "Oh, forgive me, I beseech you. There, I will think no more of Madame de Soulanges."

"You deserve that I should send you to her."

"I am off then," said the Baron, laughing, "and I shall return more devoted to you than ever. You will see that the prettiest woman in the world cannot capture the heart that is yours."

"That is to say, that you want to win Colonel Montcornet's horse?"

"Ah! Traitor!" said he, threatening his friend with his finger. The Colonel smiled and joined them; the Baron gave him the seat near the Comtesse, saying to her with a sardonic accent—"Here, Madame, is a man who boasted that he could win your good graces in one evening."

He went away, thinking himself clever to have piqued the Comtesse's pride and done Montcornet an ill turn; but, in spite of his habitual keenness, he had not appreciated the irony underlying Madame de Vaudremont's speech, and did not perceive that she had come as far to meet his friend as his friend towards her, though both were unconscious of it. At the moment when the lawyer went fluttering up to the candelabrum by which Madame de Soulanges sat, pale, timid, and apparently alive only in her eyes, her husband came to the door of the ballroom, his eyes flashing with anger. The old Duchesse, watchful of everything, flew to her nephew, begged him to give her his arm and find her carriage, affecting to be mortally bored, and hoping thus to prevent a disagreeable outburst. Before going she fired a singular glance of intelligence at her niece, indicating the enterprising cavalier who was about to address her, and this signal seemed to say, "There he is, avenge yourself!"

Madame de Vaudremont caught these looks of the aunt and niece; a sudden light dawned on her mind; she was frightened lest she was the dupe of this old woman, so cunning and so practised in intrigue. "That perfidious Duchesse," said she to herself, "has perhaps been amusing herself by preaching morality to me while playing me some spiteful trick of her own."

At this thought Madame de Vaudremont's pride was perhaps more roused than her curiosity to disentangle the thread of this intrigue. In the absorption of mind to which she was a prey she was no longer mistress of herself. The Colonel, interpreting to his own advantage the embarrassment evident in the Comtesse's manner and speech, became more ardent and pressing. The jaded old diplomats, amusing themselves by watching the play of faces, had never found so many intrigues at once to watch or guess at. The passions agitating the two couples were to be seen with variations at every step in the crowded rooms, and reflected with different shades in other countenances. The spectacle of so many vivid passions, of all these lovers' quarrels, these pleasing revenges, these cruel favours, these flaming glances, of all this ardent life diffused around them, only made them feel their impotence more keenly. At last the Baron had found a seat by Madame de Soulanges. His eyes stole a long look at her neck, as fresh as dew and as fragrant as a wildflower. He admired close at hand the beauty which had amazed him from afar. He could see a small, well-shod foot, and measure with his eye a slender and graceful shape. At that time women wore their sash tied close under the bosom, in imitation of Greek statues, a pitiless fashion for those whose bust was faulty. As he cast furtive glances at the Comtesse's figure, Martial was enchanted with its perfection.

"You have not danced once this evening, Madame," said he in soft and flattering tones. "Not, I should suppose, for lack of a partner?"

"I never go to parties; I am quite unknown," replied Madame de Soulanges coldly, not having understood the look by which her aunt had just conveyed to her that she was to attract the Baron.

Martial, to give himself countenance, twisted the diamond he wore on his left hand; the rainbow fires of the gem seemed to flash a sudden light on the young Comtesse's mind; she blushed and looked at the Baron with an undefinable expression.

"Do you like dancing?" asked the Provençal, to reopen the conversation.

"Yes, very much, Monsieur."

At this strange reply their eyes met. The young man, surprised by the earnest accent, which aroused a vague hope in his heart, had suddenly questioned the lady's eyes.

"Then, Madame, am I not overbold in offering myself to be your partner for the next quadrille?"

Artless confusion coloured the Comtesse's white cheeks.

"But, Monsieur, I have already refused one partner—a military man——"

"Was it that tall cavalry Colonel whom you see over there?"

"Precisely so."

"Oh! he is a friend of mine; feel no alarm. Will you grant me the favour I dare hope for?"

"Yes, Monsieur."

Her tone betrayed an emotion so new and so deep that the lawyer's world-worn soul was touched. He was overcome by shyness like a school boy's, lost his confidence, and his southern brain caught fire; he tried to talk, but his phrases struck him as graceless in comparison with Madame de Soulanges's bright and subtle replies. It was lucky for him that the quadrille was forming. Standing by his beautiful partner, he felt more at ease. To many men dancing is a phase of being; they think that they can more powerfully influence the heart of woman by displaying the graces of their bodies than by their intellect. Martial wished, no doubt, at this moment to put forth all his most effective seductions, to judge by the pretentiousness of his movements and gestures. He led his conquest to the quadrille in which the most brilliant women in the room made it a point of chimerical importance to dance in preference to any other. While the orchestra played the introductory bars to the first figure, the Baron felt it an incredible gratification to his pride to perceive, as he reviewed the ladies forming the lines of that formidable square, that Madame de Soulanges's dress might challenge that even of Madame de Vaudremont, who, by a chance not perhaps unsought, was standing with Montcornet vis-à-vis to himself and the lady in blue. All eyes were for a moment turned on Madame de Soulanges; a flattering murmur showed that she was the subject of every man's conversation with his partner. Looks of admiration and envy centred on her with so much eagerness that the young creature, abashed by a triumph she seemed to disclaim, modestly looked down, blushed, and was all the more charming. When she raised her white eyelids it was to look at her ravished partner as though she wished to transfer the glory of this admiration to him, and to say that she cared more for his than for all the rest. She threw her innocence into her vanity, or rather she seemed to give herself up to the guileless admiration which is the beginning of love, with the good faith found only in youthful hearts. As she danced, the lookers-on might easily believe that she displayed her grace for Martial alone, and though she was modest, and new to the trickery of the ballroom, she knew as well as the most accomplished coquette how to raise her eyes to his at the right moment and drop their lids with assumed modesty. When the movement of a new figure, invented by a dancer named Trénis, and named after him, brought Martial face to face with the Colonel—"I have won your horse," said he, laughing.

"Yes, but you have lost eighty thousand francs a year!" retorted Montcornet, glancing at Madame de Vaudremont.

"What do I care?" replied Martial. "Madame de Soulanges is worth millions!"

At the end of the quadrille more than one whisper was poured into more than one ear. The less pretty women made moral speeches to their partners, commenting on the budding liaison between Martial and the Comtesse de Soulanges. The handsomest wondered at her easy surrender. The men could not understand such luck as the Baron's, not regarding him as particularly fascinating. A few indulgent women said it was not fair to judge the Comtesse too hastily; young wives would be in a very hapless plight if an expressive look or a few graceful dancing steps were enough to compromise a woman. Martial alone knew the extent of his happiness. During the last figure, when the ladies had to form the *moulinet,** his fingers clasped those of the Comtesse, and he fancied that, through the thin perfumed kid of her gloves, the young wife's grasp responded to his amorous appeal.

"Madame," said he, as the quadrille ended, "do not go back to the odious corner where you have been burying your face and your dress until now. Is admiration the only benefit you can obtain from the jewels that adorn your white neck and beautifully dressed hair? Come and take a turn through the rooms to enjoy the scene and yourself."

Madame de Soulanges yielded to her seducer, who thought she would be his all the more surely if he could only show her off. Side by side they walked two or three times amid the groups who crowded the rooms. The Comtesse de Soulanges, evidently uneasy, paused for an instant at each door before entering, only doing so after stretching her neck to look at all the men there. This alarm, which crowned the Baron's satisfaction, did not seem to be removed till he said to her, "Make yourself easy; *he* is not here." They thus made their way to an immense picture gallery in a wing of the mansion, where their eyes could feast in anticipation on the splendid display of a meal prepared for three hundred persons. As the supper was about to begin, Martial led the Comtesse to an oval boudoir looking on to the garden, where the rarest flowers and a few shrubs made a scented bower under bright blue hangings. The murmurs of the festivity here died away. The Comtesse, at first startled, refused firmly to follow the young man, but, glancing in a mirror, she no doubt assured herself that they could be seen, for she seated herself gracefully on an ottoman.

"This room is charming," said she, admiring the sky-blue hangings looped with pearls.

"All here is love and delight!" said the Baron, with deep emotion.

In the mysterious light which prevailed, he looked at the Comtesse and detected on her gently agitated face an expression of uneasiness, modesty, and eagerness which enchanted him. The young lady smiled, and this smile seemed to put an end to the struggle of feeling surging in her heart; in the most insinuating way she took her adorer's left hand, and drew from his finger the ring on which she had fixed her eyes.

"What a fine diamond!" she exclaimed in the artless tone of a young girl betraying the incitement of a first temptation.

Martial, troubled by the Comtesse's involuntary but intoxicating touch, like a caress, as she drew off the ring, looked at her with eyes as glittering as the gem.

"Wear it," he said, "in memory of this hour, and for the love of——"

She was looking at him with such rapture that he did not end the sentence; he kissed her hand.

"You will give it to me?" she said, looking much astonished.

"I wish I had the whole world to offer you!"

"You are not joking?" she went on, in a voice husky with too great satisfaction.

"Will you accept only my diamond?"

"You will never take it back?" she insisted.

"Never."

She put the ring on her finger. Martial, confident of coming happiness, was about to put his hand round her waist, but she suddenly rose, and said in a clear voice, without any agitation—"I accept the diamond, Monsieur, with the less scruple because it belongs to me."

The Baron was speechless.

"Monsieur de Soulanges took it lately from my dressing table, and told me he had lost it."

"You are mistaken, Madame," said Martial, nettled. "It was given to me by Madame de Vaudremont."

"Precisely so," said she with a smile. "My husband borrowed this ring from me, he gave it to her, she made it a present to you; my ring has made a little journey, that is all. This ring will perhaps tell me all I do not know, and teach me the secret of always pleasing. Monsieur," she went on, "if it had not been my own, you may be sure I should not have risked paying so dear for it; for a young woman, it is said, is in danger with you. But, you see," and she touched a spring within the ring, "here is Monsieur de Soulanges's hair."

She fled into the crowded rooms so swiftly, that it seemed useless to try to follow her; besides, Martial, utterly confounded, was in no mood to carry the adventure further. The Comtesse's laugh found an echo in the boudoir, where the young coxcomb now perceived, between two shrubs, the Colonel and Madame de Vaudremont, both laughing heartily.

"Will you have my horse, to ride after your prize?" said the Colonel.

The Baron took the banter poured upon him by Madame de Vaudremont and Montcornet with a good grace, which secured their silence as to the events of the evening, when his friend exchanged his charger for a rich and pretty young wife.

As the Comtesse de Soulanges drove across Paris from the Chaussée-d'Antin* to the Faubourg Saint-Germain, where she lived, her soul was a prey to many alarms. Before leaving the Hôtel Gondreville, she went through all the rooms, but found neither her aunt nor her husband, who had gone away without her. Frightful suspicions then tortured her ingenuous mind. A silent witness of her husband's torments since the day when Madame de Vaudremont had involved him in her charade, she had confidently hoped that repentance would erelong restore her husband to her. It was with unspeakable repugnance that she had consented to the scheme plotted by her aunt, Madame de Lansac, and at this moment she feared she had made a mistake. The evening's experience had saddened her innocent soul. Alarmed at first by the Comte's look of suffering and dejection, she had become more so on seeing her rival's beauty, and the corruption of society had gripped her heart. As she crossed the Pont-Royal* she threw away the desecrated hair at the back of the diamond, given to her once as a token of the purest affection. She wept as she remembered the bitter grief to which she had so long been a prey, and shuddered more than once as she reflected that the duty of a woman, who wishes for domestic peace, compels her to bury sufferings so keen as hers at the bottom of her heart, and without a complaint.

"Alas!" thought she, "what can women do when they do not love? What is the source of their indulgence? I cannot believe that, as my aunt tells me, reason is sufficient to maintain them in such devotion."

She was still sighing when her manservant lowered the elegant carriage step down which she flew into the hall of her house. She rushed precipitately upstairs, and when she reached her room was startled by seeing her husband sitting by the fire.

"How long is it, my dear, since you have gone to balls without telling me beforehand?" he asked in a broken voice. "You must know that a woman is always out of place without her husband. You have oddly compromised yourself by remaining in the dark corner where you had ensconced yourself."

"Oh, my dear, good Léon," said she in a coaxing tone, "I could not resist the happiness of seeing you without your seeing me. My aunt took me to this ball, and I was very happy there!"

This speech disarmed the Comte's looks of their assumed severity, for he had been blaming himself while dreading his wife's return, no doubt fully informed at the ball of an infidelity he had hoped to hide from her, and, as is the way of lovers conscious of their guilt, he tried, by being the first to find fault, to escape her just anger. Happy in seeing her husband smile, and in finding him at this hour in a room where, for some time now, he had come less frequently, the Comtesse looked at him so tenderly that she blushed and cast down her eyes. Her clemency enraptured Soulanges all the more, because this scene followed on the misery he had endured at the ball. He seized his wife's hand and kissed it gratefully. Is not gratitude often a part of love?

"Hortense, what is that on your finger that has hurt my lip so much?" asked he, laughing.

"It is my diamond which you said you had lost, and which I have found."

General Montcornet did not marry Madame de Vaudremont, in spite of the mutual understanding in which they had lived for a few minutes, for she was one of the victims of the terrible fire which made famous forever the ball given by the Austrian ambassador on the occasion of Napoléon's marriage with the daughter of the Emperor Francis II.*

July 1829

The following personages appear or are mentioned
in other volumes of *The Human Comedy*:

Bonaparte, Napoléon
III: *The Vendetta*
VII: *A Woman of Thirty*
IX: *Colonel Chabert*
XXVI: *The Brotherhood of Consolation*
XXVII: *A Shadowy Affair*

Gondreville, Comte de (Malin)
III: *A Start in Life*
XXVII: *A Shadowy Affair*
XXVIII: *The Deputy for Arcis*

Keller, François
XI: *Eugénie Grandet*
XVIII: *César Birotteau*
XXIV: *The Bureaucrats*
XXVIII: *The Deputy for Arcis*

Keller, Madame François
XVII: *The Thirteen*
XXVIII: *The Deputy for Arcis*

La Roche-Hugon, Martial de
IV: *A Daughter of Eve*
XXI: *Cousin Bette*
XXV: *The Petits Bourgeois*
XXVIII: *The Deputy for Arcis*
XXX: *The Peasants*

Montcornet, Maréchal, Comte de
XVI: *Lost Illusions*
XIX: *The Splendors and Miseries of Courtesans*
XXI: *Cousin Bette*
XXIII: *A Man of Business*
XXX: *The Peasants*

Madame Firmiani
February 1831

Translated by Clara Bell

To my dear Alexandre de Berny* from his old friend
DE BALZAC

M. de Bourbonne.

Plate VII

Many tales, rich in situations, or made dramatic by the endless sport of chance, carry their plot in themselves, and can be related artistically or simply by any lips without the smallest loss of the beauty of the subject, but there are some incidents of human life to which only the accents of the heart can give life; there are certain anatomical details, so to speak, of which the delicacy appears only under the most skillful infusions of mind; then, there are portraits which demand a soul, and are nothing without the most delicate features of their changeable physiognomy; finally, there are certain things which we know not how to say, or to depict, without I know not what unconceived harmonies that are under the influence of a day or an hour, of a happy conjunction of celestial signs, or of some secret moral predispositions. Such mysterious revelations as these are absolutely required for the telling of this simple story, in which I would fain interest some of those naturally melancholy and pensive souls which are fed on tender emotions. If the writer, like a surgeon by the side of a dying friend, has become imbued with a sort of respect for the subject he is handling, why should not the reader share this inexplicable feeling? Is it so difficult to throw oneself into that vague, nervous melancholy which sheds grey hues on all our surroundings, which is half an illness, though its languid suffering is sometimes a pleasure? If you are thinking by chance of the dear friends you have lost; if you are alone, and it is night, or the day is dying, read this narrative; otherwise, throw the book aside, here. If you have never buried some kind aunt who is an invalid or without any fortune, you will not understand these pages. To some, they will be odorous as of musk; to others, they will be as colourless, as strictly virtuous, as those of Florian.* In short, the reader must have known the luxury of tears; must have felt the wordless grief of a memory that drifts lightly by, bearing a shade that is dear but remote; he must possess some of those remembrances that make us at the same time regret those whom the earth has swallowed, and smile over vanished joys. And now the author would have you believe that for all the riches of England he would not extort from poetry even one of her untruths to embellish this narrative. This is a true story, on which you may pour out the treasure of your sensibilities, if you have any.

In these days our language has as many dialects as there are men in the great human family. And it is a really curious and interesting thing to listen to the different views or versions of one and the same thing, or event, as given by the various Species which make up the monograph of the Parisian—the Parisian being taken as a generic term.

Thus you might ask a man of the Matter-of-fact type:* "Do you know Madame Firmiani?" and this man would interpret Madame Firmiani by such an inventory as this: "A large house in the Rue du Bac,* rooms handsomely furnished, fine pictures, a hundred thousand francs a year in good securities, and a husband who was formerly receiver general in the département of Montenotte."* Having thus spoken, your Matter-of-fact man—fat and round, almost always dressed in black— draws up his lower lip, so as to cover the upper lip, and nods his head, as much as to say: "Very respectable people, there is nothing to be said against them." Ask him no more! Your Matter-of-fact people state everything in figures, dividends, or real estate—a great word in their dictionary.

Turn to your right, go and question that young man, who belongs to the Flâneur species, and repeat your inquiry: "Madame Firmiani?" says he. "Yes, yes, I know her very well. I go to her soirées. She receives on Wednesdays; a very good house to know." Madame Firmiani is already metamorphosed into a house. The house is not a mere mass of stones architecturally put together; no, this word, in the language of the Flâneurs, has no equivalent. And here your Flâneur, a dry-looking man with a pleasant smile, saying clever nothings, but always with more acquired wit than natural wit, bends to your ear, and says with a knowing air: "I never saw Monsieur Firmiani. His social position consists in managing estates in Italy. But Madame Firmiani is French, and spends her income as a Parisian should. She gives excellent tea! It is one of the few houses where you really can amuse yourself, and where everything they give you is exquisite. It is very difficult to get introduced, and the best society is to be seen in her salons." Then the Flâneur emphasises his last words by gravely taking a pinch of snuff; he applies it to his nose in little dabs, and seems to be saying: "I go to the house, but do not count on my introducing you."

For the Flâneurs, Madame Firmiani keeps a sort of inn without a sign.

"Why on earth do you want to go to Madame Firmiani's? It is as dull there as it is at court. Of what use are brains if they do not keep you out of such salons, where, with poetry such as is now current, you hear the most trivial little ballad just hatched out."

You have asked one of your friends who comes under the class of Petty Autocrats*—men who would like to have the universe under lock and key, and have nothing done without their leave. They are miserable at other people's enjoyment, can forgive nothing but vice, wrongdoing, and infirmities, and want nothing but protégés. Aristocrats by taste, they are republicans out of spite, simply to discover many inferiors among their equals.

"Oh, Madame Firmiani, my dear fellow, is one of those adorable women whom nature feels to be a sufficient excuse for all the ugly ones she has created by mistake; she is bewitching, she is kind! I should like to be in power, to be king, to have millions, solely to (*and three words are whispered in your ear*). Shall I introduce you to her?"

This young man is a Student,* known for his audacious bearing among men and his extreme shyness in private.

"Madame Firmiani!" cries another, twirling his cane in the air. "I will tell you what I think of her. She is a woman of between thirty and thirty-five, face a little *passée*, fine eyes, a flat figure, a worn contralto voice, dresses a great deal, rouges a little, manners charming; in short, my dear fellow, the remains of a pretty woman which are still worthy of a passion."

This verdict is pronounced by a specimen of the genus Coxcomb, who, having just breakfasted, does not weigh his words, and is going out riding. At such moments a Coxcomb is pitiless.

"She has a collection of magnificent pictures in her house. Go and see her," says another; "nothing can be finer!"

You have come upon the species Amateur. This individual quits you to go to Pérignon's, or to Tripet's. To him Madame Firmiani is a number of painted canvasses.

A WIFE.—"Madame Firmiani? I will not have you go anywhere near her."

This phrase is the most suggestive view of all. Madame Firmiani! A dangerous woman! A siren! She dresses well, has good taste; she spoils the night's rest of every wife. The speaker is of the species Worryguts.*

AN ATTACHÉ TO AN EMBASSY.—"Madame Firmiani?

From Antwerp, is she not? I saw that woman, quite beautiful, about ten years ago. She was then at Rome." Men of the order of Attachés have a mania for utterances à la Talleyrand, their wit is often so subtle that their perception is imperceptible; they are like those billiard players who miss the balls with infinite skill. These men are not generally great talkers, but when they talk, it is of nothing less than Spain, Vienna, Italy, or Saint Petersburg. The names of countries act on them like springs; you press them, and the machinery plays all its tunes.

"This Madame Firmiani, does she not see a great deal of the Faubourg Saint-Germain?"* This is asked by a person who wishes to belong to the genus Distingué.* She adds a *de* to everybody's name—to Monsieur Dupin, senior, to Monsieur Lafayette;* she flings it right and left and spatters people with it. She spends her life in anxieties as to what is *correct,* but, for her sins, she remains in the unfashionable Marais,* and her husband was an attorney—but an attorney at the royal court.

"Madame Firmiani, Monsieur? I do not know her." This man is of the class of Dukes. He recognises no woman who has not been presented. Excuse him; he was created Duke by Napoléon.

"Madame Firmiani? Was she not a singer at the Italiens?" A man of the genus Simpleton. The individuals of this class must have an answer to everything. They would rather speak calumnies than be silent.

TWO OLD LADIES (*the wives of retired magistrates*). THE FIRST (she has a cap with bows of ribbon, her face is wrinkled, her nose sharp; she holds a prayer book, and her voice is harsh). "What was her maiden name, this Madame Firmiani?" THE SECOND (she has a little red face like a lady apple, and a gentle voice). "She was a Cadignan, my dear, niece of the old Prince de Cadignan, and cousin, consequently, to the Duc de Maufrigneuse."

Madame Firmiani then is a Cadignan. Bereft of virtues, fortune, and youth, she would still be a Cadignan. A Cadignan, just like a prejudice, is always rich and alive.

AN ECCENTRIC.—"My dear fellow, I never saw any clogs in her anteroom; you may go to her house without compromising yourself, and play there without hesitation; for if there should be any rogues, they will be people of quality, and consequently there is no quarrelling."

AN OLD MAN OF THE SPECIES OBSERVER.—"You go to Madame Firmiani's, my dear fellow, and you find a beautiful woman lounging indolently by the fire. She will scarcely move from her chair; she rises only to greet women, or ambassadors, or dukes—people of importance. She is very gracious, she charms you, she talks well, and likes to talk of everything. She bears every indication of a passionate soul, but she is credited with too many adorers to have a lover. If suspicion rested on only two or three intimate visitors, we might know which was her *cavaliere servente*.* But she is all mystery; she is married, and we have never seen her husband; Monsieur Firmiani is purely a creature of fancy, like the third horse we are made to pay for when travelling post, and which we never see; Madame, if you believe the artistes, has the finest contralto voice in Europe, and has not sung three times since she came to Paris; she receives numbers of people, and goes nowhere."

The Observer speaks as an oracle. His words, his anecdotes, his quotations must all be accepted as truth, or you risk being taken for a man without knowledge of the world, without capabilities. He will happily slander you in twenty salons, where he is as essential as the first piece on the program—pieces so often played to a room empty or half empty of spectators, but which once upon a time were successful. The Observer is a man of forty, never dines at home, and professes not to be dangerous to women; he wears powder and a maroon-coloured coat; he can always have a seat in various boxes at the Théâtre des Bouffons. He is sometimes mistaken for a Parasite, but he has held positions too high to be suspected of being a sponger, and, indeed, possesses an estate in a département, the name of which has never leaked out.

"Madame Firmiani? Why, my dear boy, she was an old mistress of Murat's!" This gentleman is a Contradictory. They supply the *errata* to every memory, rectify every fact, bet you a hundred to one, are cocksure of everything. You catch them on the same evening in flagrant acts of ubiquity: they assert that they were in Paris at the time of Mallet's conspiracy,* forgetting that half an hour before they had crossed the Berezina. The Contradictories are almost all members of the Legion of Honour;* they talk very loud, have receding foreheads, and play high.

"Madame Firmiani, a hundred thousand francs a year? Are you mad? Really, some people scatter thousands a year with the liberality of authors, to whom it costs nothing to give their heroines handsome fortunes. But Madame Firmiani is a flirt who ruined a young fellow the other day, and hindered him from making a very good marriage. If she were not beautiful, she would be penniless."

This speaker you recognise: he is one of the Envious, and we will not sketch his least feature. The species is as well known as that of the domestic *felis*. How is the perpetuity of envy to be explained? A vice which is wholly unprofitable!

People of fashion, literary *people*, very good *people*, and *people* of every kind were, in the month of January 1824, giving out so many different opinions on Madame Firmiani that it would be tiresome to report them all. We have only aimed at showing that a man wishing to know her, without choosing or being able to go to her house, would have been equally justified in the belief that she was a widow or a wife—silly or witty, virtuous or immoral, rich or poor, gentle or devoid of soul, handsome or ugly; in fact, there were as many Madames Firmiani as there are varieties in social life, or sects in the Catholic Church. Frightful thought! We are all like lithographed plates, of which an endless number of copies are pulled by slander. These copies resemble or differ from the original by touches so imperceptibly slight that, but for the calumnies of our friends and the witticisms of newspapers, reputation would depend on the balance struck by each hearer between the limping Truth and the Lies to which Parisian wit lends wings.

Madame Firmiani, like many other women of dignity and noble pride, who close their hearts as a sanctuary and scorn the world, might have been very badly judged by Monsieur de Bourbonne, an old gentleman of fortune, who had thought a great deal about her during the past winter. As it happened, this gentleman belonged to the Provincial landowner class, people who are accustomed to inquire into everything, and to make bargains with peasants. In this business a man grows keen-witted in spite of himself, as a soldier, in the long run, acquires the courage of routine. This inquirer, a native of Touraine, and not easily satisfied by the Paris dialects, was a very honourable gentleman who rejoiced in a nephew, his sole heir, for whom he planted his poplars. Their more than natural affection gave rise to much malicious gossip—which individuals of the various species of Tourangeau* formulated with much cleverness—but it would be useless to record it, as it would pale before that of Parisian tongues. When a man can think of his heir without displeasure, as he sees fine rows of poplars improving every day, his affection increases with each spadeful of earth he turns at the foot of his trees. Though such phenomena of sensibility may be uncommon, they still are to be met with in Touraine.

This much-loved nephew, whose name was Octave de Camps, was descended from the famous Abbé de Camps,* so well known to the learned, or to the bibliomaniacs, which is not the same thing. Provincial people have a disagreeable habit of regarding young men who sell their inheritances with a sort of respectable horror. This gothic prejudice is bad for speculation, which the government has hitherto found it necessary to encourage. Now, without consulting his uncle, Octave had unexpectedly disposed of an estate in favour of *La Bande Noire*.* The château of Villaines would have been demolished but for the offers made by his old uncle to representatives of Marteau's demolishing company. To add to the testator's wrath, a friend of Octave's, a distant relation, one of those cousins with small wealth and great cunning who lead their prudent neighbours to say, "I would not like to have a legal dispute with him!" had called, by chance, on Monsieur de Bourbonne and informed him that his nephew was ruined. Monsieur Octave de Camps, after dissipating his fortune for a certain Madame Firmiani, and not daring to confess his sins, had been reduced to giving lessons in mathematics, pending his coming into his uncle's legacy. This distant cousin—a sort of Charles Moor*—had not been ashamed of giving this disastrous news to the old country gentleman at the hour when, sitting before his spacious hearth, he was digesting a copious provincial dinner. But heirs do not get rid of an uncle so easily as they might wish. This uncle, thanks to his obstinacy, refusing to believe the distant cousin, came out victorious over the indigestion brought on by the biography of his nephew. Some blows fall on the heart, others on the brain; the blow struck by the distant cousin landed in the old man's gut, but produced little effect as he had a strong stomach. Monsieur de Bourbonne, as a worthy disciple of Saint Thomas, came to Paris without telling Octave, and tried to get information as to his heir's insolvency. The old gentleman, who had friends in the Faubourg Saint-Germain—the Listomères, the Lenoncourts, and the Vandenesses—heard so much slander, so much that was true, and so much that was false concerning Madame Firmiani, that he determined to call on her under the name of Monsieur de Rouxellay, the name of his estate. The prudent old man took care in going to study Octave's alleged mistress on an evening when he knew that the young man was busy completing work for some badly needed pay, for Madame Firmiani was always at home for her young friend, a circumstance that no one could account for. As to Octave's ruin, that, unfortunately, was no fiction.

Monsieur de Rouxellay was not at all like a stage uncle. As an old musketeer, a man of the best society who had his successes in his day, he knew how to introduce himself with a courtly air, remembered the polished manners of the past, had a pretty wit, and understood almost all of the Charter.* Though he loved the Bourbons with noble frankness, believed in God as gentlemen believe, and read only the *Quotidienne*,* he was by no means so ridiculous as the Liberals of his département would have wished. He could hold his own with men about the court, so long as he was not expected to talk of *Mosè*,* or the theatre, or romanticism, or local colour, or railways. He had not got beyond Monsieur de Voltaire, Monsieur le Comte de Buffon, Peyronnet,* and the Chevalier Gluck, the Queen's private musician.

"Madame," said he to the Marquise de Listomère, to whom he had given his arm to go into Madame Firmiani's room, "if this woman is my nephew's mistress, I pity her. How can she bear to live in the midst of luxury and know that he is in a garret? Has she no soul? Octave is a fool to have invested the price of the estate of Villaines in the heart of a——"

Monsieur de Bourbonne was of the Fossil species, and spoke only the language of a past day.

"But suppose he had lost it at play?"

"Well, Madame, he would have had the pleasure of playing."

"You think he has had no pleasure for his money? Look, here is Madame Firmiani."

The old uncle's brightest memories paled at the sight of his nephew's supposed mistress. His anger died in a polite speech wrung from him by the presence of Madame Firmiani. By one of these chances which come only to pretty women, it was a moment when all her beauties shone with particular brilliancy, the result, perhaps, of the glow of candlelight, of an exquisitely simple dress, of an indefinable reflection from the elegance in which she lived and moved. Only long study of the petty revolutions of an evening party in a Paris salon can enable one to appreciate the imperceptible shades that can tinge and change a woman's face. There are moments when, pleased with her dress, feeling herself brilliant, happy at being admired and seeing herself the queen of a room full of remarkable men all smiling at her, a Parisian is conscious of her beauty and grace; she grows the lovelier by all the looks she meets;, they give her animation, but their mute homage is transmitted by subtle glances to the man she loves. In such a moment a woman is invested, as it were, with supernatural power, and becomes a sorceress; an unconscious coquette, she involuntarily inspires the passion which is a secret intoxication to herself, and she has smiles and looks that are fascinating. If this excitement which comes from the soul lends attractiveness even to ugly women, with what splendour does it not clothe a naturally elegant creature: finely made, fair, fresh, bright-eyed, and, above all, dressed with such taste as artists and even her most spiteful rivals must admit.

Have you ever met, for your happiness, some woman whose harmonious tones give to her speech the charm that is no less conspicuous in her manners, who knows how to talk and to be silent, who cares for you with delicate feeling, whose words are happily chosen and her language pure? Her banter flatters you, her criticism does not sting; she neither preaches nor disputes, but is interested in leading a discussion, and stops it at the right moment. Her manner is friendly and gay, her politeness is unforced, her eagerness to please is not servile; she reduces respect to a mere gentle shade; she never tires you, and leaves you satisfied with her and yourself. You will see her gracious presence stamped on the things she collects about her. In her home everything charms the eye, and you breathe, as it seems, your native air. This woman is quite natural. You never feel an effort, she flaunts nothing, her feelings are expressed with simplicity because they are genuine. Though candid, she never wounds the most sensitive pride; she accepts men as God made them, pitying the vicious, forgiving defects and absurdities, sympathising with every age, and vexed with nothing because she has the tact to foresee every eventuality. At once tender and lively, she first constrains and then consoles you. You love her so truly, that if this angel does wrong, you are ready to justify her. Then you know Madame Firmiani.

By the time old Bourbonne had talked with this woman for a quarter of an hour, sitting by her side, his nephew was absolved. He understood that, true or false, Octave's connection with Madame Firmiani no doubt concealed some mystery. Returning to the illusions of his youth, and judging of Madame Firmiani's heart by her beauty, the old gentleman thought that a woman so sure of her dignity as she seemed was incapable of a base action. Her black eyes spoke of so much peace of mind, the lines of her face were so noble, her contours so natural, and the passion of which she was accused seemed to weigh so little on her heart, that, as he admired all the pledges given to love and to virtue by that adorable countenance, the old man said to himself, "My nephew has committed some folly."

Madame Firmiani admitted to being twenty-five years of age. But the Matter-of-facts could prove that, having been married in 1813 at the age of sixteen, she must be at least twenty-eight in 1825. Nevertheless the same persons declared that she had never at any period of her life been so desirable, so perfectly a woman. She had no children, and had never had any; the hypothetical Firmiani, a respectable man of forty in 1813, had, it was said, only his name and fortune to offer her. So Madame Firmiani had come to the age when a Parisian best understands what passion is, and perhaps longs for it innocently in her unemployed hours: she had everything that the world can sell, or lend, or give. The Attachés declared she knew everything, the Contradictories said she had yet many things to learn; the Observers noticed that her hands were very white, her foot very small, her movements a little too undulating; but men of every Species envied or disputed Octave's good fortune, agreeing that she was the most aristocratic beauty in Paris. Still young, rich, a perfect musician, witty, exquisite; welcomed, for the sake of the Cadignans, to whom she was related through her mother, by the Princesse de Blamont-Chauvry, the oracle of the aristocratic quarter; beloved by her rivals the Duchesse de Maufrigneuse her cousin, the Marquise d'Espard, and Madame de Macumer, she flattered every vanity which feeds or excites love. And, indeed, she was the object of too many desires not to be the victim of fashionable detraction and those delightful calumnies which are wittily hinted at behind a fan or in a whispered *aside*. Hence the remarks with which this story opened were necessary to mark the contrast between the real Firmiani and the Firmiani known to the world. Though some women forgave her for being happy, others could not overlook her respectability; now there is nothing so terrible, especially in Paris, as suspicion without foundation; it is impossible to kill it.

This sketch of a personality so admirable by nature can only give a feeble idea of it; it would need the brush of an Ingres to represent the dignity of the brow, the mass of fine hair, the majesty of the eyes, all the thoughts betrayed by the varying hues of the complexion. There was something of everything in this woman; poets could see in her both Joan of Arc and Agnès Sorel,* but there was also the unknown woman—the soul hidden behind this deceptive mask—the soul of Eve, the wealth of evil and the treasures of goodness, wrong and resignation, crime and self-sacrifice—the Donna Julia and Haidée of Byron's *Don Juan.**

The old musketeer very boldly remained till the last in Madame Firmiani's salon; she found him quietly seated in an armchair, and staying with the pertinacity of a fly that must be killed to be got rid of. The clock marked two in the morning.

"Madame," said the old gentleman, just as Madame Firmiani rose in the hope of making her guest understand that it was her pleasure that he should go. "Madame, I am Monsieur Octave de Camps's uncle."

Madame Firmiani at once sat down again, and her agitation was evident. In spite of his perspicacity, the planter of poplars could not make up his mind whether shame or pleasure made her turn pale. There are pleasures which do not exist without a little coy bashfulness—delightful emotions which the chastest soul would fain keep behind a veil. The more sensitive a woman is, the more she lives to conceal her soul's greatest joys. Many women, incomprehensible in their exquisite caprices, at times long to hear a name spoken by all the world, while they sometimes would sooner bury it in their hearts. Old Bourbonne did not read Madame Firmiani's agitation quite in this light, but forgive him; the country gentleman was suspicious.

"Indeed, Monsieur?" said Madame Firmiani, with one of those clear and piercing looks in which we men can never see anything, because they question us too keenly.

"Indeed, Madame, and do you know what I have been told—I, in the depths of the country? That my nephew has ruined himself for you, and the unhappy boy is in a garret, while you live here in gold and silks. You will, I hope, forgive my rustic frankness, for it may be useful to you to be informed of the slander."

"Stop, Monsieur," said Madame Firmiani, interrupting the gentleman with an imperious gesture, "I know all that. You are too polite to keep the conversation to this subject when I beg you to change it. You are too gallant, in the old-fashioned sense of the word," she added, with a slightly ironical emphasis, "not to acknowledge that you have no right to cross-examine me. However, it is ridiculous for me to justify myself. I hope you have a good enough opinion of my character to believe in the utter contempt I feel for money, though I was married without any fortune whatever to a man who had an immense fortune. I do not know whether your nephew is rich or poor; if I have received him, if I still receive him, it is because I regard him as worthy to move in the midst of my friends. All my friends, Monsieur, respect each other; they know that I am not so philosophical as to entertain people whom I do not esteem. That, perhaps, shows a lack of charity, but my guardian angel has preserved in me, to this day, an intense aversion for gossip and dishonour."

Though her voice was not quite firm at the beginning of this reply, the last words were spoken by Madame Firmiani with the cool decision of Célimène ridiculing the Misanthrope.*

"Madame," the Comte resumed in a broken voice, "I am an old man—I am almost a father to Octave—I therefore must humbly crave your pardon beforehand for the only question I shall be so bold as to ask you, and I give you my word of honour as a gentleman that your reply will die here," and he laid his hand on his heart with a really religious gesture. "Does gossip speak the truth, do you love Octave?"

"Monsieur," said she, "I should answer anyone else with a look. But you, since you are almost a father to Monsieur de Camps, you I will ask what you would think of a woman who, in reply to your question, should say, *yes?* To confess one's love to the man we love—when he loves us—well, well; when we are sure of being loved forever, believe me, Monsieur, it is an effort to us and a reward to him, but to anyone else!——"

Madame Firmiani did not finish her sentence; she rose, bowed to the good gentleman, and vanished into her private rooms, where the sound of doors opened and shut in succession was like a rebuff to the ears of the poplar planter.

"*Ah, peste!*" said the old man to himself, "what a woman! She is either a very cunning hussy or an angel," and he went down to his hired coach in the courtyard, where the horses were pawing the pavement in silence. The coachman had fallen asleep, after having cursed his customer a hundred times.

Next morning, by about eight o'clock, the old gentleman was mounting the stairs of a house in the Rue de l'Observance,* where dwelt Octave de Camps. If there was in this world a man amazed, it was the young professor on seeing his uncle. The key was in the door, Octave's lamp was still burning; he had sat up all night.

"*Monsieur le drôle,*" said Monsieur de Bourbonne, seating himself in an armchair, "how long has it been the fashion to make fools (to put it mildly) of uncles who have twenty-six thousand francs a year in good land in Touraine? and that, when you are sole heir? Do you know that formerly such relations were treated with respect? Pray, have you any fault to find with me? Have I bungled my business as an uncle? Have I demanded your respect? Have I ever refused you money? Have I shut my door in your face, saying you had only come to see how I was? Have you not the most accommodating, the least exacting uncle in France? I will not say in Europe, it would be claiming too much. You write to me, or you do not. I live on your professions of affection. I am laying out the prettiest estate in the neighbourhood, a place that is the object of envy in all the département, but I do not mean to leave it to you till the latest date possible—a weakness that is very pardonable? And Monsieur sells his property, is lodged like a groom, has no servants, keeps no style——"

"Uncle——"

"It is not a case of uncle, but of nephew. I have a right to your confidence; so have it all out at once; it is the easiest way, I know by experience. Have you been gambling? Have you been speculating on the Bourse? Come, say, 'Uncle, I am a wretch,' and we kiss and are friends. But if you tell me any lie bigger than those I told at your age, I will sell my property, buy an annuity, and go back to the bad ways of my youth, if it is not too late."

"Uncle——"

"I went last night to see your Madame Firmiani," said the old gentleman, kissing the tips of all his fingers together. "She is charming," he went on. "You have the king's warrant and approval, and your uncle's consent, if that is any satisfaction to you. As to the sanction of the Church, that I suppose is unnecessary—the sacraments, no doubt, are too costly. Come, speak out. Is it for her that you have ruined yourself?"

"Yes, uncle."

"Ah! The little minx! I would have bet upon it. In my day a woman of fashion could ruin a man more cleverly than any of your courtesans of today. I saw in her a resuscitation of the last century."

"Uncle," said Octave, in a voice that was at once sad and gentle, "you are mistaken. Madame Firmiani

149

deserves your esteem and all the adoration of her admirers."

"So hapless youth is always the same!" said Monsieur de Bourbonne. "Well, well! go on in your own way; keep telling me the same old stories. However, you should know that I am not always so chivalrous in matters such as these."

"My dear uncle, here is a letter which will explain everything," replied Octave, taking out an elegant letter case—*her* gift, no doubt. "When you have read it I will tell you the rest, and you will know Madame Firmiani as the world knows her not."

"I have not got my spectacles," said his uncle. "Read it to me."

Octave began: "My dear love——"

"Then you are very intimate with this woman?"

"Why, yes, uncle."

"And you have not quarrelled?"

"Quarrelled!" echoed Octave in surprise. "We were married—at Gretna Green."*

"Well then," continued Monsieur de Bourbonne, "why do you dine for only forty sous?"

"Let me proceed."

"Very true, I am listening."

Octave took up the letter again, and could not read certain passages without strong emotion.

"'My beloved husband, you ask me the reason of my melancholy. Has it passed from my soul into my face, or have you only guessed it? And why should you not? Our hearts are so closely united. Besides, I cannot lie, though that perhaps is a misfortune. One of the conditions of being loved is, in a woman, to be always caressing and gay. Perhaps I ought to deceive you, but I would not do so, not even if it were to increase or to preserve the happiness you give me—you lavish on me—under which you overwhelm me. Oh, my dear, my love carries with it so much gratitude! And I must love forever, without measure. Yes, I must always be proud of you. Our glory—a woman's glory—is all in the man she loves. Esteem, consideration, honour, are they not all his who has conquered everything? Well then! My angel has failed. Yes, my dear, your last confession has dimmed my past happiness. From that moment I have felt myself humbled through you—you, whom I believed to be the purest of men, as you are the tenderest and most loving. I must have supreme confidence in your still childlike heart to make an avowal which costs me so dear. Why, poor angel, your father stole his fortune, you know this, yet you keep it! And you could tell me of this attorney's triumph in a room full of the mute witnesses of our love, and you are a gentleman, and you think yourself noble, and I am yours, and you are twenty-two! How monstrous all through! I have sought excuses for you; I have ascribed your indifference to your giddy youth; I know there is still much of the child in you. Perhaps you have never yet thought seriously of what is meant by wealth and by honesty. Oh, your laughter hurt me so much! Only think, there is a family, ruined, always in grief, girls perhaps, who curse you day by day, an old man who says to himself every night, "I should not lack bread if Monsieur de Camps's father had only been an honest man."'"

"What!" exclaimed Monsieur de Bourbonne, interrupting him, "were you such an idiot as to tell that woman the story of your father's affair with the Bourgneufs? Women better understand spending a fortune than making one——"

"They understand honesty. Let me go on, uncle!"

"'Octave, no power on earth is authorised to distort the language of honour. Look into your conscience and ask it by what name to call the action to which you owe your riches.'"

And the nephew looked at his uncle, who lowered his head.

151

"'I will not tell you all the thoughts that beset me; they can all be reduced to one, which is this: I cannot esteem a man who knowingly soils himself for a sum of money whether large or small. Five francs stolen at play, or six times a hundred thousand francs obtained by legal trickery, disgrace a man equally. I must tell you all: I feel myself sullied by a love which till now was all my joy. From the bottom of my soul there comes a voice I cannot stifle. I have wept to find that my conscience is stronger than my love. You might commit a crime, and I would hide you in my bosom from human justice if I could, but my devotion would go no further. Love, my angel, is, in a woman, the most unlimited confidence, united with an almost unimaginable need to respect and venerate the being to whom she belongs. I have never conceived of love but as a fire in which the noblest feelings were yet further purified—a fire which develops them to the utmost. I have but one thing more to say: come to me poor, and I shall love you twice as much if possible; if not, give me up. If I see you no more, I know what is left to me to do. But, now, understand me clearly, I will not have you make restitution because I desire it. Consult your conscience. This is an act of justice, and must not be done as a sacrifice to love. I am your wife and not your mistress; the point is not to please me, but to inspire me with the highest esteem. If I have misunderstood, if you have not clearly explained your father's action, in short, if you can regard your fortune as legitimately acquired—and how gladly would I persuade myself that you deserve no blame—decide as the voice of conscience dictates; act wholly for yourself. A man who truly loves, as you love me, has too high a respect for all the holy inspiration he may get from his wife to be dishonourable. I blame myself now for all I have written. A word would perhaps have been enough, and my preaching instinct has carried me away. So I should like to be scolded—not much, but a little.

My dear, between you and me, are you not the authority? You alone must be aware of your faults. Well then, master of mine, can you say I understand nothing about political discussion?'"

"Well, uncle?" said Octave, whose eyes were full of tears.

"I see more writing, finish it."

"Oh, there is nothing further but such things as only a lover may read."

"Very good," said the old man. "Very good, my dear boy. I have had much good fortune with women, but please believe me when I say that I have also loved, *et ego in Arcadiâ*. Still, I cannot imagine why you give lessons in mathematics."

"My dear uncle, I am your nephew; do these words not tell you that I had indeed begun to draw on the capital left to me by my father? After reading that letter, a complete revolution took place in me: in one instant I paid up the arrears of remorse. I could never describe to you the state I was in. As I drove my cab to the woods, a voice cried to me, 'Is that horse yours?' As I ate my dinner, I said to myself, 'Have you not stolen the food?' I was ashamed of myself. My honesty was ardent in proportion to its youth. First I flew off to Madame Firmiani. Ah, my dear uncle, that day I had such joys of heart, such raptures of soul as were worth millions. With her I calculated how much I owed the Bourgneuf family, and I sentenced myself, against Madame Firmiani's advice, to pay them interest at the rate of three percent. But my whole fortune was not enough to refund the sum. We were both of us lovers enough—husband and wife enough—for her to offer and for me to accept her savings——"

"What, besides all her virtues, that adorable woman can save money!" cried the uncle.

"Do not laugh at her. Her position compels her to some thrift. Her husband went to Greece in 1820, and died about three years ago, but to this day it has been impossible to get legal proof of his death, or to lay hands on the will he no doubt made in favour of his wife; this important document was stolen, lost, or mislaid in a country where a man's papers are not kept as they are in France, nor is there a consul. So, not knowing whether she may not some day have to reckon with unscrupulous heirs, she is obliged to be extremely careful, for she does not wish to have to give up her wealth as Chateaubriand has just given up the Ministry. Now I mean to earn a fortune that shall be *mine,* so as to restore my wife to opulence if she should be ruined."

"And you never told me—you never came to me. My dear nephew, believe me, I love you well enough to pay your honest debts, your debts as a gentleman. I am the wealthy uncle who appears at the end of the play, and I will settle accounts."

"I know how you settle accounts, uncle, but let me grow rich by my own toil. If you wish to befriend me, allow me a thousand écus a year until I need capital for some business. I declare at this moment I am so happy that all I care about is to live. I give lessons that I may be no burden to anyone. Ah, if you could but know with what delight I made restitution. After making some inquiries I found the Bourgneufs in misery and destitution. They were living at Saint-Germain* in a wretched house. The old father was manager in a lottery office; the two girls did the work of the house and kept the accounts. The mother was almost always ill. The two girls are charming, but they have learnt by bitter experience how little the world cares for beauty without fortune. What a picture did I find there! If I went to the house as the accomplice in a crime, I came out of it an honest man, and I have purged my father's memory. I do not judge him, uncle; in a lawsuit there is a sort of driving force, a passion which may sometimes blind the most honest man alive. Lawyers know how to legitimise the most preposterous claims; there are syllogisms in law to humour the errors of conscience, and judges have a right to make mistakes. My adventure was a perfect drama. To have played the part of Providence, to have fulfilled one of these hopeless wishes: if only twenty thousand francs a year could drop from heaven—a wish we have all uttered in jest!—to see a sublime look of gratitude, amazement, and admiration take the place of a glance fraught with curses; to bring opulence into the midst of a family sitting round a peat fire in the evening, by the light of a wretched lamp—no, words cannot paint such a scene. My excessive justice to them seemed unjust. Well, if there be a Paradise, my father must now be happy. As for myself, I am loved as man was never loved before. Madame Firmiani has given me more than happiness; she has taught me a delicacy of feeling which perhaps I lacked. Indeed, I call her *my dear conscience*, one of those loving names that are the outcome of certain secret harmonies of spirit. Honesty is said to pay; I hope ere long to be rich myself; at this moment I am bent on solving a great industrial problem, and if I succeed I shall make millions."

"My boy, you have your mother's soul," said the old man, hardly able to restrain the tears that rose at the remembrance of his sister.

At this instant, in spite of the height above the ground of Octave's room, the young man and his uncle heard the noise of a carriage driving up.

"It is she! I know her horses by the way they pull up."

And it was not long before Madame Firmiani made her appearance.

"Oh!" she cried, with an impulse of annoyance on seeing Monsieur de Bourbonne. "But our uncle is not in the way," she went on with a sudden smile, "I have come to kneel at my husband's feet and humbly beseech him to accept my fortune. I have just received from the Austrian

Embassy a document proving Firmiani's death. The paper, drawn up by the kind offices of the Austrian envoy at Constantinople, is quite formal, and the will which Firmiani's valet had in keeping for me is subjoined. There, you are richer than I am, for you have there," and tapped her husband's breast, "treasures which only God can add to." Then, unable to disguise her happiness, she hid her face in Octave's bosom.

"My dear niece, I was in love once," said the old gentleman, "today you love. You women are all that is good and lovely in humanity, for you are never guilty of your faults; they always originate with us."

Paris, February 1831

The following personages appear or are mentioned
in other volumes of *The Human Comedy*:

Blamont-Chauvry, Princesse de
XVII: *The Thirteen*
XXXIII: *The Lily of the Valley*

Bourbonne, De
XII: *The Curé of Tours*

Camps, Octave de
XXVIII: *The Deputy for Arcis*

Camps, Madame Octave de (née Cadignan, Madame Firmiani)
IV: *A Daughter of Eve*
VII: *A Woman of Thirty*
XXIV: *The Bureaucrats*
XXVIII: *The Deputy for Arcis*

A Study of Woman
(*Étude de femme*)
February 1839

Translated by Clara Bell

*Dedicated to the Marquis Jean-Charles di Negro**

The Marquise de Listomère is a young woman brought up in the spirit of the Restoration.* She has principles, she fasts in season, she takes the Sacrament, she goes very much dressed to balls, to the Bouffons, to the Opera; her spiritual director allows her to combine the sacred and the profane. Always on good terms with the Church and the world, she is an incarnation of the present time, and seems to have taken the word *Légalité* for her motto. The Marquise's conduct is marked by exactly enough devotion to enable her, under another Maintenon, to achieve the gloomy piety of the last days of Louis XIV, and enough worldliness to adopt the manners and gallantry of the earlier years of his reign, if they ever could return. Just now she is virtuous by calculation, or, perhaps, by taste. Married some seven years since to the Marquis de Listomère, a deputy who expects a peerage, she perhaps thinks that her conduct may promote the ambitions of the family. Some women wait to pass judgment on her till Monsieur de Listomère is made Peer of France,* and till she is thirty-six—a time of life when most women discover that they are the dupes of social laws. The Marquis is an insignificant personage; he is in favour at court; his good qualities, like his faults, are negative: the former can no more give him a reputation for virtue than the latter can give him the sort of brilliancy bestowed by vice. As a deputy he never speaks, but he votes *straight*, and at home, he behaves as he does in the Chamber. He is considered the best husband in France. Though he is incapable of enthusiasms, he

161

never scolds, unless he is kept waiting. His friends nickname him *Cloudy Weather*, and, in fact, there is in him
no excessively bright light, and no utter darkness. He is
exactly like all the Ministers that have succeeded each
other in France since the Charter.* A woman with principles could hardly have fallen into better hands. Is it
not a great thing for a virtuous woman to have married
a man incapable of a folly? Dandies have been known
to venture on the impertinence of slightly pressing the
Marquise's hand when dancing with her; they met only
looks of scorn, and all have experienced that insulting
indifference which, like spring frosts, chills the germs of
the fairest hopes. Handsome men, witty men, coxcombs,
sentimental men who derive nourishment by tightly
gripping their walking sticks, men of name and men of
fame, men of high birth and of low, all have blanched
before her. She has won the right of talking as long and
as often as she pleases with men whom she thinks intelligent without being entered in the calendar of scandal.
Some coquettes are capable of pursuing this plan for
seven years on end, to gratify their fancy at last, but to
ascribe such a covert motive to Madame de Listomère
would be to calumniate her. I had been so happy as to
meet this Phoenix of a Marquise; she talks well, I am a
good listener. I pleased her, and I go to her evening parties. This was the object of my ambition. Neither plain
nor pretty, Madame de Listomère has white teeth, a brilliant complexion, and very red lips; she is tall and well
made, has a small, slender foot, which she does not display; her eyes, far from being dulled, as most eyes are in
Paris, have a soft gleam which becomes magical when
by chance she is animated. You feel there is a soul under this ill-defined personality. When she is interested
in the conversation, she reveals the grace that lies buried under the prudery of her cold demeanour, and then
she is charming. She does not crave for success, and she
gets it. We always find the thing we do not seek. This

statement is too often true not to become a proverb one day. It will be the moral of this tale, which I should not allow myself to relate if it were not at this moment the talk of every salon in Paris.

One evening, about a month since, the Marquise de Listomère danced with a young man as modest as he is heedless, full of good qualities, but showing only his bad ones; he is impassioned, and laughs at passion; he has talent, and hides it; he plays the scholar with aristocrats, and the aristocrat with scholars. Eugène de Rastignac is one of those very sensible young men who try everything, and seem to sound out other men to discover what the future will bring forth. Pending the age when he will be ambitious, he laughs at everything; he has grace and originality—two qualities which are rare, because they exclude each other. Without aiming at success, he talked to Madame de Listomère for about half an hour. While following the whims of a conversation which, after beginning with the opera *William Tell,** went on to the duties of women, he looked at the Marquise more than once in such a way as to embarrass her; then he left her, and spoke to her no more for the rest of the evening. He danced, sat down to *écarté,* lost a little money, and went home to bed. I have the honour of assuring you that this is exactly what happened. I have added, I have omitted nothing.

The next morning Rastignac woke late, remaining in bed, where he gave himself up, no doubt, to some of those morning daydreams in which a young man glides, like a sylph, behind more than one curtain of silk, wool, or cotton. At such moments, the heavier the body is with sleep, the more nimble is the fancy. Finally Rastignac got up without yawning too much, as so many ill-bred people do, rang for his manservant, ordered some tea, and drank of it immoderately—which will not seem strange to those who like tea, but, to account for this to those persons who only regard tea as a panacea for indigestion, I will add that Eugène was writing; he sat at his ease, and his feet were more often on the andirons than in his foot muff. Oh! to sit with your feet on the polished bar that rests on the two brackets of a fender and dream of your love affairs while wrapped in your dressing gown is so delightful a thing, that I deeply regret having no mistress, no andirons, and no dressing gown. When I shall have all those good things, I shall not write my experiences, I shall take the benefit of them.

The first letter Eugène had to write was finished in a quarter of an hour. He folded it, sealed it, and left it lying in front of him without any address. The second letter, begun at eleven o'clock, was not finished till noon. The four pages were written all over.

"That woman runs in my head," said he to himself as he folded the second missive, leaving it there, and intending to address it after ending his involuntary reverie. He crossed the fronts of his flowered dressing gown, put his feet on a stool, stuffed his hands into the pockets of his red cashmere trousers, and threw himself back in a delicious armchair with deep ears, of which the seat and back were set at the comfortable angle of a hundred and twenty degrees. He drank no more tea, but remained passive, his eyes fixed on the little gilt fist which formed the knob of his fire shovel, without seeing the shovel, or the hand, or the gilding. He did not even make up the fire. This was a great mistake! Is it not an intense pleasure to fidget with the fire when dreaming of women? Our fancy lends speech to the little blue tongues which suddenly burst up and babble on the hearth. We can find a meaning in the sudden and noisy language of a *bourguignon*.

At this word I must pause and insert, for the benefit of the ignorant, an explanation vouchsafed by a very distinguished etymologist, who wishes to remain anonymous. *Bourguignon* is the popular and symbolical name given, ever since the reign of Charles VI,* to the loud explosions which result in the ejection on to a rug or a dress of a fragment of charcoal, the germ of a conflagration. The heat, it is said, explodes a bubble of air remaining in the heart of the wood, in the trail of some gnawing grub. *Inde amor, inde Burgundus.** We quake as we see the charred pieces coming down like an avalanche when we had balanced them so industriously between two blazing logs. Oh! Making up a wood fire when you are in love is the material expression of your sentiments.

It was at this moment that I entered Eugène's room; he started violently, and said: "So there you are, my dear Horace. How long have you been here?"

"I have this moment come."

"Ah!"

He took the two letters, addressed them, and rang for his servant.

"Take these two notes."

And Joseph went without a remark. Excellent servant!

And we proceeded to discuss the expedition to the Morea,* in which I wanted to be employed as surgeon. Eugène pointed out that I should lose much by leaving Paris, and we then talked of indifferent things. I do not think I shall be blamed for omitting our conversation.

*   *   *   *   *

When Madame de Listomère rose at about two in the afternoon, her maid Caroline handed her a letter, which she read while Caroline was dressing her hair. (An imprudence committed by a great many young wives.)

Ah, dear angel of love, my treasure of life and happiness! On reading these words, the Marquise was going to throw the letter into the fire, but a fancy flashed through her head, which any virtuous woman will understand masterfully, namely, to see how a man who started in this way might finish. She read on. When she turned to the fourth page, she dropped her arms like a person who is tired.

"Caroline," said she, "go and find out who left this letter for me."

"Madame, I took it from Monsieur le Baron de Rastignac's manservant."

There was a long silence.

"Will Madame dress now?"

"No."

"He must be excessively impertinent!" thought the Marquise.

*   *   *   *   *

I may ask any woman to make her own commentary.

Madame de Listomère closed hers with a formal resolution to shut her door on Monsieur Eugène, and, if she should meet him in company, to treat him with more than contempt, for his audacity was not to be compared with any of the other instances which the Marquise had at last forgiven. At first she thought she would keep the letter, but, on due reflection, she burned it.

"Madame has just received such a flaming love letter, and she read it!" said Caroline to the housemaid.

"I never should have thought it of Madame," said the old woman, quite astonished.

That evening, the Marquise was at the house of the Marquis de Beauséant, where she would probably meet Rastignac. It was a Saturday. The Marquis de Beauséant was distantly related to Monsieur de Rastignac, so the young man could not fail to appear in the course of the evening. At two in the morning, Madame de Listomère, who had stayed so late solely to crush Eugène by her coldness, had waited in vain. A witty writer, Stendhal, has given the whimsical name of *cristallisation** to the process worked out by the Marquise's mind before, during, and after this evening.

Four days later Eugène was scolding his manservant.

"Look here, Joseph; I shall be obliged to get rid of you, my good fellow."

"I beg your pardon, Monsieur?"

"You do nothing but blunder. Where did you take the two letters I gave you on Friday?"

Joseph was bewildered. Like a statue in a cathedral porch he stood motionless, wholly absorbed in the travail of his ideas. Suddenly he smiled foolishly, and said: "Monsieur, one was for Madame la Marquise de Listomère, Rue Saint-Dominique, and the other was for Monsieur's lawyer——"

"Are you sure of what you say?"

Joseph stood dumbfounded. I could see that at this point I needed to interject myself, I who, by chance, still happened to be there at the moment.

"Joseph is right," said I. Eugène turned round to me. "I read the addresses quite involuntarily, and——"

"And," said Eugène, interrupting me, "was not one of them for Madame de Nucingen?"

"No, by damnation! And so I supposed, my dear boy, that your heart had pirouetted from the Rue Saint-Lazare* to the Rue Saint-Dominique."

Eugène struck his forehead with the palm of his hand, and began to smile. Joseph saw plainly that the fault was not his.

Now, there are certain moral reflections on which all young men should meditate. *Mistake the first*: Eugène thought it amusing to have made Madame de Listomère laugh at the blunder that had put her in possession of a love letter which was not intended for her. *Mistake the second*: He did not go to see Madame de Listomère till four days after the misadventure, thus giving the thoughts of a virtuous young woman time to crystallise. And there were a dozen more mistakes which must be passed over in silence to give ladies *ex professo** the pleasure of deducing them for the benefit of those who cannot guess them. Eugène arrived at the Marquise's door, but as he was going in, the porter stopped him, and told him that Madame de Listomère was out. As he was getting into his carriage again, the Marquis came in.

"Will you come up, Eugène?" said he; "my wife is at home."

Oh! Forgive the Marquis. A husband, however admirable, scarcely ever attains to perfection. Rastignac, as he went upstairs, discerned the ten fallacies in worldly logic which stood on this page of the fair book of his life. When Madame de Listomère saw her husband come in with Eugène, she could not help colouring. The young Baron observed the sudden flush. If the most modest of men never quite loses some little dregs of conceit, which he can no more get rid of than a woman can throw off her inevitable vanities, who can blame Eugène for saying to himself, "What! this stronghold too?" and he settled his head in his cravat. Though young men are not very avaricious, they all love to add a head to their collection of medals.

Monsieur de Listomère seized on the *Gazette de France,** which he saw in a corner by the fireplace, and went to the window to form, by the help of the newspaper, an opinion of his own as to the state of France. No woman, not even a prude, is long in embarrassment even in the most difficult situation in which she can find herself; she seems always to carry in her hand the fig leaf given to her by our mother Eve. And so, when Eugène, having interpreted the orders given to the porter in a sense flattering to his vanity, made his bow to Madame de Listomère with a tolerably deliberate air, she was able to conceal all her thoughts behind one of those feminine smiles, which are more impenetrable than a King's speech.

"Are you unwell, Madame? You had closed your door."

"No, Monsieur."

"You were going out perhaps?"

"Not at all."

"You are expecting somebody?"

"Nobody."

"If my visit is ill timed, you have only the Marquis to blame. I was obeying your mysterious orders when he himself invited me into the sanctuary."

"Monsieur de Listomère was not in my confidence. There are certain secrets which it is not always prudent to share with one's husband."

The firm, mild tone in which the Marquise spoke these words, and the imposing dignity of her glance, were enough to make Rastignac feel that he had been much too eager to straighten his cravat.

"I understand you, Madame," said he, laughing; "I must therefore congratulate myself all the more on having met Monsieur le Marquis; he has given me an opportunity for offering you an explanation, which would be fraught with danger, if you were not kindness itself."

The Marquise looked at the young Baron with considerable astonishment, but she replied with dignity: "On your part, Monsieur, silence will be the best excuse. On my side I promise you to forget entirely—a forgiveness you scarcely merit."

"Forgiveness is needless, Madame, when there has been no offence. The letter you received," he added in an undertone, "and which you must have thought so unseemly, was not intended for you."

The Marquise smiled in spite of herself; she wished to appear offended.

"Why tell a falsehood?" she replied with an air of disdainful amusement, but in a very friendly tone. "Now that I have scolded you enough, I am quite ready to laugh at a stratagem not devoid of skill. I know some poor women who would be caught by it. 'Good heavens, how he loves me!' they would say." She forced a laugh, and added with an indulgent air, "If we are to remain friends, let me hear nothing more of mistakes of which I cannot be the dupe."

"On my honour, Madame, you are far more so than you fancy," Eugène eagerly replied.

"What are you talking about?" asked Monsieur de Listomère, who for a minute had been listening to the conversation, without being able to pierce the darkness of its meaning.

"Oh, nothing that will interest you," said Madame de Listomère.

The Marquis quietly returned to his paper, saying, "I see Madame de Mortsauf is dead; your poor brother is at Clochegourde* no doubt."

"Do you know, Monsieur," said the Marquise, addressing Eugène, "that you have just made a very impertinent speech?"

"If I did not know the strictness of your principles," he replied simply, "I should fancy you either meant to put ideas into my head which I dare not allow myself, or to wring my secret from me; or perhaps, indeed, you wish to make fun of me."

The Marquise smiled. This smile put Eugène out of patience.

"May you always believe, Madame, in the offence I did not commit!" said he. "And I fervently hope that chance may not lead you to discover in society the person who was intended to read that letter——"

"What! Still Madame de Nucingen?" cried Madame de Listomère, more anxious to master the secret than to be revenged on the young man for his retort.

Eugène reddened. A man must be more than twenty-five not to redden when he is blamed for the stupid fidelity which women laugh at only to avoid betraying how much they envy its object. However, he said, calmly enough, "Why not, Madame?"

These are the blunders we commit at twenty-five. This confession agitated Madame de Listomère violently, but Eugène was not yet able to analyse a woman's face as seen in a glimpse, or from one side. Only her lips turned white. She rang to have some wood put on the fire, and so obliged Rastignac to rise to take leave.

"If that is the case," said the Marquise, stopping Eugène by her cold, precise manner, "you will find it difficult, Monsieur, to explain by what chance my name happened to come to your pen. An address written on a letter is not the same thing as mistakenly taking a neighbor's hat when leaving a ball."

Eugène, put quite out of countenance, looked at the Marquise with a mingled expression of stupidity and fatuousness; he felt that he was ridiculous, stammered out some schoolboy speech, and left. A few days later Madame de Listomère had indisputable proof of Eugène's veracity. For more than a fortnight she has not gone into society.

The Marquis tells everyone who asks him the reason of this change: "My wife has a gastric attack."

I, who attend her, and who know her secret, know that she is only suffering from a little nervous crisis, and takes advantage of it to stay quietly at home.

Paris, February 1839

ADDENDUM TO A STUDY OF WOMAN

The following personages appear or are mentioned
in other volumes of *The Human Comedy*:

Bianchon, Horace
I: *Letters of Two Brides*
IV: *A Second Home, The Imaginary Mistress*
V: *Honorine*
VIII: *Old Goriot*
IX: *The Atheist's Mass, The Interdiction*
XII: *Pierrette*
XIII: *The Rabouilleuse*
XIV: *The Muse of the Department*
XVI: *Lost Illusions*
XVIII: *César Birotteau*
XIX: *The Splendors and Miseries of Courtesans*
XX: *The Secrets of the Princesse de Cadignan*
XXI: *Cousin Bette*
XXIII: *A Prince of Bohemia*
XXIV: *The Bureaucrats*
XXV: *The Petits Bourgeois*
XXVI: *The Brotherhood of Consolation*
XXXII: *The Village Curé*
XXXIV: *The Magic Skin*
In addition, Monsieur Bianchon narrated the following:
V: *La Grande Bretèche*
IX: *Another Study of Woman*

Joseph
XXXIV: *The Magic Skin*

Listomère, Marquis de
XVI: *Lost Illusions*
XXXIII: *The Lily of the Valley*

Listomère, Marquise de
IV: *A Daughter of Eve*
XVI: *Lost Illusions*
XXXIII: *The Lily of the Valley*

Rastignac, Eugène de

The Imaginary Mistress
(*La fausse maîtresse*)
January 1842

Translated by Clara Bell

*Dedicated to the Comtesse Clara Maffei**

MALAGA.

LA FAUSSE MAÎTRESSE.

Plate VIII

In the month of September 1835, one of the richest heiresses of the Faubourg Saint-Germain,* Mademoiselle du Rouvre, the only child of the Marquis du Rouvre, married Count Adam Mitgislas Laginski, a young Polish exile. I allow myself to spell the names as they are pronounced, to spare the reader the sight of the fortifications of consonants by which, in the Slav languages, the vowels are protected, no doubt to secure them against loss, seeing how few they are. The Marquis du Rouvre had dissipated almost the whole of one of the finest fortunes of the nobility, to which he had formerly owed his alliance with a Mademoiselle de Ronquerolles. Hence Clémentine du Rouvre had for her uncle, on her mother's side, the Marquis de Ronquerolles, and for her aunt Madame de Sérizy. On her father's side she possessed another uncle in the eccentric person of the Chevalier du Rouvre, the younger son of the house, an old bachelor who had grown rich by speculations in land and houses. The Marquis de Ronquerolles was so unhappy as to lose both his children during the visitation of cholera.* Madame de Sérizy's only son, a young officer of the highest promise, was killed in Africa at the fight by the Macta.* In these days rich families run the risk of ruining their children if they have too many, or of becoming extinct if they have but one or two, a singular result of the Civil Code not foreseen by Napoléon. Thus, by accident, and in spite of Monsieur du Rouvre's reckless extravagances for Florine, one of the most charming actresses in Paris, Clémentine had become an heiress. The

Marquis de Ronquerolles, one of the most accomplished diplomats of the new dynasty, his sister, Madame de Sérizy, and the Chevalier du Rouvre agreed that, to rescue their fortunes from the Marquis's clutches, they would leave them to their niece, to whom they each promised ten thousand francs a year on her marriage.

It is quite unnecessary to say that the Pole, though a refugee, cost the French Government absolutely nothing. Count Adam belonged to one of the oldest and most illustrious families of Poland, connected with most of the princely houses of Germany, with the Sapiéhas, the Radziwills, the Mniszechs, the Rzewuskis, the Czartoryskis, the Leszinskis, the Lubomirskis, in short, all the great Sarmatian *skis*. But a knowledge of heraldry is not a strong point in France under Louis-Philippe, and such nobility could be no recommendation to the bourgeoisie then in power. Besides, when, in 1833, Adam made his appearance on the Boulevard des Italiens, at Frascati's, at the Jockey Club,* he led the life of a man who, having lost his political prospects, falls back on his vices and his love of pleasure. He was taken for a student. The Polish nationality, as the result of an odious government reaction, had fallen as low as the Republicans had tried to think it high. The strange struggle of Movement against Resistance*—two words which thirty years hence will be inexplicable—made a farce of what ought to have been so worthy: the name, that is, of a vanquished nation to which France gave hospitality, for which entertainments were devised, for which everyone danced or sang by subscription; a nation, in short, which at the time when, in 1796, Europe was fighting France, had offered her six thousand men, and such men! Do not conclude from this that I mean to represent the Emperor Nicholas as being in the wrong as regards Poland, or Poland as regards the Emperor Nicholas. In the first place, it would be a fairly silly thing to slip a political discussion into a tale which ought to interest or amuse.

Besides, Russia and Poland were equally right: one for aiming at unity of Empire, the other for desiring to be free again. It may be said, in passing, that Poland might have conquered Russia by the influence of manners instead of beating her with weapons, thus imitating the Chinese, who at last Chinesified the Tartars, and who, it is to be hoped, will do the same by the English. Poland ought to have Polonised the Russians; Poniatowski* had tried it in the least temperate district of the Empire.

Clémentine Laginska.

Plate IX

But that gentleman was a misunderstood king—all the more so because he did not perhaps understand himself. How was it possible not to hate the poor people who were the cause of the horrible deceit committed on the occasion of the review when all Paris was eager to rescue Poland? People affected to regard the Poles as allies of the Republican party, forgetting that Poland was an aristocratic republic. Thenceforth the party of wealth poured ignoble contempt on the Pole, who had been deified but a few days since. The wind of a riot has always blown the Parisians round from north to south under every form of government. We must remember these reversals of Parisian opinion in order to explain how the word "Polish" was, in 1835, a derogatory epithet among the people who believed themselves to be the wittiest and politest in the world, and its central luminary, in a city which today wields the sceptre of art and literature. There are, alas! two types of Polish refugees—the republican Pole, the son of Lelewel, and the noble Pole, of the party led by Prince Czartoryski.* These two kinds of Pole are as fire and water, but why blame them? Are not such divisions always to be observed among refugees whatever nation they belong to, and no matter what country they go to? They carry their country and their hatreds with them. At Brussels, two French émigré priests expressed the greatest aversion for each other, and when one of them was asked his reasons, he replied, pointing to his companion in misery, "He is a Jansenist." Dante, in his exile, would gladly have stabbed any adversary of the Bianchi.* In this lies the reason of the attacks made on the venerable Prince Adam Czartoryski by the French radicals, and that of the disapproval shown to a section of the Polish emigrants by the Caesars of the shop counter and the Alexanders of letters patent. In 1834 Adam Mitgislas Laginski was the butt of Parisian witticisms. "He is a nice fellow though he is a Pole," said Rastignac. "All the Poles are great lords," said Maxime de Trailles, "but this one pays his gambling debts; I begin to think that he must have had an estate." And without offence to the exiles, it may be remarked that the levity, the recklessness, the fluidity of the Sarmatian character justified the calumnies of the Parisians, who, indeed, in similar circumstances, would be exactly like the Poles. The French aristocracy, so admirably supported by the Polish aristocracy during the Revolution, certainly made no equivalent return to those who were forced to emigrate in 1832. We must have the melancholy courage to say that, in this, the Faubourg Saint-Germain remains Poland's debtor. Was Count Adam rich, was he poor, was he an adventurer? The problem long remained unsolved. Diplomatic circles, faithful to their instructions, imitated the silence observed by the Emperor Nicholas, who at that time counted every Polish émigré as dead. The Tuileries, and most of those who took their cue from there, gave an odious proof of this characteristic policy dignified by the name of wisdom. A Russian prince, with whom they had smoked many cigars at the time of the emigration, was ignored because, as it seemed, he had fallen into disgrace with the Emperor Nicholas. Thus placed between the prudence of the court and that of diplomatic circles, Poles of good family lived in the Biblical solitude of *Super flumina Babylonis*,* or frequented certain salons which served as neutral territory for every variety of opinion. In a city of pleasure like Paris, where amusement is to be had in every rank, Polish recklessness found twice as many pretexts as it needed for leading a dissipated bachelor life. Besides, it must be said, Adam had against him at first both his appearance and his manners. There are two types of Pole, as there are two types of Englishwoman. When an Englishwoman is not a beauty, she is horribly ugly—and Count Adam belongs to the second category. His face is small, somewhat sour, and looks as if it had been squeezed in a vice.

His short nose, fair hair, red moustaches and beard, give him the expression of a goat; all the more so because he is short and thin, and his eyes, tinged with dingy yellow, startle you by the oblique leer which Virgil's line has made famous. How is that, in spite of such unfavourable conditions, he has such exquisite manners and style? The solution of this mystery is given by his dress, that of a finished dandy, and by the education he owes to his mother, a Radziwill. If his courage carries him to the point of rashness, his mind is not above the current and trivial pleasantries of Paris conversation; still, he does not often find a young fellow who is his superior among men of fashion. These young men nowadays talk far too much of horses, income, taxes, and deputies, for French conversation to be what it once was. Wit needs leisure, and certain inequalities of position. Conversation is better perhaps at Petersburg and at Vienna than it is in Paris. Equals need no subtleties; they tell each other everything *straight out*, just as it is. Hence the ironical scoffers of Paris could scarcely discern a man of family in a light-hearted student, as he seemed, who in talking passed carelessly from one subject to another, who pursued amusement with all the more frenzy because he had just escaped from great perils, and who, having left the country where his family was known, thought himself at liberty to lead an irresponsible life without risking a loss of consideration. One fine day in 1834, Adam bought a large house in the Rue de la Pépinière.* Six months later it was on as handsome a footing as the richest houses in Paris. Just at the time when Laginski was beginning to be taken seriously, he saw Clémentine at the Italiens, and fell in love with her. A year later, he married her. Madame d'Espard's circle set the fashion of approval. Mothers of families then learned, too late, that ever since the year 900, the Laginskis had ranked with the most illustrious families of the North. By a stroke of prudence, most unlike a Pole, the young Count's mother had, at the beginning of the rebellion, mortgaged her estates for an immense sum advanced by two Jewish houses, and invested in the French funds. Count Adam Laginski had an income of more than eighty thousand francs. This put an end to the astonishment expressed in some salons at the rashness of Madame de Sérizy, of old de Ronquerolles, and of the Chevalier du Rouvre in yielding to their niece's mad passion. As usual, the world rushed from one extreme to the other. During the winter of 1836, Count Adam became the fashion, and Clémentine Laginska one of the queens of Paris. Madame de Laginska, at the present time, is one of the charming group of young married women among whom shine Mesdames de L'Estorade, de Portenduère, Marie de Vandenesse, du Guénic, and de Maufrigneuse, the very flower of Paris society, who live high above the parvenus, the bourgeois, and the fabricators of recent politics.

This preamble was necessary to define the sphere in which was carried through one of those sublime efforts, less rare than the detractors of the present time imagine—pearls hidden in rough shells, and lost in the depths of that abyss, that ocean, that never-resting tide called the world—the age—Paris, London, or Petersburg—whichever you will!

If ever the truth that architecture is the expression of the manners of a race was fully demonstrated, is it not since the Revolution of 1830, under the reign of the House of Orléans?* Great fortunes have shrunk in France, and the majestic mansions of our fathers are constantly being demolished and replaced by a sort of tenement houses, in which a Peer of France of July* dwells on the third floor, over some newly-enriched empiric. Styles are mingled in confusion. As there is no longer any court, any nobility to set a tone, no harmony is to be seen in the productions of art. On the other hand, architecture has never found more economical tricks for imitating what is genuine and thorough, never displayed more ingenuity and resource in arrangement. Ask an artist to deal with a strip of the garden of an old hôtel now destroyed, and he will build you a little Louvre crushed under its ornamentation; he will give you a courtyard, stables, and, if you insist, a garden; inside he contrives such a number of little rooms and corridors, and cheats the eye so effectually, that you fancy yourself comfortable; in fact, there are so many bedrooms, that a ducal retinue can live and move in what was only the bakehouse of a president of a law court. The Comtesse Laginska's house on the Rue de la Pépinière is one of these modern structures, with a courtyard in front and a garden behind. To the right of the courtyard are the servants' quarters, balanced on the left by the stables and coach houses. The porter's lodge stands between two handsome gates. The chief luxury of this house consists in a delightful conservatory at the end of a boudoir on the ground floor, where all the beautiful reception rooms are. It was a philanthropist driven out of England who built this architectural gem, constructed the conservatory, planned the garden, varnished the doors, paved the outbuildings with brick, filled the windows with green glass, and realised a vision like that—in due proportion—of George IV at Brighton.* The inventive, industrious, and ready Paris artisan had carved his doors and window-frames; his ceilings were imitated from those of the Middle Ages or of Venetian palaces, and there was a lavish outlay of marble slabs in external panelling. Elschoët and Klagmann* had carved the cornices of the doors and mantelpiece; Schinner had painted the ceilings with the brush of a master. The wonders of the stairs—marble as white as a woman's arm—defied those of the Hôtel Rothschild. In consequence of the disturbances, the price of this folly was not more than eleven hundred thousand francs. For an Englishman this was giving it away. All this splendour, called princely by people who do not know what a real prince is, stood in the garden of a contractor—a Croesus of the Revolution, who had died at Brussels a bankrupt after a sudden convulsion of the Bourse. The Englishman died at Paris—died of Paris—for to many people Paris is a disease; sometimes it is several diseases. His widow, a Methodist, had a perfect horror of the nabob's little house—this philanthropist had been a dealer in opium. The virtuous widow ordered that the scandalous property should be sold just at the time when the disturbances made peace doubtful on any terms. Count Adam took advantage of the opportunity, and you shall be told how it happened, for nothing could be less consonant with his lordly habits.

Behind this house, built of stone fretted like a melon, spreads the green velvet of an English lawn, shaded at the further end by an elegant clump of exotic trees, among which rises a Chinese pavilion with its mute bells and pendent gilt eggs. The greenhouse and its fantastic decorations screen the outer wall on the south side. The other wall, opposite the greenhouse, is hidden by creepers grown in arcades over poles and crossbeams painted green. This meadow, this realm of flowers, these gravelled paths, this mock forest, these aerial trellises cover an area of about twenty-five square perches, of which the present value would be four hundred thousand francs, as much as a real forest. In the heart of this silence won from Paris, birds sing; there are blackbirds, nightingales, bullfinches, chaffinches, and many sparrows. The conservatory is a vast flowerbed, where the air is loaded with perfume, and where you may walk in winter as though summer was blazing with all its fires. The means by which an atmosphere is produced at will, be it of the tropics, China, or Italy, are ingeniously concealed from view. The pipes in which the boiling water circulates—the steam, hot air, whatnot—are covered with soil, and look like garlands of growing flowers. The boudoir is spacious. On a small plot of ground the miracle wrought by the Paris fairy called Architecture is to produce everything on a large scale. The young Countess's boudoir was the pride of the artist to whom Count Adam entrusted the task of re-decorating the house. To sin there would be impossible, there are too many pretty trifles. Love would not know where to alight amid worktables of Chinese carving, where the eye can find thousands of droll little figures wrought in the ivory—the outcome of the toil of two families of Chinese artists; vases of burnt topaz mount-ed on filigree stands; mosaics that invite to theft; Dutch pictures, such as Schinner now paints again; angels im-agined as Steinbock conceives of them (but does not always work them out himself); statuettes executed by geniuses pursued by creditors (the true interpretation of the Arab myths); sublime first sketches by our greatest artists; fronts of carved chests let into the wainscot, and alternating with the inventions of Indian embroidery; gold-coloured curtains draped over the doors from an architrave of black oak wrought with the swarming fig-ures of a hunting scene; chairs and tables worthy of Madame de Pompadour; a Persian carpet, and so forth. And finally, as a crowning touch, all this splendour, seen under a softened light filtering in through lace curtains, looks all the more beautiful. On a marble slab, among some antiques, a lady's whip, with a handle carved by Mademoiselle de Fauveau,* shows that the Countess is fond of riding. Such is a boudoir in 1837, a display of property to divert the eye, as though ennui threatened to invade the most restless and unresting society in the world. Why is there nothing individual, intimate, noth-ing to invite reverie and repose? Why? Because no one is sure of the morrow, and everyone enjoys life as a prodi-gal spends a life interest.

One morning, Clémentine affected a meditative air as she lounged on one of those deep siesta chairs from which we cannot bear to rise, so cleverly has the upholsterer who invented them contrived to fit them to the curves of laziness and the comfort of *far niente*.* The doors to the conservatory were open, admitting the scent of vegetation and the perfumes of the tropics. The young wife watched Adam, who was smoking an elegant narghile, the only form of pipe she allowed in this room. Over the other door, curtains, caught back by handsome ropes, showed two magnificent rooms beyond: one in white and gold, resembling that of the Hôtel Forbin-Janson, the other in the taste of the Renaissance. The dining room, unrivalled in Paris by any but that of the Baron de Nucingen, is at the end of a corridor, with a ceiling and walls decorated in a medieval style. This corridor is reached, on the courtyard front, through a large anteroom, through whose glass door the splendour of the stairs is seen.

The Count and Countess had just breakfasted; the sky was a sheet of blue without a cloud; the month of April was drawing to a close. The household had already known two years of happiness, and now, only two days since, Clémentine had discovered in her home something resembling a secret, a mystery. A Pole, let it be repeated to his honour, is generally weak in the presence of a woman; he is so full of tenderness that, in Poland, he becomes her inferior, and though Polish women are admirable creatures, a Pole is even more quickly routed by a Parisienne. Hence, Count Adam, pressed hard with questions, had not enough artless cunning to sell the secret dear to his wife. With a woman there is always something to be got for a secret, and she likes you the better for it, as a rogue respects an honest man whom he has failed to take in. The Count, more ready with his sword than with his tongue, only stipulated that he should not be required to answer till he had finished his narghile full of *tombaki*.*

"When we were travelling," said she, "you replied to every difficulty by saying, 'Paz will see to that!' You never wrote to anybody but Paz. On my return, everyone refers me to *the Captain*. I want to go out. *The Captain!* Is there a bill to be paid? *The Captain!* If my horse's pace is rough, they will speak to *Captain* Paz. In short, here I feel as if it were a game of dominoes; everywhere Paz! I hear no one talked of but Paz, but I can never see Paz. What is Paz? Let our Paz be brought to see me."

"Then is not everything as it ought to be?" said the Count, relinquishing the *bocchettino* of his narghile.

"Everything is so quite what it ought to be, that if we had two hundred thousand francs a year, we should be ruined by living in the way we do with a hundred and ten thousand," said she. She pulled the bell cord embroidered in petit point, a marvel of skill. A manservant dressed like a minister at once appeared. "Tell Monsieur le Capitaine Paz that I wish to speak to him," said she.

"If you fancy you will find anything out in that way——," said Count Adam with a smile.

It may be useful to say that Adam and Clémentine, married in December 1835, after spending the winter in Paris, had during 1836 travelled in Italy, Switzerland, and Germany. They returned home in November, and during the winter just past, the Countess had for the first time received her friends, and then had discovered the existence—the almost speechless and unacknowledged, but most useful presence—of a factotum whose person seemed to be invisible—this Captain Paz (Paç), whose name is pronounced as it is written.

"Monsieur le Capitaine Paz begs Madame la Comtesse to excuse him; he is at the stables, and dressed in such a way that does not permit him to come at the moment; but as soon as he is dressed, Count Paz will come," said the valet.

"Why, what was he doing?"

"He was showing Constantin how to groom the Countess's horse; it was not done to his liking," replied the valet.

The Countess looked at the man; he was quite serious, and took good care not to imply by a smile the comment which inferiors so often allow themselves on a superior who seems to have descended to their level.

"Ah, he was brushing down Cora."

"You are not riding out this morning, Madame?" said the servant, but he got no answer, and went.

"Is he a Pole?" asked Clémentine of her husband, who bowed affirmatively.

Thaddée Paz.

Plate X

Clémentine lay silent, examining Adam. Her feet almost at full length on a cushion, her head in the attitude of a bird listening on the edge of its nest to the sounds of the grove, she would have seemed charming to the most blasé of men. Fair and slight, her hair curled *à l'Anglaise*, she looked like one of the almost fabulous figures in keepsakes,* especially as she was wrapped in a morning gown of Persian silk, of which the thick folds did not so effectually disguise the graces of her figure and the slenderness of her waist, as that they could not be admired through the thick covering of flowers and embroidery. As she crossed the brightly coloured stuff over her chest, the hollow of her throat remained visible, the white skin contrasting in tone with the handsome lace trimming over the shoulders. Her eyes, fringed with black lashes, emphasised the expression of curiosity that puckered a pretty mouth. On her well-formed brow were traced the characteristic curves of the Paris woman: wilful, light-hearted, well educated, but invulnerable to vulgar temptations. Her hands, almost transparent, hung from each arm of her deep chair; the tapering fingers, curved at the tips, showed nails like pink almonds that caught the light. Adam smiled at his wife's impatience, gazing at her with a look which conjugal satiety had not yet made lukewarm. This slim little Countess had known how to be mistress in her own house, for she scarcely acknowledged Adam's admiration. In her stolen glances at him, there was perhaps a dawning consciousness of the superiority of a Parisienne to this spruce, lean, and red-haired Pole.

"Here comes Paz," said the Count, hearing a step that rang in the corridor.

The Countess saw a tall, handsome man come in, well built, bearing in his features the marks of the grief which comes of strength and misfortune. Paz had dressed hastily in one of those tightly fitting coats, fastened by braid straps and oval buttons, which used to be called *polonaises*. Abundant but rather unkempt black hair covered his squarely-shaped head, and Clémentine could see his broad forehead, as shiny as a piece of marble, for he held his peaked cap in his hand. That hand was like the hand of the Hercules carrying the Infant. Robust health bloomed in a face equally divided by a large Roman nose, which reminded Clémentine of the handsome Trasteverini.* A black silk cravat put a finishing touch of martial appearance upon this mystery of five feet seven inches, with jet-black eyes as bright as an Italian's. The width of his full trousers, hiding all but the toes of his boots, showed that Paz still was faithful to the fashions of Poland. Certainly, to a romantic woman, there must have been something burlesque in the violent contrast observable between the Captain and the Count, between the little Pole with his narrow frame and this fine soldier, between the carpet-knight and the knight servitor.

"Good morning, Adam," he said to the Count with familiarity.

Then he bowed gracefully, asking Clémentine in what way he could serve her.

"Then you are Laginski's friend?" asked the lady.

"For life and death," replied Paz, on whom the young Count shed his most affectionate smile, as he exhaled his last fragrant puff of smoke.

"Well, then, why do you not eat with us? Why did you not accompany us to Italy and to Switzerland? Why do you hide yourself so as to avoid the thanks I owe you for the constant services you do us?" said the young Countess, with a sort of irritation, but without the slightest feeling.

In fact, she detected a kind of voluntary servitude on the part of Paz. At that time such an idea was inseparable from a certain disdain for a socially amphibious creature, a being at once secretary and steward, neither wholly steward nor wholly secretary, some poor relation—inconvenient as a friend.

"The fact is, Countess," he replied with some freedom, "that no thanks are owed to me: I am Adam's friend, and I find my pleasure in taking charge of his interests."

"And is it for your pleasure too that you remain standing?" said Count Adam.

Paz sat down in an armchair near the doorway.

"I remember having seen you on the occasion of our marriage, and sometimes in the courtyard," said the lady, "but why do you, a friend of Adam's, place yourself in a position of inferiority?"

"The opinion of the Paris world is to me a matter of indifference," said he. "I live for myself, or, if you choose, for you two."

"But the opinion of the world as regards my husband's friend cannot be a matter of indifference to me——"

"Oh, Madame, the world is easily satisfied by one word: eccentric! Say that." After a short pause he asked, "Do you propose going out?"

"Will you come to the park?" said the Countess.

"With pleasure."

At that word, Paz bowed and went out.

"What a good soul! He is as simple as a child," said Adam.

"Tell me now how you became friends," said Clémentine.

"Paz, my dearest, is of a family as old, as noble, and as illustrious as our own. At the time of the fall of the Pazzi,* a member of that family escaped from Florence into Poland, where he settled with some little fortune, and founded the family of the Paz, on which the title of Count was conferred. This family, having distinguished itself in the days of our royal republic, grew rich. The cutting from the tree felled in Italy grew with such vigour that there are several branches of the house of the Counts Paz. It will not, therefore, surprise you to be told that there are rich and poor members of the family. Our

Paz is the son of a poor branch. As an orphan, with no fortune but his sword, he served under Grand Duke Constantine at the time of our revolution.* Carried away by the Polish party, he fought like a Pole, like a patriot, like a man who has nothing—three reasons for fighting well. In the last skirmish, believing his men were following him, he attacked a Russian battery, and was taken prisoner. I was there. This feat of courage roused my blood. 'Let us go and rescue him!' cried I to my horsemen. We charged at the battery like freebooters, and I rescued Paz, I being the seventh. We were twenty when we set out, and eight when we came back, including Paz. When Warsaw was betrayed we had to think of escaping from the Russians. By a singular chance Paz and I found ourselves together at the same hour and in the same place on the other side of the Vistula. I saw the poor Captain arrested by some Prussians, who at that time had made themselves bloodhounds for the Russians. When one has fished a man out of the Styx, one gets attached to him. This new danger threatening Paz distressed me so much that I allowed myself to be taken with him, intending to be of service to him. Two men can sometimes escape when one alone is lost. Thanks to my name and some family connection with those on whom our fate depended—for we were then in the power of the Prussians—my flight was winked at. I got my dear Captain through as a common soldier and a servant of my house, and we succeeded in reaching Danzig. We stowed ourselves in a Dutch vessel sailing for London, where we landed two months later. My mother had fallen ill in England, and awaited me there; Paz and I nursed her till her death, which was accelerated by the disasters to our cause. We then left London, and I brought Paz to France; in such adversities two men become brothers. When I found myself in Paris with sixty-odd thousand francs a year, not to mention the remains of a sum derived from the sale of my mother's diamonds and the family pictures, I wished to secure a living for Paz before giving myself up to the dissipations of Paris life. I had discerned some sadness in the captain's eyes; sometimes even a suppressed tear floated there. I had had the opportunity to assess his soul, which is thoroughly noble, lofty, and generous. Perhaps it was painful to him to find himself bound by an act of generosity to a man six years younger than himself without being able to repay him. I, careless and light-hearted as a boy, might ruin myself at play, or let myself be ensnared by some woman; Paz and I might some day be sundered. Though I promised myself that I would always provide for all his needs, I foresaw many chances of forgetting, or being unable to pay Paz an allowance. In short, my angel, I wished to spare him the discomfort, the humiliation, the shame of having to ask me for money, or of seeking in vain for his comrade in some day of necessity. *Dunquè,** one morning after breakfast, we had our feet on the andirons, each smoking his pipe. After colouring a bit, and with great hesitation, my companion looked at me anxiously; I then handed him a bearer bond producing two thousand four hundred francs interest yearly——"

Clémentine rose, seated herself on Adam's knees, and putting her arm round his neck, kissed him on the brow, saying—"Dear heart, how noble you are! And what did Paz say?"

"Thaddée," said the Count, "turned pale and said nothing."

"Thaddée—is that his name?"

"Yes. Thaddée folded up the paper and returned it to me, saying, 'I thought, Adam, that we were as one in life and death, and that we should never part; do you wish to see no more of me?'—'Oh,' said I, 'is that the way you take it? Well, then, say no more about it. If I am ruined, you will be ruined.' Said he, 'You are not rich enough to live as a Laginski should, and do you not need a friend to take care of your concerns, someone who will be father and brother to you, and a trusted confidant?' My dear girl, as Paz spoke these words, he had in his eyes and in his voice a calm filled with motherly concern, but which betrayed the gratitude of an Arab, the devotion of a poodle, the friendship of a savage: always ready and unassuming. Well then, I laid my hand on his shoulder and kissed him on the lips as is the custom in Poland. 'For life and death, then,' said I. 'All I have is yours, do just as you will.' It was he who found me this house for almost nothing. He sold my shares when they were high, and bought when they were low, and we purchased this hovel out of the difference. He is a connoisseur of horses, and deals in them so well that my stable has cost me very little, and yet I have the finest horses, the most charming equipage in Paris. Our servants, old Polish soldiers whom he found, would pass through the fire for us. While I seem to be ruining myself, Paz keeps my house with such perfect order and economy that he has even made good some losses at play, the follies of a young man. My Thaddée is as cunning as two Genoese, as keen for profit as a Polish Jew, as prudent as a good housekeeper. I have never been able to persuade him to live as I did when I was a bachelor. Sometimes, the gentle insistence of friendship has been necessary to induce him to come to the play when I was going alone, or to one of the dinners I was giving at an inn to a party of merry companions. He does not like the life of salons."

"Then what does he like?" asked Clémentine.

"He loves Poland, and weeps over her. His only extravagance has been money sent, more in my name than in his own, to some of our poor exiles."

"Dear, how fond I shall be of that good fellow," said the Countess. "He seems to me as simple as everything that is truly great."

"All the pretty things you see here," said Adam,

praising his friend with the most generous security, "have been found by Paz; he has bought them at sales, or by some chance. Oh! he is keener at a bargain than a trader. If you see him rubbing his hands in the court-yard, it is because he has exchanged a good horse for a better. He lives in me; his delight is to see me well dressed in a dazzlingly smart carriage. He performs all the duties he imposes on himself without fuss or display. One night I had lost twenty thousand francs at whist. 'What will Paz say?' thought I to myself as I reached home. Paz gave me the sum, not without a sigh, but he did not blame me even by a look. This sigh checked me more than all the remonstrances of uncles, wives, or mothers in similar circumstances. 'You regret the money?' I asked him. 'Oh, not for you, nor for my-self; no, I was only thinking that twenty poor relations of mine could have lived on it for a year.' The family of Paz, you understand, is quite equal to that of Laginski, and I have never regarded my dear Paz as an inferior. I have tried to be as magnanimous in my degree as he in his. I never go out or come in without going to Paz, as if he were my father. My fortune is his. In short, Thaddée knows that at this day I would rush into danger to res-cue him, as I have done twice before."

"That is not a small thing to say, my dear," remarked the Countess. "Devotion is a lightning flash. Men devote themselves in war, but they no longer devote them-selves in Paris."

"Well, then," said Adam, "for Paz I am always at war. Our two natures have preserved their asperities and their faults, but the mutual intimacy of our souls has tightened the bonds, already so close, of our friend-ship. A man may save his comrade's life, and kill him afterwards if he finds him a bad companion, but we have gone through what makes friendship indissoluble. There is between us that constant exchange of pleasing impressions on both sides which makes friendship, from that point of view, a richer joy, perhaps, than love."

A pretty little hand shut the Count's mouth so suddenly that the movement was almost a blow.

"Yes, indeed, my darling," said he. "Friendship knows nothing of the bankruptcy of sentiment, the insolvency of pleasures. Love, after giving more than it has, ends by giving less than it receives."

"On both sides alike then," said Clémentine, smiling.

"Yes," said Adam. "While our friendship can only grow stronger. You need not pout: we are, my angel, as much friends as lovers; we, at least, I hope, have combined the two feelings in our happy marriage."

"I will explain to you what has made you two such good friends," said Clémentine. "The difference in your lives arises from a difference in your tastes, and not from compulsory choice—from preference, and not from the necessity of position. So far as a man can be judged from a glance, and from what you tell me, in this instance, the subordinate may at times be the superior."

"Oh! Paz is really my superior," replied Adam simply. "I have no advantage over him but that of luck."

His wife kissed him for this generous avowal.

"The perfect skill with which he conceals the loftiness of his soul is an immense superiority," the Count went on. "I say to him, 'You are a sly fellow; you have vast domains in your mind to which you retire.' He has a right to the title of Count Paz; in Paris he will only be called Captain."

"In short, a Florentine of the Middle Ages has resuscitated after three centuries," said the Countess. "There is something of Dante in him, and something of Michelangelo."

"Indeed, you are right; he is at heart a poet," replied Adam.

"And so I am married to two Poles," said the young Countess, with a gesture resembling that of a genius on the stage.

"*Chère enfant!*" said Adam, clasping Clémentine to him, "you would have distressed me very much if you had not liked my friend. We were both afraid of that, though he was delighted at my marrying. You will make him very happy by telling him that you love him—oh! as an old friend."

"Then I will go to dress; it is fine, we will all three go out," said Clémentine, ringing for her maid.

Paz led such an unobtrusive life that all the fashionable people of Paris wondered who it was that accompanied Clémentine Laginska when they saw her driving to the Bois de Boulogne* and back between him and her husband. During the drive Clémentine had insisted that Thaddée was to dine with her. This whim of an absolute sovereign compelled the Captain to dress with unusual care. On returning from her drive, Clémentine dressed with some coquettish care, in such a way as to produce an effect even on Adam as she entered the room where the two friends were awaiting her.

"Count Paz," said she, "we will go to the Opera together."

It was said in the tone which from a woman conveys, "If you refuse, we shall quarrel."

"With pleasure, Madame," replied the Captain. "But as I have not a count's fortune, call me Captain."

"Well, then, Captain, give me your arm," said she, taking it and leading him into the dining room with a suggestion of the caressing familiarity which enraptures a lover.

The Countess placed the Captain next to her, and he sat like a poor sub-lieutenant dining with a wealthy general. Paz left it to Clémentine to talk, listening to her with all the air of deference to a superior, contradicting her in nothing, and waiting for a positive question before making any reply. In short, to the Countess he seemed almost stupid, and her graces all fell flat before this icy gravity and diplomatic dignity. In vain did Adam try to rouse him by saying, "Come, cheer up, Thaddée! It might be supposed that you were not at home. You must have laid a bet that you would disconcert Clémentine?" Thaddée remained heavy and half-asleep. When the three were alone at dessert, the Captain explained that his life was arranged contrary to that of other people: he went to bed at eight o'clock and rose at daybreak; he thus excused himself, saying he was quite tired.

"My intention in taking you to the Opera was only to amuse you, Captain, but do just as you please," said Clémentine, a little nettled.

"I will go," said Paz.

"Duprez is singing in *William Tell*,"* said Adam. "Would you prefer the Variétés?"*

The Captain smiled and rang the bell; the manservant appeared. "Constantin," said Paz, "make ready the large carriage instead of the coupé. We cannot sit comfortably in it," he added, turning to the Count.

"A Frenchman would not have thought of that," said Clémentine, smiling.

"Ah, but we are Florentines transplanted to the North," replied Thaddée, with a meaning and an expression which showed that his dulness at dinner had been assumed.

But by a very conceivable want of judgment, there was too great a contrast between the involuntary self-betrayal of this speech and the Captain's attitude during dinner. Clémentine examined him with one of those keen flashes by which a woman reveals at once her surprise and her observancy. Thus, during the few minutes while they were taking their coffee in the salon, silence reigned—an uncomfortable silence for Adam, who could not divine its cause. Clémentine no longer disturbed Thaddée. The Captain, for his part, retired again into military rigidity, and came out of it no more, either on the way, or in the box, where he affected to be asleep.

"You see, Madame, that I am very dull company," said he, during the ballet in the last act of *William Tell*. "Was I not right to 'stick to my last,' as the proverb says?"

"On my word, my dear Captain, you are neither a charlatan nor a chatterbox—you are hardly a Pole."

"Leave me then to watch over your pleasures," he replied, "to take care of your fortune and your house; that is all I am good for."

"Tartuffe, begone!" cried Adam, smiling. "My dear, he is full of heart, well informed—he could, if he chose, hold his own in any salon. Clémentine, do not believe what his modesty tells you."

"Adieu, Countess. I have proved my willingness, and now will avail myself of your carriage to go to bed at once. I will send it back for you."

Clémentine bowed slightly, and let him go without replying.

"What a boor!" said she to the Count. "You are much, much nicer."

Adam pressed his wife's hand unseen.

"Poor, dear Thaddée, he has endeavoured to be a *foil* when many men would have tried to seem more attractive than I."

"Oh!" said she, "I cannot say for certain that there is no *calculation* in his conduct: his behaviour would have intrigued an ordinary woman."

Half an hour later, while Boleslas the groom was calling "The gate!" and the coachman, having turned the carriage to drive in, was waiting for the gates to be opened, Clémentine said to the Count: "Where does the Captain roost?"

"Up there," said Adam, pointing to an elegantly constructed attic extending on both sides of the gateway with a window looking on to the street. "His rooms are over the coach houses."

"And who lives in the other half?"

"No one as yet," replied Adam. "The other little suite,

over the stables, will do for our children and their tutor."

"He is not in bed," said the Countess, seeing a light in the Captain's room when the carriage was under the pillared portico, copied from that at the Tuileries, which replaced the ordinary zinc canopy painted to imitate striped ticking.

The Captain in his dressing gown, with pipe in hand, was watching Clémentine as she disappeared into the hall. The day had been a cruel one to him. Here is why: Thaddée had felt a fearful shock to his heart on the day when, Adam having taken him to the Italiens to pronounce his opinion, he first saw Mademoiselle du Rouvre; then, when he saw her in the mayor's office and at Saint-Thomas d'Aquin, he recognised in her the woman whom a man must love to the exclusion of all others—for Don Juan himself preferred one among the *mille e tre!** Hence Paz had strongly advocated the classical bridal tour after the wedding. Fairly easy all the time while Clémentine was absent, his tortures began again on the return of the happy couple. And this was what he was thinking as he inhaled his latakia from a cherry-stem pipe, six feet long, a gift from Adam: "Only I and God, who will reward me for suffering in silence, may ever know how I love her! But how can I manage to avoid alike her love or her hatred?" And he sat thinking, thinking, over this problem of the strategy of love. It must not be supposed that Thaddée lived bereft of all joy in the midst of his pain. The triumphant cunning of this day was a source of secret satisfaction. Since the Count's return with his wife, day by day he felt ineffable happiness in seeing that he was necessary to the couple, who, but for him, would have rushed inevitably into ruin. What fortune can hold out against the extravagances of Paris life? Clémentine, brought up by a reckless father, knew nothing of household management, which nowadays the richest women and the highest in rank are obliged to undertake themselves. Who in these days can afford to keep a steward? Adam, on his part, as the son of one of the great Polish nobles who allowed themselves to be devoured by the Jews, and who was incapable of husbanding the remains of one of the most enormous fortunes in Poland—where fortunes were enormous—was not of a temper to restrict either his own fancies or his wife's. If he had been alone, he would probably have ruined himself before his marriage. Paz had kept him from gambling on the Bourse, and does not that say all? Consequently, when he found that, in spite of himself, he was in love with Clémentine, Paz had not the choice of leaving the house and travelling to forget his passion. Gratitude, the clue to the mystery of his life, held him to the house where he alone could act as man of business to this heedless couple. Their long absence made him hope for a calmer spirit, but the Countess came back lovelier than ever, having acquired that freedom of thought which marriage confers on the Paris woman, and displaying all the charms of a young wife, with the indefinable something which comes of happiness, or of the independence allowed her by a man as trusting, as chivalrous, and as much in love as Adam was. The consciousness of being the working hub of this magnificent house, the sight of Clémentine stepping out of her carriage on her return from a party, or setting out in the morning for the park, a glimpse of her on the boulevards in her pretty carriage, like a flower in its nest of leaves, filled poor Thaddée with deep, mysterious ecstasies which blossomed at the bottom of his heart without the slightest trace appearing in his features. How, during these five months, should the Countess ever have seen the Captain? He hid from her, concealing the care he took to keep out of her way. Nothing is so near divine love as a hopeless love. Must not a man have some depth of soul thus to devote himself in silence and obscurity? This depth, where lurks the pride of a father—or of God—enshrines the worship of love for love's sake, as power for power's sake was the watchword of the Jesuits; a sublime kind of avarice, since it is perennially generous, and modelled indeed on the mysterious existence of the first principles of the world. The *Effect*, is it not Nature? And Nature is an enchantress: she belongs to man, to the poet, to the painter, to the lover; but the *Cause*, is it not, in the eyes of a few privileged souls and for certain towering intellects, superior to Nature? The Cause is God. In that sphere of causes dwelt the spirits of Newton, of Laplace, of Kepler, of Descartes, Malebranche, Spinoza, Buffon, of the true poets and saints of the second century of our era, of Saint Theresa of Spain and the sublime mystics. Every human emotion contains some analogy with the frame of mind in which the Effect is neglected in favour of the Cause, and Thaddée had risen to the height whence all things look different. Beset by the joys of the unknowable creator, Thaddée was, in love, what we recognise as greatest in the annals of the spirit.

"No, she is not altogether deceived," thought he, as he watched the smoke curl from his pipe. "She might involve me in an irremediable quarrel with Adam if she took a dislike to me, and if she should flirt to torment me, what would become of me?" The fatuity of this hypothesis was so unlike the Captain's modest nature and his somewhat German shyness, that he was vexed with himself for its having occurred to him, and went to bed determined to await events before taking any decisive steps. Next morning Clémentine breakfasted very well without Thaddée, and made no remark on his disobedience. That day, as it happened, was her day for being at home, and this, with her, demanded a royal display. She did not observe the absence of Captain Paz, on whom devolved all the arrangements for these great occasions. "Well and good!" said Paz to himself, as he heard the carriages rumble out at two in the morning; "the

Countess was only prompted by a Parisian's whim or curiosity." So the Captain fell back into his regular routine, disturbed for a day by this incident. Clémentine, diverted by the details of life in Paris, seemed to have forgotten Paz. For do you indeed suppose that it is a mere trifle to prevail over this inconstant city? Do you imagine, by any chance, that a woman risks nothing but her fortune over that most important game? The winter is to a woman of fashion what, of yore, a campaign was to the soldiers of the Empire. What a work of art and of genius is an outfit or a hairstyle created to make a sensation! A fragile, delicate woman wears her hard and dazzling armour of flowers and diamonds, silk and steel, from nine in the evening till two or often three in the morning. She eats little, to attract the eye by her slender shape; she cheats the hunger that seizes her during the evening with debilitating cups of tea, sweet cakes, heating ices, or heavy slices of pastry. The stomach must submit to the commands of vanity. She awakes late, and thus everything is in contradiction to the laws of nature, and nature is pitiless. No sooner is she up than the woman of fashion begins to dress for the morning, planning her dress for the afternoon. Must she not receive and pay visits, and go to the park on horseback or in her carriage? Must she not always be practising the game of smiles, straining her wits to invent compliments which seem neither stale not strained? And it is not every woman who succeeds. And then you are surprised when you see a young woman, whom the world has welcomed in her freshness, faded and blighted at the end of three years. Six months spent in the country are barely enough to heal the wounds inflicted by the winter. We hear nothing talked of but dyspepsia and strange maladies, unknown to women who devote themselves to their household. Formerly a woman was sometimes seen; now she is perpetually on the stage. Clémentine had to fight her way; she was beginning to be talked about, and amid the cares of this struggle between her and her rivals there was hardly a place for love of her husband! Thaddée might well be forgotten. However, a month later, in May, a few days before her departure to stay at Ronquerolles in Burgundy, she was returning from her drive, and saw, in a side street of the Champs-Elysées, Thaddée carefully dressed, and in raptures at seeing his beautiful Countess in her carriage, with dashing horses and splendid liveries—in short, the dear couple he admired so much.

"There is the Captain," said she to her husband.

"What a happy fellow!" said the Count. "This is his great reward! There is not a smarter equipage than ours, and he delights in seeing everybody envying us our happiness. You have never noticed him before, but he is there almost every day."

"What can he be thinking of?" said Clémentine.

"He is thinking at this moment that the winter has cost a great deal, and that we shall save a little by staying with your old uncle Ronquerolles," said Adam.

The Countess had the carriage stopped in front of Paz, and desired him to take the seat by her side in the carriage. Thaddée turned as red as a cherry.

"I shall poison you," he said, "I have just been smoking cigars."

"And does not Adam poison me?" she replied quickly.

"Yes, but he is Adam," replied the Captain.

"And why should not Thaddée enjoy the same privilege?" said the Countess with a smile.

This heavenly smile had a power which was too much for his heroic resolutions; he gazed at Clémentine with all the fire of his soul in his eyes, but tempered by the angelic expression of his gratitude—that of a man who lived solely by gratitude. The Countess folded her arms in her shawl, leaned back pensively against the cushions, crumpling the feathers of her pretty hat, and gazed out at the passersby. This flash from a soul so noble, and hitherto so resigned, appealed to her feelings. What, after all, was Adam's great merit? Was it not natural that he should be brave and generous? But the Captain! Thaddée possessed, or seemed to possess, an immense superiority over Adam. What sinister thoughts distressed the Countess when she once more observed the contrast between the fine, complete physical nature which distinguished Thaddée and the frail constitution which, in her husband, betrayed the inevitable degeneration of aristocratic families which are so mad as to persist in intermarrying! But the Devil alone knew these thoughts, for the young wife sat with vague meditation in her eyes, saying nothing till they reached home.

"You must dine with us, or I shall be angry with you for having disobeyed me," said she as she went in. "You are Thaddée to me, as you are to Adam. I know the obligations you feel to him, but I also know all we owe to you. In return for two impulses of generosity which are so natural, you are generous at all hours and day after day. My father is coming to dine with us, as well as my uncle Ronquerolles and my aunt de Sérizy; dress at once," she said, pressing the hand he offered to help her out of the carriage.

Thaddée went to his room to dress, his heart at once rejoicing and oppressed by an agonising flutter. He came down at the last moment, and all through dinner played his part of a soldier fit for nothing but to fulfil the duties of a steward. But this time Clémentine was not his dupe. His look had enlightened her. Ronquerolles, the cleverest of ambassadors next to Talleyrand,* and who served de Marsay so well during his short ministry, was informed by his niece of the high merits of Count Paz, who had so modestly made himself his friend's steward.

"And how is it that this is the first time I have ever seen Count Paz?" asked the Marquis de Ronquerolles.

"Ah! He is very sly and secretive," replied Clémentine, with a look at Paz that told him to change his demeanour.

Alas! It must be owned, at the risk of making the Captain less interesting to the reader, Paz, though superior to his friend Adam, was not a man of strong temper. He owed his apparent superiority to his misfortunes. In his days of poverty and isolation at Warsaw he had read and educated himself, had compared and thought much, but the creative power which makes a great man he did not possess—can it ever be acquired? Paz was great only through his heart, and could rise to the sublime; but in the sphere of sentiment, being a man of action rather than of ideas, he kept his thoughts to himself. His thoughts, then, did nothing but gnaw away at his heart. And what, after all, is an unspoken thought? At a word from Clémentine, the Marquis de Ronquerolles and his sister exchanged glances, with a side look at their niece, Count Adam, and Paz. It was one of those swift dramas which are played only in Italy or in Paris. Only in these two parts of the world— excepting at all courts—can the eyes say as much. To infuse into the eye all the power of the soul, to give it the full value of speech and throw a poem or a drama into a single flash, excessive servitude or excessive liberty is needed. Adam, the Marquis du Rouvre, and the Countess did not perceive this flash of observation between a past coquette and an old diplomatist, but Paz, like a faithful dog, understood its forecast. It was, you must remember, an affair of two seconds. To describe the hurricane that ravaged the Captain's heart would be too elaborate for these days. "What! The uncle and aunt already fancy that she perhaps loves me?" said he to himself. "My happiness then depends only on my own audacity. And Adam!" Ideal Love and Desire, both quite as potent as Friendship and Gratitude, rent his soul, and for a moment Love had the upper hand. This poor heroic lover longed to have his day! Paz became witty; he intended to please, and in answer to some question from Monsieur de Ronquerolles he sketched in grand outlines the Polish rebellion. Thus, at dessert, Paz saw Clémentine hanging on his lips, regarding him as a hero, and forgetting that Adam, after sacrificing a third of his immense fortune, had taken the risks of exile. At nine o'clock, having taken coffee, Madame de Sérizy kissed her niece on the forehead and took leave, carrying off Count Adam with an assertion of authority, and leaving the Marquis du Rouvre and Monsieur de Ronquerolles, who withdrew ten minutes later. Paz and Clémentine were left together.

"I will bid you good night, Madame," said Thaddée; "you will join them at the Opera."

"No," replied she. "I do not care for dancing, and they are giving an odious ballet this evening, *The Revolt of the Seraglio*."*

There was a moment's silence.

"Two years ago Adam would not have gone without me," she went on, without looking at Paz.

"He loves you to distraction——," Thaddée began.

"Oh! it is because he loves me to distraction that by tomorrow he will perhaps have ceased to love me!" exclaimed the Countess.

"The women of Paris are inexplicable," said Thaddée. "When they are loved *to distraction*, they want to be loved *rationally*; when they are loved *rationally*, they accuse a man of not knowing how to love."

"And they are always right, Thaddée," she replied with a smile. "I know Adam well; I owe him no grudge for it; he is fickle, and, above all, a great gentleman; he will always be pleased to have me for his wife, and will never thwart me in any of my tastes, but——"

"What marriage was ever without a *but?*" said Thaddée gently, trying to give the Countess's thoughts another direction.

A less conceited man would perhaps have had the thought which nearly drove this lover mad: "If I do not tell her that I love her," said he to himself, "I am an idiot!" There was silence between these two, one of those terrible pauses which seem bursting with thoughts. The Countess fixed a covert gaze on Paz, and Paz watched her in a mirror. Sitting back in his armchair, like a man given up to digestion, in the attitude of an old man or an indifferent husband, the Captain clasped his hands over his stomach, and mechanically twirled his thumbs, looking stupidly at their rapid movement.

"But say something good about Adam!" exclaimed Clémentine. "Tell me that he is not fickle, you who know him so well!"

The appeal was sublime.

"This is the opportunity for raising an insurmountable barrier between us," thought the unhappy Paz, devising a heroic lie. "Something good?" he said aloud. "I love him too well, you would not believe me. I am incapable of telling you any evil of him . . . and so . . . Madame, I have a hard part to play between you two."

Clémentine looked down, fixing her eyes on Paz's patent leather shoes.

"You northerners have mere physical courage, you have no constancy in your decisions," said she in a low tone.

"What are you going to do alone, Madame?" replied Paz, with a perfectly ingenuous expression.

"You are not going to keep me company?"

"Forgive me for leaving you."

"Why! where are you going?"

"I am going to the circus; it is the opening night on the Champs-Elysées, and I must not fail to be there . . ."

"Why not?" asked Clémentine, with a half-angry flash.

"Must I lay bare my heart?" he replied, colouring, "and confide to you what I conceal from my dear Adam, who believes that I love Poland alone?"

"What! Our dear, noble Captain has a secret?"

"A disgrace which you will understand, and for which you can comfort me."

"A disgrace! You?"

"Yes, I—Count Paz, am madly in love with a girl who was touring round France with the Bouthor family, people who have a circus in the style of Franconi's, but who only perform at fairs! I got her an engagement from the manager of the Cirque-Olympique."*

"Is she beautiful?" asked the Countess.

"In my eyes," he replied sadly. "Malaga—that is her name to the public—is strong, nimble, and supple. Why do I prefer her *to every other woman in the world?* Indeed, I cannot tell you! When I see her with her black hair tied back with blue ribbons that float over her bare olive-tinted shoulders, dressed in a white tunic with a gilt border and silk tights which make her appear a living Greek statue, her feet in frayed satin slippers, flourishing flags in her hand to the sound of a military band and flying through an enormous hoop covered with paper which crashes in the air—when her horse rushes round at a gallop, and she gracefully drops on to him again, applauded, honestly applauded, by a whole crowd—well, it excites me."

"More than a woman at a ball?" said Clémentine, with insinuating surprise.

"Yes," said Paz in a choked voice. "This splendid agility, this unfailing grace in constant peril, seem to me the greatest triumph of woman. Yes, Madame, Cinti and Malibran, Grisi and Taglioni, Pasta and Elsler,* all who reign or ever reigned on the boards, seem to me unworthy to untie Malaga's shoe strings—Malaga, who can mount or dismount a horse at a mad gallop, who slips under him from the left to reappear on the right, who flutters about the most fiery steed like a white will-o'-the-wisp, who can stand on the tip of one toe and then drop, sitting with her feet hanging, on a horse still galloping round, and who finally stands on his back without any reins, knitting a stocking, beating eggs, or stirring an omelette, to the intense admiration of the people, the true people, the peasantry and soldiers. During the walk round, Madame, that enchanting Columbine used to carry chairs balanced on the tip of her nose, the prettiest Greek nose I ever saw. Malaga is dexterity personified. Her strength is herculean: with her tiny fist or her little foot she can shake off three or four men. She is the goddess of athletics."

"She must be stupid."

"Oh!" cried Paz, "she is as amusing as the heroine of *Peveril of the Peak*.* As heedless as a gipsy, she says everything that comes into her head; she cares no more for the future than you care for the sous you throw to a beggar, and she lets slip really sublime things. Nothing will ever convince her that an old diplomat is a handsome young man, and a million francs would not make her change her opinion. Her love for a man is a perpetual flattery. Enjoying really insolent health, her teeth are thirty-two Oriental pearls set in coral. Her "muzzle"— as she calls the lower part of her face—is, as Shakespeare has it, as fresh and sweet as a heifer's snout.* And it can give bitter pain! She respects fine men, strong men— an Adolphe, an Auguste, an Alexandre—acrobats and tumblers. Her teacher, a horrible Cassandra, thrashed her unmercifully; it cost thousands of blows to give her such agility, grace, and intrepidity."

"You are drunk with Malaga!" said the Countess.

"Her name is Malaga only on the posters," said Paz, with a look of annoyance. "She lives in the Rue Saint-Lazare,* in a little apartment on the third floor, in velvet and silk, like a princess. She leads two lives: one at the fairgrounds, and one as a pretty woman."

"And does she love you?"

"She loves me—you will laugh—solely because I am a Pole. She sees in every Pole a Poniatowski, as he is shown in the print, jumping into the Elster,* for to every Frenchman the Elster, in which it is impossible to drown, is a foaming torrent which swallowed up Poniatowski. And with all this I am very unhappy, Madame——"

Clémentine was touched by a tear of rage in Thaddée's eye.

"You love the extraordinary, you men," said she.

"And you?" asked Thaddée.

"I know Adam so well that I know he could forget me for some acrobatic tumbler like your Malaga. But where did you find her?"

"At Saint-Cloud, last September, at the fair. She was standing in a corner of the stage where the performers parade themselves. Her comrades, all dressed as Poles, were making a terrific charivari. I saw her silent and dreamy, and fancied I could guess that her thoughts were melancholy. Was there not enough to make her so—a girl of twenty? That was what touched me."

The Countess was leaning in a bewitching attitude, pensive, almost sad.

"Poor, poor Thaddée!" she exclaimed. "And with the good fellowship of a really great lady," she added, not without a meaning smile, "Go, go to the circus!"

Thaddée took her hand and kissed it, dropping a hot tear, and then went out. After having invented a passion for a circus rider, he must give it some reality. Of his whole story nothing had been true but the minute's attention he had given to the famous Malaga, the rider of the Bouthor troupe at Saint-Cloud; her name had just caught his eye on an advertisement of the circus. A clown, bribed by a single five franc piece, had told Paz that the girl was a foundling, or had perhaps been stolen. Thaddée now went to the circus and saw the beautiful horsewoman again. For ten francs, a groom— they fill the place of dressers at the theater—informed him that Malaga's name was Marguerite Turquet, and that she lived in the Rue des Fossés-du-Temple,* on the fifth floor.

Next day, with death in his soul, Paz found his way to the Faubourg du Temple, and asked for Mademoiselle Turquet, in summer the understudy of the principal rider at the Cirque, and in winter a bit player in a boulevard theatre.

"Malaga!" shouted the porter's wife, rushing into the attic, "A fine gentleman for you! He is asking Chapuzot all about you, and Chapuzot is talking away at him to give me time to warn you."

"Thank you, M'ame Chapuzot, but what will he think when he sees me ironing my dress?"

"Ah, bah! When a man is in love, he loves everything about you."

"Is he an Englishman? They are fond of horses."

"No. He looks to me like a Spaniard."

"*Tant pis!* The Spaniards are down in the market they say. Stay here, Madame Chapuzot, so that I shall not look so left to myself."

"Who were you wanting, Monsieur?" said the woman, opening the door to Thaddée.

"Mademoiselle Turquet."

"My child," said the porter's wife, wrapping her shawl round her, "here is somebody asking for you."

A rope on which some linen was airing knocked off the Captain's hat.

"What is your business, Monsieur?" asked Malaga, picking it up.

"I saw you at the circus; you remind me, Mademoiselle, of a daughter I lost, and out of affection for my Héloïse, whom you are so wonderfully like, I should wish to be of use to you if you will allow me."

"Well, to be sure! But do sit down, Monsieur le Général," said Madame Chapuzot. "One cannot be more honest . . . nor more gallant."

"I am no gallant, my good lady," said Paz. "I am

213

a father in deep distress, eager to be cheated by a likeness."

"And so I am to pass as your daughter?" said Malaga, very roguishly, and without suspecting the absolute truth of the statement.

"Yes," said Paz. "I will come sometimes to see you, and that the illusion may be perfect, I will place you in handsome lodgings, nicely furnished——"

"I shall have furniture of my own?" said Malaga, looking at Madame Chapuzot.

"And servants," Paz went on, "and live quite at your ease."

Malaga looked at the stranger from under her brow.

"From what country are you, Monsieur?"

"I am a Pole."

"Then I accept," said she.

Paz went away, promising to call again.

"That is a tough one!" said Marguerite Turquet, looking at Madame Chapuzot. "But I am afraid this man is wheedling me to humour some fancy. Well, I will risk it."

A month after this whimsical scene, the fair circus rider was established in rooms charmingly furnished by Count Adam's upholsterer, for Paz wished that his folly should be talked about in the Laginski household. Malaga, to whom the adventure was like an Arabian Nights' dream, was waited on by the Chapuzot couple—at once her servants and her confidants. The Chapuzots and Marguerite Turquet expected some startling climax, but at the end of three months, neither Malaga nor the Chapuzots could account for the Polish Count's fancy. Paz would spend about an hour there once a week, during which he sat in the salon, never choosing to go either into Malaga's boudoir nor into her bedroom, which, in fact, he never entered in spite of the cleverest manoeuvring on her part and on that of the Chapuzots. The Count inquired about the little incidents that varied the horsewoman's life, and on going away he always left two forty franc coins on the mantlepiece.

"He looks dreadfully bored," said Madame Chapuzot.

"Yes," replied Malaga, "that man is as cold as frost after a thaw."

"He is a good fellow, all the same," cried Chapuzot, delighted to see himself dressed in blue Elbeuf cloth, and as smart as a minister's office boy.

By his periodic offerings, Paz made Marguerite Turquet an allowance of three hundred and twenty francs a month. This sum, added to her small earnings at the circus, secured her a splendid existence as compared with her past squalor. Strange tales were repeated among the performers at the circus as to Malaga's good fortune. The girl's vanity allowed rumours of her rent being sixty thousand francs, instead of the modest six thousand which her rooms cost the prudent Captain. According to the clowns and bit players, Malaga ate off silver plate, and she certainly came to the circus in pretty burnouses, in shawls, and elegant scarfs. And, to crown all, the Pole was the best fellow a circus rider could come across: never suspicious, never jealous, leaving Malaga perfect freedom.

"Some women are so lucky!" said Malaga's rival. "Such a thing would never happen to me, though I bring in a third of the receipts."

Malaga wore pretty berets and sometimes *held her head up a little too high* (an admirable expression from the lexicon of feminine speech) in a carriage in the Bois de Boulogne, where the youth of fashion began to observe her. Malaga soon began to be talked about in the shady world of questionable women, and there her good fortune was being attacked by malicious gossip. She was reported to be a somnambulist, and the Pole was said to be a mesmerist in search of the Philosopher's Stone. Other comments of a far more venomous taint made Malaga more inquisitive than Psyche; she reported them, with tears, to Paz.

"When I owe a woman a grudge," said she in conclusion, "I do not slander her, I do not say that a man *mesmerizes her* to find stones. I say that she is an ogress, and I prove it. Why do you get me into trouble?"

Paz was cruelly speechless. Madame Chapuzot succeeded at last in discovering his name and title. Then, at the Hôtel Laginski, she ascertained some positive facts: Thaddée was unmarried, he was not known to have a dead daughter either in Poland or France. Malaga could not help feeling a thrill of terror.

"My dear child," said Madame Chapuzot, "that monster——"

A man who was satisfied with gazing at a beautiful creature like Malaga—gazing at her by stealth—from under his brows—not daring to come to any decision—without any confidence; such a man, in Madame Chapuzot's mind, must be a monster.

"That monster is breaking you in, to lead you on to something illegal or criminal. *Dieu de Dieu!* If you were to be brought before the assizes—and it makes me shudder from head to foot to think of it, I quake only to speak of it—or in the criminal court, and your name was in the newspapers! . . . Do you know what I should do in your place? Well, in your place, to make all safe, I should warn the police."

One day, when mad notions were fermenting in Malaga's brain, Paz having laid his gold pieces on the velvet mantlepiece, she snatched up the money and flung it in his face, saying, "I will not take stolen money!"

The Captain gave the gold to the Chapuzots, and came no more. Clémentine was spending the summer on the estate of her uncle, the Marquis de Ronquerolles, in Burgundy. When the troupe at the circus no longer saw Thaddée in his seat, there was much talk among the performers. Malaga's magnanimity was regarded as folly by some, as cunning by others. The Pole's behaviour, as explained to the most experienced of the women, seemed inexplicable. In the course of a single week, Thaddée received thirty-seven letters from women of the town. Happily for him, his singular reserve gave rise to no curiosity in fashionable circles, and remained the subject of discussion only among less reputable types.

Two months later, the beautiful rider, swamped in debt, wrote to Count Paz the following letter, which the dandies of the day regarded as a masterpiece:

You, whom I still venture to call my friend, will you not take pity on me after what passed between us, which you took so ill? My heart disowns everything that could hurt your feelings. If I was so happy as to make you feel some charm when you sat near me, as you used to do, come again . . . otherwise, I shall sink into despair. Poverty has come upon me already, and you do not know what *brutish things* it brings with it. Yesterday I lived on a herring for two sous and one sou's worth of bread. Is that a breakfast for the woman you love? The Chapuzots have left me after seeming so devoted to me. Your absence has shown me the shallowness of human attachment . . . a dog that is fed leaves behind more than this! A bailiff, who turned a deaf ear to me, has seized everything on behalf of the landlord, who has no pity, and of the jeweller, who will not wait even ten days; for with you men, credit vanishes with confidence. What a position for a woman who has nothing to reproach herself for but a little amusement! My friend, I have taken everything of any value *to my aunt's*; I have nothing left but my memory of you, and the hard weather is coming on. All through the winter I shall have no fire, since nothing but melodrama is played at the boulevard, in which I have nothing to do but tiny parts, which do not *show off* a woman. How could you misunderstand my noble feelings towards you? For, after all, we do not have two ways of expressing our gratitude. How is it that you, who seemed so pleased to see me comfortable, could leave me in misery? Oh, my only friend on earth, before I go back to travel from fair to fair with the Bouthors—for so, at any rate, I can make my living—forgive me for wanting to know if I have really lost you forever. If I should happen to think of you just as I was jumping through the hoop, I might break my legs by missing *time!* Come what may, I am yours for life.

MARGUERITE TURQUET

"This letter," exclaimed Thaddée, shouting with laughter, "is well worth my ten thousand francs."

Clémentine came home on the following day, and Paz saw her once more, lovelier and more gracious than ever. During dinner the Countess preserved an air of perfect indifference towards Thaddée, but a scene took place between the Count and his wife after their friend had left. Thaddée, affecting to ask Adam's advice, had left Malaga's letter in his hands, as if by accident.

"Poor Thaddée!" said Adam to his wife, after seeing Paz make his escape. "What a misfortune for a man of his eminence to be the plaything of a street performer of the lowest class! He will love anything; he will degrade himself; he will be unrecognisable before long. Here, my dear, read that," and he handed her Malaga's letter.

Clémentine read the note, which smelt of tobacco, and tossed it away with disgust.

"However thick the bandage over his eyes may be, he must have found something out. Malaga must have played him some faithless trick."

"And he is going back to her!" cried Clémentine. "He will forgive her! You men can have no pity for any but those horrible women!"

"They want it so badly!" said Adam.

"Thaddée did himself justice—by keeping to himself!" said she.

"Oh, my dearest, you go too far," said the Count, who, though he was at first delighted to lower his friend in his wife's eyes, did not wish for the death of the sinner.

Thaddée, who knew Adam well, had begged for absolute secrecy; he had only spoken, he said, as an excuse for his dissipations, and to beg his friend to allow him to have a thousand écus for Malaga.

"He is a man of great pride," Adam went on.

"What do you mean?"

"Well, to have spent no more than ten thousand francs on her, and to wait for such a letter as that to rouse him before taking her the money to pay her debts! For a Pole, on my honour!"

"But he may ruin you!" said Clémentine in the acrid tone of a Parisian woman when she expresses her cat-like distrustfulness.

"Oh! I know him," said Adam. "He would sacrifice Malaga to us."

"We shall see," replied the Countess.

"If it was necessary for his happiness, I should not hesitate to ask him to give her up. Constantin tells me that during the time when he was seeing her, Paz, usually so sober, sometimes came in quite befuddled. If he allowed himself to take to drink, I should be as much grieved as if he were my son."

"Do not tell me any more!" cried the Countess with another gesture of disgust.

Two days later, the Captain could see in her manner, in the tone of her voice, and in her eyes, the terrible results of Adam's betrayal. Scorn had opened gulfs between him and this charming woman. And he fell forthwith into deep melancholy, devoured by this thought, "You have made yourself unworthy of her." Life became a burden to him; the bright sunshine was gloomy in his eyes. Nevertheless, under these floods of bitter thought, he had some happy moments: he could now give himself up without danger to his admiration for the Countess, who never paid him the slightest attention when, at a party, hidden in a corner, mute, all eyes and all heart, he did not lose one of her movements, not a note of her song when she sang. He lived in this enchanting life: he might himself groom the horse that *she* was to ride, and devote himself to the management of her splendid house with redoubled care for its interests. These unspoken joys were buried in his heart like those of a mother, whose child never knows anything of his mother's heart: for is it knowledge so long as even one thing remains unknown? Was not this finer than Petrarch's chaste passion for Laura,* which, after all, was well repaid by a wealth of glory, and by the triumph of the poetry she had inspired? Was not the emotion which Assas felt in dying,* in truth a whole life? This emotion Paz felt every day without dying, but also without the reward of immortality. What is there in love that Paz, notwithstanding these secret delights, was consumed by sorrow? The Catholic religion has so elevated love that she has married it inseparably, so to speak, to esteem and generosity. Love does not exist apart from the fine qualities of which man is proud, and so rarely are we loved if we are despised, that Thaddée was perishing of his self-inflicted wounds. Only to hear her say that she could have loved him, and then to die! The hapless lover would have thought his life well paid for. The torments of his previous position seemed to him preferable to living close to her, loading her with his generosity without being appreciated or understood. In short, he wanted the reward of his virtue. He grew thin and yellow, and fell so thoroughly ill, consumed by low fever, that during the month of January he kept to his bed, though refusing to see a physician. Count Adam grew extremely uneasy about his poor Thaddée. The Countess then was so cruel as to say, when they were together one day, "Let him alone; do you not see that he has some Olympian remorse?" This speech stung Thaddée to the courage of despair; he got up, went out, tried some amusement, and recovered his health. In the month of February, Adam lost a rather considerable sum at the Jockey Club, and, being afraid of his wife, he begged Thaddée to place this sum to the account of his extravagance for Malaga.

"Is it so extraordinary that this circus rider should

have cost you twenty thousand francs? It concerns no one but me. Whereas, if the Countess should know that I had lost it at play, I should fall in her esteem, and she would be in alarm for the future."

"This to crown all!" cried Thaddée, with a deep sigh.

"Ah! Thaddée, this service would make us quits if I were not already the debtor."

"Adam, you may have children. Give up gambling," said the Captain.

"Twenty thousand francs more that Malaga has cost us!" exclaimed the Countess some days after, on discovering Adam's *generosity* to Paz. "And ten thousand before—that is thirty thousand in all! Fifteen hundred francs a year, the price of my box at the Italiens, a whole fortune to many people . . . Oh! you Poles are incomprehensible!" cried she, as she picked some flowers in her beautiful conservatory. "You care no more than that!"

"Poor Paz——"

"Poor Paz, poor Paz!" she echoed, interrupting him. "What good does he do us? I will manage the house myself! Give him the hundred louis a year that he refused, and let him make his own arrangements with the Cirque-Olympique."

"He is of the greatest use to us; he has saved us at least forty thousand francs this year. In short, my dearest, he has placed a hundred thousand francs for us in Nucingen's bank, and a steward would have netted them."

Clémentine was softened, but she was no less hard on Thaddée. Some days after she desired Paz to come to her in her boudoir, where, a year since, she had been startled by comparing him with the Count. This time she received him alone, without any suspicion of danger.

"My dear Paz," said she, with the careless familiarity of fine folks to their inferiors, "if you love Adam as you say you do, you will do one thing which he will never ask, but which I, as his wife, do not hesitate to require of you——"

"It is about Malaga?" said Thaddée with deep irony.

"Well, yes, it is," she said. "If you want to end your days with us, if you wish that we should remain friends, give her up. How can an old soldier——"

"I am but thirty-five, and have not a grey hair!"

"You look as if you had," said she, "and that is the same thing. How can a man so capable of putting two and two together, so honourable . . ."

There was something terrible in how she spoke this word, with the clear intention of awakening in him the nobility of soul that she believed extinct.

"As honourable as you are," she went on, after a little pause, which a gesture from Paz forced upon her, "you allow yourself to be entrapped like a boy. Your affair with her has made Malaga famous. Well! My uncle wanted to see her, and he saw her. My uncle is not the only one; Malaga is very ready to receive all these gentlemen. I believed you to be high-minded. For shame! Come, would she be an irreparable loss to you?"

"Madame, if I knew of any sacrifice by which I might recover your esteem, it would soon be made, but to give up Malaga is not a sacrifice——"

"In your place that is what I should say if I were a man," replied Clémentine. "Well, but if I take it as a great sacrifice, there is nothing to be angry at."

Paz went away, fearing he might do some mad act; he felt his brain invaded by crazy notions. He went out for a walk, lightly dressed in spite of the cold, but failed to cool the burning of his face and brow. "I believed you to be high-minded!" He heard the words again and again. "And scarcely a year ago," said he to himself, "to hear Clémentine, I had beaten the Russians single-handed!" He thought of quitting the Laginski household, of asking to be sent on service in the spahi regiment, and getting himself killed in Africa, but a dreadful fear checked him; "What would become of them without me? They would soon be ruined. Poor Countess, what a horrible life it would be for her to be reduced even to thirty thousand francs a year! Come," said he to himself, "since she can never be yours, courage, finish your work!"

Since 1830, as all the world knows, the Carnival in Paris has grown to prodigious proportions, which has made it truly European and far more burlesque, far more lively than the departed carnivals of Venice. Is this because, since fortunes have so greatly diminished, Parisians have thought of amusing themselves collectively, just as in their clubs, they have salons for cheap, without any hostesses, and lacking in civility? Be that as it may, the month of March was lavish with these balls, where dancing, great joy, delirium, grotesque figures, and mockery made sharp by Parisian wit achieved gigantic results. This madness had its Pandemonium at that time in the Rue Saint-Honoré, and its Napoléon in Musard, a little man born to rule an orchestra as tremendous as the rampant mob, and to conduct a galop—that whirl of witches at their Sabbath, and one of Auber's triumphs, for the galop derived its form and its poetry from the famous galop in *Gustavus*.* May not this vehement finale serve as a symbol of an age when, for fifty years, everything has rushed on with the swiftness of a dream? And so, our grave Thaddée, bearing an immaculate image in his heart, went to Malaga to invite her, the queen of carnival dances, to spend an evening at Musard's ball as soon as he learned that the Countess, disguised to the teeth, was intending to come with two other young ladies, escorted by their husbands, to see the curious spectacle of one of these monstrous balls. On Mardi Gras in the year 1838, at four o'clock in the morning, the Countess, wrapped in a black domino, and seated on a bench in one of the amphitheatres of that Babylonian hall where Valentino has since given his concerts, saw Thaddée, dressed as Robert Macaire,* leading the circus rider in the costume of a savage, her head dressed with nodding plumes like a horse at a coronation, and leaping among the groups like a perfect will-o-the-wisp.

"Oh!" exclaimed Clémentine to her husband, "you Poles are not men of character. Who would not trust Thaddée? He gave me his word, not knowing that I would be here—seeing all without being seen."

Some days after this she invited Paz to dinner. After dinner, Adam left them together, and Clémentine scolded Thaddée in such a way as to make him feel that she would no longer have him about the house.

"Indeed, Madame," said Thaddée humbly, "you are quite right, I am a wretch; I had given my word. But what can I do? I put off the parting with Malaga till after the Carnival . . . and I will he honest with you, the woman has so much power over me . . ."

"A woman who gets herself turned out of Musard's by the police, and for such dancing!"

"I admit it; I sit condemned; I will quit *your* house. But you know Adam. If I hand over to you the conduct of your affairs, you will have to exert great energy. Though I have the vice of Malaga, I know how to keep an eye on your concerns, how to manage your household, and look after the smallest details. Allow me then to remain till I have seen you qualified to continue my system of management. You have now been married three years, and are safe from the first follies consequent on the honeymoon. The ladies of Parisian society, even with the highest titles, understand very well in these days how to control a fortune and a household . . . well, as soon as I am assured, not of your capacity, but of your firmness, I will leave Paris."

"It is the Thaddée of Warsaw that speaks, not the Thaddée of the circus. Come back to us cured."

"Cured? Never!" said Paz, his eyes fixed on Clémentine's pretty feet. "You cannot imagine, Countess, what spice and surprise this woman possesses in her spirit." And feeling his courage fail him, he added: "No woman of fashion, with all her pretentious airs, is worth her pure, young animal nature . . ."

"In fact, I choose not to have anything of the animal in me!" said the Countess, with a flashing look like an enraged viper.

After that day, Count Paz explained to Clémentine all her affairs, made himself her tutor, taught her the difficulties of managing her property, the real cost of things, and the way to avoid being too extensively robbed by her people. She might trust Constantin, and make him her chief steward. Thaddée had trained Constantin. By the month of May, he thought the Countess perfectly capable of administering her fortune, for Clémentine was one of those clear-sighted women whose instincts are alert, with an inborn genius for household rule.

The situation thus naturally brought about by Thaddée took a terrible turn for him, for his sufferings were not so mild as he made them seem. The hapless lover had not counted on accident. Adam fell very seriously ill. Thaddée, instead of leaving, installed himself as his friend's sick nurse. The Captain's devotion was indefatigable. A woman who would have had an interest in looking through the telescope of foresight would have seen in the Captain's heroism the sort of punishment which noble souls inflict on themselves to subdue their involuntary thoughts of sin, but women see everything or nothing, according to their frame of mind: love is their sole luminary.

For forty-five days Paz watched and nursed Mitgislas without seeming to have a thought of Malaga, for the excellent reason that he never did think of her. Clémentine, seeing Adam at death's door, and yet not dead, had a consultation with the most famous doctors.

"If he gets through this," said the most learned of the physicians, "it can only be by an effort of nature. It lies with those who nurse him to watch for the moment and aid nature. The Count's life is in the hands of his attendants."

Thaddée went to communicate this verdict to Clémentine, who was sitting in the Chinese pavilion, as much to rest after her fatigues as to leave the field free for the doctors, and not to be in their way. As he trod the gravelled paths leading from the boudoir to the rock on which the Chinese summerhouse was built, Clémentine's lover felt as though he were in one of the chasms described by Dante. The unhappy man had never foreseen the chance of becoming Clémentine's husband, and he had bogged himself in a swamp of mud. When he reached her, his face was distraught, sublime in its despair. Like Medusa's head, it communicated terror.

"He is dead?" said Clémentine.

"They have given no hope; at least, they leave it to nature. Do not go in just yet. They are still there, and Bianchon himself is examining him."

"Poor man! I wonder if I did not sometimes torment him," she said.

"You have made him very happy; be quite easy on that point," said Thaddée; "and you have been indulgent to him——"

"The loss will be irreparable."

"But, dear lady, supposing the Count should die, have you not formed your opinion of him?"

"I do not love him blindly," she said, "but I loved as a wife ought to love her husband."

"Then," said Thaddée, in a voice new to Clémentine's experience of him, "you ought to feel less regret than if you were losing one of those men who are a woman's pride, her love, her whole life! You may be frank with such a friend as I am . . . I shall miss him—I! Long before your marriage, I had made him my child, and I have devoted my life to him. I shall have no interest left on earth. But life still has charms for a widow of twenty-four."

"Why, you know very well that I love no one," said she, with the brusqueness of sorrow.

"You do not know yet what it is to love," said Thaddée.

"Oh! Husband for husband, I have sense enough to prefer a child like my poor Adam to a superior man. For nearly a month now we have been asking ourselves, 'Will he live?' These fluctuations have prepared me, as they have you, for this end. I may be frank with you? Well, then, I would give part of my life to save Adam's. Does not independence for a woman, here in Paris, mean the liberty to be taken in by the pretence of love from men who are ruined or profligate? I have prayed to God to spare me my husband—so gentle, such a good fellow, so little fractious, and who was beginning to be a little afraid of me."

"You are honest, and I like you the better for it," said Thaddée, taking Clémentine's hands, which she allowed him to kiss. "In such a solemn moment there is indescribable satisfaction in finding a woman devoid of hypocrisy. It is possible to talk to you. Consider the future; supposing God should not listen to you—and I am one of those who are most ready to cry to Him: spare my friend! For these fifty nights past have not made my eyes heavy, and if thirty days and thirty nights more care are needed, you, Madame, may sleep while I watch. I will snatch him from death, if, as *they* say, he can be saved by care. But if, in spite of you, in spite of me, the Count is dead. Well, then, if you were loved, or worshipped, by a man whose heart and character were worthy of yours——"

"I have perhaps madly wished to be loved, but I have never met——"

"Supposing you were mistaken."

Clémentine looked steadily at Thaddée, suspecting him less of loving her than of a covetous dream; she poured contempt on him by a glance, measuring him from head to foot, and crushed him with two words: "Poor Malaga!" pronounced in those tones such as fine ladies alone can find in the gamut of their contempt. She rose and left Thaddée fainting, for she did not turn round, but walked with great dignity back to her boudoir, and from there up to Adam's room.

An hour later, Paz returned to the sick man's bedside, and gave all his care to the Count, as though he had not received his own deathblow. From that dreadful moment he became silent; he had a duel to fight with disease, and he carried it through in a way that excited the admiration of the doctors. At any hour his eyes were always beaming like two lamps. Without showing the slightest resentment towards Clémentine, he listened to her thanks without accepting them; he seemed deaf. He had said to himself, "She shall owe Adam's life to me!" and it was as though he had written these words in lines of fire in the sick man's room. At the end of a fortnight, Clémentine was obliged to give up some of the nursing, or risk falling ill from so much fatigue. Paz was inexhaustible. At last, towards the end of August, Bianchon, the family doctor, answered for the Count's life.

"Ah, Madame," said he to Clémentine, "you are under not the slightest obligation to me. But for his friend we could not have saved him!"

On the day after the terrible scene in the Chinese pavilion, the Marquis de Ronquerolles had come to see his nephew, for he was setting out for Russia with a secret mission, and Paz, overwhelmed by the previous evening, had spoken a few words to the diplomat. On the very day when Count Adam and his wife went out for the first time for a drive, at the moment when the carriage was turning from the steps, a gendarme came into the courtyard and asked for Count Paz. Thaddée, who was sitting with his back to the horses, turned round to take a letter bearing the stamp of the Minister for Foreign Affairs, and put it into the side pocket of his coat, with a decision which precluded any questions on the part of Clémentine or Adam. It cannot be denied that persons of good breeding are masters of the language that uses no speech. Nevertheless, as they reached the Porte Maillot,* Adam, assuming the privilege of a convalescent whose whims must be indulged, said to Thaddée—"There can be no indiscretions between two brothers who love each other as you and I do; you know what is in that letter; tell me, I am in a fever of curiosity."

Clémentine looked at Thaddée as an angry woman can, and said to her husband, "He has been so sulky with me these two months, that I shall take good care not to press him."

"Oh, *mon Dieu!*" replied Thaddée, "as I cannot hinder the newspapers from publishing it, I may very well reveal the secret. The Emperor Nicholas does me the favour of appointing me captain on service in a regiment starting with the Khiva Expedition."*

"And you are going?" cried Adam.

"I shall go, my dear fellow. I came as captain, and as captain I return. Malaga might lead me to make a fool of myself. We shall dine together tomorrow for the last time. If I do not set out in September for St. Petersburg, I would have to travel overland, and I am not rich. I must leave Malaga her little independence. How can I fail to provide for the future of the only woman who has understood me? Malaga thinks me a great man! Malaga thinks me handsome! Malaga may perhaps be faithless, but she would go through——"

"Through a hoop for you, and land on her feet on horseback," said Clémentine, sharply.

"Oh, you do not know Malaga," said the Captain, with deep bitterness, and an ironical look which made Clémentine uneasy and silent.

"Adieu to the young trees of this lovely Bois de Boulogne, where Parisian ladies drive, and the exiles wander who have found a home here. I know that my eyes will never again see the green trees of the Allée de

Mademoiselle, or of the Route des Dames, nor the acacias, nor the cedar at the Ronds-points.* On the Asiatic frontier, obedient to the schemes of the great Emperor I have chosen to be my master, promoted perhaps to command an army, for sheer courage, for constantly risking my life, I may indeed regret the Champs-Elysées where you, once, made me take a place in the carriage, by your side. Finally, I shall never cease to regret the severity of Malaga—of the Malaga I am at this moment thinking of."

This was said in a tone that made Clémentine shiver.

"Then you love Malaga very truly?" she said.

"I have sacrificed for her the honour we never sacrifice——"

"Which?"

"That which we would fain preserve at any cost in the eyes of the idol we worship."

After this speech Thaddée kept impenetrable silence; he broke it only when, as they drove clown the Champs-Elysées, he pointed to a wooden structure and said, "There is the circus!"

Before their last dinner, he went to the Russian Embassy for a few minutes, and from there to the Ministry for Foreign Affairs, and he started for Le Havre next morning before the Countess and Adam were up.

"I have lost a friend," said Adam, with tears in his eyes, as he learned that Count Paz was gone, "a friend in the truest sense of the word, and I cannot think what has made him flee from my house as if it were the plague. We are not the sort of friends to quarrel over a woman," he went on, looking full at Clémentine, "and yet all he said yesterday about Malaga—but he never laid the tip of his finger on the girl."

"How do you know?" asked Clémentine.

"Well, I was naturally curious to see Mademoiselle Turquet, and the poor girl cannot account for Thaddée's extraordinary reserve——"

"That is enough," said the Countess, going off to her own room, and saying to herself, "I have surely been the victim of some sublime hoax."

Scarcely had she made this reflection, when Constantin placed in her hands the following letter, which Thaddée had scrawled in the night:—

Countess, to go to be killed in the Caucasus and to bear the burden of your scorn is too much: a man should die unmutilated. I loved you from the first time I saw you, as a man loves the woman he will love forever, even when she is faithless—I, under obligations to Adam, whom you chose and married—I, so poor, the volunteer steward, devoted to your household. In this dreadful catastrophe I found a delightful existence. To be an indispensable wheel in the machine, to know myself useful to your luxury and comfort, was a source of joy to me, and if that joy had been keen when Adam alone was my care, think what it must have been when the woman I worshipped was at once the cause and the effect! I have known all the joys of motherhood in my love, and I accepted life on those terms. Like the beggars on the high roads, I built myself a hut of stones on the outskirts of your beautiful home, but without holding out my hand for alms. Poor and unhappy, blinded by Adam's happiness, I was the one who gave. Yes, you were hedged in by a love as pure as that of a guardian angel; it watched while you slept; it caressed you with a look as you passed by; it was glad merely to exist; in short, you were the sunshine of home to the poor exile who is now writing to you, with tears in his eyes, as he recalls the happiness of those early days. At the age of eighteen, with no one to love me, I had chosen as an ideal mistress a charming woman at Warsaw, to whom I yielded all my thoughts and my wishes—the queen of my days and nights! This woman knew nothing of it, but why inform her? For my part, what I loved was love. You may fancy, from this adventure of my boyhood, how happy I was, living within the sphere of your influence, grooming your horse, picking out new gold pieces for your purse, superintending the splendour of your table and your entertainments, seeing you eclipse fortunes greater than your own by my good management. With what zeal did I not rush round Paris when Adam said to me, "Thaddée, *she* wants this or that!" It was one of those joys for which there are no words. You have now and again wished for some trifle within a certain time which has compelled me to feats of expedition, driving for six or seven hours in a cab, and what happiness it has been to walk in your service. When I have watched you smiling in the midst of your flowers without being seen by you, I have forgotten that no one loved me—in short, at such moments I was but eighteen again. On some days; when my happiness turned my brain, I went, at night, to kiss the place where, for me, your feet left luminous traces, just as long ago I performed miracles of thievery to go kiss the key that Countess Ladislas had touched with her hands on opening a door. The air you breathed was balsamic; to me it was fresh life to breathe it, and I felt, as they say is the case in the tropics, overwhelmed by an atmosphere charged with creative elements. I must tell you all these things to account for the strange fatuity of my involuntary thoughts. I would have died sooner than divulge my secret! You may remember those few days when you were curious, when you wanted to see the worker of the wonders which had at last struck you with surprise. I believed—forgive me, Madame—I believed that you would love me. Your kindness, your looks—interpreted by a lover—seemed fraught with so much danger to me that I took up Malaga, knowing that there are liaisons which no woman can forgive; I took the girl up at the moment when I saw that my love was inevitably infectious. Overwhelm me now with the scorn which you poured upon me so freely when I did not deserve it, but I think I may be quite sure that if, on the evening when your aunt took the Count out, I had said what I have here written, having once said it I should have been like the tame tiger who has at last set his teeth in living flesh, who scents warm blood, and . . .

Midnight

I could write no more, the memory of that evening was too vivid! Yes, I was then in a delirium! I saw Hope in your eyes; Victory and its crimson banners may have burned in mine and fascinated yours. My crime was to think such things—and perhaps wrongly. You alone can be the judge of that fearful scene when I succeeded in crushing love, desire, and the most invincible forces of manhood under the icy hand of gratitude which must be eternal. Your terrible scorn punished me. You have showed me that neither disgust nor contempt can ever be got over. I love you like a madman. I must have gone away if Adam had died; there is all the more reason since Adam is saved. I did not snatch my friend from the grave to betray him. And, indeed, my departure is the due punishment for the thought that came to me that I would let him die when the physicians said his life depended on his attendants. Adieu, Madame; in leaving Paris I lose everything, but you lose nothing in parting with yours

Most faithfully,
THADDÉE PAÇ

"If my poor Adam says he has lost a friend, what have I lost?" thought Clémentine, sitting dejected, with her eyes fixed on a flower in the carpet.

This is the note which Constantin delivered privately to the Count—

My dear Mitgislas, Malaga has told me all. For the sake of your happiness, never let a word escape you in Clémentine's presence as to your visits to the circus rider; let her still believe that Malaga costs me a hundred thousand francs. With the Countess's character, she will not forgive you either your losses at play or your visits to Malaga. I am not going to Khiva, but to the Caucasus. I have had a fit of spleen, and at the pace I mean to go, in three months I shall be Prince Paz, or dead. Adieu; though I have drawn sixty thousand francs out of Nucingen's, we are quits.

THADDÉE

"Idiot that I am! I very nearly betrayed myself just now by speaking of the circus rider!" said Adam to himself.

Thaddée has been gone three years, and the papers do not as yet mention any Prince Paz. Countess Laginska takes a keen interest in the Emperor Nicholas's expeditions; she is a Russian at heart, and reads with avidity all the news from that country. Once or twice a year she says to the ambassador, with an affectation of indifference, "Do you know what has become of our poor Count Paz?"

Alas! Most Parisian women, keen-eyed and subtle as they are supposed to be, pass by—and always will pass by—someone like Paz without observing him. Yes, more than one Paz remains misunderstood, but—fearful thought!—some are misunderstood even when they are loved. The simplest woman in the world requires some little charlatanry in the greatest man, and the most heroic love counts for nothing if it is uncut; it needs the arts of the polisher and the jeweller.

In the month of January 1842, Countess Laginska, beautified by gentle melancholy, inspired a mad passion in the Comte de la Palférine, one of the most audacious lions of present-day Paris. La Palférine understood the difficulty of conquering a woman guarded by a chimera; to triumph over this bewitching woman, he trusted to a surprise, and to the assistance of a woman who, being a little jealous of Clémentine, would lend herself to plot the chances of this surprise.

Countess Laginska, incapable with all her wit of suspecting such treachery, was so imprudent as to go with this false friend to the masked ball at the Opera. At about three in the morning, carried away by the excitement of the ball, Clémentine, for whom La Palférine had deployed all his seductions, consented to dine with him, and was getting into the carriage of her false friend. At this critical moment, she was seized by a strong arm, and in spite of her cries placed in her own carriage, which was standing with the door open, though she did not know that it was waiting.

"He has not left Paris!" she exclaimed, recognising Thaddée, who ran off when he saw the carriage drive away with the Countess.

Has a woman ever had such a romance in all her life? Clémentine is always hoping to see Paz again.

Paris, January 1842

ADDENDUM TO THE IMAGINARY MISTRESS

The following personages appear or are mentioned
in other volumes of *The Human Comedy*:

Bianchon, Horace

I: *Letters of Two Brides*
IV: *A Second Home*
V: *Honorine*
VIII: *Old Goriot*
IX: *The Atheist's Mass, The Interdiction*
XII: *Pierrette*
XIII: *The Rabouilleuse*
XIV: *The Muse of the Department*
XVI: *Lost Illusions*
XVIII: *César Birotteau*
XIX: *The Splendors and Miseries of Courtesans*
XX: *The Secrets of the Princesse de Cadignan*
XXI: *Cousin Bette*
XXIII: *A Prince of Bohemia*
XXIV: *The Bureaucrats*
XXV: *The Petits Bourgeois*
XXVI: *The Brotherhood of Consolation*
XXXII: *The Village Curé*
XXXIV: *The Magic Skin*

In addition, Monsieur Bianchon narrated the following:
IV: *A Study of Woman*
V: *La Grande Bretèche*
IX: *Another Study of Woman*

Laginski, Comte Adam Mitgislas

IX: *Another Study of Woman*
XXI: *Cousin Bette*

La Palférine, Gabriel-Jean-Anne-Victor-Benjamin-Georges-Ferdinand-Charles-Edouard-Rusticoli, Comte de

VI: *Beatrix*
XXI: *Cousin Bette*
XXIII: *A Man of Business, A Prince of Bohemia*

A Daughter of Eve
(*Une fille d'Ève*)
December 1838

Translated by George Burnham Ives

To Madame La Comtesse Bolognini, née Vimercati

If you remember, Madame, the pleasure your conversation afforded a certain traveler by reminding him of Paris at Milan, you will not be surprised to find him testifying his gratitude for the many pleasant evenings passed in your company by laying one of his books at your feet, and soliciting for it the protection of your name—a name which heretofore protected several tales of one of your old authors, dear to the hearts of the Milanese. You have a Eugénie, beautiful even now, whose thoughtful smile assures us that she will inherit from you the most precious gifts of woman, and will assuredly enjoy in her childhood all the delights which a sad-visaged mother refused to the Eugénie who figures in this story. You see that, even though the French are accused of fickleness and forgetfulness, I am a true Italian in constancy and faithful memory. As I wrote the name of Eugénie, my thoughts often carried me back to the freshly stuccoed salon and the little garden at the Vicolo dei Capuccini, *which heard the dear child's joyous laughter and our quarrels and our anecdotes. You have left the* Corso *for the* Tre Monasteri;* *I have no idea how you are situated there, and I am compelled to think of you, no longer amid the lovely things which doubtless still surround you there, but as one of the lovely figures conceived by Carlo Dolci,* Raphael, Titian or Allori, which seem like mere abstractions, they are so far removed from us.*

If this book succeed in passing across the Alps, it will bear witness to the lively gratitude and respectful friendship of

Your humble servant,

DE BALZAC

LA COMTESSE DE VANDENESSE.

UNE FILLE D'ÈVE.

Plate XI

In one of the finest houses on the Rue Neuve-des-Mathurins,* at half-past eleven in the evening, two women were sitting in front of the fire in a boudoir hung with blue velvet of soft, changing hues, such as French manufacturers have only of late years learned to make. At the doors and windows, one of those upholsterers, who are at the same time true artists, had draped soft clinging cashmere curtains of the same shade of blue as the hangings on the wall. A silver lamp, studded with turquoises, was suspended from a lovely rosette in the centre of the ceiling by three chains of beautiful workmanship. The decorative scheme was extended to the smallest details: even the ceiling itself was of blue silk with white cashmere stars, and from it long bands of white cashmere fell in graceful folds upon the wall at equal intervals, held in place by knots of pearls. The feet met the warm texture of a Brussels carpet, thick and soft as turf, and with bunches of blue flowers strewn upon a gray ground. The furniture was of carved violet wood, after the finest designs of the olden time, and its rich, warm tones relieved the lack of character in the decoration, which a painter would have called a little too *vague*. The backs of the chairs and couches were lined with thin sheets of a beautiful white silk material with raised blue flowers, boldly framed by foliage artistically carved in the wood. On either side of the window, a cabinet displayed its thousand and one priceless trifles: the flowers of the mechanical arts blossoming under the burning rays of thought. Upon the mantel of dark blue marble, the wildest creations in Saxon porcelain, shepherds on their way to never-ending wedding feasts with delicate nosegays in their hands—Chinese ideas executed in Germany—surrounded a platinum clock inlaid with arabesques. Above gleamed the beveled edges of a Venetian mirror in an ebony frame laden with figures in bas-relief, a relic of some old royal residence. Two jardinieres displayed the sickly splendor of the hothouse, pale-hued and divinely beautiful flowers, the pearls of the botanist's art. In this cold, orderly boudoir, as neat and clean as if it had been for sale, you would have looked in vain for the capricious, roguish disorder which speaks of happiness. Everything there was in harmony, for the two women were weeping. Everything in the room seemed to be in agony. The name of the proprietor, Ferdinand du Tillet, one of the wealthiest bankers in Paris, is a sufficient justification for the immoderate extravagance noticeable in this mansion, of which the boudoir we have described may serve as an illustration. Although without family, although a self-made man—God knows how!—Du Tillet had married in 1831 the youngest daughter of the Comte de Granville, one of the most illustrious names in the French magistracy, who became a Peer of France after the Revolution of July.* This marriage of ambition was purchased by the bridegroom's acknowledging in the contract the receipt of a dowry he did not obtain, as large as that of the bride's older sister, who was married to Comte Félix de Vandenesse. Now, the Granvilles had brought about the alliance with the Vandenesse family solely by the immensity of the dowry. Thus the Bank repaired the breach made in the Magistracy by the Nobility. If the Comte de Vandenesse could have looked forward three years and seen himself the brother-in-law of one Ferdinand, *called* Du Tillet, he might not have married his wife perhaps; but who could have foreseen, in the latter part of 1828, the extraordinary overturn in the political condition, the fortunes and the moral state of France that the year 1830 was destined to bring about? That man would have been deemed insane who should have told Comte Félix de Vandenesse that in that transformation scene he would lose his peer's crown only to find it again upon his father-in-law's head.

Seated upon one of the low chairs called *chauffeuses* in the attitude of one listening attentively, Madame du Tillet was holding her sister, Madame Félix de Vandenesse, close to her heart, and from time to time kissing her hand. In society the baptismal name was added to the family name in order to distinguish the Comtesse from her sister-in-law, the Marquise, wife of the one-time ambassador, Charles de Vandenesse, who had married the wealthy widow of the Comte de Kergarouët, a demoiselle de Fontaine. Half-lying upon a small sofa with a handkerchief in her disengaged hand, her breathing broken by repressed sobs and her eyes swimming with tears, the Comtesse had been confiding to her sister such things as are confided only by one sister to another when they love each other, and these two sisters did love each other dearly. We live in a time when it would be so common an occurrence for two sisters thus strangely married not to love each other, that a historian is bound to set forth the reasons of their affection, which had endured without break or impairment notwithstanding the mutual contempt of their husbands for each other and constant family discord. A rapid glance at their early years will make clear their respective positions.

Brought up in a gloomy mansion in the Marais* by a devout woman of limited intellectual powers, who, *being impregnated with her duties*—the classic phrase—had fulfilled the first obligation of a mother to her daughters: Marie-Angélique and Marie-Eugénie entered the married state—the former at twenty years, the second at seventeen—without having ever emerged from the domestic circle where the maternal glance hovered over them. Up to that time they had never been to a performance; the churches of Paris were their theatres. In short, their upbringing under their mother's roof had been as stern as it would have been in a convent. From the time they were old enough to think, they always slept in a room adjoining the Comtesse de Granville's, and the door was left open all night. The time which was not devoted to the care of their persons, to religious duties or the studies indispensable to the education of well-born young ladies, was passed in working with their needles for the poor, or in walks abroad like those which the English allow themselves to indulge in on Sundays, saying, "Let us not walk so fast, or we shall look as if we were enjoying ourselves." Their education did not go beyond the limits imposed by confessors who were selected from among the most intolerant and most Jansenist churchmen. Never were purer or more chaste girls given over to a husband's keeping; their mother seemed to have looked upon this point, which is certainly most essential, as the fulfilment of her whole duty to God and man. The two poor creatures had never read a novel before marriage, nor had they drawn anything save figures whose anatomy would have seemed to Cuvier* the culmination of the impossible, engraved in a way to make the Farnese Hercules himself turn woman. An old maid taught them to draw. A venerable priest instructed them in grammar, the French language, history, geography and the little arithmetic necessary for women to know. Their reading, all from books sanctioned by the church, like the *Lettres Édifiantes* and Noël's *Leçons de Littérature,** was done aloud in the evening, always in the presence of their mother's spiritual director, for it was possible that they might fall in with passages which, without judicious comments, would arouse their imagination. Fénelon's *Télémaque** was considered a dangerous work. The Comtesse de Granville loved her daughters enough to long to make them angels after the style of Marie Alacoque,* but her daughters would have preferred a less virtuous and more amiable mother. This education bore its natural fruit. Imposed as a yoke and presented in its most austere forms, Religion wearied with all its practices these young innocent hearts, who were treated as if they were criminals—it repressed their feelings, and although it took deep root, it was not loved. The two Maries were certain either to become imbeciles or to long for freedom; they would long to be married as soon as they could catch a glimpse of the world, and compare others' ideas with their own, but their own touching charms and their own priceless worth, of these they knew naught. They knew not their own purity, and what could they have known of life? Without arms against misfortune, as they were without experience to enable them to appreciate good fortune, they had no other source of consolation than themselves in the depths of their maternal prison. Their whispered confidences in the evening, or the few words they exchanged when their mother left them for a moment, sometimes contained more ideas than the words could give expression to. Often a glance, seen by no other eye, whereby they communicated their emotions to each other, was like a poem of bitter melancholy. The sight of the cloudless sky, the sweet odor of the flowers, the circuit of the garden arm in arm, afforded them unspeakable delight. The completion of a piece of embroidery was a source of innocent joy. Their mother's social circle, far from offering their hearts any resource or stimulating their minds, had no other effect than to cast a shadow upon their thoughts and impart a tinge of sadness to their emotions: for it was composed of narrow, strait-laced, dull old women, whose conversation turned upon the points of difference between preachers and confessors, upon their petty illnesses and upon religious incidents of too trifling importance for the *Quotidienne*

even, or the *Ami de la Religion*.* As for the men, their
faces were so cold and wore such sad and resigned expressions, that they would have extinguished the torches
of love; they were all of the age when a man is disappointed and sour, when his feelings have ceased to act
except at the table, and are concerned only with those
things which affect his physical well-being. Religious
selfishness had withered all these hearts, consecrated
to duty and entrenched behind church ceremonial.
Silent games at cards engrossed their attention most of
the evening. The two little maids, put under the ban, as
it were, by this Sanhedrin which upheld the maternal
austerity, surprised themselves by hating these depressing individuals with the sunken eyes and forbidding
faces. Against the dark shadows of this life of theirs, the
face of one man stood out in bold relief, and that man
was their music master. The confessors had decided that
music was a Christian art, born in the Catholic Church
and nurtured by it. The two little girls were permitted
therefore to learn music. A spectacled maiden who
taught vocal scales and the piano at a neighboring convent wore them out with exercises. But when the elder
of his daughters reached the age of ten, the Comte de
Granville suggested the propriety of her taking a master. Madame de Granville claimed all the credit of an
act of wifely obedience for this necessary concession; it
is a peculiarity of sanctimonious women that they make
a virtue of duties accomplished. The master was a
German Catholic, one of those men, born old, who will
never be more than fifty, even when they are eighty. His
dark, furrowed, wrinkled face still retained a trace of
childish innocence in its black depths. The deep blue of
purity gave life to his eyes, and the joyous smile of the
springtime dwelt upon his lips. His old gray hair, falling naturally like Jesus Christ's, gave to his ecstatic
expression an indescribable touch of solemnity, which
led people astray as to his character; he would have

done the most idiotic thing with the most exemplary gravity. His habits were a necessary envelope to which he paid no attention, for his eyes were too high up among the clouds ever to descend to material affairs. So this great, unknown artist may be said to have belonged to the amiable race of forgetful men, who give their time and their talents to others just as they leave their gloves upon every table and their umbrellas at every door. His hands were of the sort that look dirty immediately after they have been washed. Finally, his old body, which was awkwardly perched upon his old, rickety legs, and proved how far a man can make it the accessory of his mind, was one of those extraordinary creations which have never been painted save by a German, by Hoffmann, the poet of that which seems not to exist and yet has life. Such was Schmuke, once precentor to the Margrave of Anspach,* a scholar who underwent an examination at the hands of a religious council, and was asked if he fasted. The master would have liked to answer, "Just look at me!" but how could he trifle with devotees and Jansenist shepherds? The apocryphal old fellow occupied so great a place in the lives of the two Maries, and they became so attached to the pure-minded and great artist who was content to understand his art, that each of them, after her marriage, gave him an annuity of three hundred francs a year, which was enough to pay for his lodgings, his beer, his pipe and his clothing. Six hundred francs a year beside his lessons made the earth an Eden to him. Schmuke had never had the courage to confide his poverty and his aspirations to anybody save these two adorable maidens, these hearts which had blossomed under the snow of maternal severity and the ice of enforced piety. This fact explains Schmuke's life and the childhood of the two Maries. Later, none could say what abbé, what pious old woman discovered the German astray in Paris. As soon as the mothers of families learned that the Comtesse de Granville had found a music master for her daughters, they all asked for his name and address. Schmuke had thirty houses at which he gave lessons in the Marais. His tardy success was made manifest by shoes with bronzed steel buckles and horsehair soles, and by more frequent renewal of his linen. His artless gaiety, long repressed by noble and self-respecting poverty, reappeared. He allowed such bright little remarks as this to escape him: "Mesdemoiselles, the cats ate up the mud in Paris last night," when the frost had dried up the muddy streets over night, but he would say it in German patois, like this: "*Montemisselles, ze cads haf eaden up ze mud lazd nide een Baris!*" Well content to lay at the feet of the two angels this *vergis mein nicht*,* so to speak, culled from among the flowers of his intellect, he would assume as he offered it, a clever, knowing air which disarmed any mockery. He was so happy to make the lips of his pupils open with a smile—for the secret of their wretched lives had been fathomed by him—that he would have made himself ridiculous for that express purpose had he not been so already, for his heart could give new life to the tritest commonplaces; to adopt a happy expression of the lamented Saint-Martin,* he would have made the mire golden with his heavenly smile. In accordance with one of the most praiseworthy precepts of a religious education, the two Maries always respectfully escorted their master to the door of their apartments. There the poor girls would say a few kindly words, happy in their ability to make him happy; they could show themselves as women to none but him! So it was that, up to the time of their marriage, music was to them a life within a life, just as the Russian peasant, so it is said, takes his dreams for reality, his life for a bad dream. In their desire to defend themselves against the multitude of paltry things that threatened to swallow up their lives, against the all-consuming ascetic ideas, they recklessly attacked the difficulties of the musical art. Melody,

Harmony, and Composition, the three daughters of heaven whose chorus was led by the old music-drunken Catholic Faun, rewarded them for their labors and formed a rampart with their ethereal dances. Mozart, Haydn, Beethoven, Paësiello, Cimarosa, Hummel* and the geniuses of the second order developed in them a thousand sentiments which did not overstep the chaste circle of their veiled hearts, but which made their way into the creative sphere where they flew about with wings outspread. When they had performed some little thing almost perfectly, they would press each other's hands and kiss each other ecstatically, and their old master would call them his Saint-Cecilias.

The two Maries never attended a ball until they were sixteen, and then only four times a year at some few carefully selected houses. They did not leave their mother's side without being well provided with instructions as to the line of conduct they were to adopt toward their partners, and such strict instructions too that they could answer naught but yes or no. The Comtesse never took her eye off her daughters, and that eye seemed to divine the words they spoke simply by the movement of their lips. The poor girls had ball dresses that were beyond reproach—muslin gowns high in the neck, with an infinitude of excessively full ruches and flounces and long sleeves. This costume, by holding in leash their charms and their hidden beauties gave them a sort of vague resemblance to an Egyptian scabbard; nevertheless two faces, lovely in their melancholy, emerged from these two masses of cotton. They were furious to find themselves the objects of kindly compassion. What woman ever lived, however innocent, who did not desire to arouse envy? No perilous or unhealthy or even equivocal thought ever stained the gray matter of their brains; their hearts were pure, their hands were horribly red, they were bursting with health. Eve came not forth from God's hands more guileless than were these

two girls when they went forth from the maternal roof
to the town hall and the church, with the simple but
awe-inspiring command to render obedience in every
point to the men, at whose sides they were thenceforth,
sleeping or waking, to pass their nights. In their opinion
they could be no worse off in the strange households
to which they were to be deported than in the maternal convent. Why was it that the father of these girls,
the Comte de Granville, great and learned and upright
magistrate that he was, although sometimes carried
rather far by politics, did not protect the poor little creatures from this crushing despotism? Alas! by virtue of a
noteworthy bargain, agreed to after ten years of married
life, the husband and wife lived separate lives in their
own house. The father had stipulated that he should
himself look to his sons' education, leaving to his wife
the education of his daughters. In his eyes the application of this oppressive system was fraught with much
less danger for girls than for boys. The two Maries,
who were destined to undergo tyranny in some form,
either of love or of marriage, would lose less thereby
than boys, whose minds should be left free, and whose
mental qualities would be impaired under the violent
compression of religious ideas carried to extremes. Of
four possible victims the Comte had saved two. The
Comtesse looked upon her two sons—one of whom
was destined for a life judgeship, the other for a seat
among the magistrates of uncertain tenure—as having
been too badly brought up to be admitted to the slightest intimacy with their sisters. A rigorous surveillance
was maintained over all communication between the
poor children. Moreover, when the Comte took his sons
from school, he was very careful not to keep them at
home. The two boys came there to breakfast with their
mother and sisters; after that the magistrate provided
entertainment for them away from the house: the café,
the theatre, the museum, or excursions in the country in

the season, supplied their diversions. Except upon solemn days in the family calendar, such as the Comtesse's birthday or the Comte's, New Year's Day, or the days on which prizes were distributed, when the boys remained at the house and slept there—excessively bored, by the way, and afraid to kiss their sisters, they were so closely watched by their mother, who never left them together an instant—the poor girls saw their brothers so rarely that it was impossible that there should be any bond between them. On those days such questions as: "Where is Angélique?"—"What is Eugénie doing?"—"Where are my children?" were heard at every turn. When her two sons were mentioned, the Comtesse would raise her cold, tear-bedewed eyes to Heaven as if to implore God's forgiveness for not having wrested them from the grasp of impiety. Her exclamations, her reticence in regard to them, were as full of meaning as the most mournful verses of Jeremiah, and deceived the sisters, who believed their brothers to be utterly perverse and damned forever. When his sons were eighteen years old, the Comte gave them each a room in his own suite, and started them on the study of the law, placing them in the charge of an advocate, his secretary, who was instructed to initiate them in the secrets of their future. Thus the two Maries knew nothing of fraternity save in the abstract. At the time of their respective marriages, their brothers were both kept away by important cases, one being then public prosecutor in some distant jurisdiction, and the other just beginning practice in the provinces. Many families whose home life one might imagine to be friendly, affectionate, and coherent, really live like this: the brothers are away from home, intent upon advancement and moneymaking, or enlisted in the service of their country; the sisters are enveloped in a whirl of family interests, entirely distinct from theirs. And so all the members of the family are disunited and soon forget one another, and are bound together only by the feeble ties of memory until the time comes when pride or self-interest brings them together, or, it may be, severs them in spirit as they have heretofore been separated in body. A family united in body and spirit alike is a rare exception. Modern laws, multiplying the family by the family, have created the most horrible of all plagues: individualism.

In the profound solitude in which their youth was passed, Angélique and Eugénie rarely saw their father, and when he did appear in the spacious suite occupied by his wife on the ground floor of the house, he brought a depressing countenance with him. In his home he retained the grave and solemn expression of the magistrate on the bench. When the little girls had passed the age of dolls and playthings, when they were beginning to use their reason and had already ceased to laugh at old Schmuke—that is to say, when they were about twelve years old—they discovered the secret of the anxiety which caused the furrows on the Comte's brow, and detected beneath his mask of sternness the traces of a kindly disposition and a charming character. They came to understand that he had given way to the inroads of Religion in his household because he was disappointed in his hopes as a husband, just as he had been wounded in the most sensitive fibres of the paternal heart—a father's love for his daughters. Such sorrow produces a singularly deep impression upon young girls who are deprived of the joys of tenderness. Sometimes as they were walking about the garden together with their childish gait, each with an arm around the other's slender waist, their father would stop them under a clump of trees and kiss their foreheads one after the other. His eyes, his mouth, his whole countenance expressed at such moments the most profound compassion. "You are not very happy, my dear little girls," he would say, "but I will find husbands for you in good season, and I shall be very glad to see you leave the house."

"Papa," Eugénie would say, "we have made up our minds to marry the first man that comes along."

"And this is the bitter fruit of such a system as hers!" he would cry. "She tries to make saints, and turns out——"

He never finished the sentence. Often the girls were conscious of a most affectionate warmth in their father's manner of bidding them adieu, and in his glances when it so happened that he dined at home. They pitied this father of theirs whom they saw so rarely, and we love those whom we pity.

The austere religious education we have described was the moving cause of the marriages of the two sisters, who were welded together by unhappiness as closely as Rita-Christina* by nature. Many men, forced by circumstances to think of marriage, prefer a girl taken from the convent and saturated with religion to one reared upon worldly principles. There is no middle course. A man must marry a well-educated girl who has read and digested the newspapers, who has waltzed and danced the galop with innumerable young men, who has been to all the plays, who has devoured all the latest novels, who has had her knees bruised by a dancing master leaning his against hers, who cares but little for religion and has prepared her own code of morals, or else a pure and untutored young woman like Marie-Angélique and Marie-Eugénie. Perhaps there is as much risk with one as with the other. However, the vast majority of men who are not as old as Arnolphe much prefer a pious Agnès to a Célimène in embryo.*

The two Maries were both short and slender; they had the same figure, the same foot, the same hand. Eugénie, the younger, was fair like her mother. Angélique was dark like her father, and yet both had the same complexion; their skin was of that mother-of-pearl whiteness which proclaims the richness and purity of the blood, with veins of color standing clearly out upon flesh as firm of tissue as the jasmine, and like it finely marked and smooth and soft to the touch. Eugénie's blue eyes and Angélique's brown eyes had the same expression of guileless temerity, of unaffected wonder, mainly due to the vague way in which the pupil floated on the white fluid of the eye. They were well-shaped; their shoulders were a trifle thin, but would fill out in due time. Their throats, so long veiled, dazzled the eye by their perfect loveliness when their husbands besought them to don low-necked dresses for their first ball; the two ignorant creatures thereupon experienced the fascinating sense of shame which kept them blushing for a whole evening behind closed doors. At the time when this scene opens, when the older sister was weeping and seeking consolation from her junior, their hands and arms had become as white as milk. Each of them had nursed a child, one a boy, the other a girl. Eugénie had seemed to her mother to be very sly, and she had redoubled her watchfulness and harshness in her regard. In that dreaded mother's eyes, the proud and stately Angélique seemed to possess a lofty mind which would be its own safeguard, while the roguish Eugénie required to be held in check. There are in the world lovely creatures, misunderstood by destiny, who ought to succeed in everything they undertake, but who live and die unhappy, tormented by an evil genius, victims of unforeseen circumstances. Thus the innocent, light-hearted Eugénie had fallen under the malicious despotism of a parvenu upon emerging from the maternal prison. Angélique, who was inclined to lofty conflicts of sentiment, had been tossed into the most exalted spheres of Parisian society with a halter about her neck.

Madame de Vandenesse, who was evidently giving way under the burden of a grief that was too heavy for her heart to bear, innocent as it still was after six years of married life, was partly reclining, her legs half drawn up, her body bent double and her head wandering from side to side, as if it had lost its way, upon the back of the sofa. She had hastened to her sister's house after a brief appearance at the Italiens, and still had a few flowers in her hair, but others were scattered about on the floor with her gloves, her fur-lined silk pelisse, her muff and her hood. Tears glistened among the pearls on her white breast, and her moist eyes betokened extraordinary disclosures. Amid such luxurious surroundings, was it not horrible? The Comtesse could not summon courage to speak.

"Poor darling," said Madame du Tillet, "what a false idea you must have of my marriage to have thought of coming to me for help!"

As she listened to these words torn from the lowest depths of her sister's heart by the fury of the storm she had poured into it, just as the melting of the snow uproots the stones that are most firmly fixed in the torrent's bed, the Comtesse gazed stupidly at the banker's wife; the fire of terror dried her tears and her eyes no longer wandered.

"Do you mean that you are in purgatory, too, my angel?" she said in a low voice.

"My woes will not allay your suffering."

"Tell me them, dear child. I am not selfish enough yet to refuse to listen to you! So we are still suffering together as in our youth?"

"But we are suffering apart," replied the banker's wife in a melancholy tone. "We live in two hostile societies. I go to the Tuileries while you have ceased to go there. Our husbands belong to two opposite parties. I am the wife of an ambitious banker, a bad man, my precious treasure; you are the wife of a kind, noble, generous creature——"

"Oh! Do not reproach me," said the Comtesse. "To do that a woman must have undergone the deathly weariness of a dull, colorless life, and have left it to enter the paradise of love; she must have known the bliss one feels to realize that one's whole life is another's, to marry the infinite emotions of a poetic soul, to live a twofold life; to go and come with him in his journeys through space, in the world of ambition; to suffer in his grief, to rise upon the wings of his unbounded joys, to display one's talents on a vast stage, and to remain all the while calm and cold and serene before a curious world. Yes, my dear, one must often hold a whole ocean in her heart, when sitting, as we are now, on a sofa before the fire. And yet what bliss to have always, at every minute, an enormous interest at stake that multiplies the fibres of the heart and stretches them, to be indifferent to nothing, to find one's life depending on a drive where you will see a gleaming eye that makes the sun turn pale, to be excited by the least delay, to long to kill an unwelcome visitor who robs you of one of the rare moments when happiness beats madly in the tiniest veins! What ecstasy to live! Ah! my dear love, to live when so many women are on their knees praying for the emotions that elude them! Remember, my child, that for such poems there is but one time, youth. In a few years the winter comes and the cold. Ah! If you possessed these living riches of the heart and were threatened with the loss of them——"

Madame du Tillet had covered her face with her hands in dismay as she listened to this awful dirge.

"I had no idea of reproving you in the slightest degree, my dearest," she said at last, seeing the hot tears streaming down her sister's cheeks. "You have thrown more firebrands into my heart in a moment than my tears have extinguished. Yes, the life I lead would justify my heart in such a love as that you just described. Let me say, as I think, that we should not be where we now are if we had seen more of each other. If you had known of my suffering you would have appreciated your own good fortune; perhaps you would have emboldened me to resist, and I should be happy. Your unhappiness is an accident which a lucky chance will repair, while my unhappiness is constant and everlasting. In my husband's eyes I am the portmanteau of his splendor, the signboard of his ambition, one of the gratifications of his vanity. He has neither true affection for me nor confidence in me. Ferdinand is as cold and smooth as this marble," she said, laying her hand upon the mantel. "He distrusts me. Whatever I might ask for myself is refused in advance; but, as to anything that flatters him

Pauvre chérie, dit madame du Tillet, quelle fausse idée as-tu de mon mariage .

Plate XII

and advertises his fortune, I do not even have to express a wish; he decorates my apartments, he spends enormous sums on my table. My servants, my boxes at the theatre, every outward appearance is at the height of fashion. His vanity spares no expense; he will trim his children's swaddling clothes with lace, but he will not hear their cries or divine their needs. Do you understand me? I am covered with diamonds when I go to court; in society I wear the richest trinkets, but I have not a sou at my disposal. Madame du Tillet, who arouses jealousy, perhaps, and who seems to be swimming in gold, has not a hundred francs of her own. If the father does not trouble himself about his children, he troubles himself even less about the mother. Ah! He has done extremely well in making me feel that he has paid for me, and that my personal fortune, over which I have no control, was extorted from him. If I had nothing to do but master him, perhaps I might fascinate him, but I am subject to the influence of a third person, a woman of fifty years and more, who has claims upon him and rules him—she is a notary's widow. I have a feeling that I shall not be free until she is dead. My life here is as regular as a queen's; I am summoned to breakfast and dinner as at your chateau. I invariably go out at a certain hour to drive in the park. I am always accompanied by two servants in full livery, and must always return at a fixed hour. Instead of giving orders I receive them. At the ball, at the theatre, a footman comes and tells me: 'Madame's carriage is at the door,' and I have no choice but to go, often in the midst of my enjoyment. Ferdinand would be angry if I did not conform to the etiquette he has ordained for his wife, and he frightens me. Surrounded as I am by this accursed opulence, I regret the past and think of our mother as a kind mother; she left us at night and I could talk with you then; in short I was living with a being who loved me and suffered with me; while here, in this sumptuous mansion, I am in the midst of a desert."

At this terrible confession the Comtesse seized her sister's hand and kissed it, weeping.

"How can I help you?" Eugénie whispered. "If he should find us together, his suspicions would be aroused and he would want to know what you have been saying to me for this last hour; then we must lie to him, and that is a hard thing to do with so shrewd and treacherous a man; he would set traps for me to fall into. Let us leave my woes and think of yourself. Your forty thousand francs, my dear, would be nothing to Ferdinand, who turns millions over and over with another vulgar banker, the Baron de Nucingen. Sometimes I am present at dinner when they say things to make one shudder. Du Tillet knows how discreet I am and they talk in my presence without restraint; they are sure of my silence. Do you know murder on the highroad seems to me an act of charity compared to certain financial schemes! He and Nucingen think as little of ruining people as I think of their extravagance. Often I receive poor dupes whose cases I have heard discussed the night before, and who are plunging into enterprises where they are sure to leave their fortunes: I long to say to them, as to Léonarde in the robbers' cave:* 'Beware!' But what would become of me? I hold my tongue. This magnificent house is the resort of cutthroats. And Du Tillet and Nucingen throw away thousand-franc notes by the handful to gratify their whims. Ferdinand buys the site of the old chateau at Le Tillet, intending to rebuild it and to add to it a forest and other magnificent properties. He declares that his son shall be a count, and that his descendants in the third generation shall be noble. Nucingen is tired of his fine house on the Rue Saint-Lazare* and is building a palace. His wife is one of my friends. Ah!" she cried, "She may be of use to us; she is bold with her husband and has the control of her own fortune; she will save you."

"My dear puss, I have only a few hours; let us go there

tonight, this instant," said Madame de Vandenesse, throwing herself into Madame du Tillet's arms, and bursting into tears.

"What! Can I go out at eleven at night?"

"I have my carriage."

"What are you plotting here?" said Du Tillet, pushing open the boudoir door.

He presented to the sisters a villainous countenance, lighted up by a deceitfully affable smile. The carpet had deadened the sound of his footsteps, and the preoccupation of the two women had prevented their hearing the noise made by Du Tillet's carriage entering the courtyard. The Comtesse—in whom contact with the world and the perfect freedom of action accorded her by Félix had developed the two qualities, wit and shrewdness, whose growth was still retarded in her sister's case by the marital despotism which succeeded to that exercised by their mother—noticed that Eugénie's alarm was on the point of betraying itself, and saved her by a ready response.

"I thought my sister was richer than she is," said the Comtesse, meeting her brother-in-law's gaze. "Women sometimes get into a little trouble which they do not care to mention to their husbands, like Joséphine and Napoléon, and I came to ask her to do me a favor."

"She can easily do it, my dear sister. Eugénie is very rich," replied Du Tillet with veiled malice.

"She is rich only in your eyes, my brother," retorted the Comtesse, smiling bitterly.

"What do you want?" said Du Tillet, not sorry to get a hold upon his sister-in-law.

"You silly man, did I not tell you that we do not want to compromise ourselves with our husbands?" replied Madame de Vandenesse significantly, realizing that she was putting herself at the mercy of the man whose portrait had just been so faithfully drawn by her sister. "I will come and see Eugénie tomorrow."

"Tomorrow?" rejoined the banker coldly. "No. Madame du Tillet dines tomorrow with a future Peer of France, Baron de Nucingen, who will leave me his seat in the Chamber of Deputies."*

"Will you not allow her to accept my box at the Opera?" said the Comtesse, without even exchanging a look with her sister, so terrified was she that she would betray their secret.

"She has her own, dear sister," said Du Tillet with an offended air.

"Well, I will see her there," retorted the Comtesse.

"It will be the first time you have done us that honor," said Du Tillet.

The Comtesse felt the reproof and began to laugh.

"Never fear, we will not make you pay anything this time," said she. "Farewell, my love."

"Impertinent hussy!" cried Du Tillet, picking up the flowers that had fallen from the Comtesse's headdress. "You ought to study Madame de Vandenesse," he said to his wife. "I would like to see you as impertinent in society as your sister was here just now. You have an idiotic, bourgeois air that drives me mad."

Eugénie's only reply was to raise her eyes to heaven.

"Well, Madame, what have you two been up to here?" said the banker after a pause, pointing to the flowers. "What is going on that your sister should come to your box tomorrow?"

The poor helot took refuge in feigned sleepiness and left the room to undress, dreading a cross-examination. Du Tillet thereupon took her by the arm, led her back and placed her in front of him in the light of the candles burning in silver-gilt arms between two lovely bouquets of flowers, and fixed his keen eyes upon hers.

"Your sister came here to borrow forty thousand francs, owed by a man in whom she takes an interest, and who will be boxed up like something of value on the Rue de Clichy* inside of three days," said he coldly.

The poor woman was seized with a fit of nervous trembling which she repressed.

"You frightened me," said she. "But my sister has been too well brought up, she loves her husband too dearly to be so deeply interested in a man as that."

"You are very much mistaken," he replied drily. "Girls brought up as you two were, in restraint and religious observances, are thirsty for liberty and long for happiness, and the happiness they attain is never so great nor so enjoyable as that they dreamed of. Such girls make bad wives."

"Speak for me," said poor Eugénie in a tone of bitter mockery, "but respect my sister. The Comtesse de Vandenesse is too happy, her husband leaves her too free for her not to be attached to him. Besides, if your supposition were true, she would not have told me anything about it."

"It is true," said Du Tillet. "I forbid your doing anything whatsoever in this business. It is for my interest that the man should go to prison. Consider it settled."

Madame Du Tillet left the room.

"She will disobey me of course, and I shall know all they do by having them watched," said Du Tillet when he was left alone in the boudoir. "The poor fools really think they have a chance with us!"

He shrugged his shoulders and followed his wife, or, to speak more accurately, his slave.

Madame de Vandenesse's confidences to Madame du Tillet bore upon so many points of her life during the last six years, that they would be unintelligible without a succinct narrative of the principal events in her history.

Among the notable men who owed their fortunes to the Restoration, and whom, unluckily for itself, it neglected, as in the case of Martignac,* to admit to the secrets of government, was Félix de Vandenesse, who was banished, as were several others, to the Chamber of Peers in the last days of Charles X. This disgrace, although but momentary in his eyes, led him to think upon marriage, toward which he was impelled, as many men are, by a sort of distaste for love affairs, the wild flowers of youth. It is a supreme moment when social life appears in all its gravity. Félix de Vandenesse had been alternately lucky and unlucky, more frequently unlucky than lucky, as all men are who, at their first appearance in society, have encountered love in its most attractive form. Such privileged characters become hard to please. After having made a thorough test of life and compared the characters of many individuals, they reach a point where they are content with an *almost* and take refuge in absolute self-indulgence. They are not deceived because they no longer seek to undeceive themselves, but they resign themselves gracefully; by dint of being prepared for anything, they suffer less. Félix, however, might still be considered one of the most winning and agreeable men in Paris. He had been particularly commended to the favor of the sex by one of the noblest creatures of the age, who died, it is said, of disappointment and of love for him, but his training had been the especial care of the beautiful Lady Dudley. In the opinion of many Parisian women, Félix, a sort of hero of romance, owed many of his conquests to all the hard things that were said of him. Madame de Manerville had brought his adventurous career to a close. Without being a Don Juan, he took his leave of the lover's world as thoroughly disenchanted as he was with the world of politics. He despaired of ever falling in with his ideal of woman and of passion, which, to his undoing, had brightened and dominated his youth. As he approached his thirtieth year, Comte Félix determined to put an end to the ennui of his conquests by marrying. Upon one point his resolution was unalterable: he would take unto himself a young girl reared in the strictest tenets of Catholicism. He needed no other inducement than

263

a knowledge of the Comtesse de Granville's management of her daughters to seek the hand of the older.
He also had been subjected to a mother's despotism;
he remembered enough of his long-suffering boyhood
to discover, despite the dissimulation of feminine modesty, to what condition the maternal yoke had brought
a young girl's heart; whether the heart was disappointed, soured, rebellious, or had remained tranquil and
lovable and ready to give free access to the finer feelings. Tyranny produces two contrary effects, whose
types are found in two great figures from the slavery
of antiquity: Epictetus and Spartacus—hatred and its
accompaniment of evil sentiments, resignation and its
accompaniment of Christ-like meekness and affection.
The Comte de Vandenesse recognized his own image
in Marie-Angélique de Granville. When he took for a
wife an artless, pure, innocent girl, he resolved beforehand, like the "young old man" that he was, to combine
the affection of a father with the affection of a husband.
He felt that his own heart was withered by his experience in society and in politics, and he knew that he was
giving the remains of a worn-out life in exchange for a
blooming, youthful life. He was placing the snows of
winter beside the flowers of spring; the experience of a
graybeard beside sprightly, unreflecting imprudence.
Having made this judicious survey of his position, he
encamped in his conjugal quarters with abundant sup-
plies. Indulgence and confidence were the two anchors
upon which he relied. Mothers of families should seek
such husbands for their daughters; Intelligence is as
trustworthy a protector as the Deity, Disenchantment
as perspicacious as a surgeon, Experience as wary as
a mother. These three qualities are the divine virtues
of marriage. The delicacies and refinements which his
habits as a lady's man and a man of fashion had taught
Félix de Vandenesse, the teachings of high political office, the observations he had made during his whole

life as a man devoted to business, a thinker and a man of letters one after the other, all his powers, in short, were exerted to make his wife happy, and he devoted his whole mind to the task. Upon emerging from the maternal purgatory, Marie-Angélique was suddenly borne aloft to the conjugal paradise Félix had constructed for her on the Rue du Rocher,* in a house where the smallest things had an aristocratic savor, but where the varnish of good society imposed no restraint upon the harmonious good-fellowship for which loving young hearts yearn. In the first place Marie-Angélique enjoyed in their entirety the delights of material life, for her husband during two whole years acted as her intendant. He explained to her gradually and with much skill the meaning of life, initiated her by degrees into the mysteries of good society, taught her the genealogies of all the noble families, described the world to her, instructed her in the art of making her toilette and of conversation, took her from theatre to theatre, and put her through a course of literature and history. He educated her thus with the care of a lover, a father, a teacher and a husband, but with judicious gravity, he so managed her lessons and her recreations as not to destroy her religious sentiments. In short, he acquitted himself of his undertaking like a past master. After four years he had the satisfaction of having made the Comtesse de Vandenesse one of the most agreeable and most noteworthy women of her day. Marie-Angélique's feeling for Félix was precisely that which he desired to inspire: genuine friendship, heartfelt gratitude, and a fraternal love combined with such noble and dignified attachment as should exist between husband and wife. She was a mother, and a good one. Thus Félix bound his wife to himself by every possible tie without seeming to take her by the throat, and he relied for unclouded happiness upon the attractions of habit. Only those men who have been trained in the harsh school of life and have run through the whole gamut of political and amorous disillusionment, possess the science and can conduct themselves as he did. Moreover, he felt the same delight in his work that painters and writers and architects who rear noble structures feel in the creations of their talents; he experienced a twofold enjoyment in carrying on the work and in witnessing its success, in gazing with admiration on his wife, well-informed and artless, clever and natural, lovable and chaste, young girl and mother, perfectly free and yet in chains. The history of happy households is like that of happy peoples: it can be written in two lines and has no literary interest. And so, as happiness can be explained only by itself, the story of these four years contains nothing which is not as soft as the purple hue of undying love, as insipid as manna, and as amusing as the romance of *Astrée.**

In 1833 the edifice of happiness reared by Félix was tottering to its fall, undermined at its foundation, without the slightest suspicion on his part. The heart of the woman of twenty-five is no more identical with the heart of the girl of eighteen than that of the woman of forty is identical with that of the woman of thirty. There are four ages in a woman's life. Each age creates a new woman. Vandenesse was doubtless acquainted with the laws governing these transformations due to our modern code of morals, but he forgot them in his own case, as the most accomplished grammarian may forget the rules of grammar when he writes a book, as the greatest general on the battlefield, under fire, perplexed by the nature of the ground, may forget an invariable rule of the art of war. The man who can give enduring form to his thought by deeds is a man of genius, but the man who has the most genius does not display it at every instant—he would resemble God too closely. After four years of this life without a single heartache, without a word that produced the slightest semblance of discord in this smooth-flowing harmony of sentiment, feeling that she had attained her full development, like a lovely plant in rich soil, beneath the caresses of a glorious sun shining in a sky whose azure is never marred by a cloud, the Comtesse experienced a sort of reaction. This crisis in her life, the subject of this scene, would be incomprehensible without certain elucidations which will perhaps condone, in the eyes of women, the errors of this young countess, no less happy as a wife than as a mother, although she will appear, at first glance, to have had no excuse for them. Life is the result of the play of two contrary principles; when one is lacking the individual suffers. Vandenesse, by anticipating every want, had suppressed Desire, the king of creation, which furnishes occupation for a vast amount of moral force. Extreme heat, extreme misery, perfect happiness, all abstract principles set up their thrones in desert places; they prefer to be alone, they stifle everything that is not themselves. Vandenesse was not a woman, and women alone know the art of imparting variety to felicity, hence their coquetry, their refusals, their fears, their quarrels, and the knowing, entertaining tricks by which they raise difficulties one day about something that offered no obstacle the day before. Men may bore with their constancy, women never. Vandenesse's nature was too entirely kind to permit him wilfully to annoy a wife whom he loved, and he transported her into the bluest, most cloudless infinitude of love. The problem of everlasting beatitude is one of those whose solution is known only to God, in the other world. Here on earth the sublimest poets are forever tiring out their readers by undertaking a description of paradise. The reef upon which Dante came to grief was the same that wrecked Vandenesse; honor to courage in adversity! His wife came at last to be conscious of some monotony in an Eden so perfectly arranged; the unclouded happiness experienced by the first woman in the terrestrial Paradise gave her the same feeling of nausea that the constant use of sweet things always causes in the end, and made the Comtesse long, as Rivarol did upon reading Florian,* to fall in with a wolf in the sheepfold. This has always seemed to be the meaning of the emblematic serpent to which Eve applied, probably from ennui. This reflection will seem rather bold, perhaps, to Protestants, who take Genesis more seriously than the Jews themselves. But the position of Madame de Vandenesse can be explained without biblical metaphors; she felt that there was a vast amount of unemployed force in her heart, her happiness caused her no suffering, it pursued the even tenor of its way without care or anxiety, she did not tremble from the fear of losing it, it appeared every morning with the same clear sky, the same smile, the same pleasant words. The smooth surface of the lake was ruffled by no breath, not even by the zephyr; she would have liked to see an undulation in the mirror-like expanse. There was an indefinable childishness in her longing which might well have served as her excuse, but society is no more indulgent than the God of Genesis. Having learned to use her wits, the Comtesse realized perfectly how disgusting such a feeling must be, and she could not bear the thought of confiding it to her *dear little husband*. In her simplicity she had invented no other pet name than this, for one cannot forge in cold natures the deliciously exaggerated language that love teaches its victims amid the flames. Vandenesse, delighted with his wife's adorable reserve, detained her in the temperate latitudes of conjugal affection by his shrewd devices. Moreover, this model husband found any recourse to trickery, which would have made him greater in her eyes and earned him rewards of the heart, unworthy of a noble soul; he preferred to depend upon his own powers of pleasing, and to owe nothing to the artifices of fortune. The Comtesse Marie smiled when she saw an incomplete or poorly set up equipage in the park; her eyes would complacently return to the clock-like movement of her own horses in their English harness which left them almost free, and each keeping his proper position. Félix never lowered himself so far as to gather up the profits of the trouble he took; in his wife's eyes his love of luxury and his good taste were quite natural; she was not grateful to him for the fact that her self-esteem was not wounded. It was so with everything. Kindness is not without its disadvantages; people attribute it to one's character, and are seldom willing to see in it the secret efforts of a noble heart, while they reward evil-minded men for the harm they do not do. About this time, Madame Félix de Vandenesse reached the point where her education was so far advanced that she could lay aside the role of timid, observing, listening supernumerary which Giulia Grisi played for some time, they say, in the chorus at La Scala.* The young Comtesse felt that she was competent to essay the part of prima donna, and she made several ventures in that direction. To Félix's satisfaction she joined in conversation. Ingenious repartees and shrewd observations, sown in her mind by her intercourse with her husband, drew attention to her, and success made her bold. Vandenesse, whose wife was universally admitted to be beautiful, was delighted when she acquired a reputation for wit. On returning from a ball or a concert or a gathering at which Marie had shone, she would say to Félix with a pleased and deliberate expression, as she was undressing: "Were you satisfied with me tonight?" The Comtesse aroused some jealousy—among others on the part of her husband's sister, the Marquise de Listomère, who had patronized her at first with the idea that she was taking under her wing one who would make an excellent background against which to display her own attractions. A countess named Marie, lovely, intellectual and virtuous, a musician and not a flirt—what a victim for society! There were several women in society with whom Félix de Vandenesse had broken, or who had broken with him, but who were not indifferent to his marriage. When these women found Madame de Vandenesse to be a little bit of a creature with red hands, extremely diffident, with little to say for herself, and apparently little given to thinking, they thought they were sufficiently avenged. The disasters of July 1830 supervened, society was dissolved for two years, people of wealth remained at their estates in the country or traveled in Europe while the agony lasted, and the salons did not reopen much before 1833. The Faubourg Saint-Germain* sulked, but it looked upon some houses, among others the Austrian ambassador's, as neutral ground; legitimist society and the new society met there in the persons of their most fashionable leaders. Attached by a thousand ties of affection and gratitude to the exiled family, but strong in his matured convictions, Vandenesse did not feel called upon to imitate the absurdly extravagant performances of his party. While the danger lasted he did his duty at the risk of his life by making his way through the waves of the populace to propose terms of accommodation; so he took his wife into society where his fidelity could never be brought in question. Vandenesse's former lady friends found it difficult to recognize the young bride in the fashionable, bright, sweet-spoken Comtesse, who reappeared with the most exquisite manners of the female aristocracy. Mesdames d'Espard and De Manerville, Lady Dudley and some others less known were conscious of the awakening of serpents in the recesses of their hearts; they heard the soft hissing of angered pride, they were jealous of Félix's happiness; they would willingly have given their prettiest slippers to have some harm befall him. Instead of showing hostility to the Comtesse, these kind, malicious women thronged about her, were excessively friendly to her, and praised her to the skies to the men. Having no doubt of their real intentions, Félix kept close watch upon their relations with Marie and told her not to trust them. One and all divined the discomfort their dealings caused the Comte, they did not forgive his distrust of them, and they redoubled their attentions and devotion to their rival, who achieved a striking success through their efforts, to the great disgust of the Marquise de Listomère, who did not understand it at all. The Comtesse Félix de Vandenesse was said to be the most fascinating and cleverest woman in Paris. Marie's other sister-in-law, Marquise Charles de Vandenesse, was annoyed again and again by the confusion caused by the identity of names and the comparisons to which it gave rise. Although the Marquise was also a very beautiful and accomplished woman, her sister-in-law's rivals found it easy to make trouble between them because the Comtesse was twelve years younger. These women knew how certain the Comtesse's success was to cause unpleasantness in her relations with her sisters-in-law, who became extremely cold and uncivil to the triumphant Marie-Angélique. These were dangerous allies, intimate enemies. Everyone knows that literature was at that time defending itself against the general indifference born of the political drama, by producing works more or less Byronic which treated of little else than conjugal shortcomings. In those days infractions of the marriage vow were the main support of reviews, books, and the stage. This everlasting subject was never more fashionable. The lover, nightmare of husbands, was everywhere, except perhaps in real life, where he was less in evidence in those days of bourgeois supremacy than ever before. Do thieves select for their walks abroad the time when everybody is running to his window, shouting: "Watch!" and lighting up the street? If, during these years which were so fruitful in municipal, political, and moral agitation, matrimonial catastrophes did happen, they were exceptions and did not attract so much attention as under the Restoration. Nevertheless women talked much among themselves of the subject that then engrossed the two forms of poesy: the Book and the Stage. There was frequent discussion of the lover, that rare and much longed-for creature. Well-known affairs provided fodder for discussion, and these discussions were, as always, sustained by women of irreproachable character. A fact worthy of remark is the repugnance manifested by women who indulge in illicit enjoyment for discussions of this sort; they preserve a modest, reserved, almost timid demeanor in society; they have the air of requesting everyone to be silent, or to forgive them for their stolen pleasure. When, on the other hand, a woman takes delight in hearing of family catastrophes, when she listens to explanations of the joys which justify the culprits, be sure that she is at the crossroads of indecision and does not know which road to take. During that winter the Comtesse de Vandenesse heard the loud voice of society bellowing in her ears, the tempests roared about her. Her pretended friends, who rose above their reputations by virtue of their eminent names and rank, sketched the seductive figure of the lover to her again and again, and poured into her heart burning words about love, the key to the enigma life propounds to womankind, the great passion, according to Madame de Staël, who practised what she preached. When the Comtesse innocently asked, in a small private group, what the difference was between a husband and a lover, one of the women who wanted some misfortune to befall Vandenesse never failed to reply in such a way as to excite her curiosity, put the spur to her imagination, strike at her heart, and interest her mind.

"You exist with your husband, my dear, but you really live only with your lover," said her sister-in-law, the Marquise de Vandenesse.

"Marriage, my child, is our purgatory," said Lady Dudley; "love is paradise."

"Do not believe her," cried Mademoiselle des Touches,

"it is a perfect hell!"

"But it is a hell where one loves," observed the Marquise de Rochefide. "There is often more pleasure in suffering than in happiness; look at the martyrs!"

"With a husband, you little goose, we live our own life, so to speak; but to love is to live in another's life," said the Marquise d'Espard.

"A lover is forbidden fruit, a fact which sums up the whole thing so far as I am concerned," said pretty Moïna de Saint-Héreen, laughingly.

When she was not in attendance upon diplomatic gatherings, or at a ball at the house of some wealthy foreigner, like Lady Dudley or Princess Galathionne, the Comtesse went into society almost every evening after the Italiens or the Opera—to the Marquise d'Espard's, or Madame de Listomère's, or Mademoiselle des Touches's, or the Comtesse de Montcornet's, or the Vicomtesse de Grandlieu's, those being the only aristocratic houses then open, and she never left one of those houses without a few more poisonous seeds having been sown in her heart. They talked to her about *completing her life*—an expression much in vogue at that time; about *being understood*—another expression to which women give extraordinary meanings. She would return home restless, excited, curious and thoughtful. It seemed to her that a vague something had gone from her life, but she did not go so far as to find it a desert.

Among the salons frequented by Madame Félix, the most entertaining, and the most mixed social circle, was to be found at the Comtesse de Montcornet's, a fascinating little woman, who received illustrious artists, kings of finance, and distinguished authors, but only after subjecting them to such severe scrutiny that those who were most exacting in the matter of their associates had no reason to fear that they should meet there anybody of inferior social standing. The most exalted pretensions were free from danger there. During the winter, when society was rallying its forces, several salons, among which were Madame d'Espard's and Madame de Listomère's, Mademoiselle des Touches's and the Duchesse de Grandlieu's, had enlisted recruits among the latest celebrities in art, science, literature, and politics. Society never loses its rights, it always seeks to be entertained. At a concert given by the Comtesse, toward the end of the winter, one of the contemporaneous lights of literature and politics made his appearance in her salon—Raoul Nathan—presented by one of the cleverest but also one of the laziest authors of the age, Émile Blondet, another famous man, but only among his friends: extolled by the journalists, but unknown beyond the barriers. Blondet knew it; moreover, he indulged in no illusions, and among other disdainful remarks he was accustomed to make was this: that fame was a poison that it was well to take in small doses.

From the moment that he fought his way out into the light after a long struggle, Raoul Nathan had profited by the sudden admiration for form manifested by those dandified adulators of the Middle Ages, jocularly called Young France.* He had affected the peculiarities of a man of genius, enrolling himself among those worshipers of art whose intentions, by the way, were excellent, for, although there could be nothing more absurd than the dress of Frenchmen in the nineteenth century, it required courage to reform it. We must do Raoul the justice to say that there is in his person an indefinable something: grand, grotesque, and extraordinary, which requires a frame. His friends and his enemies, and they are about equal in number, agree that nothing could be more in accord with his mind than his body. Raoul Nathan would be more remarkable perhaps in a state of nature than he is with his surroundings. His seamed and wasted face gives him the appearance of having fought with angels or demons; it resembles the face that German painters give the dead Christ: it shows innumerable traces of an unremitting conflict between weak human nature and the powers above. But the deep wrinkles in his cheeks, the indentations on his contorted, furrowed skull, the deep hollows about his eyes and in his temples indicate no weakness of constitution. His hard muscles and prominent bones have a remarkably robust appearance, and although his skin, made sallow by dissipation, clings closely to them as if internal fires had dried and shrunken it, it covers nonetheless a formidable framework. He is tall and thin. His long hair, always disarranged, aims for effect. This unkempt, ill-made Byron has the legs of a heron, swollen knees, an exaggerated swagger, hands strong as a crab's claws, with muscles standing out like whipcord, and thin, nervous fingers.

Raoul Nathan

Plate XIII

He has Napoleonic eyes—blue eyes whose glance pierces the soul; a twisted nose, cunning beyond description; a lovely mouth, embellished with the whitest teeth a woman could ask. There is both fire and animation in his expressions and genius on his brow. Raoul is one of the few men who attract your notice as they pass, and in a salon form a luminous point on which all eyes converge. He attracts attention by his dishevelment, if we may borrow from Molière the word used by Éliante to describe the malpropre sur soi.* His clothes always look as if they had been rumpled and twisted and pulled about for the express purpose of making them harmonize with his countenance. He usually keeps one of his hands in his open waistcoat, in the attitude made famous by Girodet's portrait of Monsieur de Chateaubriand,* but he does it not so much to resemble him—for he prefers not to resemble anybody—as to disarrange the smooth folds of his shirt. His cravat is displaced in an instant by the convulsive movements of his head, which are extraordinarily quick and jerky, like those of purebred horses, fretting under their harness, who toss their heads incessantly in vain endeavors to get rid of the bit or the curb. His long, pointed beard is neither combed nor brushed nor scented nor trimmed, like those of the dandies who wear their beards fan-shaped or trimmed to a point; he leaves it as it is. His hair strays between his coat collar and his cravat, and falls luxuriantly over his shoulders, leaving a greasy mark on the spots it caresses. His dry, sinewy hands are unacquainted with the ministrations of the nail brush and the luxury of the lemon. Several journalists will have it that holy water does not often refresh their calcined skin. In a word, the redoubtable Raoul is a grotesque creature. His movements are jerky as if produced by an imperfect mechanism. His gait runs counter to all ideas of good order, with its enthusiastic zigzags and unexpected pauses which bring him in violent contact with the peaceable bourgeois walking along the boulevards. His conversation, over-flowing with caustic humor and bitter epigrams, copies the movements of his body: it suddenly abandons the revengeful tone and becomes soothing, poetic, consola-tory, and rambling; there are inexplicable pauses, and somersaults of wit which sometimes become weari-some. His manner in society is audaciously awkward, contemptuous of conventions, and he assumes a criti-cal air with regard to everything that society respects, which gives him a bad name with small-minded folk as well as with those who strive to keep alive the old-time doctrines of courtesy, but there is something original about it as there is about Chinese ornaments—some-thing that women do not dislike. Moreover, to them he sometimes displays unwonted affability, and seems to take pleasure in making them forget his outlandish appearance in achieving a victory over their antipathy which flatters his vanity, his self-esteem or his pride. "Why are you like this?" the Marquise de Vandenesse asked him one day. "Are not pearls found in shells?" he replied pompously. To another person who put the same question to him he replied: "If I were attractive to everybody, how could I make myself more so to one chosen individual?" Raoul Nathan carries into his intel-lectual life the disorder he has taken for his ensign. Its announcement is not misleading; his talent resembles that of the poor girls who apply for positions as maid-of-all-work in bourgeois households. He was, first of all, a critic, and a great critic, but he detected fraud in that trade. His articles were worth as much as books, he said. The profits of the stage next fascinated him, but, being incapable of the slow, constant work demanded of a stage manager, he was compelled to become asso-ciated with a vaudevillist, Du Bruel, who put his ideas in shape, and always succeeded in reducing them to productive little plays, running over with wit, and in-variably written for some particular actor or actress.

Between them they discovered Florine, an actress who was a great success at the box office. Humiliated by a partnership resembling that of the Siamese twins, Nathan produced, unaided, at the Théâtre-Français,* a great drama which fell with all the honors of war amid the salvos of crushing newspaper articles. In his younger days he had made an attempt to enrich the great and noble French stage with a magnificent romantic play after the style of *Pinto*, at a time when the classical fad reigned supreme, but there was so much uproar and excitement at the Odéon* for three evenings that the play was prohibited. In the eyes of many people, this second play, like the first, seemed a masterpiece, and won him more reputation than all the more profitable pieces written in collaboration with others—among people whose opinion had little weight, however, namely connoisseurs and men of genuine good taste. "Another such failure," said Émile Blondet, "and you will become immortal." But, instead of pursuing that rocky road, Raoul had from necessity fallen back upon the powder and patches of eighteenth century vaudeville, upon costume plays, and scenic reproductions of successful books. Nevertheless, he was looked upon as a great mind, who had not said his last word. Indeed he had ventured into the loftier realms of literature and had published three novels, without counting those that he kept under lock and key, like fish in an artificial pond. One of these three books—the first, as is the case with many authors who have never succeeded in writing more than one book—was brilliantly successful. This artistic work being rashly assigned the highest rank, he was accustomed to refer to it on all occasions as the finest book of the age, the only novel of the century. He complained loudly, however, of the exigencies of art; he was one of those who were most instrumental in enrolling all forms of artistic production, the picture, the statue, the book, the edifice, under the single banner of Art. He began by putting forth a collection of verses which entitled him to a place in the constellation of poets of the present day, and among which there was one mystical poem that was much admired. Being compelled by his lack of means to earn his living, he wandered from the stage to the press, from the press to the stage, dissipated and extravagant, trusting always to his lucky star. His renown therefore was not unpublished like that of a number of expiring celebrities, kept alive by the titles of forthcoming works, which will not have as many editions as they need markets. Nathan resembled a man of genius, and if he had gone to the scaffold, as he was once seized with a longing to do, he might have struck his hand against his brow after the manner of André de Chénier.* He was attacked by political ambition when he witnessed the irruption into the government of a score of authors, professors, metaphysicians, and historians, who grafted themselves on the machine during the troubles from 1830 to 1833,* and he regretted that he had not written political rather than literary articles. He deemed himself superior to these upstarts, whose elevation aroused consuming jealousy in his heart. He was one of those men who are jealous of everybody and capable of anything, whose triumphs are always stolen from them, and who go stumbling along toward one luminous point after another without establishing themselves at any one, and forever wearing out the good will of their neighbors. At this particular time, he was on his way from Saint-Simonism* to Republicanism, to return, perhaps, to ministerialism. He had his bone to gnaw in every corner, and was on the lookout for a safe place where he could bark at his pleasure, out of the reach of blows, and make himself an object of fear, but he had the humiliation of seeing that he was not taken seriously by the illustrious De Marsay, who was then at the head of the government and had no consideration for authors in whom he could not detect what Richelieu called the spirit of sequence, or, better still, sequence in his ideas. Furthermore, any ministry must have taken into account the constant confusion of Raoul's affairs. Sooner or later, necessity would bring him to the point where he must submit to conditions instead of imposing them. Raoul's real but sedulously hidden character is in accord with his public performance. He is an actor in good faith, as self-satisfied as if the State were *he*, and a very clever declaimer. No one knows better than he how to feign sentiment, to pride himself upon false grandeur, to deck himself out with fine moral aphorisms, to maintain his dignity in words, and to pose as an Alceste while adopting the methods of a Philinte.* His selfishness trots along, protected by this armor of painted pasteboard, and often attains the secret goal at which it aims. Slothful to the last degree, he has never done anything except when goaded by the spear points of necessity. He knows nothing of the unremitting toil necessarily expended upon the creation of a monument, but in the paroxysm of rage brought on by a wound inflicted upon his vanity, or at a crisis precipitated by a creditor, he leaps the Eurotas,* he triumphs over the deepest deficiencies of the spirit. Then, worn out and amazed to find that he has really created something, he falls back into the slough of Parisian dissipation. His necessities become alarming; he has expended all his strength, so he descends from his high estate and compromises himself. Induced by a mistaken idea of his own grandeur and his future, which he measures by the exalted fortune of an old comrade of his, one of the few men with a genius for administration brought to light by the Revolution of July, he so far demeans himself, in order to get clear of the difficulty, as to play unconscionable tricks upon people who are attached to him—tricks that are buried in the mysteries of private life, and of which no one ever speaks or complains. The frivolity of his heart, the effrontery of the grasp of his hand, in which are gathered all the vices, unhappiness, and treachery in every guise, and every shade of opinion, have made him as inviolable as a constitutional king. The venial sin, which would raise a hue and cry at the heels of a man of high character, is of no consequence in him; an indelicacy is almost nothing, and everybody makes excuses for himself by excusing him. The very man who might be tempted to despise him offers him his hand, fearing that he may need him. He has so many friends that he longs for foes. His apparent good-fellowship, which attracts newcomers and interferes with no act of treachery, which takes great liberties and justifies everything, which cries aloud at an injury and forgives it, is one of the distinguishing characteristics of the journalist. This *camaraderie*, a word invented by a bright man, corrodes the noblest hearts; it eats away their pride, destroys the active principle of great exploits, and makes of mental cowardice a sacred thing. By exacting this pliability of conscience from everybody, certain people seek to obtain absolution for their own treachery and backsliding. That is how the most enlightened portion of a nation may become the least estimable. From a literary standpoint Nathan lacks style and thoroughness. Like the majority of young men ambitious of literary renown, he disgorges today what he learned yesterday. He has neither the time nor the patience to write; he has not been an observant man, but he listens well. Incapable of constructing a vigorous, well-knit plot, he saves his reputation perhaps by the fervid enthusiasm of his sketch. He plays at passion—to use a bit of literary slang—because in genuine passion everything is true, while it is the mission of genius to seek among the chance developments of the true for what is likely to seem probable to everybody. Instead of awakening novel ideas, his heroes are simply exaggerated personalities, who arouse only momentary sympathy; they have no relation to the important interests of life, and for that reason they represent nothing, but he maintains his position by the rapid working of his mind, by those lucky hits which billiard players call flukes. None so skilful as he, at shooting on the wing, the ideas that hover over Paris or that Paris beats up. His fertility is not his own, but the time's: he lives upon passing events, and, in order to control them, stretches them too far. In short, he is not genuine; his words are false; there is, as Comte Félix said, something of the sleight-of-hand artist about him. We can feel that his pen gets its ink in an actress's closet. Nathan is a fair type of the literary youth of today, its fictitious grandeur and its real misery; he represents it with its faulty beauty and its crushing failures, its life of foaming torrents, sudden reverses, unhoped-for triumphs. He is the true child of this jealousy-ridden age, when innumerable rivalries under the cover of projects of all sorts are nourishing for their own benefit the hydra of anarchy, born of all their errors—the age which seeks fortune without labor, glory without talent, success without strife, but which, after many rebellions and many skirmishes, its vices are forcing to trim down the Budget at the pleasure of Power. When so many youthful ambitions set out on foot, and are all bound for the same point, there is a constant clashing of wills, incredible suffering, desperate strife. In this ghastly struggle, the most violent or the most wary egoism gains the victory. The example thus set is envied, justified despite all the outcry, as Molière would say: one follows it. When Raoul made his appearance in Madame de Montcornet's salon in the capacity of an enemy of the new dynasty, his apparent grandeur was in a flourishing condition. He was accepted as the political critic of the De Marsays, the Rastignacs, the La Roche-Hugons, who formed the government. Émile Blondet, Nathan's sponsor, always the victim of his fatal hesitation and of his repugnance to do anything that concerned himself alone, was still playing the role of scoffer, took sides with nobody and was on good terms with everybody. He was Raoul's friend, Rastignac's friend, Montcornet's friend. "You are a political triangle," a laughing De Marsay once said to him when he met him at the Opera, "that particular geometrical figure is suitable only for God, who has nothing to do, but ambitious men should always follow a curved line, the shortest road in politics." Seen at a distance, Raoul Nathan was a very striking meteor. Fashion authorized his manners and his apparel. His borrowed Republicanism gave him for the moment the Jansenist asperity assumed by the defenders of the popular cause—at whom he sneered internally—and which is not without a certain fascination in a woman's eyes. Women love to perform miracles, to crush stones, to melt natures that seem to be of bronze. Thus Raoul's moral attire was at this time in harmony with his bodily garb. He was fitted to be and was, for the Eve wearied of her paradise on the Rue du Rocher, the glistening, many-hued serpent—he of the honeyed words, magnetic eyes, and graceful motions, who destroyed the first woman. As soon as the Comtesse Marie's eyes fell upon Raoul, she was conscious of an internal commotion so violent as almost to terrify her. This pseudo-great man, by his glance alone, exerted a physical influence upon her that reached to her heart and caused a turmoil there. The turmoil affected her pleasantly. The purple cloak that fame threw for a moment over Nathan's shoulder dazzled the guileless creature. When the time for serving tea arrived, Marie left the place where she had been sitting with several ladies who were busily talking; she was disturbing herself about this extraordinary being. Her silence was noticed by her pretended friends. She approached the square divan in the centre of the salon where Raoul was holding forth. She remained standing, leaning on the arm of Madame Octave de Camps, a dear, good woman, who never breathed a word as to the involuntary trembling that betrayed her intense excitement. Although the eye of a woman in love or taken by surprise allows glances of incredible sweetness to escape it, Raoul was discharging at that moment a veritable shower of fireworks; he was too much engrossed by his epigrams which went off like bombs, by his accusations, darting hither and thither like spluttering suns, by the flaming portraits he was drawing in fiery strokes, to remark the artless admiration of a poor little Eve, hidden in the group of women that surrounded him. Such curiosity as theirs, the counterpart of that which would cause all Paris to rush to the Jardin-des-Plantes to see a unicorn if one should be found in the famous Mountains of the Moon,* still untrodden by European feet—such curiosity intoxicates second-rate minds as much as it saddens the truly lofty-minded, but it enchanted Raoul; he was therefore too devoted to all the ladies to be devoted to a single one.

"Take care, my dear," whispered Marie's kind, thoughtful companion, "you had better go."

The Comtesse looked at her husband to ask him for his arm with one of the glances husbands do not always understand: Félix took her away.

"My dear boy," said Madame d'Espard in Raoul's ear, "you are a lucky rascal. You have made more than one conquest tonight, and among others, the charming woman who left us so abruptly."

"What do you suppose the Marquise d'Espard undertook to tell me?" Raoul asked Blondet, repeating the great lady's remark to him when they were almost alone, between one and two o'clock in the morning.

"Why, I heard that the Comtesse de Vandenesse had fallen madly in love with you. You are not to be pitied."

"I did not see her," said Raoul.

"Oh! You will see her, you rascal," said Blondet, roaring with laughter. "Lady Dudley made you promise to go to her great ball so that you may meet her."

Raoul and Blondet left the house with Rastignac, who offered them seats in his carriage. All three laughed heartily at the idea of an eclectic under secretary of state in company with a ferocious Republican and a political atheist.

"Suppose we take supper at the expense of the existing order of things?" suggested Blondet, who wished to restore suppers to favor.

Rastignac took them to Véry's,* sent away his carriage, and they took their seats around the festive board, analyzing society as it is today, and laughing with Rabelaisian glee. In the course of the supper, Rastignac and Blondet advised their supposititious foe not to neglect such a capital opportunity as was offered him. The two rakes gave him a satirical sketch of Marie de Vandenesse's history: with the scalpel of the epigram and the keen point of the bon mot they dissected her innocent childhood, her happy married life. Blondet congratulated Raoul upon having met a woman who was as yet guilty of nothing worse than wretched drawings in red chalk, paltry watercolor landscapes, slippers embroidered for her husband, and sonatas executed with the purest intentions; tied for eighteen years to her mother's petticoat, preserved in religious ceremonial, dressed by Vandenesse, and cooked to a turn by marriage, to be tasted by love. At the third bottle of champagne, Raoul Nathan became more communicative than he had ever been with anybody.

"My friends," said he, "you know my relations with Florine, you know what my life is, and you will not be surprised to hear my confession that I have absolutely no idea of the color of a countess's love. I have often felt deeply humiliated to think that I could not take to myself a Beatrice or a Laura* except in poetry! A pure, noble woman is like an unsullied conscience which shows us to ourselves in attractive guise. We may sully ourselves, you know, but with such a woman we remain great and proud and immaculate. We lead wild lives, but with such a woman we find tranquillity and refreshment and the verdure of the oasis."

"Come, come, my boy," said Rastignac, "give us the prayer of *Moïse** on the fourth string, à la Paganini."

Raoul sat silent, his eyes staring into vacancy.

"This low-lived minister's apprentice does not understand me," he said, after a pause.

Thus, while the poor Eve of the Rue du Rocher lay between the swaddling clothes of humiliation, terrified at the thought of the pleasure with which she had listened to this sham great poet, and hesitating between the stern voice of her gratitude to Vandenesse and the honeyed words of the serpent, these three shameless wits were trampling on the tender, white flowers of her nascent love. Ah! If women but knew what a cynical tone these men, who are so patient and wheedling in their presence, adopt when they are out of sight, how they would mock at what they now adore! How they tore the blooming, fascinating, modest creature to pieces and analyzed her in their facetious way! But what a triumph for her, too! The more veils she lost, the more beauties she disclosed.

Marie at that moment was comparing Raoul to Félix, with no suspicion of the risk run by the heart in drawing such parallels. No two men in the world afforded a more striking contrast than the powerful, dishevelled Raoul and Félix de Vandenesse, curled and combed like any dandy, arrayed in clothes of faultless cut, endowed with charming *disinvoltura*,* a disciple of the English school of elegance to which Lady Dudley had long ago admitted him. Such a contrast pleases the imagination of women who are sufficiently interested to pass from one extreme to the other. The Comtesse, a virtuous and pious woman, forbade herself to think of Raoul, accusing herself the next day, in her paradise, of being a detestably ungrateful creature.

"What do you think of Raoul Nathan?" she asked her husband at breakfast.

"A mere sleight-of-hand performer," was the Comte's reply; "one of those volcanoes that can be made to subside with a little gold dust. The Comtesse de Montcornet did wrong to admit him to her house." This reply was the more crushing to Marie in that Félix, who was thoroughly posted in literary matters, supported his opinion by proofs, relating what he knew of Raoul Nathan's hand-to-mouth life, bound up with that of Florine, a famous actress. "If the man has genius," he concluded, "he has neither the application nor the patience which consecrate it and make it a divine thing. He tries to impose upon society by placing himself on a level where he cannot maintain himself. Men of genuine talent— studious, honorable men—do not do as he does; they go their way courageously, accept their poverty, and do not cover it up with tinsel."

A woman's mind is endowed with incredible elasticity: when it receives a stunning blow, it bends, seems utterly crushed, and soon resumes its original shape. "Félix is right, of course," the Comtesse said to herself at first. But three days later she was thinking of the serpent once more, led back to him by the sweet, yet painful emotion Raoul had awakened in her, and which Vandenesse had been foolish enough never to cause her to feel. The Comte and Comtesse went to Lady Dudley's great ball, at which De Marsay made his last appearance in society, for he died two months later, leaving behind him the reputation of a most eminent statesman, whose capacity, said Blondet, was past comprehension. Vandenesse and his wife found Raoul Nathan in that assemblage, which was particularly remarkable for the presence of several characters in the political drama of the day who were much surprised to find themselves together. It was one of the first solemn functions in high society. The salons presented a magic spectacle; flowers, diamonds, gorgeous headgear, all the emptied jewel cases, all the resources of the toilette brought under contribution. The whole might be compared to one of those artistic hothouses in which wealthy horticulturists collect the loveliest exotics. Here was the same brilliancy of color, the same delicacy of tissue. Human handicraft seemed eager for the conflict with animate works of nature. On all sides were gauzes, white or colored like the wings of the loveliest of dragonflies, crêpes, laces, silks, tulles as many-hued as the caprices of nature in bird life, pinked and waved and flounced, gold and silver spiders' webs, waving mists of silk, flowers embroidered by fairies or brought to perfection by imprisoned genii, feathers dyed by the fierce tropical sun waving like weeping willows over haughty heads, strings of pearls woven into mats, and dress stuffs smooth and rough and ribbed, as if the genius of arabesques had acted as adviser to the French manufacturers. This magnificence was in harmony with the beautiful women assembled there as if to form a keepsake. The eye beheld the whitest of shoulders, some of the hue of amber, others so glossy that it seemed as if they must have been passed between heavy cylinders, these with the sheen of satin, those dead-white and plump as if Rubens had prepared the paste—in short, all the variations of white known to mankind. There were eyes that sparkled like the onyx or the turquoise, bordered with black velvet or with a fringe of long, blonde lashes; faces of many shapes which recalled the most attractive types of the different countries; foreheads sublime and majestic, or with a graceful outward curve as if thought abounded there, or flat as if resistance unsubdued were there enthroned, and then, the thing that adds so much to the attractiveness of a fete designed for show, there were breasts that overlay each other as George IV liked them, or separated after the fashion of the eighteenth century, or with a tendency to draw near each other, as Louis XV preferred them, but exhibited without shame and without covering, except perhaps one of the pretty little ruffled tuckers to be seen in Raphael's portraits, the triumph of his patient pupils. The prettiest of feet tensed for the dance, waists abandoned to the waltzer's arm, stimulated the attention of the most indifferent. The melodious hum of sweetest voices, the rustling of dresses, the murmurs of the contradanse, the rhythmic beat of the waltz furnished a fantastic accompaniment to the music. It seemed as if a fairy's wand must have called into being this scene of overpowering witchery, this melody of sweet odors, the lights that were reflected in all the colors of the rainbow in the crystal sconces where the candles twinkled, and the pictures multiplied by the mirrors. This throng of lovely women and lovely clothes stood out in bold relief against the black mass of the men, where the blonde moustaches and serious faces of the English were mingled with the clean-cut, refined, classic profiles of the nobles, and the gracious countenances of the French aristocracy. All the orders of Europe gleamed upon their breasts, hanging about their necks, worn like a sautoir, or falling at the hip. To one who closely scrutinized this great assemblage, it not only presented the brilliant hues of magnificent attire—it had a soul, it lived and thought and felt. Hidden passions imparted to it features of its own: you would have seen malevolent glances exchanged, giddy, inquisitive young girls in white betraying a desire, jealous women wagging their evil tongues behind their fans or paying one another fulsome compliments. Society—arrayed, curled, and perfumed—indulged in a festive frenzy that went to the brain like an intoxicating vapor. It was as if from every brain, as from every heart, emotions and ideas found vent, and were condensed into a solid mass which reacted upon the least imaginative persons and excited them. At the moment when the animation of this soul-stirring festivity was at its height, in a corner of the gilded salon where one or two bankers, ambassadors, former ministers, and wicked old Lord Dudley, whose presence was accidental, were playing cards, Madame Félix de Vandenesse was irresistibly impelled to enter into conversation with Nathan. It may be that she fell a victim to the ballroom intoxication which has often extorted confessions from the most discreet women.

At the sight of this festive throng and the splendors of a world to which he had never before been admitted, Nathan's ambition redoubled and gnawed at his heart. When he looked upon Rastignac, whose younger brother had just been appointed bishop at twenty-seven years of age, whose brother-in-law, Martial de la Roche-Hugon, was in the ministry, and who was himself an undersecretary of state and was to marry, so rumor had it, the Baron de Nucingen's only daughter; when he saw in the diplomatic corps an unknown scribbler who translated foreign newspapers for a journal that had come over to the new dynasty in 1830; when he saw editorial writers admitted to the Council of State,* professors made Peers of France, he sadly concluded that he was on the wrong tack preaching the overthrow of this aristocracy where fortunate talents shone, and speeches were crowned by success and genuine superiority. Blondet, who was so unfortunate, so thoroughly worked out in journalism, but so well received at that house—he could still, if he chose, make a fresh start on the road to fortune as a result of his liaison with Madame de Montcornet—was in Nathan's eyes a striking example of the power of social connections. Deep down in his heart he determined to snap his fingers at opinions after the fashion of the De Marsays, Rastignacs and Blondets, and of Talleyrand,* the leader of the sect; to accept nothing but facts; to twist them to serve his own purposes, to see in every scheme a weapon, and not to disturb so well-constituted, attractive, and natural a society. "My future," he said to himself, "depends upon a woman who belongs to this circle." Acting upon this thought, conceived in the flames of a frenzied desire, he fell upon the Comtesse de Vandenesse like a vulture upon its prey. The charming creature, so pretty in her headdress of marabou feathers which produced the deliciously *soft* effect of Lawrence's paintings,* quite in harmony with her sweet disposition, was carried away by the ambition-mad poet's seething energy. Lady Dudley, whom nothing escaped, shielded this *aside* by handing the Comte de Vandenesse over to Madame de Manerville. This lady, strong in her former ascendancy, steered Félix out upon the broad waters of a quarrel accompanied with much enticement, with whispered confidences embellished by blushes, with regrets shrewdly tossed at his feet like flowers, and with recriminations whereby she put herself in the right for the sake of being put in the wrong. These two disunited lovers spoke for the first time from ear to ear. While her husband's former mistress was digging among the ashes of extinct pleasures, trying to find a few live coals there, Madame Félix de Vandenesse was experiencing the violent palpitations of the heart caused by a woman's certainty that she is doing wrong and is treading on forbidden ground: emotions which are not without charm and which awaken many slumbering powers; today, as in the tale of Bluebeard, all women love to use the blood-stained key, a magnificent mythological idea, one of the glories of Perrault.

The sorry dramatist, who knew his Shakespeare thoroughly, unfolded his wretchedness, described his struggle with men and things, hinted at his baseless greatness, his unsuspected genius for politics, his life which contained no lofty sentiment. Without expressing it in words, he suggested to this charming creature the idea of playing for him the sublime role played by Rebecca in *Ivanhoe*: of loving and shielding him. The whole interview was carried on in the ethereal regions of sentiment. The myosotis is no bluer, the lily is no purer, the brow of the seraph no fairer than were the images, the words and the animated, radiant brow of this artist, who might have sent his conversation to his publisher. He played his role of reptile to perfection, he dangled before the Comtesse's eyes the brilliant colors of the fatal apple. Marie left the ball suffering from remorse that was akin to hope, tickled by compliments that flattered her vanity, moved to the deepest recesses of her heart, entrapped by her very virtues, seduced by her pity for misfortune.

Perhaps Madame de Manerville had guided Vandenesse to the salon where his wife was talking with Nathan; perhaps he had been there of his own motion, looking for Marie to take her home; perhaps his conversation had given new life to deadened chagrin. However that may be, when she went to him to ask him for his arm, his wife found him in a reverie, with clouded brow. The Comtesse feared that she had been seen. As soon as she was alone in the carriage with Félix, she bestowed her most coaxing smile upon him and said: "Were you not talking with Madame de Manerville, my dear?" Félix had not emerged from the underbrush into which his wife led him by a delicious little quarrel on that theme when the carriage drove into their courtyard. It was the first stratagem dictated by love. Marie was overjoyed with her triumph over the man who had hitherto seemed so superior to her. She tasted the first thrill of delight afforded by indispensable success.

In a passageway between the Rue Basse-du-Rempart* and the Rue Neuve-des-Mathurins, on the third floor of a narrow, ugly house, Raoul had a small, comfortless, bare, uninviting suite of rooms, where his home was for the general public, for literary neophytes, for his creditors, and for the different varieties of pests and bores who should be kept at the threshold of a man's private life. His real domicile, the scene of his grandeur, the stage upon which he acted, was at Mademoiselle Florine's, a second-rate actress to whom Nathan's friends, certain newspapers, and some few authors had for ten years past awarded a place among illustrious artists. For ten years Raoul had been so closely attached to this woman that he passed half his life with her; he took his meals there when he had no friend to entertain and no invitation to dine out. Florine combined absolutely corrupt morals with exquisite wit, which constant dealings with artists had developed, and which became keener every day. Wit is supposed to be a rare accomplishment among actors. It is so natural to suppose that people who spend their lives displaying everything on the outside have nothing within! But, if we consider the small number of actors and actresses in every generation, and the multitude of dramatic authors and fascinating women these people have furnished, it is easy to refute that opinion, which is founded upon a criticism everlastingly made upon dramatic artists, who are charged, one and all, with losing sight of their personal feelings in the mechanical expression of the passions, whereas they really employ no other forces than those of wit, memory, and imagination. Great artists, as Napoléon said, are beings who intercept at will the communication established by nature between the feelings and the thought. Molière and Talma* in their old age were more amorous than the average man. Compelled to listen to journalists who divine everything by calculation, to authors who foresee and talk about everything, and to watch certain political characters, who made the most of every sally he heard in her salon, Florine presented a combination of angel and devil which made her worthy to receive these rakes; she enchanted them by her sang-froid. Her abnormal qualities of mind and heart pleased them beyond description. Her house, enriched by tributes from her lovers, was furnished with the exaggerated magnificence characteristic of women who care little for the price of things, but only for the things themselves, and estimate their value by their caprice—who in a fit of rage shatter a fan or a vinaigrette a queen might envy, but raise an uproar if you break a porcelain dish worth ten francs, out of which their little dogs lap. Her dining room, filled to overflowing with the choicest offerings, will serve to convey an idea of the chaotic aspect of this disdainful, royal magnificence. Everywhere, even on the ceiling, was a carved wainscoting of natural oak, relieved by mouldings of unburnished gold, the panels framed with children playing with chimeras, in which lights twinkled, shining here upon a sketch by Decamps, there upon a plaster angel holding a *bénitier* presented by Antonin Moine; farther on, a dainty picture by Eugène Devéria, the sombre figure of a Spanish alchemist by Louis Boulanger, an autographed letter from Lord Byron to Caroline in an ebony frame carved by Elschoët;* opposite, a letter from Napoléon to Joséphine. All this arranged with no attempt at symmetry, but with imperceptible art. One's wits were taken by surprise, as it were. There was a touch of coquetry and a free-and-easy air, two qualities which are found together only in an artist's quarters. Upon the beautifully carved wooden mantelpiece there was nothing but a curious Florentine statue of ivory, attributed to Michelangelo, representing Pan finding a woman in the dress of a young shepherd, the original of which is in the Treasury at Vienna; on each side were torch holders carved by some chisel of the Renaissance. A Boule clock,* upon a tortoiseshell pedestal incrusted with arabesques of copper, glistened in the centre of a panel, between two statuettes escaped from some dismantled abbey. In the corners, lamps of regal magnificence burned upon their pedestals, by which some manufacturer had paid for a few resounding advertisements as to the necessity of having lamps perfectly fitted to Japanese vases. Upon a marvelous étagère was paraded a valuable service of plate doughtily won in battle where some English lord had acknowledged the ascendancy of the French nation; there too, were porcelain ornaments with raised figures; in short, the exquisite luxury of the artist who has no other capital than her furniture. The violet chamber was like the dream of a ballet dancer at her debut: velvet curtains lined with satin and draped over a misty veil of tulle; a ceiling of white cashmere with raised figures in violet satin; at the foot of the bed, a rug of ermine; in the bed, whose curtains were like a lily turned upside down, was a lantern by which to read the newspapers before the public saw them. A yellow salon, embellished with ornaments of the color of Florentine bronze, was in perfect harmony with all this splendor, but an exact description would make these pages resemble the announcement of a sale by judicial decree. To find the like of all these lovely things one must have gone a few steps away, to Rothschild's.

Sophie Grignoult, christened Florine by a process of baptism not unusual on the stage, made her first appearances at second-rate theatres, notwithstanding her beauty. Her success and her fortune she owed to Raoul Nathan. The close association of these two destinies, which is not of rare occurrence in the dramatic and literary world, in no way injured Raoul, who observed the proprieties like a man of excellent judgment. But there was no stability to Florine's fortune. Her uncertain income depended upon her engagements and her vacations, and barely paid for her clothes and her housekeeping. Nathan contributed some small sums levied upon new industrial enterprises, but, although he was always gallant to her and took care of her, there was nothing regular or certain about his patronage. This uncertainty, this life in the air, did not terrify Florine. Florine believed in her talent, she believed in her beauty. Her robust faith had something comical in it to those who heard her mortgage her future thereon when they ventured to remonstrate with her. "I shall have annuities when it suits my pleasure to have them," she would say. "I have fifty francs in the funds already." No one understood how she could have been neglected for seven years, lovely as she was, but the fact is that Florine was employed as a bit player at thirteen, and made her debut at an obscure theatre on the boulevards two years later. At fifteen, neither beauty nor talent exists; a woman is all promise. At the time of which we are writing she was twenty-eight, the age at which a French woman's beauty is at its height. What painters noticed first of all about Florine was a pair of lustrous white shoulders, with an olive tinge about the base of the neck, but hard and smooth; the light was reflected in them as in watered silk. When she turned her head, magnificent folds, the admiration of sculptors, were formed in her neck. Upon that magnificent neck was perched the little head of a Roman empress, the well-poised, graceful, delicate, wilful head of Poppaea,* intelligent, regular features, the smooth brow of the unreflecting woman who banishes care, but who can also be as obstinate as a mule and at such times will listen to nothing. This brow of hers, which seemed to have been fashioned with a single blow of the chisel, displayed to the best advantage her lovely chestnut hair which was almost always raised in front in two masses of equal height, *à la Romaine*, and arranged in a knot behind the head to give the head an appearance of greater length, and to relieve the whiteness of the neck by its color. Delicate black eyebrows, drawn by some Chinese painter, framed a pair of soft eyes with a network of pink blood vessels. Her pupils, blazing with vivid light, but marked with brown stripes like a tiger's skin, gave to her glance the cruel fixity of a wild beast's, and revealed the cool cunning of the courtesan. Her adorable gazelle-like eyes were of a beautiful gray, fringed with long black lashes, a charming contrast which made still more apparent their expression of watchful, calm licentiousness; there were black rings that told of weariness, but the artistic way in which she could roll the pupil into the corner or to the top of her eye, to watch or to assume an air of meditation, her manner of keeping it perfectly still and causing it to gleam its brightest without moving her head or disturbing the immobility of her countenance—a trick learned on the stage—and the animation of her gaze when it seemed to embrace a whole great hall as she looked about in search of some person, made hers the most terrible, the softest and the most extraordinary eyes in the world. Rouge had destroyed the delicious, transparent coloring of her cheeks, whose flesh was very delicate, but, if she could no longer blush or turn pale, she had a slender nose, intersected by passionate pink nostrils, made to express the irony and the mockery of Molière's servants. Her sensual, dissipated mouth was embellished by the ridges of the furrow that attached the upper lip to the nose. Her white chin, somewhat coarse in outline, indicated the violence of her passions. Her hands and arms were worthy of a queen. But she had the short, thick foot which is an indelible sign of obscure birth. Never did inheritance cause more anxiety. Florine had tried everything, except amputation, to change it. Her feet were as obstinate as the Bretons to whom she owed her birth; they resisted all the professors, all varieties of treatment. She wore long shoes stuffed with cotton inside to make it appear that she had a curving instep. She was of medium height, threatened with plumpness, but erect and well-made. Morally speaking, she was thoroughly at home in all the pretty tricks and petty quarrels, the condiments and sweetmeats of her trade; she imparted a particularly delicious flavor to them when she played the child and interjected bits of mischievous philosophy in the midst of her innocent laughter. Apparently ignorant and frivolous, she was very strong in figures and in all the details of commercial jurisprudence. She had descended from stage to stage before the dawning of her precarious success! She knew life in all its forms, from that which begins with Brie to that which toys disdainfully with pineapple fritters; from that which cooks and washes in the chimney corner of an attic with a clay oven to that which summons the ban and arriere-ban of pot-bellied chefs and impudent scullions. She had kept her credit in repair without killing it. She knew all about the things that honest women know nothing of, she spoke all languages; she was of the People by virtue of her experience, and Noble by virtue of her distinguished beauty. It was difficult to take her by surprise, for she always imagined everything, as a spy does, or a judge, or an old statesman, and thus was able to see into everything. She knew what method to adopt with tradespeople and their wiles, she knew the value of things as well as a professional appraiser. When she was stretched out in her long chair, like a fair and blooming young bride, holding her lines in her hand and committing them to memory, you would have said she was a child of sixteen, artless and ignorant and weak, without other artifice than her innocence. But let an importunate creditor appear, she would sit up like a startled fawn and swear a good round oath. "Look here, my dear man! Your impertinence is a high rate of interest to pay for the money I owe you," she would say; "I am tired of seeing you; send me some bailiffs, I prefer them to your idiotic face!"

Florine gave delightful dinners, concerts, and very popular evening parties, where the gambling was fast and furious. Her friends of her own sex were all beautiful. No old woman was ever seen under her roof; she was an entire stranger to jealousy and looked upon it as an admission of inferiority. She had known Coralie and La Torpille, she knew the Tullias, Euphrasie, the Aquilinas, Madame du Val-Noble, Mariette—the women who pass through Paris like the gossamer threads that float about in the air, without anyone knowing from whence they come or whither they go—queens today, slaves tomorrow, and the actresses too, her rivals, and the singers, in short, all the unconventional female society, good-humored, and attractive in its recklessness, whose Bohemian existence absorbs all those who allow themselves to be drawn into the mad whirl of its impetuosity and fervor and its contempt for the future. Although the Bohemian mode of life with all its lack of order held sway in her house, encouraged by the cheery laughter of the actress, the queen of the salon had ten fingers of her own and knew how to count better than any of her guests. There were held the secret saturnalia of literature and art combined with politics and finance. There Desire reigned supreme; there, Spleen and Caprice were held as sacred as honor and virtue in a bourgeois household. To that place came Blondet, Finot, Étienne Lousteau, her seventh lover and supposed to be the first, Félicien Vernou, the newspaper writer, Couture, Bixiou, Rastignac at an earlier period, Claude Vignon the critic, Nucingen the banker, Du Tillet, Conti the composer, in brief, the whole devil-ridden legion of the most pitiless schemers of every sort; then there were the friends of the singers, dancers and actresses whom Florine knew. All these people loved or hated one another according to circumstances. This house of common resort, where celebrity in some direction was sufficient to entitle any one to admission, was, as it were, the brothel of wit, the galleys of intelligence; no one could enter there who had not stolen his fortune by legal means, or lived through ten years of poverty, or slaughtered two or three passions, or acquired celebrity of some sort by his books or his waistcoats, by a drama or a handsome turnout. Base plots were hatched there, and ways of making money eagerly sought; they laughed at the disturbances they had fomented the day before, and weighed the chances of a rise or fall in the funds. Every man, on leaving the house, resumed the livery of his opinions, but there he could, without compromising himself, criticize his own party, admit the science and skilful play of his opponents, formulate thoughts which no one avows—say anything, in short, with the air of a man who could do anything. Paris is the only place in the world where such eclectic houses as this exist, houses where every taste, every vice, every opinion is made welcome with an appearance of decency. It cannot be said either, that Florine is still a second-rate actress. Her life is not idle or to be envied. Many people, misled by the magnificent pedestal upon which the Theatre places a woman, fancy that her life is as joyous as a perpetual carnival. In many a porter's lodge, under the eaves of more than one attic, poor creatures, returning from the play, dream of pearls and diamonds, of gold-threaded dresses with sumptuous corded belts; they seem to see themselves with jewels shining in their hair, they fancy themselves applauded, purchased, worshipped, removed from their surroundings—but they know nothing of the realities of this life of a riding school horse, in which the actress is required to attend rehearsals under penalty of a fine, to listen to the reading of plays, and constantly to study new parts, at a time when two or three hundred plays a year are produced in Paris. Florine has to change her costume two or three times during every performance, and is often completely exhausted, half-dead, when she returns to her dressing room. Then she is obliged to remove the red or white paint by profuse applications of cosmetic, and to wash off the powder if she has been playing an eighteenth-century part. She has hardly had time to dine. When she is playing, an actress can neither dress, nor eat, nor speak. Florine no longer has time for dinner parties. When she returns home after one of the performances which, in these days of ours, end the next day, does she not have to make her toilette for the night and to give her orders for the next day? After going to bed at one or two o'clock in the morning, she must rise sufficiently early to look over her lines, select her costumes, inspect them, and try them on; then breakfast, read her billets-doux, answer them, labor with the stage managers for applause, to be sure that her entrances and exits are properly looked after, and settle the account for the triumphs of the past month while purchasing in bulk those of the current one. In the time of Saint-Genest, a canonized actor, who fulfilled his religious duties and wore a hair shirt,* it is fair to suppose that the Theater did not demand such ferocious activity.

Là venaient Blondet, Finot, Étienne Lousteau ... Bixiou, Félicien Vernou.

Plate XIV

Florine is often obliged to say she is sick in order to be able to go into the country, bourgeois fashion, to pick wild flowers. But these purely mechanical occupations are nothing at all in comparison with the scheming to be carried on, the mortifications of wounded vanity, the preferences accorded by authors, roles taken away or forced upon one, the exacting demands of actors, the malice of a rival, the fusillade of managers and newspaper critics who demand that two days' work be done in one. Hitherto there has been no thought of art, of the expression of the passions, of the details of mimicry, of the essential requirements of the stage, where the blemishes that mar every manifestation of splendor are revealed by thousands of opera glasses—requirements that Talma, Lekain, Baron, Contat, Clairon, Champmeslé* devoted their thoughts and their lives to satisfying. In those infernal wings, self-esteem has no sex; the triumphant artist, man or woman, finds men and women against him. As regards fortune, though Florine could command a reasonably large salary, it did not cover the cost of her stage toilette, which, to say nothing of costumes, required an enormous supply of shoes and long gloves, and included both evening dresses and street dresses. One-third of an actress's life is passed in begging, another in maintaining herself, and the last in defending herself: it is all work. If happiness is enjoyed with great gusto when it comes to such lives, it is because it is stolen, as it were, rarely attained, long hoped for, and found at last by chance amid hateful counterfeited pleasures and smiles at the pit. To Florine, Raoul's power was like a protecting sceptre: he spared her much ennui and much anxiety, as the great nobles did for their mistresses in the old days, and like some old men today, who run and throw themselves at the feet of the critics when a word in some petty newspaper has alarmed their idol. She clung to him more than to a lover, she clung to him as to a pillar of strength, she cared for him as if he were her father, she deceived him as if he were her husband, but she would have sacrificed all for him. Raoul could do everything for her vanity as an actress, for the tranquillity of her self-esteem, for her future on the stage. Without the intervention of a great author, no great actress—we owed Champmeslé to Racine, as we owed Mars to Monvel and Andrieux.* Florine could do nothing for Raoul, but she would have been very glad to be useful or necessary to him. She relied upon the allurements of habit, she was always ready to open her salons, to display all her magnificence for his friends or in aid of his projects. In short, she aspired to be to him what Madame de Pompadour was to Louis XV. Other actresses envied Florine's position just as certain newspaper men envied Raoul's. Now, those who have observed the inclination of the human mind toward contrasts and contraries, will understand how it was that after ten years of this disorderly Bohemian existence, full of ups and downs, of feasts and executions for debt, of sobriety and orgies, Raoul was irresistibly attracted toward a pure, chaste passion, toward the peaceful and harmonious abode of a great lady, just as the Comtesse Félix longed to introduce the torments of passion into her life, which had become monotonous by virtue of its abounding happiness. This law of life is the law of all the arts, which exist only by contrasts. A work accomplished without that resource is the supreme expression of genius, as the cloister is the greatest effort of the Christian.

Upon returning home, Raoul found a short note from Florine, brought by her maid, but an unconquerable desire to sleep prevented him from reading it; he sought his couch, filled with delicious thoughts of the fresh, sweet love that was lacking in his life. Some hours later he read in that note important news which neither De Marsay nor Rastignac had divulged. The actress had learned from an indiscreet remark that the Chamber was to be dissolved after the session. Raoul went at once to

Florine's and sent for Blondet. In the actress's boudoir, Raoul and Émile, with their feet on the andirons, analyzed the political situation in France in 1834. On which side was the best opportunity for making one's fortune? They considered the pure Republicans, the Republicans who would have a presidency, the Republicans without a republic, the *Constitutionnels* without a dynasty, the *Constitutionnels* with a dynasty, ministerial conservatives, ministerial absolutists; from these they passed to the Right favoring concessions, the aristocratic Right, the legitimist Right, the *Henriquinquiste* Right, the Carlist Right. As between the Party of Resistance and the Party of Movement,* it was impossible to hesitate: it would have been as sensible to discuss the respective merits of life and death.

At this time, a multitude of newspapers, established to suit every possible shade of opinion, were crying out against the frightful political muddle, which a soldier might have called *a fine mess*. Blondet, the most judicious mind of the age, but judicious in the interests of others always, never in his own, like those advocates who manage their own business badly, was sublime in such private discussions as this. He advised Nathan not to change sides abruptly.

"Napoléon said that young republics are not made with old monarchies. So, my dear fellow, become the hero, the mainstay, the creator of the Left Centre in the Chamber that is to be, and you will get ahead in politics. Once admitted, once in the government, you are whatever you choose to be, you hold every opinion that prevails!"

Nathan decided to found a daily newspaper devoted to politics, to be the absolute master of it, to attach to it one of the small newspapers in which the Press abounds, and to establish connections with a review. The Press had been the means of making so many fortunes among his acquaintants that he paid no heed to the advice Blondet gave him, not to trust to it. Blondet declared that it was a wretched speculation, the number of newspapers fighting for subscribers at that time was so great, and the press seemed to him to be such a worn out weapon. Raoul, relying upon his pretended friendships and his courage, rushed boldly into the scheme; he rose to his feet with a burst of pride and said: "I shall succeed!"

"You have not a sou!"

"I shall write a drama!"

"It will fail."

"Very well then, it will fail," said Nathan.

He made the circuit of Florine's apartment, followed by Blondet, who believed him mad; then he glanced with a covetous eye at the wealth that was piled up there; Blondet understood him.

"There is a hundred thousand francs and more here," said he.

"Yes," said Raoul sighing, as he stood by Florine's sumptuous bed, "but I would prefer to pass the rest of my life peddling knickknacks on the boulevards and live on fried potatoes, than sell a single peg out of this room."

"Not a peg," said Blondet, "but everything! Ambition is like death, it must lay its hand on everything, for it knows that life is close at its heels."

"No! A hundred times no! I would accept anything from my countess of yesterday, but to steal Florine's shell?"

"Pull down her mint," said Blondet with a tragic air, "smash the dies and stamps—that is a serious matter."

"As far as I can understand, you propose to go into politics instead of sticking to the theatre," said Florine, suddenly making her appearance.

"Yes, my girl, yes," said Raoul good-humoredly, putting his arm around her neck and kissing her on the forehead. "What! You pout? Shall you lose anything by it? Will the minister not be better able than the journalist to get the queen of the boards a good engagement? Won't you have plenty of parts and plenty of vacations?"

"Where will you get the money?" said she.

"At my uncle's," Raoul replied.

Florine knew Raoul's *uncle*. That word symbolized the usurer, as *aunt*, in vulgar parlance, signifies pawnbroker.

"Do not you disturb yourself, my little jewel," said Blondet, tapping Florine on the shoulder, "I shall get Massol to help him, an advocate who, like all advocates, wants to be Keeper of the Seals* for a day; Du Tillet, who wants to be a deputy; Finot, who is still at the helm of a small newspaper; and Plantin, who wants to be Master of Requests* and is dabbling in a review. Yes, I will save him from himself; we will have Étienne Lousteau here and get him to write the literary article, and Claude Vignon for critic; Félicien Vernou will be the paper's cleaning lady, the advocate will work, Du Tillet will look after the Bourse and Industry, and we will see where all these slaves and passions come together."

"To the insane asylum or the ministry, where all those who are ruined in body or mind bring up," said Raoul.

"When will you settle matters with them?"

"Here," said Raoul, "five days hence."

"You must tell me what amount of money you will need," said Florine simply.

"Why, the advocate and Du Tillet and Raoul cannot go into the thing without a hundred thousand francs each," said Blondet. "The paper will go on then for eighteen months, the time it takes a man to rise or fall here in Paris."

Florine gave a little nod of approbation. The two friends took a cab to kidnap associates, pens, brains, and interests. The fair actress meanwhile sent for four wealthy dealers in furniture, curiosities, pictures, and jewels. These men entered the sanctuary and inventoried everything therein contained, as if Florine were dead. She threatened them with a sale at public auction in case they should do violence to their consciences in expectation of a better opportunity. She had made an impression, she told them, upon an English nobleman by her acting in a play of the Middle Ages, and wanted to get rid of all her movable wealth in order to make him think she was poor and induce him to give her a magnificent house which she would furnish in a way to rival Rothschild. But in spite of all she could do to inveigle them, they would give her only seventy thousand francs for the whole lot, which was worth a hundred and fifty thousand. Florine, who would not have given two sous for it, agreed to deliver it all in a week's time for eighty thousand. "You can take it or leave it," said she. The bargain was concluded. When the tradesmen had decamped, Florine leapt for joy like the little hills of King David.* She committed a thousand follies, for she had no idea she was so rich. When Raoul returned, she pretended to be angry with him. She said that she had thought it over, and that he had deserted her; men did not go from one party to another, nor from the Theater to the Chamber without a motive; she had a rival! How unerring is instinct! She made him swear eternal love to her. Five days later, she gave the most splendid banquet imaginable. The new journal was baptized under her roof in oceans of wine and jests, of oaths of fidelity, of good-fellowship and serious cooperation. The name, forgotten today as are the *Libéral*, the *Communal*, the *Departemental*, the *Garde National*, the *Féderal*, the *Impartial*, was something ending in *al*, which was destined to be very ephemeral. After the numerous descriptions of orgies which marked this literary era—so few of which took place in the attics where they were written—it is a difficult matter to describe this one of Florine's. A single word only. At three o'clock in the morning, Florine was able to undress and go to bed as if she were alone, although no one had gone away. All these lights of the age were sleeping like beasts. When the packers and porters and draymen arrived, early in the morning, to remove all the famous actress's magnificence, she laughed heartily as she saw them lift up these celebrities like heavy pieces of furniture and deposit them on the floor. Thus all the lovely things vanished. Florine banished all her souvenirs to the shops, where no passerby could tell from their appearance where or how those flowers of luxury had been paid for. By agreement, certain specified things were left with Florine until evening: her bed, and her table and crockery, so that she could give her guests their breakfast. Having fallen asleep under the luxurious canopy of wealth the famous wits awoke surrounded by the cold, dismantled walls of poverty, covered with the marks of nails and disfigured by the odd, incongruous things that collect behind hangings like the ropes and cords behind the decorations at the Opera.

"Why, Florine, the poor girl, has had a foreclosure in here!" cried Bixiou, one of the revellers. "Hands in your pockets! A collection!"

As he spoke, the whole party leaped to their feet. All their pockets turned inside out produced thirty-seven francs, which Raoul jocosely handed to the smiling hostess. The happy courtesan raised her head from her pillow, and pointed to the coverlet where there was a pile of banknotes, as thick as in the days when a courtesan's pillow was worth as much, in both good years and bad. Raoul called Blondet.

"I understand," said the latter. "The rascal levied on herself without saying a word. Well done, my little angel!"

This exploit caused the actress to be carried in triumph,

en déshabillé as she was, to the dining room by the few friends who remained. The advocate and the bankers had taken their leave. That evening, Florine had a dazzling triumph at the theatre. The story of her sacrifice had spread through the hall.

"I should rather be applauded for my talent," her rival said to her in the foyer.

"That is a very natural desire for an artist who has never been applauded as yet for anything but her good-nature," she retorted.

Ce trait fit porter l'actrice en triomphe et en déshabillé dans la salle à manger...

Plate XV

During the evening, Florine's maid had moved her belongings to Raoul's apartment on the Passage Sandrié.* The journalist was to take up his quarters in the house where the offices of the newspaper had been opened.

Such was the rival of the chaste and pure Madame de Vandenesse. Raoul's caprice bound the actress and the Comtesse together as with a ring: a ghastly bond which a duchess severed, in the days of Louis XV, by causing Adrienne Lecouvreur to be poisoned*—a sweet revenge easily understood when one considers the enormity of the offence.

Florine did not interfere with the early stages of Raoul's passion. She anticipated financial complications in the difficult undertaking on which he had embarked, and applied for a furlough of six months. Raoul conducted the negotiation for her with great ardor and achieved success in a way to make him still dearer to Florine. With the good sense of the peasant in La Fontaine's fable,* who makes sure of his dinner while his betters are thinking about it, the actress went into the provinces and abroad to secure the ducats, in order to support the famous man while he was on the hunt for power.

Until now, only a few painters have attacked the subject of love as it exists in the more exalted social spheres, abounding in grandeur and secret misery, terrible in its desires defeated by the most absurd, most commonplace accidents, and often shipwrecked by weariness. Perhaps we may catch a few glimpses of it here. On the day following Lady Dudley's ball, although not a word in the nature of the most timid declaration had been spoken on either side, Marie believed that Raoul loved her, according to the tenor of her dreams, and Raoul knew that Marie had chosen him for her lover. Although neither of them had arrived at that advanced stage at which men and women alike cut short the preliminaries, they were both making rapid progress toward the goal. Raoul, surfeited with pleasure, was bound for an ideal world, while Marie, who was as far removed as possible from the thought of sinning, did not dream that she could leave that world behind her. Thus there never was a passion more innocent and purer, in fact, than the love of Raoul and Marie, nor was there ever one more ardent or more delightful in anticipation. The Comtesse's mind was filled with ideas suited to the days of chivalry, but completely modernized. In the spirit of her role, her husband's antipathy for Nathan ceased to be an obstacle to her love. The less deserving of esteem Raoul had proved to be, the grander she would have been. The poet's impassioned conversation had awakened more of an echo in her breast than in her heart. Charity was aroused by the voice of Desire. That queen of all the virtues almost justified in the Comtesse's eyes the emotions, the joys, the violent impulses of love. She thought it was a glorious thing to be a sort of human Providence to Raoul. What a sweet thought! To sustain with her feeble white hand this colossus whose feet of clay she would not see, to supply life where it was lacking, to be in secret the creator of a great fortune, to assist a man of genius to contend with fate and overcome it, to embroider his scarf for the joust, to furnish him with weapons, to give him an amulet against sorcery, and a healing balm for his wounds! In the case of a woman educated as Marie had been, and devout and noble-souled as she was, love was certain to take the shape of a sort of voluptuous charity. Herein lies the explanation of her forwardness. Virtuous sentiments compromise themselves with superb disdain not unlike the shamelessness of a courtesan. As soon, therefore, as she had satisfied herself, by specious sophistry, that she was not violating her conjugal faith, the Comtesse plunged heart and soul into the pleasure of loving Raoul. Thereupon the most trivial incidents of life acquired a charm for her. Her boudoir, where she sat and thought of him, she transformed into a sanctuary. There was nothing there, even to her dainty writing desk, that did not awaken in her heart the thousand and one delights of such a connection; she would have letters to read and hide and answer. The toilette, the sublime poetry of a woman's life, whose charm had worn off or was unappreciated by her, reappeared, endowed with a magic power hitherto unsuspected. Her toilette suddenly became to her what it is to all women, a constant manifestation of her inmost thoughts, a language, a symbol. How much pleasure may be derived from a costume designed to please *him*, to do *him* honor! She devoted her attention most innocently to the fascinating little artifices which occupy so large a part of the lives of Parisian women and which give ample meaning to everything you see at their homes or upon their persons. Very few women run about to silk merchants and milliners and fashionable dressmakers in their own interest alone. When they are old they no longer think of their dress. When you see, as you walk along the street, a female figure stopping for a moment in front of a shop window, look carefully at her: "Would he like me better in that?" is a phrase writ large upon her cheerful face, in her eyes glistening with hope, in the smile that plays about her lips.

Lady Dudley's ball took place on a Saturday evening; on Monday the Comtesse went to the Opera, drawn there by the certainty that she should see Raoul. And there he was, planted on one of the staircases leading to the amphitheatre stalls. He lowered his eyes when the Comtesse entered her box. With what bliss did Madame de Vandenesse take note of the unwonted care her lover had bestowed upon his toilette! That scoffer at the laws of fashion exhibited a well-combed head of hair with perfumed oil glistening in the curves of his myriad curls; his waistcoat conformed to the prevailing style, his cravat was securely tied, the folds of his shirt were irreproachably clean and smooth. His hands seemed very white beneath the yellow gloves he wore in obedience to the decree then in force.* His arms were folded across his chest as if he were posing for his portrait, superbly indifferent to the whole great audience, but bursting with ill-restrained impatience. His eyes, although cast down, seemed to be turned toward the red velvet box railing on which Marie's arm rested. Félix, seated in the other corner of the box, had his back turned to Nathan. The clever Comtesse had seated herself so that she could fix her eyes upon the pillar against which Raoul was leaning. And so, all in a moment, Marie had caused this man of brains to abjure his cynicism in the matter of clothing.

Il ont tenait les bras croisés sur sa poitrine.

Plate XVI

The most humble as well as the most exalted of women is deeply moved to see the first manifestation of her power in such a metamorphosis as this. Every change is a confession of subjection. "They were right, there is much happiness in being understood," she said to herself as she thought of her hateful mentors. When the two lovers had taken in the whole hall with the swift glance that sees everything, they exchanged a look of intelligence. It was to both as if the dew from heaven had fallen in a refreshing shower upon their hearts, parched by long waiting. "I have been here for an hour in hell and now the gates of heaven are opening," said Raoul's eyes. "I knew you were here, but am I my own mistress?" the Comtesse's eyes replied. Thieves, spies, lovers, diplomats—in short, slaves of all kinds, but no others, know the resources and the delights of the glance. They alone know all the possibilities in the way of tenderness, mutual understanding, wrath and malice contained in the modifications of that soul-laden ray of light. Raoul felt his passion wince under the spur of necessity, but wax greatly at the sight of the obstacles in its path. Between the step on which he stood and the box of the Comtesse Félix de Vandenesse, the distance was scarcely thirty feet, but it was impossible for him to ignore that distance. In the breast of a man of fierce passions, who hitherto had found but a brief interval between a desire and its gratification, that stern and impassable abyss aroused a fierce longing to leap with a tiger's spring to where the Comtesse sat. In a paroxysm of rage, he tried to feel the ground. He bowed openly to the Comtesse, who responded with one of those slight, disdainful movements of the head, with which women put an end to any inclination their adorers may have to begin again. Comte Félix turned to see who had attracted his wife's attention; he saw Nathan, did not bow to him, but seemed rather to call him to account for his audacity, and turned slowly around again, saying a few words evidently in approbation of his wife's feigned contempt. It was clear that the door of the box was closed to Nathan, who darted a threatening glance at Félix. Anyone who saw this glance would have interpreted it by repeating a remark of Florine's: "Before long you will not be able to put your hat on!" Madame d'Espard, one of the most impertinent women of her day, had seen the whole episode from her box; she raised her voice, exclaiming "Bravo!" Raoul, who stood below her, at last turned his head; he bowed to her and received in return a gracious smile which said to him so plainly: "If they shut you out there, come here!" that he left his pillar and paid a visit to Madame d'Espard. It was well for him to show himself there in order to teach that wretched little Monsieur de Vandenesse that Celebrity was of equal value with Nobility, and that all emblazoned doors turned upon their hinges when Nathan knocked at them. The Marquise forced him to sit facing her at the front of the box. She proposed to put him to the question.

"Madame Félix de Vandenesse is enchanting this evening," she said, complimenting him upon her toilette as she might have complimented him upon a book he had published the day before.

"Yes," said Raoul carelessly, "the marabou feathers are wonderfully becoming, but she is very faithful to them, she wore them night before last," he added with a nonchalant air, as if to repudiate by this criticism the sweet complicity of which the Marquise accused him.

"You know the proverb?" she replied. "Every pleasure has its tomorrow."

At the game of repartee, literary celebrities are not always as strong as marquises. Raoul adopted the course of pretending to misunderstand, the last resource of men of wit.

"The proverb is true in my case," he said, glancing at the Marquise with a gallant air.

"My dear boy, your declaration comes too late for me to accept it," she said, laughingly. "Come, come, do not be such a prude; you thought Madame de Vandenesse was lovely in marabou feathers at the ball yesterday morning; she knows it, so she wears them again for your benefit. She loves you and you adore her; it is a little sudden, but I do not see why it is not perfectly natural. If I were mistaken you would not be twisting one of your gloves about like a man who is half-crazy because he is sitting by my side instead of being in his idol's box—from which he has just been turned away by a formal expression of scorn—and listening to me say in a whisper what he would like to hear said aloud." Raoul was, in fact, twisting one of his gloves and exhibiting an astonishingly white hand. "She has induced you," she said, staring at his hand in the most impertinent way, "to make sacrifices that you never made to society at large. She ought to be enchanted with her success; no doubt she will be a little proud of it, but if I were in her place I might be even more so. She was nothing but a bright woman, and now she is going to be held up as a woman of genius. You are going to paint her for us in one of the charming books you know so well how to write. My dear, do not forget Vandenesse—do it for me. Upon my word, he is too sure of himself. I would not put on that radiant expression for the Olympian Jupiter, the only one of the heathen gods who was exempt from accident, they say."

"Madame," cried Raoul, "you give me credit for a very base heart, if you deem me capable of making a business matter of my feelings or my love. I should prefer to such literary baseness as that, the English custom of putting a rope around a woman's neck and leading her to market."

"But I know Marie—she will ask you to do it."

"She is incapable of it," said Raoul hotly.

"Do you know her so well, pray?"

Nathan began to laugh at himself, he a deviser of scenes, for allowing himself to be caught by a stage trick.

"The comedy is being played here in your box, and not there," he said, pointing to the footlights.

He took her opera glass and began to survey the audience to keep himself in countenance.

"Are you angry with me?" said the Marquise, looking at him out of the corner of her eye. "Should I not have known your secret all the same? We shall easily be reconciled. Come and see me; I receive on Wednesdays; the dear Comtesse will not miss an evening as soon as she finds you are likely to be there. I shall be the one who gains from it. Sometimes I see her between four and five o'clock, and I shall be a good girl and add you to the small number of particular friends I admit at that hour."

"Well, well," said Raoul, "what people there are in the world! They told me you were a wicked creature."

"Wicked!" said she, "So I am when there is occasion for it. Should I not defend myself? But as to your Comtesse, I adore her; you will be satisfied with her, for she is charming. You will be the first man whose name has been engraved on her heart with the childish joy that leads all lovers, even corporals, to carve their ciphers on the bark of trees. A woman's first love is a delicious fruit. Later on, you see, there is a touch of science in our affections and our coquetry. An old woman like me can say whatever she pleases, for she is afraid of nothing, not even a journalist. In the autumn of life we know how to make you happy, but when we begin to love, we are happy ourselves, and thus we flatter your pride in a thousand ways. At such times, everything is unexpected and enchanting, for our hearts are overflowing with artlessness. You are too much of a poet not to prefer the flower to the fruit. I shall expect you six months from now."

Raoul, like all criminals, resorted to a system of denial, but he thereby furnished this bold fencer with additional weapons. Finding himself involved before long in the meshes of one of the cleverest and most dangerous of those private conversations in which Parisian women excel, he feared lest he might be surprised into making admissions which the Marquise would at once make the most of with her mocking tongue, and so he discreetly withdrew as Lady Dudley entered the box.

"Well," said the Englishwoman to the Marquise, "how far along are they?"

"They are madly in love with each other. Nathan has just told me so."

"I would have liked to have him uglier than he is," said Lady Dudley, casting a viperish glance at Félix. "Otherwise he is just what I wanted: he is the son of a Jew pawnbroker who died bankrupt soon after his marriage, but his mother was a Catholic, and unfortunately she made a Christian of him."

These facts concerning his origin, which Nathan was at such pains to conceal, Lady Dudley had succeeded in discovering, and she was enjoying in anticipation the pleasure it would afford her to extract them from some crushing epigram against Vandenesse.

"To think that I just now invited him to come to my house!" exclaimed the Marquise.

"Did I not receive him yesterday?" rejoined Lady Dudley. "There are pleasures which cost us very dear, my love."

The news of the mutual passion of Raoul and Madame de Vandenesse was industriously circulated among the people of fashion during the evening, not without arousing incredulity and contradiction, but the Comtesse was defended by her friends, Lady Dudley, Mesdames d'Espard and De Manerville, with ambiguous warmth well calculated to induce belief in the report. Impelled by necessity, Raoul went to Madame d'Espard's on

Wednesday evening, and met the aristocratic company usually to be found there. As Félix did not accompany his wife, Raoul was able to exchange a few words with Marie, words more expressive by reason of the tone in which they were uttered than of the ideas conveyed by them. The Comtesse, warned by Madame Octave de Camps to be on her guard against evil tongues, realized her position in the eyes of the world and made Raoul realize it.

Amid that gorgeous throng, the only pleasure enjoyed by either consisted in the sensations, so keenly relished at such times, that are aroused by the voice, the gestures, the attitudes, the ideas of a person who is dear to one. The heart grasps madly at trifles. Sometimes the eyes of both are fixed upon the same object, embodying therein, so to speak, a thought conceived, transmitted, and understood. We remark with admiration the foot put slightly forward during a conversation, the restless hand, the fingers busily occupied in taking up and putting down and toying with some knickknack in a significant way. Ideas no longer speak, nor words, but things: they say so much that a man in love often leaves it for others to bring a cup of tea or the sugar bowl or the thousand and one things his beloved may ask for, because he fears that he may reveal his confusion to eyes that seem to see nothing, but see everything. A thousand desires, wild wishes, and passionate thoughts are compressed in a glance. The pressure of the hand, unseen by the thousand Argus eyes, acquires the eloquence of a long letter, the rapture of a kiss. Love grows on all that it denies itself, and leans upon every obstacle to renew its strength. And finally these obstacles, more often cursed than crossed, are cut down and cast into the fire to keep it alive. At such times, women can measure the extent of their power in the small dimensions to which a boundless passion is reduced, as it recoils upon itself, conceals itself in a thirsty glance, in a contraction of the nerves, behind a commonplace courteous phrase. How many times, upon the lowest step of a staircase, is a man rewarded by a single word for all the unheard of torture, the meaningless conversation of a whole evening! Raoul, a man who cared little for society, gave free rein to his wrath in his speech, and was in a fever of excitement. Everyone heard the roars inspired by the restraint which artists find it so hard to endure. This frenzy, à la Roland,* this wit that crushed and shattered everything, using epigram as a club, intoxicated Marie and entertained the company as if they were watching the mad career of a bull, decked out with flags in a Spanish bull ring.

"It is of no use for you to knock everybody down; you will not succeed in creating a solitude," said Blondet.

This hint restored Raoul's presence of mind, and he ceased to make an exhibition of his vexation. The Marquise came and offered him a cup of tea, and said so that Madame de Vandenesse could hear: "Really you are very amusing, pray come and see me some day at four o'clock."

Raoul took offence at the word *amusing*, although it was used as a pretext for the invitation. He began to listen like those actors who stare about the theatre instead of keeping their thoughts on the stage. Blondet had compassion on him.

"My dear fellow," said he, taking him into a corner, "you act in society as if you were at Florine's. Here it simply will not do to lose your temper or make long speeches, but you should say a clever word or two now and then, assume a tranquil expression just when you feel the greatest desire to throw people out of the window, jest mildly, make a pretence of paying marked attention to the woman you adore, and not roll over on your back like a donkey in the middle of the road. Here, my dear fellow, we love according to rule. Either carry off Madame de Vandenesse, or act like a gentleman. You are too much like the lover in one of your books."

Nathan hung his head as he listened; he was like a lion caught in a net.

"I will never set my foot inside these doors again," said he. "This paper-mâché Marquise sells her tea too dear. She thinks me amusing! I understand now why Saint-Just guillotined all such people."

"You will come again tomorrow."

Blondet was a true prophet. The passions are as cowardly as they are cruel. The next day, after wavering a long while between: "I will go," and "I will not go," Raoul left his associates in the middle of an important discussion, and hurried to Madame d'Espard's on the Faubourg Saint-Honoré.* When he saw Rastignac's stylish cabriolet drive in as he was paying his cabman, his vanity was wounded; he determined to have a stylish cabriolet himself and the tiger to go with it.* The Comtesse's carriage was in the courtyard. At that sight, Raoul's heart swelled with delight. Marie was going forward under the impulsion of her desires like the hand of a clock kept in motion by its spring. She was stretched out in an easy chair at the corner of the fireplace in the small salon. Instead of looking up at Nathan when he was announced, she looked at him in the mirror, feeling sure that the mistress of the house would turn toward him. Love is hunted down so persistently in society that it is forced to resort to such little stratagems; it gives life to mirrors and muffs and fans, to a multitude of things whose utility is not at once demonstrated and which many women wear out without making use of them.

"Monsieur le Ministre," said Madame d'Espard to Raoul, introducing De Marsay to him by a glance, "was insisting, just as you came in, that the Royalists and the Republicans understand one another; you ought to know something about it?"

"Suppose it should be so," said Raoul, "where is the harm? We hate the same object; we are agreed in our hatred, but we differ in our love. That is the whole story."

"It is a curious alliance at all events," said De Marsay, embracing Comtesse Félix and Raoul in a single glance.

"It will not last long," said Rastignac, who thought a little too much about politics, like all new recruits.

"What do you say to it, my dear friend?" Madame d'Espard asked the Comtesse.

"I do not understand politics at all."

"You will go into it, Madame," said De Marsay, "and then you will be our enemy twice over."*

Nathan and Marie did not understand the allusion until De Marsay had gone. Rastignac followed him, and Madame d'Espard accompanied them to the door of her first salon. The two lovers forgot the minister's epigrams, for they found that they were blessed with a few moments to themselves. Marie quickly drew off her glove and gave her hand to Raoul, who took it and kissed it as if he were only eighteen. The Comtesse's glance expressed such whole-hearted, noble affection that Raoul's eyes were wet with the tears that men of a nervous temperament always have at their command.

"Where can I see you? Where can I speak to you?" he said. "I shall die if I must always disguise my voice, my look, my heart, my love."

Marie, deeply moved by his tears, promised to drive in the park whenever the weather was not too bad. This promise gave Raoul more happiness than Florine had given him in five years.

"I have so much to say to you! I suffer so from the silence to which we are condemned!"

The Comtesse was gazing at him as if fascinated, unable to reply, when the Marquise returned.

"How is this! You could not find any answer for De Marsay?" she said as she came in.

"We must respect the dead," said Raoul. "Do you not

see that he is on his last legs? Rastignac is his nurse, he hopes to be mentioned in the will."

The Comtesse pretended that she had calls to make; she was anxious to be gone in order not to betray herself. For that quarter of an hour Raoul had sacrificed precious time and his most pressing interests. Marie as yet knew nothing of the details of this life of a bird on the tree, combined with most complicated business interests and most exacting toil. When two persons united by undying love lead lives knit together more closely every day by bonds of confidence, by scrutinizing together such difficulties as arise; when two hearts exchange regrets each night and morning, as their mouths exchange sighs, share the same agonies of suspense, beat fast together at sight of an obstacle, then everything counts; a woman knows how much love may be expressed in an averted glance, how much effort expended in a rapid journey; she keeps her hands busy, goes and comes, hopes, suffers with the hard-working, worried man; her complaints are addressed to things; she does not doubt, for she knows and appreciates the details of life. But at the outset of a passion in which so much ardor and suspicion and unreasonableness are displayed, and where neither party really knows the other—with lazy women, at whose door love must always be doing sentry duty; with women who have an exaggerated idea of their dignity and are determined to be obeyed in everything, even when they give orders for the commission of a crime that may ruin a man— love, in Paris in our time, demands the performance of impossible tasks. Women of the world have remained under the sway of the traditions of the eighteenth century, when everyone had a fixed and definite position. Few women know anything whatsoever of the perplexities that beset the existences of most men, all of whom have a position to make for themselves, a fortune to establish on a firm basis, glory in embryo. Today, the men whose fortune is established can be counted; only the old men have time to love, the young are rowing in the galleys of ambition, even as Nathan was pulling an oar there. The women, still unresigned to this change in manners, loan the time of which they have an over-supply to those who have not enough; they have no conception of any other occupations, any other aim than their own. Although the lover may have overcome the Lernean hydra to reach their feet, he has no credit for it; everything else is blotted out by the joy of seeing him; they are grateful to him only for their own emotions, without taking the trouble to ascertain what they may have cost. If they have invented, during their hours of idleness, one of those stratagems which they have at their command, they exhibit its brilliancy as if it were a jewel. You have wrenched aside the iron bars of neces-sity, while they were putting on the mittens or adjusting the cloak of a ruse; to them goes the prize, and do not seek to wrest it from them. They are right too, for how can we refuse to sever every tie for a woman who does as much for us? They demand as much as they give. Raoul realized when he came to himself how difficult it would be for him to conduct a love affair in society, the ten-horse chariot of journalism, his dramatic pro-ductions, and his unsavory business affairs.

"The paper will be detestable tonight," he said to him-self as he left the house; "there will not be a single article by myself, and it is the second number too!"

Madame Félix de Vandenesse went three times to the Bois de Boulogne* without seeing Raoul there, and re-turned home in despair and sorely troubled. Nathan did not choose to make his appearance there otherwise than with all the splendor of a prince of the press. He spent the whole week in finding two horses and a suit-able cabriolet and groom, in convincing his partners of the necessity of saving such valuable time as his, and in having his equipage charged to the general expenses of the newspaper. His partners, Massol and Du Tillet, acceded to his request so readily that he thought they were the best fellows in the world. Without this assistance, life would have been impossible to Raoul; it was becoming so hard a life, however, although with an admixture of the most delectable pleasures of ideal love, that many people, even those endowed with the strongest constitutions, would have been unable to stand up under such dissipation. A vehement and requited passion occupies much space in an ordinary existence, but when its object is a woman in Madame de Vandenesse's position, it may be expected to exhaust the vitality of a man with so many demands upon his time as Raoul. These are the duties which his passion placed before all others. He must appear on horseback in the Bois de Boulogne almost every day between two and three o'clock, in the guise of a gentleman of leisure. There he would learn at whose house or at which theatre he could see Madame de Vandenesse again in the evening. He never left the salons until around midnight after pouncing upon a word or two long awaited, a few morsels of tenderness bestowed by stealth under the table, between two doors, or as she entered her carriage. Most of the time, Marie, who had launched him in the first society, procured invitations for him to dine at certain houses at which she was a frequent guest. Was it not a simple matter? Raoul, dominated by his passion, was restrained by pride from speaking of his work. He was compelled to obey the most capricious behests of this innocent sovereign, and at the same time to follow the parliamentary debates and the torrent of politics, keep an eye on the management of the newspaper, and produce two plays, the receipts from which were indispensable to him. Madame de Vandenesse had but to pout when he tried to escape attendance at a ball, a concert, or a drive, and he at once sacrificed his interests to her good pleasure. When he quitted the gay world between one

and two o'clock in the morning, he would return home
to work until eight or nine, sleep almost not at all, and
then be on his feet again to decide upon the opinions to
be espoused by the newspaper in concert with the influential men upon whom its existence depended, and
to discuss the innumerable details of the management.
In these days, journalism has a hand in everything:
manufactures, public and private concerns, new enterprises, the productions of literary men and everything
that touches their self-esteem. When Nathan had been
running all day from his editorial office to the theatre,
from the theatre to the Chamber, from the Chamber to
some of his creditors, tired out and worried as he was,
he must appear before Marie with a tranquil, blissful
mien, gallop up to her door with the serenity of a man
who has no cares and knows no weariness, save that of
happiness. When, as his reward for all this unsuspected
devotion, he received nothing more than the sweetest
of words, the most touching assurances of everlasting
attachment, a warm pressure of the hand, stolen during
a few seconds of solitude, a passionate word or two in
exchange for his own, he felt that he was cheating himself by leaving her in ignorance of the enormous price
he was paying for what our fathers would have called
these *trifling testimonials.* The opportunity for an explanation was not long in coming. One lovely day in April,
the Comtesse accepted Nathan's arm in an out-of-the-
way corner of the Bois de Boulogne; she had to make
one of those charming little quarrels about nothing out
of which women can build mountains. Instead of greet-
ing him with a smile upon her lips, her face radiant with
happiness, her eyes lighted up with some ingenious,
joyous thought, she was grave and serious.

"What is wrong with you?" said Nathan.

"Do not concern yourself about such trifles," said she;
"you must know that women are children."

"Have I offended you?"

"Should I be here?"

"But you do not smile at me, you do not seem glad to see me."

"I sulk, do I not?" said she, looking at him with the resigned air which women adopt when they wish to pose as victims.

Nathan walked forward a few steps with a feeling of apprehension that saddened him and made his heart sick.

"It must be," he said after a pause, "some trivial fright, one of the vague suspicions that you place above the greatest concerns of life; you have the power to change the world's course with a feather or a straw!"

"Irony? I expected it," said she, hanging her head.

"Marie, my angel, do you not see that I said that to tear your secret from you?"

"My secret will still be a secret even after you have been entrusted with it."

"Well, tell me——"

"I am not loved," she retorted, glancing at him out of the corner of her eye with the cunning, mischievous expression with which women cross-examine the men they wish to torture.

"Not loved?" cried Nathan.

"No, you have too many irons in the fire. Where am I in the midst of all the excitement? Neglected at every turn. Yesterday I came to the Bois and waited for you——"

"But——"

"I wore a new dress for your benefit, and you did not come; where were you——"

"But——"

"I had no idea. I went to Madame d'Espard's and I did not find you there."

"But——"

"In the evening, at the Opera, I never took my eyes off the balcony, every time the door opened my heart beat as if it would burst."

"But——"

"What an evening! You have no conception of these tempests in the heart."

"But——"

"Such emotion wears one's life away——"

"But——"

"Well?" said she.

"True, it does wear one's life out," said Nathan, "and before many months you will have consumed mine. Your insane reproaches extort my secret from me too— you say I do not love you? Ah! I love you too well."

He painted his position in vivid colors, told her of his vigils, enumerated his engagements at stated hours, and explained the necessity of success, the insatiable demands of a newspaper which is called upon to pass judgment, before all others, upon current events and to make no mistake under pain of losing its power, and the innumerable rapid studies he was required to make upon the questions which succeeded each other as swiftly as clouds in that consuming age.

Raoul was put in the wrong in a moment. As the Marquise d'Espard had told him, nothing is more art-less than a first love. He soon found that the Comtesse was guilty of loving too much. A loving woman responds to everything with a confession, an endearment, or a caress. The Comtesse, when this prodigious life was un-rolled before her, was overwhelmed with admiration. She had made Nathan a very great man in her thoughts, she found him sublime. She accused herself of loving too much, begged him to come at his own time; she smoothed his ambitious labors by raising her eyes to heaven. She would wait! Thenceforth she would sacrifice her own pleasures. Although her desire was to be only a stepping stone, she was an obstacle! She wept with despair.

"Women," she said with tears in her eyes, "can do nothing but love, while men have a thousand things to occupy them; we can only think and pray and adore."

Such a wealth of love deserved a reward. She looked around, like the nightingale as he flies down from his branch to a spring, to see if they were alone in the solitude, if no spy were hidden in the silence; then she raised her head to Raoul, who bent his to meet it; she allowed him to take a kiss, the first, the only one she was destined to bestow clandestinely, and she was happier at that moment than she had been for five years. Raoul felt that all his labors were rewarded. They walked along together on the road from Auteuil to Boulogne, without any definite idea where they were going; they were obliged at last to return to their carriages, walking with the regular, rhythmical step which lovers know. Raoul had confidence in that kiss, bestowed with the modest willingness that sanctity of sentiment imparts. All the harm came from the world, and not from this woman who was so entirely his. Raoul no longer regretted the trials of his tempestuous life, which Marie was certain to forget in the heat of her first desire, like all women who are not constant witnesses of the terrible struggles of such exceptional lives. Under the sway of the grateful admiration, characteristic of a woman's love, Marie trod the fine sand of a bypath with a quick, firm step, saying, as did Raoul, very few words, but heartfelt and full of meaning. The sky was without a cloud, the great trees were budding, and here and there a speck of green gave life to their myriads of slender brown twigs. The shrubs, the birches, the willows, the poplars were putting forth their first tender, still diaphanous shoots. Such harmony no soul can resist. Love explained Nature to the Comtesse as it had explained Society to her.

"I wish that you had never loved anyone but me!" said she.

"Your wish is gratified," Raoul replied. "We have taught each other what true love is."

He spoke the truth. In posing as a pure man before this youthful heart, Raoul had resort to high-flown phrases of lofty sentiment. At first, purely speculative and self-seeking, his passion had become sincere. He began by lying, he ended by speaking the truth. There is, however, in every writer a sentiment, difficult to restrain, that leads him to admire what is morally beautiful. In short, by dint of making sacrifices, a man becomes interested in the person who demands them. Women of the world have an instinctive perception of this truth, just as courtesans have; indeed it may be that they put it in practice without knowing it. So it was that the Comtesse, after her first burst of gratitude and surprise, was enraptured to find that she had inspired so many sacrifices, had caused him to overcome so many obstacles. She was beloved by a man who was worthy of her. Raoul did not know all that his false grandeur required of him, for women do not allow their lovers to descend from their pedestals. A god can not be pardoned for the slightest baseness. Marie did not know the keyword of the enigma Raoul gave his friends at the supper party at Véry's. This low-born writer's struggle for existence had occupied the first ten years of his youth; he longed to be beloved by one of the queens of the world of fashion. Vanity—without which love is very weak, says Champfort*—kept his passion alight and added fuel to it from day to day.

"Can you swear to me that you do not and never will belong to any other woman?" said Marie.

"There would be no more time in my life than there is room in my heart for another woman," he replied, believing that he was telling the truth, so great was his contempt for Florine.

"I believe you," said she.

When they reached the avenue where the carriages were waiting, Marie dropped Nathan's arm, and he assumed a respectful attitude as if he had just met her; he escorted her to her carriage, hat in hand, then followed her along the Avenue Charles X, breathing the dust raised by her horses and gazing at her feathers, drooping like the weeping willow, as the wind blew them about. Notwithstanding Marie's noble self-denial, Raoul, inflamed by his passion, went wherever she was; he adored the reproachful yet happy expression the Comtesse assumed in an ineffectual attempt to scold him, when she saw him wasting the time that was so valuable to him. Marie undertook the direction of his labors, gave him explicit orders as to the employment of his time, and remained at home in order to deprive him of all excuse for dissipation. She read his paper every morning and became the herald of the renown of Étienne Lousteau the feuilletonist, whom she thought delightful, of Félicien Vernou, Claude Vignon and all the editors. She advised Raoul to do justice to De Marsay when he died, and read with rapture the noble and eloquent eulogy he wrote of the dead minister, although he blamed his Machiavellianism and hatred for the masses. Naturally she was present, in a front seat at the Gymnase,* at the first performance of the play upon which Nathan relied to support him in his undertaking, and which seemed to make a tremendous hit. She was deceived by the hired applause.

"You have not said farewell to the Italiens, have you?" said Lady Dudley, to whose house she went after the performance.

"No, I have been to the Gymnase. It was the first night of a new play."

"I cannot endure vaudevilles. I feel the same way about them that Louis XIV felt about Teniers's pictures,"* said Lady Dudley.

"For my part," said Madame d'Espard, "I think that our authors are making progress. The vaudevilles of today are delightful comedies, bubbling over with wit, and they demand first-rate talent; I enjoy them very much."

"The actors are excellent, too," said Marie. "They acted

extremely well at the Gymnase tonight; the play suited them, for the dialogue is very bright and clever."

"Like Beaumarchais," said Lady Dudley.

"Monsieur Nathan is not a Molière yet, but——" said Madame d'Espard with a glance at the Comtesse.

"He makes vaudevilles," said Madame Charles de Vandenesse.

"And unmakes ministries," added Madame de Manerville.

The Comtesse said nothing; she tried to reply with some biting epigram; she felt that her heart was in a ferment of rage; she could find nothing better to say than: "He will make them perhaps."

All the women exchanged mysterious glances of intelligence. When Marie de Vandenesse had taken her leave, Moïna de Saint-Héreen exclaimed: "Why, she worships Nathan!"

"She makes no mystery of it," observed Madame d'Espard.

The month of May arrived and Vandenesse took his wife away to his estate in the country, where her only consolation was the receipt of passionate letters from Raoul, to whom she wrote every day.

The Comtesse's absence might have saved him from the chasm he had stepped into if Florine had been with him, but he was alone in the midst of friends who became his secret enemies as soon as he exhibited a purpose to domineer over them. His collaborators hated him for the moment, ready to hold out a helping hand and console him if he failed; ready to fall down and fawn upon him if he succeeded. So goes the literary world. There, no man loves anybody save his inferiors. Every man is the foe of anyone who seeks to rise. This general jealousy increases tenfold the opportunities of mediocre men who arouse neither envy nor suspicion, but burrow along like moles, and, however stupid they may be, find themselves gazetted in the *Moniteur** for three or four lucrative places, while the men of talent are still fighting at the door to prevent one another from going in. The underground hostility of these pretended friends, whom Florine would have detected with the innate genius of the courtesan for putting her hand upon the truth among a thousand hypotheses, was not the greatest danger by which Raoul was threatened. His two associates, Massol the advocate and Du Tillet the banker, had conceived the scheme of harnessing his ardor to the chariot in which they were showing themselves off, intending to eject him as soon as he ceased to be in a condition to carry on the newspaper, or to deprive him of that great power as soon as they wanted to make use of it. In their eyes, Nathan stood for a certain sum of money to be consumed, a literary force as effective as ten pens to be employed. Massol, one of those advocates who mistake the faculty of speaking at indefinite length for eloquence, who possess the secret of wearying their hearers whatever they may say, the pest of assemblies where they cheapen everything, and who are determined to become personages at any price, no longer aimed at being Keeper of the Seals; he had seen five or six of them succeed one another in four years, and had taken a dislike to the robe. He desired, even as he desired money in his purse, a chair in the Department of Public Instruction, a seat at the Council of State, the whole seasoned by the Cross of the Legion of Honor.* Du Tillet and Baron de Nucingen had guaranteed the Cross and his appointment as Master of Requests if he would enter into their plans; he deemed them better able to fulfill their promises than Nathan, and he obeyed them blindly. The better to pull the wool over Raoul's eyes they allowed him to manage the paper without interference. Du Tillet used it only to forward his stock-jobbing interests, which Raoul understood nothing about, but he had already given Rastignac to understand through Baron de Nucingen that the sheet would be tacitly indulgent to the government, on the single condition that support should be given his candidacy for the succession to Monsieur de Nucingen, soon to be made a Peer of France, who sat in the Chamber for a sort of rotten borough with very few electors, where the paper was sent gratis in profusion. Thus Raoul was fooled by the banker and the lawyer, who took infinite delight in seeing him on his throne at the office of the newspaper, making the most of all his chances, reaping all the fruits of selfishness or of other qualities. Nathan was delighted with them, and, as at the time of his request for funds with which to stock his stable, thought them the best fellows in the world; he believed that he was fooling them. Men of imagination, to whom hope is the essence of life, are never willing to say to themselves that the most perilous moment in matters of business is that when everything seems to be going on in accordance with their wishes. It was a moment of triumph by which Nathan profited, for he made his appearance in the political and financial world: Du Tillet presented him at Nucingen's house. Madame de Nucingen welcomed Raoul with warmth, less on his own account than on Madame de Vandenesse's, but when she let drop a word or two concerning the Comtesse, he thought that he was wonderfully clever to use Florine as a screen; he descanted with fatuous generosity upon his relations with the actress, which it was impossible for him to break. Does a man abandon certain happiness for the coquetries of the Faubourg Saint-Germain? Nathan, hoodwinked by Nucingen and Rastignac, by Du Tillet and Blondet, pompously accorded his support to the Doctrinaires* in the formation of one of their ephemeral cabinets. Then, in order to go into business with clean hands, he declined, with a great show of disdain, to accept a share in certain enterprises that were floated with the assistance of his paper—a man who did not hesitate to compromise his friends and to deal in a way that showed no nice sense of honor with certain manufacturing concerns at various critical moments! Such contrasts, engendered by vanity or by ambition, are to be found in many similar lives. The outer cloak must be made to appear magnificent to the public, so a man borrows cloth from his friends to cover the holes. Nevertheless, two months after the Comtesse's departure, Raoul had a certain *quart d'heure de Rabelais** which caused him some anxiety in the midst of his triumph. Du Tillet had advanced a hundred thousand francs. The money furnished by Florine, a third of the original capital, had been eaten up by the public charges and the enormous expenses attending the first establishment of the paper. It was necessary to provide for the future. The banker accommodated the editor by taking his notes of hand at four months for fifty thousand francs. Thus Du Tillet held Raoul by the halter of the note of hand. This supplementary contribution supplied the paper with funds for six months. In the eyes of some writers, six months are an eternity. Moreover, by ingenious advertising, by employing a number of agents, and by offering illusory advantages to subscribers, they had scraped together two thousand of them. This partial success encouraged Raoul to throw banknotes into the furnace. Given a little more talent, let a political prosecution be undertaken against them, or something that might pass for persecution, and Raoul would become one of the modern *condottieri* whose ink is more effective today than the gunpowder of former days. Unfortunately this arrangement was made before Florine returned with about fifty thousand francs. Instead of creating a reserve fund, Raoul, sure of success, because he saw that success was necessary, humiliated at having already accepted money from the actress, dazzled by the insidious laudation of his flatterers, and feeling in his heart that his love had ennobled him, deceived Florine as to his position and forced her to use the money in refurnishing her house. Under the existing circumstances it was essential to make a magnificent show. The actress, who did not need to be urged, burdened herself with debts to the amount of thirty thousand francs. She had a charming house all to herself, on the Rue Pigalle,* where all her former coterie reassembled. The house of a damsel in Florine's position was neutral ground, very favorable for the ambitious politicians, who did as Louis XIV did in Holland: made treaties under Raoul's roof without Raoul. Nathan had held in reserve for Florine's reappearance a play in which the principal part was admirably suited to her abilities. This vaudeville-drama was to be Raoul's farewell to the stage. The newspapers, who incurred no expense by reason of this act of complaisance for Raoul, premeditated such an ovation to Florine that the Comédie-Française talked about offering her an engagement. The critics declared that Florine was the heir of Mademoiselle Mars. This triumph turned the actress's head to a sufficient extent to interfere with her study of the course Nathan was pursuing; she was living in a whirl of fêtes and banquets. Queen of a court filled with a pressing throng of petitioners, one for his book, another for his play, another for his ballet dancer, another for his theatre, another for his enterprise, another for an article, she abandoned herself to all the delights of the power of the press, seeing therein the dawn of ministerial influence. To judge from what was said by those who frequented her salon, Nathan was a great politician. Nathan had shown good judgment in his venture, he would be a deputy, and certainly a minister before long, like so many others before him. Actresses rarely say no to anyone who flatters them. Florine was credited with too much talent in the feuilleton to distrust the paper and those who conducted it. She knew too little of the mechanism of the press to trouble herself about the means. Girls of Florine's stamp never look at anything but results. As for Nathan, he believed, from that time on, that at the next session he would take a hand in affairs, with two former journalists, one of whom, then a minister, was trying to turn out his colleagues in order to strengthen himself. Nathan was delighted to see Florine again after her six months' absence, and nonchalantly fell back into his old ways. The coarse woof of his life he secretly embellished with the loveliest flowers of his ideal passion, and with the pleasure Florine strewed upon it. His letters to Marie were masterpieces of love, grace, and style. Nathan made her the light of his life, he undertook nothing without consulting his good genius. In despair at being on the popular side, there were moments when he longed to espouse the cause of the aristocracy, but, accustomed though he was to feats of agility, it seemed to him absolutely impossible to leap from the Left to the Right; it was easier to become a minister. Marie's precious letters were deposited in one of the portfolios with secret compartments put on the market by Huret or Fichet, the two inventors who were carrying on a war of advertisements and placards in Paris as to which could make the safest and most reliable locks. This portfolio was kept in Florine's new boudoir, where Raoul worked. No one is so easy to deceive as a woman to whom one is accustomed to tell everything; she is suspicious of nothing, because she thinks that she sees and knows everything. Moreover, since her return the actress was a witness of Raoul's whole life, and could see nothing irregular in it. She would never have imagined that the portfolio, which she had hardly noticed, and which was kept locked without any affectation of mystery, contained treasures of love, a rival's letters, which, at Raoul's request, the Comtesse directed to the office of the paper. Nathan then seemed to occupy an extremely brilliant position. He had many friends. Two plays written in collaboration, which had just been successful, provided funds to gratify his luxurious tastes and banished all anxiety for the future. Nor did he worry at all concerning his debt to his friend Du Tillet.

"How can a man distrust a friend?" he would say, when Blondet, as sometimes happened, expressed some apprehension, induced by his habit of analyzing everything.

"But we have no need to distrust even our enemies," said Florine.

Nathan defended Du Tillet. Du Tillet was the kindest, the most obliging, the most upright of men. This sort of ropewalker's existence without a balancing pole would have horrified anyone, even the most indifferent, if he could have penetrated the mystery, but Du Tillet contemplated it with the stoicism and dry eye of a parvenu. There was a sort of fiendish mockery in the friendly good-humor of his treatment of Nathan. One day he shook hands with him as they left Florine's house together and watched him enter his cabriolet.

"That fellow goes to the Bois de Boulogne in magnificent style," he said to Lousteau, the envious man par excellence, "and in six months' time perhaps he will beat Clichy."

"He? Never!" cried Lousteau, "Florine is on hand."

"How do you know, my boy, that he will keep her? As for you, you are worth a thousand of him, and you will certainly be our editor-in-chief six months from now."

In October, the notes of hand fell due; Du Tillet obligingly renewed them, but for two months only, and increased in amount by the discount and a new loan. Sure of victory, Raoul drained the very springs dry. Madame Félix de Vandenesse was to return in a few days, a month earlier than usual, drawn back to Paris by a frenzied longing to see Nathan, who did not choose to be at the mercy of a lack of money when he resumed his contentious life. Correspondence, in which the pen is always bolder than the tongue—in which thought, clothed in its flowers, touches upon every subject and can say what it will—had brought the Comtesse to the highest pitch of exaltation; she saw in Raoul one of the most transcendent geniuses of the age: an exquisite, misunderstood heart, without stain and worthy of adoration; she saw him fearlessly putting forth his hand to stay the prodigality of the ruling powers. Soon that voice, so sweet in love, would thunder from the tribune. Marie's life ran in interlaced circles like those of a sphere, at whose centre is the world. With no inclination for the tranquil pleasures of home, she welcomed the excitement of this tempestuous life, communicated by a clever, loving pen; she kissed the letters penned amid the smoke of battles of the press, in moments stolen from his hours of study; she was conscious of their value; she was sure that she filled his whole heart, that she had no rivals save glory and ambition; she found means in her solitude to exert all her strength, she was happy that she had chosen well: Nathan was an angel. Fortunately her absence in the country and the obstacles that existed between Raoul and herself had silenced the slanderous tongues of the world. So during the last days of autumn, they resumed their drives in the Bois de Boulogne; they could meet nowhere else until the salons were once more thrown open. Raoul was able to enjoy more at ease the pure, exquisite delights of his ideal life and conceal it from Florine: he worked a little less as matters were running smoothly at the newspaper office and each editor knew what he had to do. He involuntarily made comparisons, always to the advantage of the actress, and yet the Comtesse lost nothing in his sight. Overspent anew by the manoeuvres which his passion of head and heart for a woman at the top of the social ladder compelled him to perform, Raoul put forth superhuman efforts in order to be in three places at once: in society, at his office, and in the wings. At the time when Florine, who was grateful to him for everything, who almost shared his labors and his anxiety, was flitting in and out, pouring out genuine happiness upon him in streams, without high-flown phrases, without any accompaniment of remorse, the Comtesse, with her insatiable eyes and her chaste corsage, forgot his gigantic labors and the pains he often took to see her for an instant. Instead of domineering over him, Florine allowed him to take her up and put her down and take her up again like a cat that falls upon its feet and shakes its ears. Such easy-going morals are in admirable accord with the inclinations of men who live by their thoughts, and any artist would have made the most of them, as Nathan did, without abandoning the pursuit of his beautiful ideal love, that noble passion which fascinated his poetic instincts, his secret dreams of grandeur, his social vanity. Fully realizing the crash that would follow any indiscretion, he would say to himself: "Neither the Comtesse nor Florine will ever know anything about it!" They were so far removed from each other! With the beginning of winter, Raoul reappeared in society at his apogee: he was almost a personage. Rastignac, who had fallen with the ministry when it went to pieces at De Marsay's death, leaned upon Raoul and bolstered him up by his laudation. Madame de Vandenesse thereupon determined to find out if her husband had changed his opinion with regard to him, a year having elapsed. So she questioned him anew, thinking to be revenged on him in brilliant style—a thing that all women, even the noblest, the least worldly, thoroughly enjoy, for it would be perfectly safe to wager that the angels do not lay aside their self-esteem when they gather about the Holy of Holies.

"The only thing he lacked was to be the dupe of schemers," the Comte replied.

Félix, whose experience of the world and of politics made him very clear-sighted, had fathomed Raoul's position. He calmly explained to his wife that Fieschi's exploit* had resulted in attaching many lukewarm men to the interests threatened in the person of King Louis-Philippe. Newspapers, whose colors were not sharply defined, would lose subscribers, for journalism was going to be simplified with politics. If Nathan had put his fortune into his newspaper, he would soon come to the end of his rope. This opinion was so clear and so reasonable, although expressed in few words as an off-hand answer to a question in which he took no interest, by a man who was a shrewd calculator of the chances of all parties, that it alarmed Madame de Vandenesse.

"Are you so deeply interested in him?" Félix asked his wife.

"Only as a man whose wit amuses me and whom I like to talk with."

This reply was made in so perfectly natural a tone that the Comte suspected nothing.

The next day at four o'clock, at Madame d'Espard's, Marie and Raoul had a long, whispered conversation. The Comtesse expressed fears which Raoul dissipated, only too happy to crush Félix's conjugal grandeur with epigrams. He proceeded to take his revenge. He described the Comte as a man of small mind and behind the times, who would measure the Revolution of July with the yardstick of the Restoration, who refused to recognize the triumph of the middle class, the new force in society, and a genuine force whether temporary or lasting. Great noblemen were no longer possible, the reign of actual superiority had arrived. Instead of taking to heart the indirect, impartial judgment of an experienced politician dispassionately replying to questions, Raoul strutted about on stilts and draped himself in the purple robes of his success. What woman is there who has not more faith in her lover than in her husband? So Madame de Vandenesse, relieved of her apprehensions, entered upon the life of repressed vexations, of trifling stolen pleasures, of clandestine pressures of the hand, her sustenance of the preceding winter—a life which ends in leading a woman beyond bounds when the man she loves has some resolution and is impatient of obstacles. Luckily for her, Raoul, appeased by Florine, was not dangerous. Moreover, he was bound hand and foot by important interests which made it impossible for him to take advantage of his good fortune. Nevertheless, any sudden disaster befalling him, fresh obstacles, or a fit of impatience, might hurry the Comtesse into an abyss. Raoul caught a glimpse of such a tendency on her part when Du Tillet, toward the end of December, called for payment of his notes. The rich banker, who said that he was pressed for money, advised Raoul to borrow the money for a fortnight from a usurer—Gigonnet, for instance—the providence at twenty-five percent of all youths in straitened circumstances. In a few days, the paper would effect its grand January renewals, there would be money in the cash box, and then Du Tillet would see. Indeed, why should not Nathan write a play? From sheer pride, Nathan was determined to pay the notes at any price. Du Tillet gave him a letter to the usurer, whereupon Gigonnet advanced the money on notes of hand drawn at twenty days. Instead of seeking for an explanation of his readiness to oblige, Raoul was angry with himself for not asking for more. Many men of the most eminent intellectual powers act in the same way; they see food for jesting in matters of serious importance; they seem to keep their mind in reserve for their works, and make no use of it in everyday life for fear of cheapening it. Raoul described his morning's experience to Florine and Blondet; he sketched out Gigonnet for them in his entirety: his little bit of Réveillon wallpaper,* his staircase, his asthmatic bell and the stag's foot bellpull, his little worn-out straw pallet, his hearth, where there was no more fire than in his eyes; he made them laugh heartily over this new uncle of his; they were not disturbed at the thought of Du Tillet in need of money or of a usurer so ready to open his cash box. It was all caprice!

"He only charged you fifteen percent," said Blondet, "and you ought to be very grateful to him. At twenty-five percent we stop bowing to them; usury begins at fifty percent: at that figure we despise them."

"Despise them!" said Florine. "Who is there among your friends who would loan you money at that rate without posing as your benefactor?"

"She is right, I am lucky not to owe Du Tillet anything anymore," said Raoul.

Why is it that men who are accustomed to looking thoroughly into everything are so deficient in penetration in their own private affairs? Perhaps it is that the mind can not be completely equipped in every direction, perhaps artists live too entirely in the present to study the future, perhaps they keep their eyes too closely upon trivial things to see a trap, and believe that no one dares play a trick on them. The future was not slow in arriving. Twenty days later, the notes were protested, but at the Tribunal de Commerce, Florine demanded and obtained twenty-five days in which to provide for their payment. Raoul looked about to see where he stood, and requested an accounting; the result was that the receipts of the newspaper covered two-thirds of the expenditures, and that the subscription list was dwindling. The great man became anxious and gloomy, but only to Florine, to whom he confided his troubles. Florine advised him to realize on the plays he was writing by selling them outright, and to assign his receipts from his other plays. In this way, he procured twenty thousand francs and reduced his debt to forty thousand. On February 10th, the twenty-five days expired. Du Tillet, who did not choose to have Nathan for a rival in the electoral college at which he proposed to offer himself as a candidate, leaving to Massol another college that was at the disposal of the ministry, ordered Gigonnet to pursue him to the last ditch. A man imprisoned for debt cannot offer himself as a candidate for the

Chamber. The debtor's prison at Clichy was destined to swallow the future minister. Florine herself was in constant communication with the bailiffs by reason of her personal debts, and in this crisis she had no other resource than the *Moi!* of Medea,* for her furniture was seized. The ambitious creature heard the cracking sounds of approaching destruction in all parts of his newly-erected structure, built with no foundation. He knew that he lacked the necessary strength to carry on so vast an undertaking, much less was he capable of beginning it anew; so he must perish in the ruins of his dream. His love for the Comtesse still afforded him some few gleams of life: it gave animation to his mask, but within, hope was dead. He did not suspect Du Tillet, he saw nobody's hand but the usurer's. Rastignac, Blondet, Lousteau, Vernou, Finot, Massol were careful not to enlighten a man who could on occasion exhibit such perilous activity. Rastignac, who wanted to return to power, made common cause with Nucingen and Du Tillet. The others experienced infinite delight in contemplating the death agony of one of their equals, guilty of having attempted to be their master. Not one of them would have said a word to Florine; on the other hand, they praised Raoul to her. "Nathan's shoulders were broad enough to hold up the world, he would get out of it, and everything would go on all right!"

"We have two new subscribers as of yesterday," said Blondet gravely; "Raoul will be a deputy. As soon as the budget is voted, the order for dissolution will appear."

As Nathan had been sued, he could no longer expect assistance from usurers. As Florine's furniture had been seized, she had nothing to look to, save the chance of inspiring a passion in some idiot, who never turns up at the proper time. Nathan's friends were all men without money or credit. An arrest would destroy his hopes of political advancement. To cap the climax of his woes, he was pledged to perform a vast amount of work for which he had been paid in advance; he could see no bottom to the abyss of misery in which he was soon to be plunged. In the presence of so many threatened disasters, his audacity deserted him. Would the Comtesse de Vandenesse cleave to him, would she fly with him? Women are never impelled to take that step unless by absolute, undivided love, and their passion had not knitted them together by the mysterious ties of happiness. But even if the Comtesse should go abroad with him, she would be without means, stripped bare of all her property, and would be an additional burden. A second-rate mind, a vain man like Nathan, was certain to see, and he did thereupon see, in suicide the blade that would cut these Gordian knots. The idea of falling from his pedestal in the sight of the social circle into which he had made his way and which he had sought to master, of leaving the Comtesse there, triumphant, and of becoming once more a base foot soldier, was not to be endured. Folly danced and jingled her bells at the door of the imaginary palace in which the poet dwelt. In his extremity, Nathan awaited a possible stroke of luck and did not propose to kill himself until the last moment.

During the last days, while the judgment was being certified and the petition for arrest and order thereon issued, Raoul's face wore, wherever he went, the ominously indifferent expression which keen observers have noticed in all men predisposed to suicide, or who are contemplating it. The ghastly ideas they are caressing cause grayish clouds to settle upon their brow; their smile has an indefinable suggestion of fatality; their movements are solemn. The wretched creatures seem to be determined to consume the gilded fruit of life to the core; their eyes search the heart on every occasion; they hear their funeral knell in the air and are unmindful of their surroundings. Marie noticed these alarming symptoms one evening at Lady Dudley's; Raoul had remained behind, alone, upon a divan in the boudoir, while everybody was talking in the salon; the Comtesse went to the door, he did not raise his head; he heard neither her breath nor the rustling of her silk dress; he was staring at a flower in the carpet with eyes dazed with suffering; he preferred death to abdication. Not everyone has Saint Helena for a pedestal. Moreover, suicide was king in Paris at this time; is it not always the last word of societies wavering in their faith? Raoul had made up his mind to die. Despair is proportioned to the hopes that it succeeds, and Raoul's had no other issue than the tomb.

"What is the matter?" said Marie, flying to his side.

"Nothing," he replied.

There is a way of saying that word *nothing*, between lovers, that means just the opposite. Marie shrugged her shoulders.

"You are a perfect child!" said she. "Has anything gone wrong with you?"

"Not with me. However, you will know it all too soon, Marie," he replied, affectionately.

"What were you thinking about when I came in?" she demanded authoritatively.

"Do you want to know the truth?" She nodded. "I was thinking of you; I was saying to myself that many men in my place would have insisted upon being loved unreservedly: I am, am I not?"

"Yes," she said.

"And I leave you pure and with no remorse," continued Raoul, putting his arm around her and drawing her to him to kiss her forehead, at the risk of being surprised. "I might drag you into the pit, but you will remain in all your glory without a stain, on the brink. There is one thought that troubles me, however——"

"What is it?"

"You will despise me." She smiled superbly. "Yes, you will never believe in the holiness of my love, and then people will abuse me, I know. Women do not imagine that from the depths of our slime we raise our eyes to heaven, there to worship with our whole heart, a Marie. They mix up this sanctified love with paltry questions, they do not understand that men of lofty intelligence and poetic temperament can detach their minds from mere enjoyment in order to keep it in reserve, to worship at some cherished altar. But, Marie, the worship of the ideal is more fervent with us than with you: we find it in the woman who does not look for it in us."

"Why this deliverance?" said she jestingly, like a woman who was sure of herself.

"I am leaving France; tomorrow you will learn why and how, by a letter that my valet will bring you. Adieu, Marie."

He rushed from the room after pressing the Comtesse to his heart in a fierce embrace, and left her stupefied with grief.

"Pray, what has happened, my dear," said the Marquise d'Espard, entering the room in search of the Comtesse; "what did Monsieur Nathan say to you? He left us with a most melodramatic air. You are too reasonable, perhaps, or too unreasonable."

The Comtesse took Madame d'Espard's arm and returned to the salon, taking her departure a few moments later.

"Perhaps she is going to her first rendezvous," suggested Lady Dudley to the Marquise.

"I will find out," replied Madame d'Espard, and she too left the house and followed the Comtesse's carriage.

But Madame de Vandenesse's coupe went in the direction of the Faubourg Saint-Honoré. When Madame d'Espard entered her own courtyard, she saw the Comtesse Félix driving on through the faubourg on her way to the Rue du Rocher. Marie went to bed, but was unable to sleep, and passed the night reading a voyage to the North Pole without understanding a word of it. At half-past eight she received a letter from Raoul and hurriedly tore it open. The letter began with these classic words:

My dearest love, when you receive this letter, I shall be no more.

She did not finish, but crumpled the paper nervously in her hand, rang for her maid, hastily donned a peignoir, thrust her feet into the first shoes that came to hand, wrapped herself in a shawl, and put on a hat; then she went out, bidding her maid to tell the Comte that she had gone to see her sister, Madame du Tillet.

"Where did you leave your master?" she asked Raoul's servant.

"At the office of his newspaper."

"Let us go there," she said.

To the great astonishment of her servants, she left the house on foot, before nine o'clock, evidently under the influence of intense excitement. Luckily for her, the maid informed the Comte that Madame had just received a letter from Madame du Tillet which gave her a terrible shock, and that she had hurried off to her sister's with the servant who brought her the letter. Vandenesse awaited his wife's return to find out what it all meant. The Comtesse entered a cab and was driven rapidly to the office of the newspaper. At that hour, the huge rooms occupied by the paper, in an old mansion on the Rue Feydeau,* were deserted; nobody was to be found but an office boy, who was greatly astonished to see a pretty young woman rushing wildly through the rooms, asking where Monsieur Nathan was.

"He is at Mademoiselle Florine's, of course," he replied, taking the Comtesse for a jealous rival who was intending to make a scene.

"Where does he work when he is here?" she asked.

"In an office, the key of which he carries in his pocket".

"I wish to go there."

The boy led her to a small, dark room looking out on a rear courtyard, formerly a dressing room attached to a large bedroom, the alcove of which had not been destroyed. The office was at right angles with the bedroom. By opening the window of the latter, the Comtesse could look through the office window and see what was taking place there: Nathan was sitting in the armchair of the editor-in-chief, writhing in the death agony.

Raoul sortit après avoir pressé la comtesse sur son cœur.

Plate XVII

"Break in the door and say nothing! I will buy your silence," she said. "Don't you see that Monsieur Nathan is dying?"

The boy ran to the printing office for an iron form with which to break in the door. Raoul was dying of suffocation, like a common seamstress, through the medium of a chafing dish of charcoal. He had just finished a letter to Blondet in which he begged him to give it out that his suicide was a stroke of apoplexy. The Comtesse arrived in time; she ordered Raoul to be carried out to the cab, and having no idea where to take him to procure proper care, she drove to a hotel, took a room there and sent the office boy for a doctor. In a few hours, Raoul was out of danger, but the Comtesse did not leave his bedside until she had obtained from him a general confession. After the ambitious castaway had poured into her heart the pitiable elegiacs of his sorrow, she returned home a prey to all the torturing thoughts that had besieged Raoul the night before.

"I will arrange everything," she had said to him, to induce him to live.

"Well, what is the matter with your sister?" Félix asked his wife when she joined him. "There is a tremendous change in you, I should say."

"It is a terrible story and I must keep it absolutely secret," she replied, summoning all her strength in order to appear calm.

In order to be alone and to think at her ease, she went in the evening to the Italiens, and thence to pour out her heart into Madame du Tillet's, to whom she described the scene of the morning, asking her advice and assistance. Neither of them knew that Du Tillet had kindled the fire in the vulgar chafing dish, the sight of which had terrified Comtesse Félix de Vandenesse.

"He has nobody but me in the world," said Marie to her sister, "and I shall not fail him."

That declaration contains the secret of all women's

hearts: they are heroic when they are certain that they are all the world to a great man of irreproachable character.

Du Tillet had heard the story, more or less proba-ble, of his sister-in-law's passion for Nathan, but he was one of those who denied it or deemed it incompat-ible with the liaison between Raoul and Florine. The actress would be sure to drive away the Comtesse, or vice versa. But when, upon returning home that eve-ning, he found there his sister-in-law, in whose face he had noticed at the Italiens, abundant evidences of intense emotion, he guessed that Raoul had confided his plight to her; in that case the Comtesse was in love with him and had come to ask Marie-Eugénie for the amount due Gigonnet. Madame du Tillet, who was un-acquainted with the secret of what seemed supernatural penetration, exhibited such dismay that Du Tillet's sus-picions changed to certainty. The banker believed that he could soon hold in his hand the thread of Nathan's intrigues. No one knew the poor fellow lying in bed in a furnished hotel on the Rue du Mail,* under the name of the office boy, to whom the Comtesse had promised five hundred francs if he held his tongue about the events of the night and morning. So François Quillet had taken the precaution to say to the concierge that Nathan had been taken sick as the result of overwork. Du Tillet was not surprised that he did not find Nathan at the office. It was natural that the journalist should go into hiding to elude the people sent to arrest him. When the spies arrived to make inquiries, they learned that a lady had come in the morning and taken the editor-in-chief away. Two days passed before they discovered the number of the cab, questioned the driver, found and searched the hotel where the debtor was coming back to life. Thus the wise measures taken by Marie had procured Nathan a reprieve of three days.

Each of the two sisters passed a miserable night. Such

a catastrophe casts the gleam of its charcoal over the whole life: it lights up the shoals and reefs, rather than the mountain tops which have thus far engrossed the attention. Deeply impressed by the horrible spectacle of a young man dying in his chair, before his journal, writing down his last thoughts just as a Roman might have, poor Madame du Tillet could think of nothing but assisting him and restoring life to that heart in which her sister lived. It is natural to the human mind to look to effects before analyzing causes. Eugénie, upon reflection, thought well of her plan of applying to Baronne Delphine de Nucingen, with whom she was to dine the next night, and she did not doubt that she should be successful. Madame du Tillet, great-hearted, as are all those who have not been crushed between the polished steel rollers of modern society, resolved to take everything upon herself.

The Comtesse, happy in that she had already saved Nathan's life, passed the night inventing schemes to procure forty thousand francs. At such crises, women are sublime. Guided by sentiment, they arrive at combinations that would surprise thieves, business men, and usurers, if those three classes of toilers, licensed or not, were ever surprised at anything. The Comtesse thought she would sell her diamonds and wear false ones. She decided to ask Vandenesse for the money for her sister, whom she had already compromised, but she had too much nobility of soul not to recoil from dishonorable means; they were conceived only to be rejected. Vandenesse's money to Nathan! She jumped up in her bed, terrified at her own wickedness. Wear false diamonds! Her husband would discover it sooner or later. She would go to the Rothschilds who had so much money and ask them for the amount she needed, to the Archbishop of Paris whose duty it was to succor the poor—rushing from one religion to another, imploring help from all. She deplored the fact that her family was no longer in the government; the time had been when she could have borrowed the money on the outskirts of the throne. She thought of applying to her father. But the old magistrate had a horror of anything illegal; his children had learned at last how little he sympathized with the misfortunes of love; he would not allow them to be mentioned, he had become a misanthrope; he held every sort of intrigue in abomination. As for the Comtesse de Granville, she was living in retirement in Normandy, on one of her estates, ending her days between priests and bags of gold, cold to the last. Even if Marie had had time to reach Bayeux, would her mother give her so much money without knowing what use would be made of it? Would she imagine it was to pay debts? Yes, perhaps she would allow herself to be softened by her favorite. Well then, in case of failure, the Comtesse would go to Normandy. The Comte de Granville would not refuse to furnish her with an excuse for the journey by sending her word of a fictitious serious illness from which his wife was supposed to be suffering. The lamentable spectacle that had horrified her in the morning, the care she had lavished upon Nathan, the hours passed at his bedside, his broken narratives, the death agony of a noble mind, the theft of genius arrested in its career by a commonplace, ignoble obstacle—everything crowded in upon her memory to stimulate her love. She reviewed her emotions and felt that she was even more captivated by misery than by grandeur. Would she have kissed that brow if it had worn the crown of success? No. To her mind, there was infinite nobleness in the last words Nathan had said to her in Lady Dudley's boudoir. What sanctity in that farewell! How noble to sacrifice happiness which would have become a means of torture to her! The Comtesse had longed for emotion in her life; it abounded there, intense and cruel, but dear to her heart. She lived more completely by sorrow than by joy. With what ecstasy she said to herself: "I have saved him once,

I will save him again!" She heard him crying: "Only the unfortunate know how far love can go!" when he felt her lips laid upon his forehead.

"Are you sick?" her husband asked her, when he went to her room to summon her to breakfast.

"I am horribly upset by the drama that's being enacted at my sister's," said she, without telling a falsehood.

"She has fallen into bad hands; it's a disgrace to the family to have a Du Tillet in it, a base-born creature; if anything should happen to your sister she would get very little pity from him."

"What woman is satisfied with pity?" said the Comtesse with a convulsive movement. "When you show no pity, your severity is a boon to us."

"I have known your nobleness of heart before today," said Félix, kissing his wife's hand, and deeply touched by this outburst of pride. "A woman who thinks like that doesn't need to be watched."

"Watched!" she repeated. "More shame that reacts upon you."

Félix smiled, but Marie blushed. When a woman is doing wrong in secret, she carries her woman's pride in public to the highest possible point. It is a little piece of dissimulation for which we must bear her no ill will. Deception at such times abounds in dignity, if not in grandeur. Marie wrote a line to Nathan, under the name of Monsieur Quillet, to tell him that all was going well, and sent it by a messenger to the Hôtel du Mail. In the evening, at the Opera, the Comtesse reaped the benefit of her falsehoods, for it seemed perfectly natural to her husband that she should leave her box to call upon her sister. Félix waited until Du Tillet had left his wife alone before he gave her his arm to escort her there. With what intense emotion Marie's heart was filled as she hurried through the corridor, entered her sister's box, and took her seat there with a calm and serene expression before the world of fashion, which opened its eyes to see them together!

"Well?" said she.

Marie-Eugénie's face was an answer in itself; it fairly beamed with artless delight which many people attributed to satisfied vanity.

"He will be saved, my dear, but for three months only, and, in the meantime, we'll think up some way to assist him more permanently. Madame de Nucingen wants four notes for ten thousand francs each signed by anybody, no matter who it is, so that you shall not be compromised. She explained to me how they must be made; I did not understand a word of it, but Monsieur Nathan will write them for you. I simply thought Schmuke, our old teacher, might help us out of the difficulty; he would sign them. If you send with the four notes a letter in which you guarantee their payment, Madame de Nucingen will let you have the money tomorrow. Do everything yourself, don't trust a soul. I don't think Schmuke will have any objections to make. To avoid suspicion on her part, I said that you wanted to oblige our old music teacher, a German who has had bad luck. So I was justified in asking her to keep the matter a profound secret."

"You are as clever as an angel! If only the Baronne de Nucingen does not talk about it until she has given me the money!" said the Comtesse, raising her eyes as if to implore God's assistance, although she was at the Opera.

"Schmuke lives on the Petite Rue de Nevers, that short street on the Quai Conti,* do not forget, and go there yourself."

"Thank you, dear," said the Comtesse, pressing her sister's hand. "Ah! I would give ten years of my life——"

"To have in your old age——"

"To put an end to such agony forever," said the Comtesse, smiling at the interruption.

All those who had their glasses fixed upon the sisters at that moment, would have believed, observing with admiration their ingenuous laughter, that they were discussing the most trivial matters, but one of those idlers who frequent the Opera rather to scrutinize the clothes and the faces than to enjoy the music, might have guessed the Comtesse's secret, had he remarked the violent emotion that suddenly extinguished the joyous expression of those two lovely faces. Raoul, who had no occasion to fear the bailiffs at night, appeared, pale and wan, with restless eye and clouded brow, upon the step of the staircase where he usually stood. He looked for the Comtesse in her box, saw that it was empty and hid his face in his hands, resting his elbow on the rail.

"As if she could be at the Opera!" he thought.

"Pray look at us, you poor great man," said Madame du Tillet in an undertone.

As for Marie, at the risk of compromising herself, she fixed upon him that piercing, steadfast gaze, in which the will gushed from the eyes, as the waves of light gush from the sun, and which, according to the mesmerists, penetrates the being of the person at whom it is directed. Raoul seemed to have been touched by a magic wand; he raised his head and his eye suddenly met those of the two sisters. With the adorable ready wit that never abandons a woman, Madame de Vandenesse seized a cross that lay against her throat, and held it up to him with a rapid, meaning smile. The jewel cast a gleam upon Raoul's brow, and he replied with a joyful expression; he understood.

"Is it not worth while, Eugénie," said the Comtesse to her sister, "to restore a dead man to life in this way?"

"You are entitled to join the Society to Relieve Shipwrecked Sailors," replied Eugénie, with a smile.

"How sad and downcast he was when he came, but how happy he will go away!"

"Well, how are you getting on, my dear boy?" said Du Tillet, accosting Raoul with every appearance of friendliness, and pressing his hand.

"Why, like a man who has just received most encouraging reports of the elections. I shall be elected," replied Raoul, with radiant face.

"Delighted," rejoined Du Tillet. "We must have some money for the paper soon."

"We shall find some," said Raoul.

"Women have the devil on their side!" said Du Tillet without seeming to heed Raoul's words, whom he had dubbed *Charnathan*.

"What's the matter?" asked Raoul.

"My sister-in-law is in my wife's box," said the banker; "there is some deviltry at hand. The Comtesse seems to be very fond of you, she bows to you across the whole hall."

"Look," said Madame du Tillet to her sister, "he is lying about us; my husband is wheedling Monsieur Nathan, and he is the man who's trying to put him in prison!"

"And men accuse us!" cried the Comtesse. "I shall enlighten him."

She rose, took Vandenesse's arm—he was waiting for her in the corridor—and returned with radiant face to her box; then she left the Opera, ordered her carriage to be ready before eight o'clock in the morning, and at half-past eight was on the Quai Conti, having taken the Rue du Mail on the way.

The carriage could not drive into the Petite Rue de Nevers, but as Schmuke lived in a house at the corner of the quay, the Comtesse was not compelled to walk in the mud; she could almost jump from her carriage step to the filthy, ruinous hall of the dingy old house, which was patched up with iron rivets like a concierge's crockery, and leaned over the street in a way to alarm passersby. The old precentor lived on the fourth floor, and enjoyed a lovely view of the Seine, from the Pont Neuf to the hill of Chaillot.* The good creature was so surprised when the footman announced his former pupil that, in his stupefaction, he allowed her to enter his apartment. The Comtesse had never imagined nor suspected the manner of existence suddenly revealed to her eyes, although she had long known Schmuke's profound contempt for dress and his very slight interest in the things of this world. Who could have conceived the absolute freedom and heedlessness of such a life? Schmuke was a musical Diogenes, he was not ashamed of his lack of order; he would have denied it, he was so used to it. The incessant use of a great German pipe had spread over the ceiling, over the wretched paper on the walls, scratched in numberless places by a cat, a yellowish tint, which gave everything in the room the aspect of golden harvests of Ceres. The cat, clothed in a magnificent coat of long, tangled, silky hair that would have made a concierge green with envy, was present like the mistress of the house, undisturbed, with a grave bearded face. From the top of a fine Vienna piano where he was sitting magisterially, he cast upon the Comtesse, when she entered, the same simpering yet indifferent glance with which any woman amazed at her beauty would have greeted her. He did not move, he simply waggled the silver threads of his straight moustaches and carried his golden eyes back to Schmuke. The piano, which was a decrepit affair, with a wooden frame painted black and gold, but dirty and dingy and cracked, exhibited a set of keys worn like an old horse's teeth, and yellowed by the fumes of pipe smoke. Little heaps of ashes on the keyboard told how Schmuke had ridden the old instrument to some musical debauch the night before. The floor, covered with dried mud, torn papers, pipe ashes, and other inexplicable rubbish, resembled the floor of a boarding school when it has not been swept for a week, from whence the servants eject piles of litter fitted for some place between the dung heap and the ragbag. A more practised eye than the Comtesse's would have learned something concerning Schmuke's life from the chestnut shells, apple parings, and eggshells in plates carelessly broken and dirty with sauerkraut. This German *detritus* formed a carpet of unclean particles which cracked under the feet and centred about a heap of ashes that descended majestically from a fireplace of painted stone, where a great lump of pit coal sat enthroned with two sticks of wood pretending to burn in front of it. Over the fireplace was a pier glass in which faces seemed to be dancing a saraband; on one side hung the glorious pipe; on the other, was a Chinese jar in which the professor kept his tobacco. Two armchairs purchased at second-hand, as was the thin, flat couch, the worm-eaten commode with no marble top, and the rickety table on which were the remains of a frugal breakfast, composed the furniture of the apartment, simple as that of a Mohican's wigwam. A shaving glass hanging on the sash of the curtainless window, surmounted by a tattered cloth streaked with dirt where the razor had been cleaned upon it, pointed to the only sacrifice Schmuke was accustomed to make to the Graces* and to society. The cat, a feeble creature and his protege, was the better favored; he revelled in an old sofa cushion beside which were a cup and plate of white porcelain. But the thing that no words can describe was the condition to which Schmuke, his cat, and his pipe, a living trinity, had reduced these articles of furniture. The pipe had burned the table here and there. The cat and Schmuke's head had smeared the green Utrecht velvet of the two armchairs with grease so thoroughly as to remove its rough surface. Except for the cat's splendid tail, which did its share of the housekeeping, the uncovered places on the commode and the piano would never have been swept. In a corner stood a pile of shoes which only an epic could enumerate.

The tops of the commode and piano were littered with music books, with cracked worm-eaten backs, and mouldy, whitened corners, where the myriad layers of the pasteboard could be seen. The walls were plastered with great wafers to hold pupils' addresses. The number of wafers without papers represented addresses that had ceased to be. On the wallpaper were calculations made in chalk. The commode was adorned with beer jugs emptied the night before, which looked new and shiny amid all the old lumber and waste paper. Hygiene was represented by a jug of water covered with a towel and a piece of common white soap, streaked with blue, which had spotted the rosewood in several places. Two hats of equal age were hanging on a hat rack, where the same old box coat with three capes, that the Comtesse had always seen Schmuke wear, was also hanging. On the windowsill were three pots of flowers, German flowers of course, and nearby a walking stick of holly. Although the Comtesse's sight and smell were disagreeably affected, Schmuke's smile and glance concealed these wretched details from her with rays of celestial light which made the yellow tints a blaze of glory and vivified the chaos. The soul of this divine creature, who knew and revealed so many divine things, sparkled like a sun. So frank, so artless was his laughter at the sight of one of his Saint Cecilias, that it gave off bursts of youth, gaiety, and innocence. He poured forth man's dearest treasures and made with them a cloak to hide his poverty. The most disdainful parvenu might well have deemed it a base thing to think of the frame in which this glorious apostle of the religion of music was set.

"*Ah! Py vat chance to you gome here, tear Montame la Gondesse?*" said he. "*Must I zing de zong of Zimeon ad my atche?*" This idea caused a renewed immoderate outburst of laughter. "*Am I in gut lug?*" he continued with a cunning look. Then he began to laugh again like a child. "*You gome vor de musik und nod vor ein boor man. I know,*" he said in a melancholy tone; "*put gome for vat you vill, you know dat here everyding is for you, poty unt soul unt broberdy!*"

He took the Comtesse's hand, kissed it, and deposited a tear upon it, for in the honest creature's mind every day was but the day after a benefaction. His joy had deprived him of his memory for a moment, only to restore it in all its force. He at once seized the chalk, leaped upon the armchair that stood by the piano, and wrote on the paper, as rapidly as a young man, in large letters: 17 FEBRUARY 1835. This pretty, ingenuous movement was executed in such a frenzy of gratitude that the Comtesse was deeply moved.

"My sister is coming to see you," she said.

"*De oder alzo! Ven? Ven? May it pe pefore I tie!*"

"She will come to thank you for a very great favor which I am going to ask you to do for her," she continued.

"*Gwick, gwick, gwick, gwick!*" cried Schmuke. "*Vat moost I to? Go to de teufel?*"

"Nothing but write: *Accepted for the sum of ten thousand francs* on each of these papers," she said, taking from her muff four notes of hand drawn in proper form by Nathan.

"*Ha! Dat vill pe zoon made,*" replied the German, as meek as a lamb. "*Pud I know not vere are mein bens unt mein ink. Get you avay vrom dere, Meinherr Mirr,*" he cried to the cat, who stared coldly at him. "*Dat ist mein kat,*" he said, pointing him out to the Comtesse. "*Eed eez de boor animal vat leefs mit boor Schmuke! He ees hantzoom?*"

"Yes," said the Comtesse.

"*Vood you lige him?*" said he.

"How can you think of such a thing?" she replied. "Is he not your friend?"

The cat, who was hiding the inkstand, seemed to understand that Schmuke wanted it, and leaped on to the bed.

"*He ees meesjefus as ein mongey!*" said Schmuke pointing to him on the bed. "*I call him Mirr, to clorivy our crate Hoffmann of Perlin,* whom I ferry vell knew.*"

The worthy man signed the notes with the unquestioning obedience of a child who does what his mother tells him to do, without understanding anything about it, but sure that he is doing right. He was much more interested in the cat's introduction to the Comtesse than in documents by virtue of which, according to the provisions of the law relative to foreigners, he might be deprived of his liberty forever.

"*You azzure me dat deze liddle ztampt babers——*"

"Do not be in the least alarmed," said the Comtesse.

"*I am not alarmt,*" he replied sharply. "*I zay vill dese liddle ztampt babers bleaze Montame ti Dilet?*"

"Oh! yes," said she, "you are doing her as great a service as if you were her father——"

"*Den I am ferry habby to pe to her ofe zome zerfiss. Hear me blay!*" he exclaimed, laying the papers on the table and leaping to his piano.

The old archangel's hands were already galloping over the old keys, his eyes were already gazing through the roof to the skies, the most enchanting of songs was already springing into life in the air and making its way into the heart, but the Comtesse did not allow this childlike interpreter of things celestial to make the keys and chords sing—as Raphael's Saint Cecilia does for the listening angels—after the ink had had time to dry: she slipped the notes into her muff and called her radiant master back from the ethereal realms through which he was soaring, by putting her hand on his shoulder.

"My dear Schmuke," said she.

"*Alretty!*" he cried, with pitiable resignation. "*Vy haf you gome ad all?*"

He did not complain; he stood up like a faithful dog, to listen to the Comtesse.

"My dear Schmuke," she continued, "it is a matter of

life and death; every minute is a saving of blood and tears."

"*Alvays de same*," said he. "*Go, anchel! Try de dears of oders! Be zhur dat boor Schmuke abbrezhiates your fizid more dan your benzhun!*"

"We shall meet again," said she; "you must come and play for us and dine with us every Sunday, under pain of making bad blood between us. I expect you next Sunday."

"*Druly?*"

"I beg you to come, and my sister will doubtless appoint a day also."

"*Den my habbiness vill pe gombleed*," said he, "*for I only haf zeen you at de Champs-Hailyssées ven you haf bast dat vay in ein garritch, ferry zeldom!*"

This thought dried the tears that were collecting in his eyes, and he offered his arm to his lovely pupil, who felt the old man's heart beating wildly.

"So you think of us sometimes?" said she.

"*Alvays ven eading my pret!*" he replied. "*In de furst blaize az my penefacdresses, unt den as de du furst mädchens voordy to pe lofed I haf effer known!*"

The Comtesse dared say no more. There was an indescribable solemnity—respectful, faithful, religious—in that phrase. The smoky, dirt-encumbered room was a temple inhabited by two divinities. Pure sentiment was growing hour by hour there, unknown to those who inspired it.

"Here we are loved, dearly loved," she thought.

The emotion with which old Schmuke watched the Comtesse enter her carriage, was shared by her, and with the ends of her fingers she sent him one of the dainty kisses with which ladies bid one another good morning at a distance. That sight kept Schmuke planted upon the sidewalk long after the carriage had disappeared. A few moments later, the Comtesse drove into the courtyard of Madame de Nucingen's mansion. The

Baronne was not up, but, in order not to keep a lady of such high rank waiting in her anteroom, she arrayed herself in a peignoir and threw on a shawl.

"I come in the interest of a kind action, Madame," said the Comtesse, "so that promptness is a great favor; except for that I would not have disturbed you so early."

"Why, I am only too happy," said the banker's wife, taking the four notes and the Comtesse's guaranty. She rang for her maid. "Thérèse, tell the cashier to bring me forty thousand francs himself, instantly."

Then she placed Madame de Vandenesse's letter in a secret drawer of her table, after sealing it.

"You have a lovely room," said the Comtesse.

"Monsieur de Nucingen is going to take it away from me; he is building a new house."

"You will give this one to your daughter, no doubt. They say she is to marry Monsieur de Rastignac."

The cashier appeared just as Madame de Nucingen was about to reply; she took the banknotes and handed him the four notes of hand.

"That will make your accounts balance," she said to the cashier.

"*All put de tiscound,*" said the cashier. "*Dis Schmuke ees ein musicien von Anspach,*" he added as he saw the signature, thereby causing the Comtesse to shudder.

"Am I in business, pray?" said Madame de Nucingen, rebuking the cashier with a haughty glance. "This is my affair."

The cashier gazed in vain from the Comtesse to the Baronne; their features betrayed nothing.

"Go, leave us. Be good enough to remain a few moments in order not to make them think that you had any interest in this matter," said the Baronne to Madame de Vandenesse.

"I will ask you to add to your very great kindness the further favor of keeping this transaction secret," rejoined the Comtesse.

"For a kind action, that goes without saying," replied the Baronne with a smile. "I am going to send your carriage round to the rear of the garden without you; then we will walk across the garden together and no one will see you leave the house; it will make the whole affair perfectly inexplicable."

"You are as charitable as one who has suffered," said the Comtesse.

"I do not know if I am charitable, but I have suffered terribly," said the Baronne. "Your suffering has been to better purpose, I trust."

As soon as the order was given, the Baronne put on her fur-lined slippers and a pelisse, and escorted the Comtesse to the gate at the rear of her garden.

When a man has concocted a scheme like that Du Tillet had concocted against Nathan, he confides it to no one. Nucingen knew something of it, but his wife was an entire stranger to these Machiavellian manoeuvres. But the Baronne knew that Raoul was financially embarrassed, and she was not fooled by the sisters; she had a shrewd idea whose hands the money would go to and she was delighted to oblige the Comtesse; indeed, she had profound compassion for embarrassment of that description. Rastignac, who was in a position to fathom the schemes of the two bankers, came to breakfast with her. Delphine and Rastignac had no secrets from each other, and she described her interview with the Comtesse. Rastignac, incapable of imagining that the Baronne could ever be involved in this affair, which was in his eyes subsidiary to the main scheme—one means among many—enlightened her concerning it. Delphine had perhaps ruined Du Tillet's chances of election and rendered of no avail the trickery and sacrifices of a whole year. Rastignac, thereupon, informed the Baronne fully, and urged her to keep silent as to the mistake she had made.

"If only the cashier does not mention it to Nucingen," said she.

A few moments before noon, while Du Tillet was at lunch, Gigonnet was announced.

"Show him in," said the banker, although his wife was at the table.

"Well, my old Shylock, is our man boxed up?"

"No."

"What? Did I not tell you he was in the Rue du Mail, Hôtel——"

"He has paid," said Gigonnet, taking forty banknotes from his pocket. Du Tillet's face assumed a desperate expression. "We must never turn a cold shoulder on good money," said Du Tillet's unemotional associate; "that may bring bad luck."

"Where did you get that money, Madame?" said the banker, glaring at his wife in a way that made her blush to the roots of her hair.

"I do not know what you mean by such a question," said she.

"I will get to the bottom of this mystery," he retorted, leaving the table in a rage. "You have upset my most cherished plans."

"You will upset your own lunch," said Gigonnet, seizing the tablecloth, which was entangled with the skirt of Du Tillet's dressing gown.

Madame du Tillet coolly rose to leave the room, for his words terrified her. She rang, and a footman appeared.

"My horses," said she. "Send for Virginie; I wish to dress."

"Where are you going?" snarled Du Tillet.

"Well-bred husbands do not question their wives," she retorted, "and you pretend to act like a gentleman."

"I no longer recognize you these last two days, since you have seen your impertinent sister twice."

"You ordered me to be impertinent," said she; "I am

making a trial on you."

"Your servant, Madame," said Gigonnet, but little interested in a family quarrel.

Du Tillet gazed fixedly at his wife, who returned his gaze without lowering her eyes.

"What does this mean?" said he.

"That I am no longer a little girl whom you can frighten," she replied. "I am and shall be all my life a good and loyal wife to you; you can be a master, if you choose, but a tyrant, no!"

Du Tillet went out. Marie-Eugénie returned to her apartments, worn out after this effort. "If it had not been for my sister's danger," she said to herself, "I should never have dared to defy him thus, but, as the proverb says, every cloud has a silver lining." During the night, Madame du Tillet had gone over in her mind her sister's confidential conversation with her. Sure of Raoul's safety, her mind was no longer dominated by the thought of that imminent danger. She remembered the terrible earnestness with which the Comtesse had spoken of flying with Nathan to console him for his disaster, if she could not prevent it. She realized that the man might induce her sister, by the very excess of his gratitude and love, to do what the sage Eugénie looked upon as downright madness. There were recent instances in high life of such flights, which purchased a little uncertain pleasure at the cost of remorse and the loss of consideration suffered by those who occupy a false position; Eugénie remembered their frightful results. Du Tillet's words increased her alarm beyond measure; she feared that the whole thing would be discovered; she saw the Comtesse de Vandenesse's signature in the portfolio of the Nucingen establishment; she determined to implore her sister to confess everything to Félix. Madame du Tillet did not find the Comtesse. Félix was at home. A voice in her heart cried out to Eugénie to save her sister. Tomorrow, perhaps, it would be too late. She took a great deal upon herself, but she resolved to tell the Comte the whole story. Would he not be indulgent when he found that his honor was still untarnished? The Comtesse was misled rather than perverted. Eugénie feared that she was a coward and traitress to divulge secrets which all classes of society agree in respecting, but she looked forward to her sister's future, she trembled at the thought of finding her some day alone, ruined by Nathan, poor, ill, unhappy, in despair; she hesitated no longer, but sent to request the Comte to receive her. Félix, surprised at her visit, had a long conversation with his sister-in-law, during which he seemed so calm and so self-controlled that she trembled lest he should decide upon some terrible resolution.

"Have no fear," Vandenesse said to her, "I will conduct myself in such a way that the Comtesse will bless you some day. However disinclined you may be to conceal from her the fact that you have told me, give me credit for a few days. A few days are necessary to enable me to go to the bottom of certain mysterious circumstances which you do not perceive, and more than all else to enable me to act with prudence. Perhaps I shall clear up everything in a moment! I alone am guilty, my sister. All lovers play their little game, but all women are not fortunate enough to see life as it is."

Madame du Tillet took her leave, much comforted. Félix de Vandenesse went at once to the Banque de France and drew forty thousand francs; he hurried to Madame de Nucingen's, found her at home, thanked her for the confidence she had placed in his wife, and paid back the money. He explained this mysterious loan as due to the extravagant demands of a benevolence to which he had determined to put bounds.

"You need give me no explanation, Monsieur, as Madame de Vandenesse has confessed everything to you," said the Baronne de Nucingen.

"She knows all," thought Vandenesse.

The Baronne handed him the letter of guaranty and sent for the four notes. Vandenesse, during this brief interval, bestowed upon the Baronne the penetrating glance of a statesman; he almost disturbed her equanimity, and he deemed the moment propitious for negotiation.

"We live in a time when nothing is sure, Madame," he said. "Thrones rise and disappear in France with frightful rapidity. Fifteen years make an end of a great empire, a monarchy, and a revolution as well. No one would dare take it upon himself to answer for the future. You know my attachment to *la Légitimité*.* There is nothing extraordinary about these words coming from my mouth. Suppose anything should happen: would you not be glad to have a friend in the triumphant party?"

"Most assuredly," she replied with a smile.

"Very well, do you care to have in me a debtor who could retain for Monsieur de Nucingen, if need be, the peerage to which he aspires?"

"What do you want me to do?" she cried.

"Very little," was the reply. "Tell me all you know about Nathan."

The Baronne repeated the conversation she had had that morning with Rastignac, and said to the ex-Peer of France as she handed him the four notes of hand brought to her by the cashier: "Don't forget your promise."

Vandenesse was so far from forgetting that magical promise that he dangled it before the Baron de Rastignac's eyes as a means of obtaining some additional information from him.

When he left the Baron's house, he dictated to a public scrivener the following letter to Florine:

If Mademoiselle Florine wishes to know the first part she is to play, she is requested to attend the next ball at the Opera, and to procure the escort of Monsieur Nathan.

Having put the letter in the post, he went to his man of business, a very clever, keen-witted fellow, albeit perfectly honest; he asked him to play the part of a friend of Schmuke, to whom the German, feeling apprehensive somewhat tardily as to the meaning of the words: *Accepted for ten thousand francs*, repeated four times, had confided the secret of Madame de Vandenesse's visit; in that capacity he was to go and ask Monsieur Nathan for a note for forty thousand francs as security. It was a bold game to play. Nathan might be already informed as to how matters had been arranged, but it was necessary to venture a little to gain much. In her excitement, Marie might very well have forgotten to ask her Raoul for any document to protect Schmuke. The man of business went at once to the newspaper office and returned triumphantly to the Comte's house at five o'clock with a note for forty thousand francs; at the first words he exchanged with Nathan he found he could safely say that the Comtesse sent him.

The success of this manoeuvre made it necessary for Félix to prevent his wife from seeing Raoul until the Opera ball, to which he intended to take her and there let her discover for herself Nathan's relations with Florine. He knew the Comtesse's jealous pride: he preferred to make her abandon her passion of her own volition, to give her no reason to blush beneath his eyes, and to show her in due time her own letters to Nathan sold by Florine, from whom he expected to be able to purchase them. This judicious plan, conceived so rapidly, already partly executed, was destined to fail through a trick of Chance which modifies everything in this world. After dinner Félix led the conversation to the Opera ball, remarking that Marie had never been to one of them, and he proposed that amusement to her for the next evening.

"I shall give you someone to poke fun at," said he.

"Ah! You will add greatly to my pleasure."

"To make the joke as enjoyable as possible, a woman ought to attack an illustrious victim, a celebrity, a man of intellect, and make him wish the devil had him. Would you like me to hand Nathan over to you? I shall have, from someone who knows Florine, secrets enough of his to drive him mad."

"Florine," said the Comtesse, "the actress?"

Marie had already heard the name in the mouth of Quillet, the office boy: it passed through her mind like a flash.

"Why, yes, his mistress," replied the Comte. "Is that very surprising?"

"I thought Monsieur Nathan was too busy to have a mistress. Do authors have time to love?"

"I do not say that they love, my dear, but they are compelled to *lodge* somewhere, like all other men, and when they have no home of their own, when the bailiffs are after them, they *lodge* with their mistresses; that may seem rather free to you, but it's infinitely better than to *lodge* in prison."

The fire was less red than the Comtesse's cheeks.

"Will you have him for a victim? You would frighten him," the Comte continued, paying no heed to his wife's face. "I will put you in a way to prove to him that your brother-in-law Du Tillet is playing with him like a child. The wretch is trying to get him into prison, so as to make it impossible for him to come forward as his rival in the electoral district from which Nucingen was elected. I know from a friend of Florine's, the amount realized from the sale of her furniture, which she gave him to found his journal; I know what she sent him out of the harvest she reaped last year in the provinces and in Belgium—money which eventually benefits Du Tillet and Nucingen and Massol. The three together have sold the paper to the ministry in advance, they are so sure of ejecting this great man."

"Monsieur Nathan is incapable of accepting money from an actress."

"You hardly know these people, my dear," said the Comte, "he will not deny the fact to you himself."

"I will certainly go to the ball," said the Comtesse.

"You will be much amused," Vandenesse rejoined. "With such weapons, you will be able to give Nathan's self-esteem a good shaking-up, and you will do him a service, too. You will see him fly into a rage, try to restrain himself, and squirm under your stinging epigrams! In a joking way you can enlighten an intelligent fellow as to the danger that threatens him, and you will have the pleasure of beating the horses of the *juste-milieu* in their own stable—you are not listening to me, my dear child."

"On the contrary, I am listening too intently," she replied. "I will tell you later why I am anxious to be sure of all this."

"Sure?" Vandenesse repeated. "Keep on your mask, and I will arrange it so that you will take supper with Nathan and Florine: it will be very amusing for a woman in your position to mystify an actress, after you have had a bout with a famous author and have kept his wits prancing about such momentous secrets; you can harness them both to the same mystification. I must try and get on the track of Nathan's infidelities. If I can learn the details of a recent adventure of his, you will enjoy the spectacle of a courtesan's wrath, a magnificent thing—Florine's will boil and seethe like an Alpine torrent: she adores Nathan, he is everything to her; she clings to him like the flesh to the bones, like a lioness to her cubs. I remember in my younger days seeing a famous actress who wrote like a cook come to one of my friends and demand her letters; I have never seen such a sight since—the tranquil fury, the majestic impertinence, the attitude of a savage—are you ill, Marie?"

"No; they have made too much fire."

The Comtesse threw herself upon a couch. Suddenly, with an impulsive movement impossible to foresee, suggested doubtless by the corroding pains of jealousy, she stood erect upon her trembling legs, folded her arms and walked slowly to her husband.

"What do you know?" she asked. "You are not the man to torture me, you would crush me without making me suffer if I were guilty."

"What do you want me to know, Marie?"

"Well, as to Nathan?"

"You think you love him, but you love a phantom constructed with words."

"Then you know——?"

"Everything," said he.

That word fell upon Marie's head like a club.

"If you prefer, I will never know anything," he continued. "You are in a mess, my child, and we must get you out of it; I have been at work already. Look."

He took from his pocket the letter of guaranty and Schmuke's four notes of hand, which the Comtesse recognized, and threw them into the fire.

"What would have become of you, poor Marie, three months from now? You would have found yourself being dragged by bailiffs before the courts. Don't hang your head, don't humble yourself; you have been led astray by the noblest sentiments, you have flirted with poetic ideas and not with a man. All women—all, do you hear, Marie?—would have been fascinated as you were. Would it not be rather absurd of us men, who have committed innumerable follies in twenty years, to insist that you should not be imprudent a single time in your whole lives? God forbid that I should triumph over you, or overwhelm you with pity, which you repelled so earnestly the other day. Perhaps the poor wretch was sincere when he wrote you, sincere in his suicide, sincere in going back to Florine the same evening. We are not to be compared with you. I am not speaking for myself at this moment, but for you. I am indulgent, but Society is not; it avoids the woman who makes a scandal, it does not choose that the same person shall enjoy perfect happiness and social consideration. I can't say that it is just. The world is cruel, that is all. Perhaps it is more envious as a body than when taken in detail. A thief sitting in the pit applauds the triumph of innocence and will steal its jewels when he leaves the theatre. Society refuses to put down the evils it engenders; it awards honors to skilful trickery, and has no reward to bestow upon unassuming devotion. I know and see all this, but, if I cannot reform the world, at all events it is in my power to protect you against yourself. We have to do with a man who brings you nothing but misery, and not one of those holy, consecrated passions which sometimes command us to sacrifice ourselves, and which carry their own excuses with them. It may be that I have done wrong not to give more variety to your life, not to show you the difference between tranquil happiness and the more exciting forms of enjoyment, traveling, diversions of all sorts. But I can account for the feeling that drew you toward a famous man by the jealousy you have caused certain women. Lady Dudley, Madame d'Espard, Madame de Manerville, and my sister-in-law Émilie have had a hand in it all. Those women, against whom I tried to put you on your guard, have cultivated your curiosity more to annoy me than to expose you to storms which have howled all about you without harming you, I trust."

As she listened to these words, instinct with kindness, the Comtesse was stirred by a thousand conflicting emotions; but the dominant force in the hurricane was ardent admiration for Félix. Proud and noble hearts are not slow to recognize the delicacy with which they are treated. Tact of this sort is to the emotions what grace is to the body. Marie appreciated the grandeur of soul that hastened to humble itself at an erring woman's feet in order not to see her blushes. She fled like a madwoman, but returned at once, impelled by the thought of the pain her action might cause her husband.

"Wait," she said to him, and disappeared.

Félix had adroitly prepared an excuse for her and he was soon rewarded for his good judgment, for his wife returned with all Nathan's letters in her hand, and gave them to him.

"Judge me," said she, kneeling at his feet.

Tu sais donc ? — Tout, dit-il.

Plate XVIII

"Is a man qualified to judge when he is in love?" was his reply. He took the letters and threw them into the fire, for he knew that in the future his wife would never be able to forgive him for having read them. Marie laid her head upon the Comte's knees and burst into tears. "Where are yours, my child?" he said, raising her head.

At that question the Comtesse ceased to feel the intolerable heat in her cheeks; she turned cold.

"In order that you may not suspect your husband of slandering the man you thought worthy of you, I will see that they are returned to you by Florine herself."

"Oh! Why should he not return them at my request?"

"But suppose he should refuse?"

The Comtesse hung her head.

"I am sick of the world," she said, "I do not care to go into society any more; I will live alone with you if you forgive me."

"You might be bored again. Besides, what would the world say if you were to turn your back on it abruptly? In the spring we will travel; we will go to Italy and all over Europe, waiting until you have more than one child to bring up. We must still go to the Opera ball tomorrow, for we cannot get your letters in any other way without compromising ourselves, and by the very act of bringing them to you, will not Florine demonstrate her power?"

"And I will see this?" said the horrified Comtesse.

"The day after tomorrow, in the morning."

The next night, toward midnight, at the Opera ball, Nathan was promenading in the foyer with a mask leaning on his arm, and with a decidedly marital air. After two or three turns, two masked women accosted them.

"Poor fool! You are ruining yourself; Marie is here and looking at you," said Vandenesse, who was disguised as a woman, in Nathan's ear.

"If you take my advice you will find out what Nathan is keeping secret from you, and that will show you what great danger threatens your love for him," said the Comtesse in a trembling voice to Florine.

Nathan had abruptly dropped Florine's arm to follow the Comte, who passed out of sight in the crowd. Florine took a seat beside the Comtesse, who led her to a bench where Vandenesse, having returned to protect his wife, was already sitting.

"Explain yourself, my dear," said Florine, "do not think to keep me waiting here long. No one on earth will ever take Raoul from me, you see, for I hold him by habit, which is every whit as strong as love."

"In the first place, are you Florine?" said Félix, resuming his natural voice.

"*Belle question!* If you do not know that, how do you expect me to believe you, you fool?"

"Go and ask Nathan, who is now looking for the mistress I am talking about, where he passed the night three days ago! He tried to suffocate himself, my dear, without your knowledge, for want of money. That is how much you know about the affairs of a man you say you love, and you leave him without a sou, and he kills himself—or rather he does not kill himself, he misses it. An unsuccessful suicide is as ridiculous as a duel without a scratch."

"You lie," said Florine. "He dined with me that day, but after sunset. The bailiffs were after the poor boy. He was in hiding, that is all."

"Well, then, go to the Hôtel du Mail on the Rue du Mail and ask if he wasn't brought there in a dying condition by a beautiful woman with whom he has been more or less intimate for a year, and your rival's letters are hidden right under your nose in your own house. If you would like to give Nathan a good lesson, we shall all three go to your house; there I will prove to you with the documents in my hand, that you can very soon prevent him from going to the Rue de Clichy, if you will be a good girl."

"Try to get somebody besides Florine to go with you, my boy. I am certain that Nathan cannot be in love with anyone."

"You would make me believe that he has been more attentive than ever to you for some time past, but that is the very fact that proves that he is very much in love——"

"With a woman in society, he?" said Florine. "A little thing like that doesn't disturb me."

"Well, would you like to have him come and tell you that he will not take you home this morning?"

"If you get him to tell me that, I shall take you home with me and we shall look for those letters, which I will not believe in till I see them."

"Stay here," said Félix, "and watch."

He took his wife's arm and stationed himself a few steps away from Florine. Soon Nathan, who was rushing up and down the foyer, looking everywhere for his mask like a dog in search of his master, returned to the spot where he had received the hint. Reading his very evident preoccupation in his face, Florine took her stand like a wall in front of the journalist, and said to him in an imperious tone: "I do not want you to leave me; I have my reasons."

"Marie!" the Comtesse, at her husband's suggestion, thereupon exclaimed in Raoul's ear. "Who is this woman? Leave her instantly, go out and wait for me at the foot of the staircase."

In this horrible extremity, Raoul shook Florine's arm violently; she was not expecting that manoeuvre, and although she tried hard to hold him, she was obliged to let him go. Nathan at once plunged into the crowd and disappeared.

"What did I tell you?" cried Félix in the stupefied Florine's ear, as he offered her his arm.

"Whoever you are, come," said she. "Have you a carriage?"

For all reply, Vandenesse hurried Florine from the room, and they joined his wife at a spot previously agreed upon under the peristyle. In a few moments the three masks, driven at full speed by Vandenesse's coachman, reached the actress's house, where she removed her mask. Madame de Vandenesse could not repress a start of surprise at the sight of Florine choking with rage, superb in her wrath and jealousy.

"There is a certain portfolio," said Vandenesse, "the key of which has never been entrusted to you; the letters should be in that."

"To tell the truth, I am puzzled; you know something that has been troubling me for several days," said Florine, hurrying into the dressing room to get the portfolio.

Vandenesse saw his wife turn pale under her mask. Florine's bedroom had more to say as to the intimacy between the actress and Nathan than an ideal mistress would have cared to know. The female eye can see to the bottom of things of that sort in a moment, and the Comtesse saw, in the promiscuous condition of things, a proof of what Vandenesse had told her. Florine returned with the portfolio.

"How am I to open it?" said she.

She sent for her cook's carving knife, and when the maid brought it to her, waved it above her head, saying in a mocking tone: "This is what they kill *chickens* with!"*

That remark, which made the Comtesse shudder, explained to her even more clearly than her husband had done the day before, the depth of the abyss into which she had almost fallen.

"What an idiot I am!" said Florine; "his razor will do better."

She went to fetch the razor Nathan used for shaving,

and cut a slit in the morocco large enough to allow Marie's letters to pass through. Florine took up one of them at random.

"Yes, this is certainly from a proper woman. It looks to me as if there is not a word spelled wrong."

Vandenesse took the letters and handed them to his wife, who went to a table to look them over and see if they were all there.

"Do you care to let me have them in exchange for this?" said Vandenesse, handing Florine the note for forty thousand francs.

"What a fool he is to sign such things! Take your letters," said Florine as she read the note. "Ah! I will give you countesses! And to think that I was killing myself body and soul in the provinces to scrape money together for him, and that I let a broker put the screws on me to save him! That is a man: when you damn yourself for him, he will walk over you! He shall pay me for this."

Madame de Vandenesse had made her escape with the letters.

"*Hé!* Look here, my handsome mask! Leave me just one of them to convince him."

"That is not possible," said Vandenesse.

"Why not?"

"That mask is your ex-rival."

"Well, she might at least have thanked me!" cried Florine.

"Why, what do you take the forty thousand francs for?" said Vandenesse, saluting her.

It very rarely happens that young people, driven to attempt suicide, try it again after they have once undergone the agony of it. When the suicide fails to cure himself of the disease called life, he becomes cured of voluntary death. So it was that Raoul no longer had any desire to kill himself, even when he found that he was in a much more horrible position than that from which he had just been relieved, being confronted with the Schmuke note in Florine's possession, who had evidently received it from the Comte de Vandenesse. He tried to see the Comtesse again to explain to her the nature of his love, which burned in his heart more ardently than ever. But the first time she met Raoul in society she gazed at him with the contemptuous stare that places an impassable chasm between a man and a woman. Despite his assurance, Nathan did not venture, during the rest of the winter, to speak to the Comtesse, or even to go near her.

He opened his heart to Blondet, however: he insisted upon talking to him about Laura and Beatrice, apropos of Madame de Vandenesse. He paraphrased the beautiful passage for which we are indebted to the pen of one of the most noteworthy poets of our day: "O my ideal, blue flower, with the heart of gold, whose fibrous roots, a thousand times more fine than fairies' silken tresses, plunge to the deep recesses of the heart to drink its purest essence; sweet and bitter flower! We cannot pluck thee that thou dost not cause the heart to bleed, and from the broken stem red drops ooze forth! Ah! Cursed flower, how it has twined its roots about my heart!"*

"You are raving, my dear fellow," said Blondet; "I agree that it was a pretty flower, but it was not ideal, and, instead of singing like a blind man in front of an empty niche, you had better think about washing your hands so as to make your submission to the government and fall into line. You are too great an artist to be a politician, and you have been made a fool of by men who are not your equals. Think about being made a fool of again, but in another place."

"Marie cannot prevent me from loving her," said Nathan. "I will make her my Beatrice."

"My dear man, Beatrice was a small girl of twelve whom Dante never saw again; except for that, would she have been Beatrice? To make a divinity of a woman we do not want to see her in a cloak today, tomorrow in a low-necked dress, and the day after on the boulevard, haggling over the price of toys for her youngest. When one has Florine, who is, at one time or another, a vaudeville duchess, a bourgeoise of melodrama, a negress, a marquise, a colonel, a Swiss peasant, and a Virgin of the Sun in Peru*—her only way of being a virgin, by the way—I do not know how one can take chances with a society woman."

Du Tillet, in the jargon of the Bourse, *closed out* Nathan's contracts, and the journalist parted with his share in the newspaper for lack of money. The illustrious man had but five votes in the college which elected the banker.

When the Comtesse de Vandenesse returned to Paris the following winter, after a long and happy trip through Italy, Nathan had justified all of Félix's anticipations: following Blondet's advice he was negotiating with the government. His personal affairs were in such confusion that the Comtesse Marie saw her former adorer on the Champs-Élysées one day, on foot, in the most lamentable array, with Florine on his arm. A man to whom a woman is indifferent is passably ugly in her eyes, but when she has ceased to love him, he is horrible to her, especially when he resembles Nathan. Madame de Vandenesse's cheeks flushed with shame at the thought that she had ever been interested in Raoul. If she had not been cured of all extraconjugal passion, the contrast between the Comte and that other man who had already forfeited his claim to public favor would have sufficed to make her prefer her husband to an angel.

Today the ambitious youth, so rich in ink and so poor in will power, has at last capitulated and taken refuge in a sinecure, like any man of moderate parts. After giving his support to all sorts of attempts at disorganization, he lives in peace in the shadow of a ministerial journal. The Cross of the Legion of Honor, once a fruitful subject of pleasantry to him, now adorns his buttonhole. The *peace at any price* policy,* upon which he had kept alive a revolutionary newspaper, is today the object of laudatory articles from his pen. Hereditary right, once so fiercely attacked during his Saint-Simonian periods, he defends today with the authority of common sense. This illogical conduct has its origin and its cause in the about-face on the part of certain men, who, during our latest political developments, have acted in the same way.

Les Jardies,* December 1838

ADDENDUM TO A DAUGHTER OF EVE
The following personages appear or are mentioned
in other volumes of *The Human Comedy*:

Aquilina
XXXIV: *The Magic Skin*
XXXV: *Melmoth Reconciled*

Bidault (known as Gigonnet)
III: *The Vendetta*
VII: *Gobseck*
XVIII: *César Birotteau, The Firm of Nucingen*
XXIV: *The Bureaucrats*

Blondet, Émile
II: *Modeste Mignon*
IX: *Another Study of Woman*
XVI: *Lost Illusions*
XVIII: *The Firm of Nucingen*
XV: *Jealousies of a Country Town*
XIX: *The Splendors and Miseries of Courtesans*
XX: *The Secrets of the Princesse de Cadignan*
XXX: *The Peasants*

Blondet, Virginie
IX: *Another Study of Woman*
XVI: *Lost Illusions*
XV: *Jealousies of a Country Town*
XX: *The Secrets of the Princesse de Cadignan*
XXVIII: *The Deputy for Arcis*
XXX: *The Peasants*

Bruel, Claudine Chaffaroux, Madame du (Tullia)
I: *Letters of Two Brides*
XIII: *The Rabouilleuse*
XVI: *Lost Illusions*
XXIII: *A Prince of Bohemia*
XXV: *The Petits Bourgeois*

385

Vignon, Claude

Appendix I:

"The Affair of the Diamond"

an episode from the Eleventh Amusement of
Charles Dufresny's *Amusemens sérieux et comiques* (1707)

Translated by R.J. Allinson

Because "L'Aventure du diamant" does not have a specific start-ing point in Dufresny's work, a little background to this anecdote is helpful for placing it in context.

Charles Dufresny's Amusemens sérieux et comiques *(2nd ed., 1707) is a satirical prose narrative divided into twelve "amuse-ments," each focusing on a particular sphere of French life such as the Paris social scene, the university, the opera, the royal court, and so forth. In these various settings, the narrator's companion, a Siamese traveller who is wont to appear and disappear at the whim of the author (and who does not really figure into this particular story), provides an outsider's view of life in France, often revealing its absurdity and hypocrisy.*

"L'Aventure du diamant" or "The Affair of the Diamond" forms part of the eleventh amusement, which is subtitled "the Bourgeois Circle." Shortly before the episode takes place, a group of ladies are growing bored listening to a Senator preaching about the deleteri-ous effects of gambling, when a handsome, young, and exquisitely attired Cavalier enters, arousing their curiosity. The Siamese trav-eller expresses surprise and dismay at the women's fickle behavior as they lose their composure and flock to the Cavalier. After an au-thorial digression, the narrator explains to his companion that it is the fickle curiosity of women rather than any romantic sentiment for the Cavalier that has made them act so impetuously; they take interest in his fine clothes, but soon grow bored when it becomes clear that he possesses nothing more than empty charms. The la-dies quickly discard their idol, and the Cavalier then moves on to his next encounter . . .

Thinking only of showing off his great charm, the Cavalier makes his way into the adjoining room, but there finds himself struck by the charms of a young woman—he besieges her with his eyes, he simpers at her, and finally he makes his approach.

The Lady is very reserved, but just as charming as her parish Cavalier; his manner does not alarm her at all, and once again it is curiosity which exposes her to the risk of a tête-à-tête with him: she therefore readies herself to listen to the Adventurer. Let us now see how our Cavalier will conduct himself with her.

He must be quite unsure of himself in the presence of this woman, for she seems full of spirit, and she will not easily buy into appearances. Nevertheless, we see here that even the most intelligent do not despise a handsome exterior: so our dashing Cavalier convinces himself that as he is persuading her that he loves her, he will also easily persuade her that she must love him. He makes use of the finest turns of phrase, and the most touching expressions of the silent language of mannerism: his natural language that he speaks so well. But the beautiful Lady does not seem open to this; what will it take for him to express himself more clearly? On his finger he wears an expensive diamond; he must now find a gallant means of offering it to her: he takes on a playful and light-hearted air, and gestures in such a way to make the diamond ring sparkle in the eyes of the disinterested lady. She is dazzled and turns away; such goings-on annoy her, it is nevertheless the sole recourse of the fool. He is greatly astonished to find a woman who will put a man like himself to the test, as well as a diamond like his; this is certainly a cold woman, an insensitive woman.

At the very moment when he despairs of this enterprise, this cold and insensitive woman suddenly seizes his hand for a closer look at the diamond from which she had first averted her eyes—what a change of fortune for this rejected lover! He takes heart, and so as to make his declaration short and to the point, he pulls the ring from his finger and presents it to her. It is taken; so as to better observe her, he redoubles his effort: he redoubles his hope and his boldness, he believes himself to be entitled to kiss the hand which received his diamond. The Lady examines it so carefully that she does not even think to become angry: on the contrary, she smiles, and without further ceremony, places the ring on her finger.

And now that his conquest is assured, the Cavalier, transported with joy, proposes a time and place for their rendezvous.

"I am charmed by this diamond, Monsieur," says the Lady with great composure, "and I accepted it from you without scruple, for it belongs to me. Yes, Monsieur, the diamond is mine; my husband took it from my toilette three months ago, and then made me believe he had lost it."

"This cannot be!" exclaims the coxcomb, "it was a Marquise who exchanged the ring with me."

"You are correct, Monsieur," the Lady continues, "my husband knows this Marquise of yours; he exchanged my diamond with her, the Marquise then exchanged it with you, and now I take it from you for nothing, although my husband certainly would have been deserving had I been in the mood to give you the same prize he received from the Marquise."

At this unexpected blow, our handsome Cavalier is dumbfounded and confused. On this occasion I forgive him for being speechless; even a man of intelligence would surely be at a loss.

Appendix II:

An extended excerpt from
Balzac's Preface to the 1839 Souverain edition of
A Daughter of Eve: A Scene from Private Life

Translated by R.J. Allinson

Scenes from Private Life would have been less complete without the principal work of this publication: *A Daughter of Eve*. This sketch was previously advertised by the *Revue de Paris*, but within a fortnight, this title, which also belongs to a charming little tale by Du Cerceau, appeared on a poster at the Théâtre des Variétés, which thus kept the author from carrying on with his work.*

A Daughter of Eve is intended to paint a situation in which some women are driven into an illicit passion by a host of more or less extenuating circumstances, but who, not seeing themselves too seriously compromised, are wise enough to return to conjugal life. The misfortunes of passion have taught them the pleasures of a happy household.

When the author published this work in a newspaper,* many readers were expecting emotional catastrophes—pages filled with tragedies, as they say—but the actual conclusion, although rather abrupt, made this scene seem rather innocent, and therefore a bit bland. How could the author demand that the public, nowadays so distracted, so disinterested in literature, pay attention to his *Scenes From Private Life*, which depict none of the acts of violence or spicy condiments that are to be found in a *Scene From Parisian Life?* In the plan adopted by the author, the *Scenes From Private Life* are intended to represent the phase of human life which encompasses the emotions of Childhood, those of Youth, early missteps, and beginnings in society; this plan should not have to present the depiction of any deeply-rooted vice, or of some long-standing passion, but rather the beginnings of lives, the errors which come less from some sort of system than from a desire whose driving force is not calculated, but instead caused by the inexperience of life. The author includes in his work enough of these denouements that are in harmony with the laws that govern the poetics of the novel to allow himself to follow, here and there, those outcomes of a more social nature, where everything seems to be tied together neatly and where everything concludes by resolving itself in a rather bourgeois fashion, usually with only the smallest of disruptions.

He has therefore not wanted to abandon here the principles which he had already adopted in the *Scenes of Private Life*, and which have perhaps been instrumental in the welcome they received. Later on, the differences in tone, shade, color, and outline that will distinguish the six parts of this work will perhaps be felt and appreciated, and the contrasts which will result from them will undoubtedly not be without effect. Until the day when this lengthy story of modern manners in action comes to an end, the author is forced to receive in silence the thoughtless critics who persist in judging in isolation parts of a work intended to be compatible with a greater whole, becoming something else by virtue of juxtaposition, by the addition or the proximity of a fragment still in progress. There are better critics—some full of goodwill and to whom the overall plan was not known—who found some parts of *Scenes From Private Life* a bit too lively; they did not consider the necessity which obliges the author to have at his disposal certain figures from this part of the work who must mature over time and would seem false later on if at first they did not show themselves with their true characters.

There is, however, a flaw in this voluminous work of mine—a flaw without remedy—which the public should be made aware of. It is now possible to evaluate the interwoven structure of *Studies of Manners in the Nineteenth Century*. This great book will contain more than one hundred distinct works—even *The Thousand and One Nights* is not so broad in its scope—for our civilization is vast in all its details, and of course a society such as ours did not exist in the Orient of Arab confabulations—confabulations which encompassed their entire world. Indeed, Scheherazade seems to be present only by accident: she is locked away, the house is walled, there is only the bazaar and the Caliph's palace where the traveller may enter, for the man of the Orient only received the foreign traveller in a special apartment. These customs dominated private life until the advent of Jesus Christ, whose religion created another set of morals. The Arab storyteller also depends upon talismans and strange coincidences to create interest; all the wonderment he brings is inspired by the imprisonment of women. For us, in times past, the novel also used to come up against some basic principles which were few and quite simple. Walter Scott has exhausted all the possibilities of the historical novel: the struggle of the serf or the bourgeoisie against the nobility, the nobility against the clergy, or the nobility and the clergy against the monarchy. The kings, queens, and great men of history, with their points of coherence as well as their weaknesses, were all necessary for him to achieve such great effects. Once everything was simplified by the monarchical institutions, these characters were simply divided up among the bourgeoisie, the merchant or artisan class, the free nobility, and the enslaved peasantry—and there one has traditional European society; it contributed little to the incidents which make up the novel. Thus you see what the novel was until the reign of Louis XV. Today, Equality in France creates countless nuances. Formerly caste gave to each a physiognomy which defined the individual; today the individual only maintains his physiognomy as himself. Societies no longer have anything picturesque about them: there are no longer either costumes or banners; there is nothing more to conquer; the social sphere is everything. There is nothing more original than that which exists in one's profession, nothing more comical than in one's habits. This lack of form necessitated that literature throw itself into the painting of an idea, and look for the most delicate emotions of the human heart. This is why the author has chosen French society for the subject of his work: it alone offers the spirit and spontaneity in normal situations where each can rediscover his mind and his nature. Such fecundity does not exist in England, the only country where modern doctrines are in effect as they are in France. In England, society's head is bowed under customs which deprive it of grace and the leave to go to the heart; it is under the influence of duty. Italy has no freedom, and its only possible novel has already been written, and admirably so: *The Charterhouse of Parma*. In Germany, where the old conventions struggle silently against the new, everything is still without character and formless like molten metal. In Russia, autocratic power constricts manners; there, there is only a single nature, that of the rich, and it entails little opposition. Spain is struggling more visibly than Germany between two opposing systems, and so France is the only country truly fitting for the novel. The author still knows of no observer who has noticed how French manners are, in literary terms, so far above those of other countries with regard to a variety of attributes, such as drama, spirit, and action—everything is said here, everything is thought here, everything is done here. The author here does not judge, he does not reveal the secret of his political thought, entirely contrary to the majority of France, but to which we will perhaps arrive at before long. The time is not far distant when the costly deception of constitutional government will be recognized. The author is simply acting as a historian, nothing more. He congratulates himself for the greatness, the variety, the beauty, and the fecundity of his subject, however deplorably it may confuse the most contradictory of facts, the abundance of its many elements, and the impetuousness of its actions. This disorder is a source of beauty. Thus, it is neither for national glory nor for patriotism that he has chosen the manners of his country, but because his country has presented, first of all, THE MAN OF SOCIETY under more numerous aspects than anywhere else. France is perhaps the only country which does not suspect the greatness of its role, the magnificence of its time, the variety of its contrasts.

And so this long story, wherein the reading public is the sultan, wherein the author resembles Scheherazade dreading every new evening, not to see oneself beheaded, but, what is worse, to see oneself dismissed as being a mere driveller, will unfortunately have, in the eyes of certain reasonable people, a most capital vice. Perhaps this vice will later pass for beauty.

Here you will find, for example, the actress Florine painted in the middle of her life in *A Daughter of Eve* in *Scenes From Private Life*, and you will see her in her debut in *Lost Illusions* in *Scenes From Provincial Life*. Here the tremendous figure of De Marsay appears as Prime Minister, but in *The Marriage Contract* he is in his beginnings; further back, in *Scenes From Provincial* or *Parisian Life*, he appears at the age of eighteen or at thirty as the most trivial and idle of dandies, who can only amuse himself by wearing out either his boots on the Boulevard des Italiens* or the shoes of his horse rushing off to the Bois. In *A Daughter of Eve*, characters like Félix de Vandenesse and Lady Dudley meet, characters whose circumstances would be eminently dramatic and replete with social comedy if their story were known, but the reader will not have the opportunity to read it until the final part of the work, *The Lily of the Valley*, which belongs to *Scenes From Country Life.* In summation, you will have the middle of a life before its beginning, the beginning after the end, and the story of death before that of birth.

Such is the case here in the social world. In the middle of a salon, perhaps you will meet a man whom you have lost sight of for ten years who formerly had no finesse in matters public or private, nor even a coat to his name, who is now a minister or a man of business; you admire him in all his glory, you are astonished at his good fortune or his many talents, and then, after retiring to a corner of the salon, you encounter a delightful storyteller of society who will paint for you, in the space of half an hour, a picturesque tale of ten or twenty years that you did not know. You will then find yourself recounting this story, be it scandalous or respectable, beautiful or unpleasant, the following day or a month later, perhaps even a few times at parties. There is nothing that is simply a single tile in this world, everything here is a mosaic. One can only tell the story of times past chronologically, a system that is inapplicable to the present which proceeds from it. Before him as a model, the author has the nineteenth century, a model which is extremely restless and difficult to fix in place. The author awaits the year 1840 when the reader will finally be able to finish these adventures, their denouement having taken him no less than three years to write. Literature cannot create time, the secret of restaurateurs who blow the dust of fantastical wine cellars upon young bottles of Bordeaux or Spanish wine. The book's publisher has said, rather wittily, that at a later date we should include with *Studies of Manners* a biographical index, which would assist the reader in finding his way through this immense labyrinth by means of a series of articles so designed.

RASTIGNAC, (Eugène Louis) eldest son of the Baron and the Baronne de Rastignac, born at Rastignac, Charente dé-partement, in 1799; comes to Paris in 1819 to study law, resides at La Maison Vauquer, becoming acquainted there with Jacques Gollin, known as Vaturin, and with the celebrat-ed physician Horace Bianchon. He falls in love with Madame Delphine de Nucingen, the daughter of Sieur Goriot, an old manufacturer of vermicelli, just as she is abandoned by De Marsay; Rastignac pays for her father's burial. He is one of the lions of high society (*see Tome IV*); he becomes acquaint-ed with all the eminent young people of his time, such as De Marsay, Baudenord, d'Esgrignon, Lucien de Rubrempré, Émile Blondet, du Tillet, Nathan, Paul de Manerville, Bixiou, and so forth. The story of his fortune is found in *The House of Nucingen*; he reappears in almost every scene in *The Cabinet of Antiquities* and in *The Interdiction*. He marries off his two sisters, one to Martial de la Roche-Hugon, a dandy from the days of the Empire, one of the characters in *Domestic Peace*; the other to a minister. His younger brother is Gabriel de Rastignac, secretary to the Bishop of Limoges in *The Village Curé*, whose activities take place in 1828; he is named bishop in 1832 (see *A Daughter of Eve*). Although from an old family, he accepts a position of undersecretary of state in the ministry of De Marsay, after 1830 (see *Scenes From Political Life*), etc.

We shall not continue with this lark intended to emphasize the drawbacks that the author has had the good faith to point out himself, and that shall perhaps seem instead like profun-dities when this *Story of Manners* finally receives the attention it is due—a situation assuming, however, that it can find read-ers in a time, difficult to foresee, when the French language of today might require commentary—something we cannot safely hope for. For the moment, its graces are in question and its drawbacks are genuine, or at the very least they will be so until such time as the author will have the pleasure of seeing the first three series republished with all their various developments, which, according to certain audacious book-sellers, will not be long in coming. In a few days, the author will have published *Béatrix or Love Under Duress* which will advance many of the *Scenes From Private Life*, the proper place for this work as well as *A Daughter of Eve*.

Besides, why would the author refrain from confessing his ambition to create a work worthy of being read more than once, a work which offers such attractions to those who will try to understand it, that this second reading becomes the occasion for a victory won over the indifference of his time with regard to serious literature? Is there not a little modesty in asking for this triumph of skillful combinations: a vast imbroglio similar to that which takes place before our very eyes, every single day in the great comedy of our century?

The author has often been heard to reproach some of the characterizations of his work, but his critics do not even consider that this so-called flaw stems from an excessive ambition: he endeavors to paint an entire country while painting men, to describe the most beautiful of places and the principal towns of France to foreigners, to record the state of nineteenth century buildings, both ancient and modern, to explain the three different systems which have, over the course of fifty years, given a particular appearance to houses and the furnishings they contain. Thanks to the care that he has taken, perhaps, one will know in 1850 what Paris in the days of the Empire was like. Because of him, archaeologists will learn the location of the Rue du Tourniquet-Saint-Jean* and the state of the adjacent quarter, now completely demolished. There is, in his story, an archaeological painting of houses which used to exist in Paris, the likes of which, in 1850, one would not believe had existed, had he not depicted them in their original state. This will also be the case for a few corners of the provinces, for some details of Military Life, and for historical figures whose immensity will never be truly taken into account. Because of the pleasure that they take at these local paintings, a number of illustrious foreigners have begged the author to consider those for whom France is the land of dreams—those who wish to know some of the places, persons, or things—and to persist with courage and tenacity in the manner in which he began. He has always believed that one of the glories of France is her ability to bestir Europe by the pen as it has been bestirred by the sword. Finally, are not the accessories of existence often some of the things of the greatest importance in the eyes of the following centuries? Our archaeologists commit the most serious of offenses by attributing strange customs to the furnishings of the Middle Ages or Roman Society. What value does Petronius's satire* not have in our eyes, which is after all but another Scene of Private Life of the Romans? How many books does one have to devour to acquire knowledge of the terrible use that the women of Rome made of the long golden needles with which they adorned their hair! What a treasure for us it would have been if some Roman author had had the courage to expose himself to the critics who would undoubtedly have taken him to task for relating the lives of the Romans *to* the Romans, for writing a Study of Manners encompassing the first century of the Christian era, between the reign of Caesar and Nero, and recounting the thousand details— lives both typical and grandiose—of this vast empire. Here, it is also the primary task of the author to achieve a synthesis by analysis, to portray and to gather together the elements of our lives, to establish patterns and to reveal them all together, to finally map out the vast physiognomy of a century by depicting some of its main personages. The approbations of certain men, all of whom have found a science satisfactory to them in the reading of this or that particular work, have gathered slowly. For quite some time the author believed in the joining of art and science for no other purpose than his personal satisfaction, yet every day he returns to the same misconception, while learning that it is only by conscientious work that he will receive his reward, sooner or later. Not long from now, a great and illustrious doctor will tell him how much he has been struck by the care with which he has built the medical physiques of his characters, by not giving to a blond-haired man, as do so many other authors, the passions and ideas, the morals or idiosyncrasies which are suitable for a man with brown hair; by not endowing a weak man with strong shoulders and a cyclopean chest; by not presenting as a strong man a character with a slender chest or cold white hands. Sometimes a scientist recognizes a serious study of the most profound issues. The public is ignorant of the travails of conception an author commits himself to as he pursues the truth and all its consequences, and how many slowly acquired observations must be buried in epithets, indifferent to all appearances, but intended to be discovered by one man in a thousand. Such is the case with a phrase from a portrait, as in *La Torpille** for example, which might cost a night's work, the reading of several volumes, and which perhaps poses major scientific questions. Has this not been the case for this very page?

"Only those races that are native to the desert have in their eyes the power of fascination. Their eyes preserve, no doubt, something of the infinitude they have gazed upon. Has nature, in her foresight, armed their retinas with some reflective ability that enables them to endure the mirage of the sands, the torrents of sunshine, and the burning cobalt of the Ether? Or, do human beings, like other creatures, derive something from the surroundings in which they develop, and preserve for ages the qualities they have drawn from them? The great solution of this problem of race lies perhaps in the question itself. Instincts are living facts, and their origins dwell in past necessity: variety in animals is the result of the exercise of these instincts. To convince ourselves of this long-sought-for truth, it is enough to extend to the herd of mankind the observation recently made on flocks of Spanish and English sheep which, in low meadows where pasture is abundant, feed side by side in close array, but on mountains, where grass is scarce, scatter apart. Take these two kinds of sheep, and transfer them to Switzerland or France; the mountain breeds will feed apart even in a lowland meadow of thick grass, the lowland sheep will keep together even on an alp. Several generations pass by before these acquired and transmitted instincts are reformed. After a century, the highland spirit reappears in a refractory lamb, just as, after eighteen centuries of exile, the spirit of the East shone in Esther's Jewish eyes and features."*

Another reader will notice the care with which the names are appropriate to the characters—the author has at least seen this imperceptibly appreciated in his work. Perhaps, as a novelist, he will be accepted also as a historian in one of those promotions that public opinion makes from time to time. But this most distinguished honor will necessarily delay itself until someone has finally understood this long work.

[the remainder of the preface is primarily concerned with *Massimilla Doni*]

*

Endnotes

References that can be found in an unabridged English dictionary, or are otherwise self-explanatory, are not included here unless they bear some special relevance to the author or the text.

A Second Home: **Textual History & Notes**

Manuscript: The Lovenjoul Collection, now housed at the Institut de France in Paris, is a vast library of French books, literary journals, newspapers, letters, and manuscripts assembled by Belgian scholar Charles de Spoelberch de Lovenjoul (1836-1907), and includes the papers of Balzac, Flaubert, Gautier, Sainte-Beuve, George Sand, and others. Due to Lovenjoul's efforts, nearly all of Balzac's original manuscripts and corrected proofs have been assembled in the collection and preserved for posterity. The original manuscript of *Une double famille* in 36 handwritten leaves (the first two pages are missing) forms part of this collection. The story ends differently in this earliest version, as follows: "Some time after this scene, the Comte de Grandville [*sic*] was dismissed from his position and separated from his wife, but kept his sons with him. He was appointed deputy, and proved himself to be one of the fiercest antagonists of the *Pères de la Foi* [The Fathers of the Faith]." The Comte de Grandville's first name here is given as "Victor."

Periodical: *Une Double Famille* first appeared as a fragment entitled "La Grisette parvenue" in *Le Voleur*, 5 April 1830; the title can be roughly translated as "The Grisette Who Came Up in the World."

1st edition: appearing as *La Femme vertueuse* (*The Virtuous Woman*) in *Scènes de la vie privée*, in vol. 2 of 2 (Paris, Mame et Delaunay-Vallée, April 1830); the work is initially divided into ten separate episodes and a conclusion. The Comte's first name is changed from Victor to Eugène.

2nd edition: as *La Femme verteuse* in *Scènes de la vie privée*, expanded edition, in vol. 2 of 4 (Paris, Mame-Delaunay, May 1832); changed to eight episodes and a conclusion.

3rd edition: as *La Femme vertueuse* in *Études de moeurs au XIXe siècle: Scènes de la vie parisienne*, in vol. 9 of 12 (Paris, Madame Charles-Béchet, November 1835); there are now only two parts and a conclusion. Eugène is changed to Roger.

4th edition: as *La Femme vertueuse* in *Scènes de la vie parisienne*, revised and corrected edition, in vol. 2 of 2 (Paris, Charpentier, December 1839).

5th edition: as *Une double famille* in *La Comédie humaine* (*Scènes de la vie privée*), in vol. 1 of 17 (Paris, Furne, June 1842); Balzac does away with all previous divisions, and the spelling of Grandville changes to Granville.

Sequence: The Furne edition, the last to be printed during Balzac's lifetime, has the novel as the sixth work of the *Comédie*, while the "definitive" French Pléiade edition, which arranges the works in the final state the author left them in before his death, places it in the ninth position.

Readers of *Une double famille* may wish to pay special attention to "the two Maries," Marie-Angélique de Granville and Marie-Eugénie de Granville, as the character of their early lives in this story will have important repercussions that manifest themselves in *A Daughter of Eve*, the last work in this volume.

1   To Madame la Comtesse Louise de Turheim: a friend of Balzac's eventual wife, Ewelina Hańska (1805-1882), known as "Loulou" to her intimates; she was said to be one of the women on whom the eponymous character in *Modeste Mignon* was based.

3   *The Rue du Tourniquet-Saint-Jean . . . the Hôtel-de-Ville . . . the Rue du Martroi*: the Rue du Tourniquet-Saint-Jean was a Parisian street of the old 9th arrondissement located in the Hôtel-de-Ville, a quarter named for the Paris city hall. The first part of the street's name, as Balzac explains, comes from the turnstile that used to stand there; Saint-Jean refers to the Église Saint-Jean-en-Grève, a church that was situated behind the Hôtel-de-Ville, near the shore of the Seine. The building was demolished between 1797-1800. This street and the nearby Rue du Martroi, formerly a site where criminals were executed (the old French word *martroi* means "place of martyrdom"), were incorporated into the Rue Lobau, the name by which it is known today, in 1838. The Hôtel-de-Ville itself can trace its origins to the 14th

century, and over time has been the site of numerous, highly significant historical events, among them the attempted suicide and capture of Robespierre.

the fête given in honour of the Duc d'Angoulême: Louis-Antoine, Dauphin of France and Duke of Angoulême (1775-1844), was the eldest son of Charles X and the legitimist pretender to the throne of France from 1836-1844. He fought for the reinstatement of his cousin Ferdinand VII during the Spanish War of Independence.

Rue de la Tixéranderie: Parisian street, no longer extant, dating to the 12th or 13th century that formed the border between the old 7th and 9th arrondissements, named for the weavers (*tisserands*, the craft of weaving is *tisseranderie*) who lived there.

the Marais: literally "the Marsh," a quarter of what was then Paris's 8th arrondissement, initially named because the area was a floodplain of the Seine. It was the site of highly fashionable aristocratic residences beginning in the 17th century, but had gone into decline by the early 19th.

the Rue du Chaume, the Rues de l'Homme-Armé, des Billettes, and des Deux-Portes: Parisian streets of the old 7th arrondissement. The first two were located in the Mont-de-Piété quarter, the latter two in the Marché-Saint-Jean quarter. The Rue du Chaume, variously known as the Porte de Braque, the Porte du Chaume, the Porte-Neuve, La Grande Rue de Braque, Rue de la Chapelle-de-Braque, and the Rue du Grand-Chantier-du-Temple, traces its origins to the late 13th century, and had been known as the Rue du Chaume since the 16th century; it was later absorbed by the present-day Rue des Archives.

The Rue de l'Homme-Armé, literally "the Street of the Armed Man," apparently took its name from a sign, perhaps a tavern's, that, like the street itself, is no longer extant.

3   The Rue des Billettes was formerly known as the Rue
     des Jardins in the 13th century and in the 15th as the
     Rue Où-Dieu-fut-Bouilli ("the Street Where God was
     Boiled," so named because it was where a Jew had al-
     legedly committed sacrilege by dropping the Host into
     a cauldron of boiling water); "billettes" refers to either
     a tollbooth that may have stood there at one point, or,
     perhaps more likely, to the rectangular scapulars worn
     by members of the Temple des Billettes, a church that
     would later become Protestant in the early 19th centu-
     ry. As with the Rue du Chaume, the Rue des Billettes
     and the Rue des Deux-Portes-Saint Jean were also in-
     corporated into the Rue des Archives in 1890.

6   *the Quartier-Latin*: not an actual quarter, but an area
     around the Sorbonne in the old 11th arrondissement,
     named for the language predominately spoken by stu-
     dents and their instructors until the Revolution.

     the Palais de Justice: the French name for "law courts;" in
     this particular case it refers to the judicial institution for
     the city of Paris. The building, which dates to the 13th
     century, is located on the Île de la Cité, in what was
     then the Cité quarter of the old 9th arrondissement.

8   *Lavater*: a finely-bound copy the Swiss theologian's
     L'Art de connaître les hommes par la physionomie (*The Art
     of Knowing Men by Their Physiognomy*, 1778), translat-
     ed from the original German into French, was one of
     Balzac's favorite books.

13   *that dearth of grain was beginning to be felt which made
     the year 1816 so hard on the poor*: the "*Année sans été*" or
     the "Year without a summer" was the name given to a
     famine caused by unusual climatic changes that took
     place in the summer of 1816, with Western Europe and
     France in particular being especially hard hit.

16   *Montmorency* (Val-d'Oise) is a French commune locat-
     ed to the north of Paris, famous for hosting Rousseau
     while he wrote *Émile*.

the Rue du Faubourg-Saint-Denis and the Rue d'Enghien: the first street, still in existence, formed the border between the old 3rd and 5th arrondissements, and is an extension of the Rue Saint-Denis, a road which leads to the Basilique Saint-Denis, for which it is named; the second was located in the Faubourg-Poissonnière quarter of the old 3rd arrondissement, and exists to this day. Formerly known as the Rue Mably, it was renamed in 1814 in honor of Louis Antoine Henri de Bourbon-Condé, Duc d'Enghien (1772-1804), who had been mistakenly linked to a Royalist conspiracy by the French police and was summarily executed on Napoléon's orders. This act outraged the courts of Europe, and definitively turned aristocratic opinion against the First Consul.

17 *Saint-Leu-Taverny . . . Saint-Denis*: both French communes located to the north of Paris. Saint-Leu-Taverny is situated in the Valley of Montmorency in what is today the Val-d'Oise département, and originally consisted of two towns, Saint Leu-la-Forêt and Taverny, which merged in 1806, but are today once again separate. The town's castle, the Château de Saint-Leu, was once home to Napoléon's brother Louis and his wife Hortense. The château was known for the extensive gardens on its grounds (see Plate XIX).

Eaubonne: French commune to the northwest of Paris in the valley of Montmorency.

19 *the taste of Queen Hortense*: Hortense Eugénie Cécile de Beauharnais (1782-1837), the Queen of Holland, was the daughter of Joséphine de Beauharnais from her union with Alexandre de Beauharnais, the French general who was executed during the Reign of Terror, and thus Napoléon's stepdaughter. Her husband was Louis Bonaparte, the Emperor's brother and King of Holland, with whom she had three sons, one of them being Napoléon III. She composed the melody for "*Partant pour la Syrie*" ("Leaving for Syria"), which served as a de facto national anthem for the Second Empire.

Plate XIX:
Saint-Leu (Seine-et-Oise)

Plate XX:
A dress *à la Grecque*

21   *Sambre-et-Meuse*: during the period of the Directory and the Empire, a département of France located in what is today southern Belgium.

      The Bourbons returned: the Restoration of Louis XVIII of the Bourbon dynasty to the French throne after the Revolution and the Napoleonic Wars.

22   *the* little Corporal *has sat where you are sitting*: a reference to Napoléon.

      a ribbon and cross . . . l'autre: The *Ordre national de la Légion d'honneur*, founded by Napoléon in May 1802, was a decoration that could be awarded to soldiers and civilians based on their merits and service to France, and, significantly, did not require the wearer to be a member of the nobility. The Order is divided into five degrees: Chevalier, Officer, Commander, Grand Officer, and Grand Cross; its motto is *Honneur et Patrie* (Honor and Fatherland). During the Restoration, Louis XVIII decided to keep the order, but changed the design of the medals so that images of Napoléon were no longer displayed; those loyal to the Emperor felt that it was awarded rather freely by the King, thus diminishing its importance. The award has gone through a number of subtle changes over the years, but to this day remains the highest honor France can grant to an individual.
      L'autre: the other, another reference to Napoléon.

24   *the Rue Taitbout*: extant Parisian street located in what was then the Chaussée-d'Antin quarter of the 2nd arrondissement, apparently named for a clerk of the court. In Balzac's *Splendeurs et misères des courtisanes*, the Rue Taitbout is the home of Lucien de Rubempré's mistress, Esther van Gobseck.

26   Ombres Chinoises: "Chinese shadows," or shadow puppets.

27   *the Feydeau Theatre*: originally known as the Théâtre de Monsieur because of its royal patronage, the Théâtre Feydeau, located on the street of the same name in the old 2nd arrondissement, was an opera house founded in 1788 by Italian composer and violinist Giovanni Battista Viotti; the theater specialized in the presentation of Italian operas and French plays. By the time of the story, the Feydeau had actually been merged with the Opéra-Comique for some time.

29   *the tiger's gold lace*: *tigre*, a groom in fancy dress.

31   *this little estate in the Gâtinais*: a historical region of France corresponding to parts of the present-day Loiret, Seine-et-Marne, Essonne, and Yonne départements to the south of Paris.

34   *the Rue Saint-Louis, in the Marais*: the Rue Saint-Louis-au-Marais, a street of the old 8th arrondissement known variously as the Rue de l'Égout ("Sewer Street"), the Rue de l'Égout-Couvert ("Covered Sewer Street"), and the Rue Neuve-Saint-Louis. During the Revolution, its name was changed to the Rue de Turenne after Henri de la Tour d'Auvergne, Vicomte de Turenne, a 17th century Marshal General of France, before reverting back to the Rue Saint-Louis during the Restoration.

Jardin Turc: an enclosed garden in the Temple quarter of the old 6th arrondissement, located between the Rue du Vendôme and the Boulevard du Temple, that served as a café as well as a musical venue; it was sumptuously decorated in the Turkish style, and noted for its pavilions with colored glass windows.

35   *Auvergnat*: a denizen of Auvergne, a former province located in south central France.

38   bouillotte: *bouillotte* is an early form of poker that originated around the time of the Revolution. A table lamp known as a bouillotte lamp was invented for use during

game play; its shade was designed so that it could be lowered as the candles burned down. It was usually made from brass or bronze, and had a base in the form of a dish where tokens could be placed.

39 *Quai des Augustins*: the Quai des Grands-Augustins, a wharf that runs alongside the Seine, still extant, located in what was then the École-de-Médecine quarter of the 11th arrondissement. The quay dates to the 14th century and was named for the Augustinian monastery that was situated nearby until the Revolution, when the building was declared national property and sold.

40 *the Councillor of State:* a member of the *Conseil d'État*, an institution which dates from the time of the French Consulate. Under the direction of the Consuls it was "responsible for drafting bills and regulations of public administration, and [resolving] difficulties that arise in administrative matters." The council was preserved under the Restoration as an administrative court, but had significantly less prominence. The July Monarchy saw some increase in its influence.

41 *the Rue Notre-Dame-des-Victoires*: Parisian street, still in existence, located in what was then the Mail quarter of the 3rd arrondissement. It was formerly known as the Chemin Herbu in the 17th century, and later named for the Basilique Notre-Dame-des-Victoires.

42 *the Rue Teinture*: street of the French town of Bayeux, named for the dyers who once plied their trade there. Balzac's sister Laure lived on this street after marrying in 1820; responding to a letter from her brother, full of questions about her new home, Madame Surville described it as being "full of bigots" or "full of sanctimonious women" ("plein de dévotes"), which is probably why he chose this street to be the home of the Comte de Granville's future wife, Angélique.

the Peace of Utrecht: treaties signed on 11 April and 13 July 1713 ending the War of Spanish Succession.

43   *a Dominiquin*: Domenichino, an Italian artist of the Bolognese School of Baroque painting.

46   *an air from the opera of* Rose et Colas: an opéra comique by Michel-Jean Sedaine (1719-1797) and Pierre-Alexandre Monsigny (1729-1817) that debuted in March 1764; the story concerns the quarrels of two lovers living in the countryside.

50   Va-t-en voir s'ils viennent: *"Va-t-en voir s'ils viennent, Jean"* ("Go see if they're coming, Jean"), the title of a popular song and its refrain; the phrase is a figure of speech used to humorously express disbelief; a contemporary equivalent would be along the lines of "yeah, right!"

      retours de noce: a celebratory event that usually takes place about a week after a wedding, during which time visits are paid to the bride and groom's birthplaces, symbolically uniting the two families.

      the Vieille-Rue-du-Temple and the Rue Neuve-Saint-François: the Vieille-Rue-du-Temple begins in what was the Marché-Saint-Jean quarter of the old 7th arrondissement and continues north, forming what was then the border between the Mont-de-Piété and Marais quarters; the street owes its name to the nearby Maison du Temple, a Templar fortress dating to the late 12th century. During the Revolution, its tower served as a jail for Louis XVI, Marie Antoinette, and other members of the royal family; this was demolished on Napoléon's orders in 1808, to prevent it from attracting royalist sympathizers, though remains of the building survived until 1860.
      The Rue Neuve-Saint-François was a Parisian street of the old 8th arrondissement, located in the Marais and named for François Lefebvre de Mormans, a 17th century "Président des Trésoriers de France."

the Rue d'Orléans: the Rue d'Orléans-au-Marais, a Parisian street of the old 7th arrondissement, no longer extant, that was actually located in the Mont-de-Piété quarter, near the Marais. It was named for Orléans, a historical French province.

the Chaussée-d'Antin: a quarter of the old 2nd arrondissement.

53 *Normande*: the name for a female inhabitant of Normandy.

65 *the Keeper of the Seals*: though the exact nature of the position varied over time, the *Garde des Sceaux* was the title given to the person entrusted with the seals of France, including the Great Seal of France, that were used to stamp official documents, necessary for marking laws and orders as official. French Kings of the Ancien Régime each had their own unique seal that bore their likeness; during the Revolution the royal seal was destroyed and replaced with one that depicted the goddess of Liberty.

67 *He showed a spring to Hagar when He had driven her into the desert*: Genesis 16:7. It was in fact Sarai that drove Hagar away, not God.

73 *Will you put on a dress* à la Grecque: the French name for a fashion in women's dresses, known more commonly in the English-speaking world as the Empire silhouette, which featured bare arms, a fitted bodice with a waistline raised to under the bust, and a loose, flowing skirt (see Plate XX).

the Rue Gaillon: Parisian street of the old 2nd arrondissement situated in what was then the Feydeau quarter, named for the Hôtel Gaillon: a great house that no longer stands.

73   *the Rue Saint-Lazare*: Parisian street of what was then the 1st arrondissement, dating to the 12th century and still in existence to this day, that formed the border between Roule and the Place-Vendôme, then continued into the old 2nd arrondissement, bisecting the Chaussée-d'Antin quarter. It was named for the Maison Saint-Lazare, a leper colony which was converted into a prison during the Revolution.

74   *the Palais-Royal or the Cercle des Étrangers*: Palais-Royal can refer to the 17th century palace, formerly known as the Palais-Cardinal, built for Cardinal Richelieu and used as his residence; a quarter of the old 2nd arrondissement that is named for the palace; or, in this case, a vast arcade of shops, cafés, theaters, brothels, and gambling dens (one of the most exclusive of which was the Cercle des Étrangers) built around the palace and its gardens at the direction of its owner and inheritor, Louis-Philippe II, Duke of Orléans, around 1780. Because of its royal status, police were not allowed on its premises, and the Palais thus became a magnet not only for pleasure-seekers, but also for revolutionaries. It became the Palais de l'Égalité during the Revolution, and Napoléon made it the seat of the Tribunat in 1800. The Palais was returned to the House of Orléans during the Restoration and was renovated at the direction of Louis-Philippe, but by this point had become a much tamer version of its earlier self.

75   *I think more of Taglioni's grace*: either Filippo (1777-1871) or Marie Taglioni (1804-1884)—Balzac is probably referring to the latter—the former was a dancer, choreographer, and teacher of Marie, his daughter, a famous and influentual ballerina of the Romantic era.

76   *Are you a match for Talma*: François-Joseph Talma (1763-1826) was a celebrated French actor, famous for his portrayals of Nero in Racine's *Britannicus* (1669), Augustus in Corneille's *Cinna* (1639), and many others. As a close personal friend of Napoléon's, there

was some speculation that Talma had given the First Consul lessons in public speaking and had shown him how to comport himself in a commanding and imperial manner.

78   *the Rue de la Chaussée-d'Antin*: street that formed the border between the Place-Vendôme quarter of the old 1st arrondissement and the Chaussée-d'Antin quarter of the old 2nd. The street was named for Louis Antoine de Pardaillan de Gondrin, the 1st Duc d'Antin (1665-1736). During the Revolution, in 1791, it was renamed the Rue de Mirabeau to honor the French politician who died there, and then changed again to the Rue du Mont-Blanc two years later after it was discovered that Mirabeau had had a secret association with the King. Its original name was restored in 1815, and is still in existence.

    In his *Histoire et Physiologie des Boulevards de Paris* (1846), Balzac wrote "the heart of present-day Paris . . . beats between the Rue de la Chaussée-d'Antin and the Rue du Faubourg-Montmartre."

One of those children of the night . . . during the Revolution, facetiously called members of the Committee of Research: the *Comité des recherches*, as it was known, was an institution created for the purpose of detecting anti-revolutionary conspiracies; vagrants, or those dressed as such, were (presumably) employed by the Committee to lurk about the streets, listening for and reporting on any speech or action that might be considered seditious.

a . . . face worthy of those immortalised by Charlet in his caricatures of the sweepers of Paris: Nicolas-Toussaint Charlet (1792-1845) was a French printmaker and painter who specialized primarily in depictions of military life and popular scenes. Charlet was an ardent Bonapartist, and his works did much to solidify the Napoleonic myth after the fall of the Empire (see Plate XXI).

Plate XXI:
École du balayeur by Nicolas-Toussaint Charlet

Plate XXII
Madame Laure de Berny by Henri Nicolas van Gorp

Domestic Peace: Textual History & Notes

Manuscript: the Lovenjoul Collection contains Balzac's complete handwritten text of *La Paix du ménage*, comprising 21 numbered leaves; there is no record of the story appearing in a periodical.

1st edition: in *Scènes de la vie privée*, vol. 2 of 2 (Paris, Mame et Delaunay-Vallée, April 1830); the story is divided into three parts, and ends on a much lighter note.

2nd edition: in *Scènes de la vie privée*, expanded edition, vol. 2 of 4 (Paris, Mame-Delaunay, May 1832).

3rd edition: in *Études de moeurs au XIXe siècle: Scènes de la vie privée*, vol. 2 of 12 (Paris, Madame Charles-Béchet, November 1835); some corrections made, the divisions are removed. The story ends abruptly with the revelation of the diamond's true owner.

4th edition: in *Scènes de la vie privée*, revised and corrected edition, vol. 1 of 2 (Paris, Charpentier, October 1839).

5th edition: in *La Comédie humaine: Scènes de la vie privée*, vol. 1 of 17 (Paris, Furne, June 1842); further revisions. The abrupt ending, not unlike the fate met by Rosalie de Watteville at the end of *Albert Savarus*, makes its first appearance here.

Sequence: The story was revised and corrected for the Furne edition of *La Comédie humaine* in 1842, appearing once again within the *Scènes de la vie privée* in the seventh position. The Pléiade edition places it in the tenth position.

The origin of Balzac's short novel can be traced to a work by French playwright Charles Rivière Dufresny (1648-1724) entitled *Amusements sérieux et comiques* (1699), a collection of interconnected short works divided into twelve satirical "amusements." A portion of the eleventh amusement, subtitled *"Le Cercle Bourgeois,"* or "The Middle Class Circle," contains the episode, *"L'aventure du diamant,"* or "The Affair of the Diamond" (see Appendix I), and it is from this anecdote that Balzac took his inspiration for *La Paix du ménage,* which he completed at La Bouleaunière, the country estate of Laure de Berny, in July 1829 (see note at the beginning of *Madame Firmiani* for more about Madame de Berny).

85   *Dedicated to my dear niece Valentine Surville*: the younger of Balzac's sister Laure Surville's (1800-71) two

daughters (the elder being Sophie, to whom *Ursule Mirouët* was dedicated). Valentine had, according to Balzac biographer Juanita Helm Floyd, "a good voice for singing and literary talent," though her uncle worried that her great beauty would cause her to become spoiled and indolent. She lived from 1830-1885; in 1859 she married the lawyer Louis Duhamel, with whom she had two children. She was responsible for the publication of her uncle's correspondence.

87   *The trumpet blasts of Wagram . . . Peace was being signed between France and the Coalition*: the Battle of Wagram (5-6 July 1809) resulted in a great but costly victory for Napoléon's forces, which had fought against the Austrian army led by Archduke Charles (1771-1847). The Treaty of Schönbrunn, signed on 14 October, marked the end of the Fifth Coalition, made up of the European powers arrayed against Napoléon, which included Austria, the United Kingdom, Spain, Sicily, Sardinia, and others.

a magnificent experiment in the power he afterwards displayed at Dresden: presumably the Battle of Dresden is meant, wherein the French fought against the Sixth Coalition (made up of the same nations that comprised the Fifth Coalition, along with Russia, Prussia, Sweden, and Portugal) on 26-27 August 1813, resulting in another, though less definitive, victory for Napoléon.

the sovereign's marriage with an Austrian archduchess: Marie-Louise of Austria, the daughter of Holy Roman Emperor Francis II, whom Napoléon married in 1810 in the hopes of producing an heir, as the Empress Joséphine was unable to bear children.

a few yards of red ribbon: possibly intended as a reference to the Legion of Honor (see note to page 22, *a ribbon and cross*).

88   *certain malcontents of the Faubourg Saint-Germain*: a quarter of Paris's old 10th arrondissement. A traditionally wealthy Paris neighborhood, it takes its name from the Abbaye de Saint-Germain-des-Prés, a Benedictine church built in the 6th century.

89   *the* Sénat Conservateur: a self-selecting legislative body that existed during the time of the French Consulate (1799-1804). Charged with protecting the Constitution of the Year VIII (and subsequently those of the Years X and XII which established Napoléon as First Consul for Life, and then as Emperor of the First French Empire, respectively), it was composed of permanent members who were entirely loyal to Napoléon.

Napoléon would have kept his word but for the scene which had broken out . . . between him and Joséphine, etc.: on 30 November 1809 (evidently the date on which the story takes place) Napoléon informed the Empress of his decision to divorce her so that he could marry Marie-Louise of Austria in the hopes of producing an heir. Upon hearing this, according to one source, Josephine is said to have cried out: *"Non, je n'y survivrai point!"* ("No, I will not survive this!") before fainting and being carried to her room.

90   *a young lady with her hair drawn back* à la Chinoise: a woman's hairstyle done "in the Chinese fashion;" the hair being pulled back into a topknot of curls in a manner that was certainly fashionable, but quite uncomfortable to wear.

91   *Monsieur le Maître des Requêtes*: Master of Appeals.

Dyle: a département of the French Empire which is today known as Brabant, the Belgian province in which Brussels is situated.

94   *Ravrio's work; Isabey made the design*: André-Antoine Ravrio (1759-1814) was a French sculptor specializing

in bronze furnishings (such as the French Empire mantel clock) who counted Napoléon among his many
famous and well-to-do patrons.

Jean-Baptiste Isabey (1767-1855) was a French painter
specializing in portrait miniatures. He too counted
Napoléon and Josephine among his clients, and was
given a part in directing the pair's coronation in 1804.

95   *you affect the Lovelace*: Robert Lovelace is a duplicitous
      gentleman appearing in Samuel Richardson's wildly
      popular epistolary novel *Clarissa* (1748), who continu-
      ously seeks to undermine the eponymous heroine's
      virtue.

99   *the Restoration*: see note to page 21, *The Bourbons*.

101   *the Princesse de Wagram*: Duchess Maria Elizabeth
      Amalie Franziska Wagram in Bavaria, Princess of
      Wagram and Neuchâtel (1784–1849), the wife of Louis-
      Alexandre Berthier (1753-1815), a Marshal of France
      and Napoléon's Chief of Staff.

105   bouillotte: see note to page 38.

107   *the Grand Duchess of Berg*: in full, Maria Annunziata
      Carolina Murat, née Bonaparte, Grand Duchess Consort
      of Berg and Cleves, Queen Consort of Naples and Sicily
      (1782-1839), usually known as Caroline Bonaparte, was
      Napoléon's youngest sister and the wife of Joachim
      Murat.

112   *The younger branch of the house of Navarreins bears quar-
      terly with the arms of Navarreins those of Lansac . . . etc.*:
      in the terminology of heraldry known as blazon, this
      means that the coat of arms is divided vertically, half
      blue and half silver, with the border between con-
      taining diagonal crenelations. The six spearheads are
      probably lined up vertically to either side of the center
      divide. These arms would occupy two quarters of the
      shield, the other two being occupied by the arms of the
      elder house of Navarreins, which are not described.

116   *as the Duc d'Albe once said, one salmon is worth a thousand frogs*: Fernando Álvarez de Toledo, 3rd Duke of Alba (1507-1582), known as "the Iron Duke," was a Spanish general charged with putting down Protestant revolts in the Netherlands. The saying that is attributed to him meant that he preferred striking at powerful figures rather than at the masses.

123   *the* moulinet: a dance figure in which four dancers join hands in a cross formation and then rotate.

126   *the Chaussée-d'Antin*: see note to page 50, *the Chaussée-d'Antin*.

    As she crossed the Pont-Royal: Parisian bridge located in the city's center that crosses the Seine and joins the Right and Left banks.

128   *she was one of the victims of the terrible fire . . .* , etc.: Karl Philipp, Prince of Schwarzenberg (1771-1820), was an Austrian Field Marshal and Minister of State who had fought at the Battle of Wagram. It was Schwarzenberg who arranged the marriage between Napoléon and Marie-Louise of Austria, and on 1 July 1810 a ball was given by the Prince at the Austrian embassy in Paris to celebrate their union. At about midnight, a candle accidentally set a curtain on fire, and despite vigorous efforts on the part of some officers to put out the blaze, it quickly spread to the rest of the building. The Prince's sister-in-law and the Russian ambassador were among those killed.

Madame Firmiani: Textual History & Notes

Manuscript: *Madame Firmiani* is one of the few original manuscripts of Balzac's that the Lovenjoul Collection does not possess, though it does contain pages from the second edition that bear corrections intended for the Furne. Two pages of the original manuscript are kept at the Bibliothèque municipale de Nancy.

Periodical: the shory story was published in the 19 February 1832 issue of the *Revue de Paris*.

1st edition: in *Nouveaux Contes philosophiques* (Paris, C. Gosselin, October 1832); appearing alongside *Maître Cornélius*, *L'Auberge rouge*, and *Louis Lambert*. Octave's character is initially named Jules; the uncle's name is given as Monsieur le Comte de Valesnes.

2nd edition: in *Études de moeurs au XIXe siècle: Scènes de la vie parisienne 4*, vol. 12 of 12 (Paris, Madame Charles-Béchet, May 1835); Jules's name is changed to Octave.

3rd edition: in *Scènes de la vie parisienne*, revised and corrected, vol. 1 of 2 (Paris, Charpentier, December 1839).

4th edition: in *La Comédie humaine: Scènes de la vie privée*, vol. 1 of 17 (Paris, Furne, June 1842); the Comte de Valesnes becomes Monsieur de Bourbonne.

Sequence: *Madame Firmiani* is the fifth work of the Furne edition of the *Comédie;* the Pléiade edition places it in the eleventh position.

In her *Women in the Life of Balzac* (1921), Juanita Helm Floyd states that "It is doubtless Madame de Berny whom Balzac had in mind when in *Madame Firmiani* he describes the heroine." To provide some context for this statement, the following has been freely adapted from Ms. Floyd's book:

Laure-Louise-Antoinette de Berny, née Hinner (1777-1836), was the daughter of a harpist at the court of Louis XVI and a lady in waiting to Marie Antoinette. Having been brought up in the midst of royal society, she was privy to all manner of the plots, intrigues, and secrets that Balzac would later make such effective use of in his stories. In 1793 she married Gabriel de Berny, a magistrate who was almost nine years her senior, and of the oldest nobility. Despite having nine children with her husband, their union was unhappy. She and her family were imprisoned for nine months during the Reign of Terror, and were not released until after the fall of Robespierre.

Balzac met his *Dilecta*, as he referred to her in his letters, perhaps as early as 1819, when the two families lived near each other in Villeparisis, a suburb of Paris. When Balzac went to reside there, he became tutor to his younger brother Henri, while at the same time giving lessons to Monsieur and Madame de Berny's son Alexandre, to whom the story is dedicated. It was under these circumstances that the great friendship between the aspiring writer and the grande dame would first begin to bloom. During the year 1825, Madame de Berny loaned Balzac 9,250 francs so that he could start a type-foundry, and on Monsieur de Berny's recommendation his venture gained official approval. The endeavor was a failure, requiring a further 45,000 francs from the De Berny's, and Alexandre was given charge of the business. Nonetheless, the two remained very close friends until 1832 when Madame de Berny began to feel that their relationship had become overly intimate. After 1834 Madame de Berny's health failed rapidly, and her last days were full of sorrow. On his return to France from a journey to Italy, Balzac was overcome with grief at the news of her death. "I have lost the being whom I love most in the world," he wrote ". . . She whom I have lost was more than a mother, more than a friend, more than any human creature can be to another; it can only be expressed by the word *divine*."

Although Madame de Berny was of great help to Balzac in the financial and social worlds, of greater value was her literary influence over him. She, too, was a writer and may have collaborated with him in the writing of the *Physiologie du Marriage* and *La Femme de trente Ans*, though to what extent is not clear. Balzac's conception of woman was formed largely from his association with Madame de Berny in his early manhood, and her reflection can be seen throughout his works in characters such as (but not limited to) Pauline de Villenoix (*Louis Lambert*), Pauline Gaudin (*La Peau de Chagrin*), and Madame de Mortsauf (*Le Lys dans la Vallée*). It would have doubtless given Madame de Berny great pleasure to know that she was the basis for the mature beauties about whom he so often wrote, and whose characterizations won for him so many feminine admirers (see Plate XXII).

131   To my dear Alexandre de Berny: Laure de Berny's son (see above).

134   *Florian*: Jean-Pierre Claris de Florian (1755-1794) was a French fabulist and writer of pastorals, also noted for his popular translation of *Don Quixote*. He became a member of the Académie française in 1788, but was imprisoned during the Revolution, and died shortly

thereafter. Balzac often makes reference to him in connection with French epigrammatist Antoine de Rivarol (1753-1801).

134   *the Matter-of-fact type*: *les Positifs* in the original.

the Rue du Bac: Parisian street of the old 10th arrondissement that ran through the Saint-Thomas d'Aquin and Faubourg Saint-Germain quarters; it leads to the Pont Royal, a bridge connecting the left and right banks. The street was named after the ferry that crossed the Seine at that location before the bridge was built.

the département of Montenotte: former French département that existed from 1805-1814 during the Consulate and First French Empire, traditionally a region of northwestern Italy.

135   *the class of Petty Autocrats*: *les Personnels* in the original.

136   *This young man is a Student*: *Lycéen* in the original, the French equivalent of a high school or sixth-form student.

The speaker is of the species Worryguts: the word used to describe this class of person in the French text is "*Tracassiers*," from *tracasser*: "to worry." The translator had originally rendered this as "Shrew" which seems to miss the mark; "worryguts," like the more familiar "worrywart," is likely an anachronism, but seems closer to what Balzac had in mind.

137   *utterances à la Talleyrand*: the "Prince of Diplomats," as he was known, Charles Maurice de Talleyrand-Périgord, 1st Prince de Bénévent (1754-1838), was a highly skilled French statesman who served in governments before, during, and after the Revolution, despite their widely disparate politics and aims. Some of his more famous quotations are: "*Ce n'est pas un événement, c'est une nouvelle*" ("This is not an event, it is a piece of

news," upon learning of Napoléon's death); "*Je connais quelqu'un qui a plus d'esprit que Napoléon, que Voltaire, que tous les ministres présents et futurs: c'est l'opinion"* ("I know where there is more wisdom than is found in Napoléon, Voltaire, or all the ministers present and to come: it is in public opinion"); and, perhaps most famously, "*C'est le commencement de la fin*" ("This is the beginning of the end").

the Faubourg Saint-Germain: see note to page 88.

the genus Distingué: there is no satisfactory English equivalent, which would otherwise have to be something like "the genus *distinguished*," or "the genus of *distinguished ones*," etc.

She adds a de *to everybody's name—to Monsieur Dupin, senior, to Monsieur Lafayette*: French names with the preposition *de* usually (but not always) denote a person with some degree of royalty in their family, and can also indicate an ancestral place of origin.

André Marie Jean Jacques Dupin (1783-1865), usually known as Dupin the Elder, was a French lawyer and politician. Successively he served as President of the Chamber of Deputies and of the newly-formed Legislative Assembly; as a close advisor to Louis-Philippe, Dupin was an important political actor during the July Monarchy.

Lafayette's name, in full, is Marie-Joseph Paul Yves Roch Gilbert du Motier de Lafayette, Marquis de Lafayette.

the unfashionable Marais: see note to page 3, *the Marais*.

138   cavaliere servente: literally an "obliging knight," a swain who is openly in love with a married woman and attends to her every whim.

139   *at the time of Mallet's conspiracy*: Claude-François Malet (1754-1812) was a French brigadier general who had

grown disenchanted with Napoléon as he became more politically powerful. In 1812, during the abortive French invasion of Russia, Malet took advantage of the Emperor's absence and planned to install a provisional government. Using a series of forged documents to support his claim, the General informed the head of the *Garde national* that Napoléon had died, and that he was taking command. The plot progressed successfully until a senior military police officer recognised Malet as a former prisoner (he had previously been imprisoned for belonging to the Philadelphes, an anti-Bonapartist secret society) and took him into custody. He and his co-conspirators were later executed.

139   *members of the Legion of Honour*: see note to page 22, *a ribbon and cross*.

140   *the various species of Tourangeau:* a native of Tours.

141   *the famous Abbé de Camps*: François de Camps (1643-1723), the Abbé of Signy, an antiquarian and numismatist.

La Bande Noire: "the Black Gang;" a group of land speculators who bought up old estates after the Revolution and tore them down for building materials.

a sort of Charles Moor: Karl Moor, the protagonist of Schiller's *Die Räuber* (*The Robbers*, 1781). After being swindled out of his inheritance by his younger brother Franz, Karl joins a band of outlaws and becomes a Robin Hood-like character who fights against corrupt authorities.

142   *he . . . understood almost all of the Charter*: a reference to the Charter of 1814, a constitution required by the Congress of Vienna as a precondition for Louis XVIII's restoration to the throne. The Charter retained some of the freedoms gained during the Revolution and the Empire, but as it had the King still holding the lion's share of power, the constitutional monarchy that it

promulgated would ultimately prove to be an unsatisfactory compromise between old ways and new.

the Quotidienne: an ultra-royalist newspaper. After merging with two other papers it became known as the *Union monarchique* in 1847, and in the same year Balzac had his novel *L'Élection* (later to be known as *Le Député d'Arcis*) serialized in its pages. The *Quotidienne* was also the newspaper in which Balzac first responded to an anonymous letter from Ewelina Hańska, one of his many admiring correspondents, who would eventually become his wife in 1850.

Mosè: *Mosè in Egitto* (Moses in Egypt, 1818), an opera by Rossini. The composer made some changes to the work, and retitled it *Moïse et Pharaon, ou Le passage de la Mer Rouge* in 1827.

Peyronnet: Pierre-Denis, Comte de Peyronnet (1778-1854), was a French Ultra-royalist politician and magistrate who served as Minister of the Interior on four separate occasions. He was an architect of the Anti-Sacrilege Act of 1825, and was one of the signatories of the July Ordinances, a set of royal decrees that, among other things, greatly restricted freedom of the press and dissolved the Chamber of Deputies, the lower legislative house; their issuance led directly to the July Revolution of 1830.

146 *Agnès Sorel*: mistress to Charles VII of France, the first woman to be officially accepted in that role. She bore the King three children and died at the age of 28 in 1450.

the Donna Julia and Haidée of Byron's Don Juan: the former is a married woman who has an affair with Don Juan and is consequently sent to live in a convent; the latter is a beautiful Greek maiden who nurses Don Juan back to health after he manages to swim ashore from his sunken ship. There, on the Aegean Island of

Cyclades, the two fall in love, but are discovered by
Haidée's father Lambro, who sends Don Juan away
on a slave ship, an act which causes his daughter to go
mad and die.

147   *the cool decision of Célimène ridiculing the Misanthrope*:
      Célimène is a coquette in Molière's *Le Misanthrope* who
      flirts with Alceste, the misanthrope of the title.

148   *the Rue de l'Observance*: Parisian street that was located
      in the Banque quarter of the old 4th arrondissement
      dating to the late 17th century. Between 1793 and 1796
      it was known as the Rue de Marseille and then as the
      Rue de l'Ami-du-Peuple after Marat, "the friend of the
      people," whose printing press was located nearby.

150   *We were married at Gretna Green*: Scottish village located
      near the English border which was a popular rendez-
      vous for young couples, who were legally allowed to
      marry there without parental consent.

153   et ego in Arcadiâ: a Latin phrase initially written as "*Et
      in Arcadia ego*," ("I, too, have been in Arcadia,") wrong-
      ly attributed to Virgil. In that form, the phrase first
      appears as the title of a painting (c.1622) by Guercino
      (1591-1666) which depicts two shepherds contemplat-
      ing a skull; Poussin completed a similarly-themed
      painting of the same title in 1638. Originally intended
      as a memento mori (as though the skull were saying
      "I, too, dwell in Arcadia"), the phrase came to mean
      something more along the lines of "I was young once,"
      and so Balzac is employing this phrase incorrectly, but
      was certainly not the first to do so.

154   *Saint-Germain*: Saint-Germain-en-Laye, a French com-
      mune situated about 12 miles to the west of Paris.

A Study of Woman: Textual History & Notes
Manuscript: the manuscript for *Étude de femme* is not extant.
Periodical: *La Mode,* 12 March 1830; the Marquis de Beauséant,

the Marquis and Marquise de Listomère, Madame de Nucingen, and Rastignac are initially "the Marquis de L . . .," "the Comte and Comtesse de ***," "the Vicomtesse de B," and "Ernest de M . . . ," respectively. The anecdote of the *bourguignon* is written as a footnote.

1st edition: in *Romans et contes philosophiques*, volume 3 of 3 (Paris, C. Gosselin, September 1831).

2nd edition: as *Profil de marquise* in *Études de moeurs au XIXe siècle: Scènes de la vie parisienne 4*, vol. 12 of 12 (Paris, Madame Charles-Béchet, May 1835); the above character's names are changed, the *bourguignon* footnote is incorporated into the text.

3rd edition: as *Profil de marquise* in *Scènes de la vie parisienne*, revised and corrected, vol. 2 of 2 (Paris, Charpentier, December 1839).

4th edition: as *Étude de femme* in *La Comédie humaine: Scènes de la vie privée*, vol. 1 of 17 (Paris, Furne, June 1842); Horace Bianchon's character is introduced into the story, and a brief mention of Madame de Mortsauf is inserted.

Sequence: The Furne edition has the story in the 9th position, the Pléiade in the 12th.

159　　*the Marquis Jean-Charles di Negro*: Gian Carlo Di Negro (1769-1857), as he was known in Italian, was a Genoese nobleman and man of letters responsible for the building of the Villetta di Negro, a grand park located in the district of Castelletto in Genoa that attracted famous visitors from far and wide.

161　　*the Restoration*: note to page 21.

　　　　till Monsieur de Listomère is made Peer of France: the *Pairie de France* was an honor granted by the King to certain distinguished members of the nobility. This distinction was reinstated after the Revolution by a provision of the Charter of 1814; its members, who could have either hereditary or lifetime appointments, formed the Chamber of Peers, the upper house of the French Parliament (the lower house being the Chamber of Deputies). Inherited peerages were abolished after the

July Revolution of 1830 (see note to page 142, *Peyronnet*), and after the Revolution of 1848 the Chamber of Peers was permanently dissolved.

162   *like all the Ministers . . . in France since the Charter*: see note to page 142, *the Charter*.

163   William Tell: the opera, with its famous overture, is by Rossini.

164   *the sudden and noisy language of a* bourguignon . . ., etc.: *bourguignon* is the French demonym for a Burgundian, a native of Burgundy. Balzac is here referring to the Armagnac–Burgundian Civil War (1407-1435), a conflict between two parties that took place during the reign of Charles VI of France. The war broke out soon after the King's brother, Louis I, Duke of Orléans, was assassinated by agents of John the Fearless, the Duke of Burgundy.

165   Inde amor, inde Burgundus: perhaps a play on *Inde amor, inde Venus*.

     the expedition to the Morea: between 1828 and 1833 French troops were sent to the Morean peninsula, now known as the Peloponnese, to fight alongside the Greeks in their war of independence against the Ottoman Empire.

166   cristallisation: in his *De l'Amour* (1822), Stendhal uses the following anecdote (as translated by Gilbert and Suzanne Sale for The Merlin Press in 1957) to illustrate this concept: "At the salt mines of Salzburg, they throw a leafless wintry bough into one of the abandoned workings. Two or three months later they haul it out covered with a shining deposit of crystals. The smallest twig, no bigger than a tom-tit's claw, is studded with a galaxy of scintillating diamonds. The original branch is no longer recognizable.

What I have called crystallization is a mental process which draws from everything that happens new proofs of the perfection of the loved one."

167   *the Rue Saint-Lazare*: see note to page 73, *the Rue Saint-Lazare*.

ex professo*:* Latin, "by profession."

168   *the* Gazette de France: known variously as *La Gazette nationale de France*, *Le Peuple français*, *L'Étoile de la France*, and simply *La Gazette,* the *Gazette de France* was France's first weekly periodical and was founded by French physician and journalist Théophraste Renaudot (c.1586-1653) in 1631 with the backing of Cardinal Richelieu. Largely an instrument of the government, the paper did not report the storming of the Bastille, and in later years served the legitimist cause; its final issue was printed on 30 September 1915.

170   *your poor brother is at Clochegourde*: Balzac based the Château de Clochegourde on the Manoir de Vonnes, a "little castle" located in France's Loire Valley. Though only mentioned in passing here, it is featured more prominently in *Le Lys dans la vallée*, a novel appearing much later in the *Comédie*.

The Imaginary Mistress: Textual History & Notes

Manuscript: the complete handwritten manuscript comprising 38 folios is held by the Lovenjoul Collection.

Periodical: serialized in five installments in *Le Siècle*, 24-28 December 1841, Nos. 355-359; the chapter titles are "*Un mystère dans le bonheur*," "*Deux nouveaux amis du Monomotapa*," "*Malaga*," "*Un homme incompris*," and "*Paz partout*."

1st edition: in *La Comédie humaine: Scènes de la vie privée*, Vol. 1 of 17 (Paris, Furne, June 1842).

2nd edition: appears alongside *Un début dans la vie* in an un-approved edition by Louis-Fortuné Loquin (June 1844); here the story has been artificially divided into ten parts, and many liberties have been taken with the text.

Sequence: The Furne has *La Fausse Maîtresse* in the 8th position, the Pléiade in the 13th.

Thaddée Wylezynski was a relation of Ewelina Hańska, the woman Balzac married shortly before his death in 1850 (see note to page 142, *the* Quotidienne). It was evident that the Polish gentleman carried a torch for his cousin, and when he died in 1844, Balzac wrote the following in a missive to Madame Hańska: "The death of Thaddée, which you announce to me, grieves me. You have told me so much of him, that I loved one who loved you so well, *although!* You have doubtless guessed why I called Paz, Thaddée. Poor dear one, I shall love you for all those whose love you lose!"

175   Dedicated to the Comtesse Clara Maffei: Elena Clara Antonia Carrara Spinelli (1814-1886) was an Italian *salonnière* and woman of letters remembered for her passionate support of the Risorgimento. Balzac first made her acquaintance in Milan in 1837 and was quite enchanted by her, much to the consternation of her husband, Italian poet and translator Count Andrea Maffei (1798-1885).

177   *the Faubourg Saint-Germain*: see note to page 88.

The Marquis de Ronquerolles was so unhappy as to lose both his children during the visitation of cholera: probably a reference to what is now known as the second cholera pandemic, a worldwide outbreak of the disease lasting from 1829-1851, which claimed 100,000 victims in France alone.

the fight by the Macta: the Battle of Macta, which took place on 28 June 1835 by the Macta River in western Algeria. Retreating French forces under the command of General Camille Alphonse Trézel (1780-1860) were routed by tribal fighters led by Emir Abd al-Qadir (1808-1883). A fictionalized scene from this battle serves as an important plot point in *A Start in Life*.

178 *Boulevard des Italiens, at Frascati's, at the Jockey Club*: the first is a Parisian street that was located in the old 2nd arrondissement and formed part of the border between the Chaussée-d'Antin and Feydeau quarters. To the east, it turns into the Boulevard Montmartre, home to Frascati's, a gambling den and café known for its fancy garden and sumptuous decor. The Jockey-Club de Paris was a prestigious gentleman's club created, as the name may suggest, to promote horse racing.

The strange struggle of Movement against Resistance: see the final paragraph of the note to page 304.

179 *Poniatowski*: Stanisław Antoni Poniatowski (1732-1798), who reigned as Stanisław II August, was the last King of Poland before the country was partitioned between Austria, Prussia, and Russia in 1795. Elected as king with Russia's support, he made several attempts to reform the Polish government but was opposed by conservative factions, leading to conflicts which resulted in the First and Second Partitions of Poland. The defeat of the Kościuszko Uprising, which attempted to liberate Poland from foreign influence and which Poniatowski felt obligated to support, led to the Third and final Partition of Poland, after which he abdicated and lived out his days in St. Petersburg.

180 *There are . . . two types of Polish refugees—the republican Pole, the son of Lelewel, and the noble Pole, of the party led by Prince Czartoryski*: Joachim Lelewel (1786-1861) was a Polish historian and political activist of Prussian descent who served as a deputy in the Sejm of Congress Poland and supported the abortive November Uprising against Russia in 1830.

Adam Jerzy Czartoryski (1770-1861) was a Polish-Lithuanian noble who served important roles in several countries' governments. Under Tsar Nicholas I he was the Minister of Foreign Affairs of Imperial Russia and active in creating the Third Coalition opposing Napoléon. Later, in Poland, he became president of the provisional government during the 1830 uprising and was subsequently exiled by the Russians. Moving to the United Kingdom and then Paris, he remained active in advocating for an independent Poland.

180 *Dante, in his exile, would gladly have stabbed any adversary of the Bianchi*: a reference to the Guelphs, an Italian political party active between the 12th and 15th centuries who backed the Pope and opposed the Ghibellines, supporters of the Holy Roman Emperor. The Guelphs eventually split into two factions, the Bianchi and the Neri. As a member of the Bianchi, who wanted a democratic Florence free from both papal and imperial influence, Dante was exiled from the city, on pain of death, by the ruling Neri in 1302; the city council of Florence revoked the poet's sentence in 2008.

181 *the Biblical solitude of* Super flumina Babylonis: Latin: "By the Rivers of Babylon," Psalm 137.

182 *the Rue de la Pépinière*: an existing Parisian street of the old 1st arrondissement in the Roule quarter, named for the royal plant nursery.

183 *the Revolution of 1830 . . . the House of Orléans*: the final years of Louis XVIII's reign and the succession of Charles X saw the gradual erosion of liberties gained from the Charter of 1814 (see note to page 142, *the Charter*) as well as an attempt to restore the old pre-revolutionary order. The July Monarchy of Louis-Philippe, the "Citizen King," a more moderate constitutional monarchy than that of Louis XVIII, began with the July Revolution of 1830 and lasted until 1848.

   The House of Orléans is a junior branch of the House of Bourbon, to which Louis-Philippe belonged.

   a Peer of France of July: see note to page 161, *Monsieur de Listomère*.

184 *George IV at Brighton*: a reference to the Brighton
Pavilion, a royal residence built in the Indo-Saracenic
style at the direction of George IV, located in the
English seaside town of the same name.

Elschoët and Klagmann: Jean-Jacques Elschoët (also
spelled Elshoecht, 1797-1856) and Jean-Baptiste-Jules
Klagmann (1810-1867) were French sculptors; both
distinguished themselves with public projects such as
fountains.

186 *Mademoiselle de Fauveau*: Félicie de Fauveau (1801-1886)
was a French sculptor whose work is considered to be
a stylistic precursor to the pre-Raphaelite movement.

187 far niente: Italian, "doing nothing."

tombaki: a Persian variety of tobacco.

190 *her hair curled* à l'Anglaise . . . *keepsakes*: a hairstyle
with long sausage curls on either side of the face, inspired, in part, by gift publications from England
known as "keepsakes," which, according to Carol
de Dobay Rifelj's *Coiffures: Hair in Nineteenth-century
French Literature and Culture*, were steel plate engrav-
ings featuring images of women in fashionable dress
accompanied by French prose and verse. This style,
which remained fashionable into the 1850s, would
have been time-consuming to create, but was considered attractive and seductive.

191 *the handsome Trasteverini*: the demonym for inhabitants
of Trastevere, a district of Rome that lies to the west of
the Tiber River.

192 *At the time of the fall of the Pazzi*: a prominent Tuscan
noble family that plotted unsuccessfully against the
ruling Medici family in the late 15th century and was
subsequently expelled from Florence.

193   *he served under the Grand Duke Constantine at the time of our Revolution*: Grand Duke Constantine Pavlovich of Russia (1779-1831), was the brother of Tsars Alexander I and Nicolas I; the death of the former, and Constantine's subsequent abdication, led to the Decembrist Revolt of 1825. Given the post of *de facto* viceroy of Poland, he was seen by the Poles as the face of heavy-handed Russian control of their country, discontent with which led to the November Uprising of 1830.

194   Dunquè: Italian, therefore.

198   *the Bois de Boulogne*: A large park which at the time was several miles to the west of Paris, and today is part of the city. Originally used as a royal hunting ground, the woods were heavily deforested by occupying British and Russian troops after the defeat of Napoléon. In the subsequent years it was reforested and beautified, and became a popular recreational spot. When characters in Balzac's stories speak of "going to the park" or "going to the bois," and are in Paris, they are likely referring to the Bois de Boulogne.

199   *Duprez is singing in* William Tell: Gilbert-Louis Duprez (1806-1896) was a French tenor famous for being the first to sing a high C from the chest, a technique he debuted while playing the part of Arnold in *William Tell*.

     the Variétés: the Théâtre des Variétés, a Parisian theater dating to 1807 which remains open to this day and at the same address: at No. 7 Boulevard Montmartre, in what was then the Feydeau quarter of the 2nd arrondissement.

201   *Don Juan himself preferred one among the* mille e tre: the mythical Spanish nobleman was said to have made love to no less than one thousand and three women during the course of his many adventures.

206   *the cleverest of ambassadors next to Talleyrand*: see note to
       page 137, *Talleyrand.*

208   *The Revolt of the Seraglio*: *La révolte au Sérail* (1833), a
       three act ballet by Théodore Labarre (1805-1870), a
       French composer and harpist, and Filippo Taglioni (see
       note to page 75).

210   *the Bouthor family, people who have a circus in the style of*
       Franconi's . . . the Cirque-Olympique: Antonio Franconi
       (1738-1836) was an Italian performer who founded the
       Cirque-Olympique in 1807, a company specializing in
       equestrian acts, which perfomed at a number of differ-
       ent venues throughout Paris.

       Cinti and Malibran, Grisi and Taglioni, Pasta and Elsler:
       Laure Cinti-Damoreau (1801-1863), Maria Malibran
       (1808-1836), and Giuditta Pasta (1797-1865) were cel-
       ebrated opera singers from France, Italy, and Spain,
       respectively. There were several famous members of
       the Grisi family: Giuditta (1805-1840) and Giulia (1811-
       1869) were opera singers and Carlotta (1819-1899) was
       a ballet dancer. For Taglioni see note to page 75. Sisters
       Fanny (1810-1884) and Therese (1808-1878) Elssler were
       ballet dancers. Many, if not all, were associated with
       Rossini and his works.

211   *the heroine of* Peveril of the Peak: a lengthy historical
       novel by Walter Scott taking place in the late 17th
       century in which Alice Bridgenorth, the daughter of
       a Roundhead, falls in love with the Cavalier Julian
       Peveril.

       Her "muzzle" . . . is, as Shakespeare has it, as fresh and
       sweet as a heifer's snout: there does not appear to be an
       equivalent line in any of Shakespeare's works.

       the Rue Saint-Lazare: see note to page 73, *the Rue Saint-*
       Lazare.

Plate XXIII:
The Death of Poniatowski by January Suchodolksi

Plate XXIV
Chateaubriand by Girodet

212   *She sees in every Pole a Poniatowski . . . jumping into the Elster*: not the Polish King mentioned above, but his nephew, Prince Józef Antoni Poniatowski (1763-1813), a general and Marshal of the French Empire who led Polish troops under Napoléon. During the Battle of Leipzig in 1813, he defended the city against armies of the Sixth Coalition, but was forced to retreat towards the Weisse Elster River. His French allies had prematurely blown up the bridge, forcing a wounded Poniatowski to attempt a fording of the river on horseback, causing him to drown. He became a highly romanticized, even Napoleonic, figure to Poles fighting for freedom against foreign occupiers, especially during the November Uprising of 1830 (see Plate XXIII).

213   *Rue des Fossés-du-Temple*: Parisian street located in the Temple quarter of the old 6th arrondissement that ran parallel to the Boulevard du Temple, passing behind the Cirque-Olympique.

220   *Petrarch's chaste passion for Laura*: Laura was an idealized figure of a young girl (who may or may not have been based on a real person) who is the subject of the Italian poet's 14th century work *Il Canzoniere*.

      the emotion which Assas felt in dying: Louis d'Assas du Mercou (1733-1760) was a French aristocrat and Captain of the Régiment d'Auvergne. While on patrol before the Battle of Kloster Kampen, he is credited with warning French troops of the presense of the enemy by crying "To me, Auvergne! Here is the enemy!" before being killed by English soldiers.

223   *the Rue Saint-Honoré . . . Musard . . . the famous galop in Gustavus*: the Rue Saint-Honoré is a Parisian street (sections of which date back as far as the early 14th century) that ran through parts of what were then the 1st, 2nd, and 4th arrondissements; known by various names over its long history, its current appellation comes from a church that formerly stood within

the Cloister of Saint-Honoré. Balzac situates César Birotteau's perfume shop, known as "The Queen of Roses," at No. 397 on this street.

Philippe Musard (1792-1859) was a French composer and conductor, known as *le Napoléon du quadrille*, remembered for his lively and unconventional performance style. His performances included antics such as firing pistols in the air to signal the final galop of a piece. During Carnival each year he would host a series of masked balls where guests would don fancy costumes and participate in wild dancing.

Gustave III, ou Le bal masqué (1833), is a historical opera by Auber dramatizing the assassination of the Swedish King during a masked ball.

223   *Valentino . . . Thaddée, dressed as Robert Macaire*: Henri-Justin-Joseph Valentino (1787-1865) was a French musician who conducted at the Paris Opera and the Opéra-Comique. He went on to produce a series of more affordable classical concerts aimed at wider audiences, which came to be known as "Concerts Valentino."

Robert Macaire was a character created by French playwright Benjamin Antier (1787-1870) for a drama entitled *L'Auberge des Adrets* (1823). Macaire was originally depicted as a tattered thief, but evolved into a well-dressed financial swindler famously depicted by the artist Daumier. A stock villain in a number of French plays, he came to symbolize the perceived hypocrisy of the July Monarchy.

229   *the Porte Maillot*: A gate at the northeast corner of the Bois de Bologne, at the time located outside of Paris to the west.

the Khiva Expedition: the Khanate of Khiva was a region which encompassed parts of present-day Uzbekistan, Kazakhstan, and Turkmenistan. In 1839 Tsar Nicholas I sent an expedition to Khiva with a twofold purpose: to free captured Russians who had been sold into slavery by Turkmen raiders, and the expansion of Russia's borders in an attempt to counter Great Britain's growing influence in the area.

230   *the Allée de Mademoiselle . . . the Route des Dames . . . the cedar at the Ronds-points*: names of pathways in the Bois de Boulogne.

A Daughter of Eve: Textual History & Notes

Manuscript: the Lovenjoul Collection has the entire manuscript, which bears the subtitle "*Scène inédite de la vie privé*" and is dated December 1838.

Periodical: serialized in 13 installments in *Le Siècle*, 31 December 1838-14 January 1839, bearing the titles "*Les Deux Marie* [sic]," "*Confidences de Deux Soeurs*," "*Un Homme Célèbre*," "*Florine*," "*L'Amour aux prises avec le Monde*," "*Le Suicide*," "*L'Amant Sauvé et Perdu*," and "*Le Triomphe du Mari*;" five of the installments are untitled.

1st edition: in *Une fille d'Eve: Scène de la vie privée*, 2vos. (Paris, Hyppolite Souverain, August 1839); this edition also contains *Massimilla Doni*, and commences with a collective preface to the two works by Balzac, the greater part of which can be found in Appendix II.

2nd edition: in *La Comédie humaine: Scènes de la vie privée*, Vol. 2 of 17 (Paris, Furne, September 1842).

Sequence: The Furne edition places this work in the 12th position, the Pléiade in the 14th.

Une fille d'Ève is an autobiographically inspired piece that may have some of its origins in Balzac's illicit romance with the Countess Sarah Guidoboni-Visconti (née Lovell), an Englishwoman married to a disinterested Italian count, with whom he may have had an illegitimate son, Lionel Richard. However, the boy shared his forename with the Comte de Bonneval, another man with whom the Countess had had an affair.

239   the Tre Monasteri: Via Trei Monasteri was the address of Contessa Clara Maffei's famous salon in Milan (see note to page 175).

239   *one of the lovely figures conceived by Carlo Dolci . . . or Allori*: Carlo Dolci (1616-1686) was a Florentine painter of religious subjects in the late baroque style; Allori is either Angelo Allori, better known as Bronzino; Alessandro Allori (1535-1607), his adopted son and pupil; or Cristofano Allori (1577-1621), the son of Alessandro. All are Florentine painters of the Mannerist school; Balzac is probably referring to one of the latter two.

241   *the Rue Neuve-des-Mathurins*: Parisian street located in what was then the Place-Vendôme quarter of the old 1st arrondissement, named for the Mathurins, a religious order of Trinitarian friars who owned land that ran alongside it. In *Les Paysans*, Balzac places a mansion belonging to General de Montcornet on this street. George Sand, a close friend of Balzac's, lived here in 1823 at No. 56, the Hôtel Florence, today known as the Hôtel George Sand.

242   *a Peer of France after the Revolution of July*: see notes to page 161, *Monsieur de Listomère* and 183, *Revolution of 1830*.

243   *a gloomy mansion in the Marais*: see note to page 3, *the Marais*.

244   *Cuvier*: As a young man, Balzac attended at least one of Cuvier's lectures at the Natural History Museum in Paris and was so impressed after hearing him speak that, along with Napoléon and Irish politician Daniel O'Connell, he considered the naturalist to be one of the three greatest men who had ever lived (Balzac himself hoped to become the fourth). Cuvier is mentioned frequently throughout the *Comédie*.

       the Lettres Édifiantes *and Noël's* Leçons de Littérature: The *Lettres édifiantes et curieuses* (1702-1776) was a collection of letters written by Jesuit missionaries who were stationed in distant and exotic locations such as China, India, and the Americas.

The *Leçons françaises de littérature et de morale* (1804) was an anthology of prose and verse from the 17th and 18th centuries compiled by French politician François Noël (1756-1841); the selections it contains are today considered to be rather undistinguished.

Fénelon's Télémaque: *Les Aventures de Télémaque* (1699) was a didactic novel written by the French archbishop and theologian in which Telemachus, the son of Ulysses, is guided by the goddess Minerva (in the guise of his tutor Mentor) in the ways of virtue and good governance. The book was written for the benefit of Fénelon's pupil, the young Louis de France, the Duke of Burgundy (1682-1712), and was seen as a rebuke to his father, Louis XIV, who, among others, saw the work as seditious.

245 *Marie Alacoque*: a French Catholic nun and saint of the 17th century who claimed to have visions of the Sacred Heart of Jesus: a symbol of love and sacrifice.

246 *the* Quotidienne . . . *the* Ami de la Religion: for the former, see note to page 142, *the* Quotidienne. *L'Ami de la Religion et du roi: journal ecclésiastique, politique et littéraire* was, as its name might suggest, an ultramontanist and ultraroyalist periodical. Founded at the beginning of the Restoration (see note to page 21, *The Bourbons*), it quickly became the most important Catholic journal in France. The paper appeared biweekly, and generally contained accounts of missionary activity as well as lists of books considered antithetical to the teachings of the Church. Becoming somewhat more liberal over time, the paper went into decline during the 1840s, and appears to have ceased publication in 1862.

247 *Anspach:* Ansbach, a city of western Bavaria situated near the Franconian Rezat, a tributary of the Main River.

248   vergis mein nicht: *vergissmeinnicht,* German for "forget-me-not."

      the lamented Saint-Martin . . ., etc.: presumably Claude de Saint-Martin (1743-1803), "*le philosophe inconnu,*" as he was known, was a French philosopher and mystic of the Iluminist school, whose doctrines were a mix of Gnosticism, Neoplatonism, and Swedenborgianism. Balzac became familiar with Saint-Martin through works contained in his mother's library, and may have learned more about the philosopher from eclecticist Victor Cousin while attending his lectures at the Sorbonne. *Séraphîta,* appearing much later in the *Comédie,* is greatly influenced by Saint-Martin's thought. The source of the quote attributed to him is not known.

249   *Hummel*: Johann Nepomuk Hummel (1778-1837), a German pianst and composer who studied with Mozart, Haydn, and Salieri.

253   *Rita-Christina*: conjoined twins, each supposedly of opposite temperaments—one happy, the other sad—born in Sardinia in 1829. They were brought to Paris by their desperately poor parents, who wanted to exhibit them in the hopes of making money, but shows of that sort had been made illegal, and the twins died soon thereafter.

      men who are not as old as Arnolphe much prefer a pious Agnès to a Célimène in embryo: Arnolphe is a character from Molière's comedy *L'école des femmes* (*The School for Wives*, 1662), a middle-aged gentleman who carefully arranges to have his young ward Agnès brought up in such a way that she will be incapable of being unfaithful to him as a wife and mistress. See note to page 147 for Célimène.

259   *as to Léonarde in the robbers' cave*: a character in Le Sage's *L'Histoire de Gil Blas de Santillane* (1715-1735), usually

known simply as *Gil Blas*. Léonarde is the cook for a band of highwaymen that the title character has been forced to join up with.

his fine house on the Rue Saint-Lazare: see note to page 73, *the Rue Saint-Lazare*.

261   *the Chamber of Deputies*: during the Restoration and the July Monarchy, the lower legislative house.

the Rue de Clichy: Parisian street that formed the border between what were then the old 1st and 2nd arrondissements, named for the suburb to which it still leads. As implied, it was the site of a debtor's prison.

262   *as in the case of Martignac*: Jean Baptiste Gay, Vicomte de Martignac (1778-1832), was a moderate royalist statesman. As Prime Minister of France under Charles X from 1828-9, he tried to steer a middle course between right and left, but was ultimately ineffective. He was succeeded by the reactionary Prince de Polignac (1780-1847).

265   *the Rue du Rocher*: extant Parisian street located in what was then the Roule quarter of the old 1st arrondissement.

266   *the romance of* Astrée: *Astræa* or *L'Astrée* (1607-1628) by Honoré d'Urfé (1568-1625) is a pastoral romance set in 5th century Gaul concerning the heroine of the title and her troubled relationship with the devoted but misunderstood Céladon.

268   *as Rivarol did upon reading Florian*, etc.: Antoine de Rivarol (1753-1801) was a French epigrammatist notorious for attacking and ridiculing many of the popular writers of his day, Jean-Pierre Claris de Florian (see note to page 134, *Florian*) being one of his many literary targets. "The wolf in the sheepfold" quote that Balzac frequently makes reference to cannot be directly

attributed to Rivarol, however there is an anecdote concerning the two along the same lines: "It is said that Rivarol once overtook Florian, who was walking in front of him, a manuscript half sticking out of his pocket, and exclaimed: 'Ah, Monsieur, it would be a temptation to rob you if we did not know you.'"

269   *the role . . . which Giulia Grisi played . . . in the chorus at La Scala*: for Giulia Grisi see note to page 210, *Grisi*; La Scala is a famous Milanese opera house.

270   *The Faubourg Saint-Germain*: see note to page 88.

274   *those dandified adulators of the Middle Ages, jocularly called Young France*: a creative group espousing romanticism, centered around the authors Pétrus Borel, Gautier, and Nerval. They favored unconventional fashion and promoted the concept of "art for art's sake".

276   *He attracts attention by his dishevelment, if we may borrow from Molière the word used by Éliante to describe the* malpropre sur soi: Éliante is a character from *Le Misanthrope*; the lines Balzac is referring to can be found in Act 2, Scene 5 of the play:

> *La malpropre sur soi, de peu d'attraits chargée*
> *Et mise sous le nom de beauté négligée*

Henry Baker and James Miller's venerable prose translation of *The Misanthrope* (1755) has these lines as follows:

> the naturally Slattern who has few Charms, is plac'd under the Name of a negligent Beauty

the attitude made famous by Girodet's portrait of Monsieur de Chateaubriand: Anne-Louis Girodet de Roussy-Trioson (1767-1824) was a French Romantic painter renowned for his portraits of Napoléon and Chateaubriand (see Plate XXIV for his picture of the latter); Girodet was Balzac's favorite painter, and he is mentioned frequently throughout the *Comédie*.

278   *the Théâtre-Français*: known variously as the Théâtre-Nautique, the Théâtre de la République, La maison de Molière, and most commonly as the Comédie-Française, the Théâtre Français was founded by Louis XIV in 1680. Since 1799 it has been housed in the Salle Richelieu, a hall located next to the Palais-Royal (see note to page 74) in the old 2nd arrondissement.

    a magnificent romantic play after the style of Pinto . . . *the Odéon*: *Pinto ou la Journée d'une conspiration* (1800) is the title of a historical comedy by French poet and dramatist Népomucène Lemercier (1771-1840) concerning the Portuguese Revolution of 1640.

    The Odéon is a theater dating to 1782, located in what was then the École-de-Médecine quarter of the old 11th arrondissement. It occupied a series of three buildings, the last of which remains in use to this day.

279   *he might have struck his hand against his brow after the manner of André de Chénier*: the martyred French poet is famously depicted in this pose in a painting by Charles Müller (1815-1892) entitled *L'appel des dernières victimes de la Terreur à la prison Saint-Lazare le 7-9 Thermidor an II* (see Plate XXV).

    the troubles from 1830 to 1833: a reference to the July Revolution, and perhaps also to other revolutionary activity taking place throughout Europe during those years in Belgium, Poland, Italy, and Germany. "When France sneezes, Europe catches cold," as Metternich said.

    Saint-Simonism: Saint-Simonianism, a philosophy named for the French economist and philosopher, which envisioned a society of equals centered around science and industry rather than traditional authority.

280   *to pose as an Alceste while adopting the methods of a Philinte*: for the former, see note to page 147. Philinte is another character from *Le Misanthrope*, a friend of Alceste's, and his opposite, who values social graces.

Plate XXV
André Chénier

Plate XXVI
Charles Rivière Dufresny

280   *he leaps the Eurotas*: the Eurotas is a Greek river located in the Peloponnese named for a Spartan hero. Balzac may be making reference to a couplet from the second canto of Byron's "Childe Harold's Pilgrimage:"

> O, who that gallant spirit shall resume,
> Leap from Eurotas' banks, and call thee from the
>   tomb?

284   *the Jardin-des-Plantes . . . the famous Mountains of the Moon*: the former is the main botanical garden in France, dating to 1626, which also includes a small zoo, originally made up of animals transferred from the Royal Menagerie at Versailles. Notably, the first giraffe in France was displayed there in 1827; the latter is the name given by the Ancient Greeks to an unspecified mountain range in east Africa where the source of the Nile was thought to be located.

285   *Rastignac took them to Véry's*: Chez Véry, "the palace of all restaurants," as it was known, located in the Palais-Royal. Balzac dined here on a number of occasions, always tipping generously and then sending the bill to his publisher. An anecdote attached to this establishment relates how a Prussian general ordered a cup of coffee "from which no Frenchman had drunk," and was brought his drink in a chamber pot.

   a Laura: see note to page 220, *Petrarch's chaste passion*.

286   *the prayer of* Moïse: see note to page 142, Mosè.

   disinvoltura: Italian, "ease of manner."

290   *the Council of State*: see note to page 40.

   Talleyrand: see note to page 137, *Talleyrand*.

291   *the deliciously soft effect of Lawrence's paintings*: Thomas Lawrence (1769–1830), an English portraitist.

292   *the Rue Basse-du-Rempart*: Parisian street that was located in the Place Vendôme quarter of the old 1st arrondissement.

293   *Talma*: see note to page 76.

294   *Decamps . . . a* bénitier *presented by Antonin Moine . . . Eugène Devéria . . . Louis Boulanger . . . letter from Lord Byron to Caroline . . . Elschoët*: Alexandre-Gabriel Decamps (1803-1860), Eugène Devéria (1805-1865), and Louis Boulanger (1806-1865) were French Romantic painters; Boulanger painted a portrait of Balzac in 1836. Antonin-Marie Moine (1796-1849) was a French Romantic sculptor; a *bénitier* is a vessel for holy water. Lady Caroline Lamb (1785-1828) was a novelist who had a brief affair with Lord Byron in 1812 and coined the phrase "mad, bad, and dangerous to know" in describing him. For Elschoët, see note to page 184, *Elschoët*.

    A Boule clock: a clock encased in wood marquetry containing inlaid brass and tortoiseshell; the style's name is derived from André Charles Boulle (1642-1732), a French cabinetmaker who was a master of the technique.

296   *the . . . wilful head of Poppaea*: Poppaea Sabina (30-65), the wife of Nero.

301   *Saint-Genest, a canonized actor, who fulfilled his religious duties and wore a hair shirt*: a 3rd century Roman actor who converted to Christianity onstage and was afterwards martyred; his story was the subject of several French plays.

302   *Lekain, Baron, Contat, Clairon, Champmeslé*: Lekain was stage name of French actor Henri Louis Cain (1728-1778); Michel Baron (1653-1729) was a French actor and playwright and a protégé of Molière; Louise Contat (1760-1813), La Clairon (1723-1803), whose real

name was Clair Josèphe Hippolyte Leris, and Marie Champmeslé (1642-1698) were French actresses.

303   *as we owed Mars to Monvel and Andrieux*: Mademoiselle Mars was the stage name of Anne Francoise Hyppolyte Boutet (1779-1847), an accomplished actress of the Comédie-Française; the actor and playwright who went by the name Monvel (Jacques Marie Boutet, 1745-1812) was her father. François Guillaume Jean Stanislaus Andrieux (1759-1833) was a French lawyer, poet, playwright, and a member of the French Academy. His best known play is the comedy *Les Étourdis* (1787). Andrieux was asked to review the manuscript of Balzac's first play *Cromwell* (1819), on which the elder man of letters wrote: "The author should do anything he likes, but not literature."

304   *the political situation in France in 1834 . . . the pure Republicans, the Republicans who would have a presidency, the Republicans without a republic . . .*, etc.: this passage provides an interesting window into the many-hued political spectrum of the July Monarchy (see note to page 183, *the Revolution of 1830*) in 1834, a year in which a legislative election for the Chamber of Deputies (see note to page 261, *the Chamber of Deputies*) took place. It is important to note that none of the various "sides" mentioned here were true political parties, but rather groupings of like-minded deputies that would generally coalesce around certain individuals.

The Republicans, those who followed the ideals of the French Revolution, were subjected to a great deal of repression during this period, particularly after the Second Canute Revolt, an uprising of silk workers, which began in Lyons in April 1834 and quickly spread to other cities. The uprising was blunted, and the election of 21 June resulted in the Republicans being essentially shut out of the government (rather ironically, Citizen King Louis-Philippe had agreed to rule under the historically Republican tricolor flag as part of his compromise regime, sometimes referred to as "*le juste milieu*").

Balzac's reference to the *Constitutionnels* perhaps betrays a somewhat incomplete knowledge of the politics of his day. This party, as its name may suggest, supported a constitutional monarchy, and appears to have been active during parts of the Revolution and the Restoration, but not during the July Monarchy. Moderate constitutional monarchists, who opposed the extremes of both the aristocracy and the left, would have been known as Orléanists.

Ministerialists were those who occupied the Center-right portion of the spectrum. The aristocratic, legitimist, *Henriquinquiste*, and Carlist Right were essentially synonyms for those who supported the old Bourbon monarchy. Carlists, specifically, favored Charles X, but since he and his son had abdicated, Salic Law dictated that the King's grandson, Henri d'Artois (1820-1883), known to French legitimists as Henry V (hence *Henriquinquiste*), was the rightful heir to the throne. However, Henri was only 10 years old at the time of the July Revolution, and so was passed over in favor of Louis-Philippe.

The Party of Resistance and the Party of Movement, as they have been traditionally known, were Orléanist "factions" embodying two tendencies: the former wished to leave the balance of power as it stood, the latter wanted to expand suffrage and increase the power of the Chamber of Deputies in relation to the King.

306   *Keeper of the Seals*: see note to page 65.

  Master of Requests: a mid-level member of the Conseil d'État (see note to page 290, *the Council of State*).

307   *the little hills of King David*: Psalms 114:4.

310   *the Passage Sandrié*: passage that was located in the Place Vendôme quarter of the old 1st arrondissement.

  a ghastly bond which a duchess severed . . . causing Adrienne Lecouvreur to be poisoned: Maria Karolina Sobieska,

Duchess of Bouillon (1697-1740), was suspected of poisoning the actress Adrienne Lecouvreur (1692-1730), her rival for the love of the Marshall Maurice de Saxe (1696-1750).

the peasant in La Fontaine's fable . . . , etc.: perhaps Balzac is thinking of the French fabulist's fable *The Ant and the Grasshopper*.

313   *the yellow gloves he wore in obedience to the decree then in force*: at that time kid gloves were a mark of the aristocracy and may also have been worn to show support for Charles X. *Gants jaunes* was also a nickname given to dandies and so-called "moderate bourgeois republicans."

320   *This frenzy*, à la Roland: in Aristo's *Orlando Furioso* (1532), the mythicized paladin becomes mad with grief when his beloved Angelica runs away with the injured Saracen Medoro. Roland then goes on a killing spree before his sanity is brough back from the moon in a bottle by the English crusader Astolfo.

321   *the Faubourg Saint-Honoré*: quarter of the old 4th arrondissement.

      a stylish cabriolet . . . and the tiger to go with it: see note to page 29.

322   *"Vous vous y mettrez, madame, dit de Marsay, et vous serez alors doublement notre ennemie."* in the original French.

324   *the Bois de Boulogne*: see note to page 198.

330   *Vanity—without which love is very weak, says Champfort*: Sébastien-Roch Nicolas de Chamfort (1741-1794) was a French dramatist and essayist; the quote made reference to, in full is: *Otez l'amour-propre de l'amour, il en reste trop peu de choses. Une fois purgé de vanité, c'est un convalescent affaibli, qui peut à peine se traîner* (Take away

461

love's pride, and little remains. Once purged of vanity, love is a weakened convalescent which can scarcely drag itself about).

331   *a front seat at the Gymnase*: founded in 1820 by French playwright Delestre-Poirson (1790-1859), the Théâtre du Gymnase began as a theater for students of the Conservatoire National Supérieur d'Art Dramatique, but over time expanded its repertoire to include plays by established writers. After the July Revolution of 1830, it was known as the Gymnase Dramatique.

   I feel the same way about them that Louis XIV felt about Teniers's pictures: of David Teniers the Younger's (1610-1690) works, at least one of which depicted costumed apes, the King is said to have exclaimed: "*Otez-nous ces magots!*" ("Take away these baboons!").

332   *the* Moniteur: *Le Moniteur Universel*, sometimes known as the *Gazette Nationale*, was a moderate and highly influential daily newspaper, founded by French writer Charles-Joseph Pancoucke (1736-1798) on 24 November 1789, which published the texts of the debates of the National Assembly. Under the Consulate it became the official government newspaper, replacing political news with that of the Grande Armée. The focus shifted back to the debates during the July Monarchy, but the paper remained under government control.

333   *the Cross of the Legion of Honor*: see note to page 22, *a ribbon and cross*.

334   *Doctrinaires*: a party active during the Restoration that endeavored to harmonize the liberties gained under the Revolution with royal power in the form of a constitutional monarchy.

335   *a certain* quart d'heure de Rabelais: *le mauvais quart-d'heure de Rabelais* or "Rabelais's disagreeable quarter of an hour" is an expression that refers to the period of

time between the end of a meal at a restaurant and the presenting of the bill, especially when the guest does not have enough money to pay. When the famous satirist once found himself in this position, as the story goes, he was able to extricate himself by declaring his intent to poison the King; when hauled in front of the monarch, Rabelais explained his ruse and was allowed to go free.

336 *the Rue Pigalle*: Parisian street that was located in the Chaussée-d'Antin quarter of the old 2nd arrondissement, known variously as the Rue Royale, the Rue de la République, Rue de l'An Huit, and today as the Rue Jean-Baptiste-Pigalle, named for the French sculptor.

340 *Fieschi's exploit*: Giuseppe Fieschi (1790-1836) was a Corsican soldier and the would-be assassin of King Louis-Philippe. His *machine infernale* was composed of twenty or twenty-five gun barrels, attached to a frame, which could be triggered simultaneously. It was fired from the window of a house on the Boulevard du Temple on 28 July 1835, slightly injuring the King and members of his entourage, but killing the eminent Marshal Mortier. Eighteen bystanders were also killed and dozens wounded, including Fieschi himself. He and his accomplices were promptly arrested, tried, and guillotined.

342 *his little bit of Réveillon wallpaper*: Jean-Baptiste Réveillon (1725-1811) was a French businessman who made his fortune by importing fashionable wallpaper from England before eventually manufacturing his own. His meeting with Étienne Montgolfier led to a collaboration on the construction of the envelope of the first hot air balloon, which was launched from Réveillon's garden on 12 September 1783. On 28 April 1789, Réveillon's factory was the scene of a riot when one of his speeches was misunderstood as advocating lower wages for his workers.

344 *the* Moi! *of Medea*: an exchange from Corneille's *Médée* (1635). The line that Balzac refers to is from Act I Scene V:

NÉRINE (Medea's maidservant):
Your country hates you, your husband is faithless;
In such a great reverse what remains to you?

MÉDÉE
Myself!
Myself, I say, and that is enough.

348 *the Rue Feydeau*: an extant Parisian street located in what was then the Feydeau quarter of the old 2nd arrondissement. Originally known as the Rue Neuve-des-Fossés-Montmartre, its name was changed in 1713 to honor an ancient noble family; it has no connection to the French playwright Georges Feydeau as one might initially suppose.

351 *the Rue du Mail*: an extant Parisian street dating to the 17th century that was located in the Mail quarter of the old 3rd arrondissement.

355 *the Petite Rue de Nevers . . . the Quai Conti*: the Rue de Nevers (the location of the *Petite* Rue de Nevers is not entirely clear, though it was, or is, likely nearby) is an extant Parisian street located in what was then the Monnaie quarter of the old 10th arrondissement; the quay, which runs alongside the Seine, lies adjacent to the Rue de Nevers, and is also still in existence. The street takes its name from the Hôtel de Nevers, which itself is named for Louis IV de Gonzague-Nevers (1539-1595), an Italian Prince.

358 *from the Pont Neuf to the hill of Chaillot*: the Pont Neuf is a bridge that crosses over the western tip of the Île de la Cité, connecting Paris's Left and Right Banks; Chaillot is a suburb to the west of the city.

359   *the Graces*: Aglaea, Euphrosyne, and Thalia–Greek god-
desses personifying Splendor, Mirth, and Good Cheer
respectively.

362   *I call him Mirr, to clorivy our crate Hoffmann of Perlin*:
a reference to the German fantasist's unfinished final novel entitled, in full: *Lebens-Ansichten des Katers
Murr nebst fragmentarischer Biographie des Kapellmeisters
Johannes Kreisler in zufälligen Makulaturblättern* (*The
Life And Opinions of the Tomcat Murr Together with a
Fragmentary Biography of Kappelmeister Johannes Kreisler
on Random Sheets of Waste Paper*, 1819-21), a work in the
same vein as Sterne's *Tristram Shandy*. Hoffmann's real-
life pet (and surrogate child) provided the inspiration
for the book's comical narrator: a tomcat who takes an
interest in his master's writing desk, and consequently teaches himself to read and write before deciding to
pen his autobiography. Murr unwittingly uses pages
torn from one of the books (a biography of the afore-
mentioned Kapellmeister) in his master's library for his
writing paper, and the two texts become intermingled
and printed in a single volume.

369   la Légitimité: the belief that the rule of Louis-Philippe
was in violation of the traditional rules of royal succession. See note to page 183, *the Revolution of 1830,* etc.

379   *This is what they kill chickens with*: "*C'est avec ça qu'on
égorge les poulets!*" In French, "*les poulets*" can mean
"love letters" as well as "chickens."

381   *O my ideal, blue flower, with the heart of gold*, etc.: a passage from *Mademoiselle de Maupin* (1836) by Théophile
Gautier, a novel based upon the real life antics of Julie
d'Aubigny (1670-1707), a cross-dressing swordswom-
an. Despite its racy subject matter, the book is actually
more famous for its preface, a manifesto advocating
"art for art's sake."

    An earlier version of *Un Fille d'Ève* has Gautier men-
tioned by name in the text, but Balzac later decided to

refer to his friend only as "one of the most noteworthy poets of our day", letting the quote speak for itself.

The blue flower is a traditional symbol of Romanticism, first used by the German poet Novalis.

382   *Virgin of the Sun in Peru*: a reference to *La Périchole, ou La Vierge du soleil* (1835), a one act comedy by Emmanuel Théaulon (1787-1841), a French playwright who also adapted Balzac's *Le Père Goriot* for the stage. As *La Périchole* is set in Peru, the play perhaps takes its subtitle from a work by French writer Françoise de Graffigny (1695-1758), *Lettres d'une Péruvienne* (*Letters of a Peruvian Woman*, 1747), whose main character is the kidnapped Incan Princess Zilla, also known as the Virgin of the Sun.

The peace at any price *policy*: "*La paix à tout prix,*" a political slogan that, in general, summed up the foreign policy of Louis-Philippe. This approach was exercised not for lack of nationalistic or militaristic sentiment, but due to the fact that the forced abdication of Charles X in 1830 had caused alarm throughout Europe, and the King of the French took great pains to reassure his fellow monarchs that France no longer wished to antagonize its neighbors with any expansionist activity or to undermine their power with any form of renewed revolutionary fervor.

383   *Les Jardies*: the name Balzac gave to his makeshift country estate. Having grown weary of Paris, Balzac purchased some land in the vicinity of Sèvres to the west of the city towards the end of 1837 and proceeded to commission the building of a "Hermit's villa" upon the scenic hillside he had chosen for his new home. It was an eccentric dwelling described by biographer Frederick Lawton: "Three rooms, one over another, composed the main building. The ground floor served as drawing room; above it was the anchoret's bedroom; and the top story was used as a study . . . The whole stood in its own grounds, fenced in with walls, half of

which, being situated on the steepest portion of the declivity, persisted in tumbling. One curious feature of the house was its outside staircase . . . being a sort of broad ladder."

The cost of building and maintaining the villa was well beyond his means, and in 1840 the property was seized by creditors. Among the more notable of Balzac's works that were completed during this period were the first and second parts of *Lost Illusions*, and *The Firm of Nucingen*.

Appendix I:
"The Affair of the Diamond" Notes

Charles Rivière Dufresny (1648-1724), the author of *Amusemens sérieux et comiques d'un Siamois* (*The Serious and Comical Amusements of a Siamese Traveller*, 1699), was a French dramatist. On the basis of his claim of descent from one of Henri IV's mistresses, he was made a valet de chambre by Louis XIV, who also put him in charge of designing the royal gardens. A spendthrift by nature, he was obliged to sell his royal offices to pay his debts. After leaving the royal court in Versailles, he went to live in Paris where he turned his talents to the writing of comic dramas in partnership with the significantly more talented playwright Jean-François Regnard (1655-1709). For a time he also served as the director of the *Mercure Gallant*, a French review.

Although he is often described primarily as being a comic dramatist, his plays are not generally considered memorable; it is instead his *Amusements*, a prose work perhaps best described as a collection of intertwined satirical fictions, that he is now remembered for, perhaps in large part because they were the inspiration for Montesquieu's *Persian Letters* (1721).

Appendix II:
Balzac's Preface to *A Daughter of Eve* Notes

The preface Balzac wrote to the Souverain edition of *A Daughter of Eve*, though not included as part of the Furne edition, is generally considered to be more noteworthy than the novel itself.

399   *This sketch was previously advertised by the Revue de Paris
       . . . Du Cerceau . . . the Théâtre des Variétés . . .*, etc.: the
       Revue de Paris was a literary journal founded by French
       journalist and politician Louis-Désiré Véron (1798-
       1867) in 1829; Balzac's *Père Goriot* was serialized in its
       pages beginning in December 1834, and several of the
       author's other works also made their first appearance
       there.

       For the Théâtre des Variétés, see note to page 199, *the
       Variétés*.

       An endnote in Nicole Cazauran's *Catherine de Médicis
       et son temps dans La Comédie Humaine* (1976) provides
       some explanation for this rather enigmatic statement:
       Balzac is misremembering (perhaps intentionally) the
       title of *La Nouvelle Eve*, a story by Jean-Antoine du
       Cerceau (1670-1730), an 18th century author whom he
       was possibly confusing with his son, Jacques Androuet
       du Cerceau, evidently a contemporary. Furthermore,
       the vaudeville Balzac claims to have seen advertised,
       according to Bourdin and Loubinoux's *La scène bâ-
       tarde: entre Lumières et romantisme* (2004), was indeed
       also titled *Une Fille d'Ève*, but had been written in
       1833 by Dumanoir and Pillet, not by any member of
       the Du Cerceau family. It is unclear exactly why this
       should have "kept the author from carrying on with
       this work;" it seems likely that Balzac is simply fab-
       ricating an excuse for a missed deadline. The title of
       Une Fille d'Ève can be found in some of Balzac's notes
       dating to 1831, and the fact that it shares a name with
       a vaudeville whose story is completely different from
       that of the novel would seem to be nothing more than
       a coincidence.

       Le Siècle, a daily newspaper founded by French jour-
       nalist Armand Dutacq (1810-1856) in 1836 that was
       politically aligned with the constitutional monarchy
       of Louis-Philippe.

403   *the Boulevard des Italiens*: see note to page 178.

405   *the Rue du Tourniquet-Saint-Jean*: see note to page 3, *The Rue du Tourniquet-Saint-Jean*.

406   *Petronius's satire*: The *Satyricon* (1st century, a.d.), a lengthy satirical prose work written in Latin, now surviving only in fragments, which details the many misadventures of Encolpius, a former gladiator, and his servant Giton.

407   La Torpille . . ., etc.: *La Torpille* was the title Balzac originally gave to the work that would in time become *Splendeurs et misères des courtisanes*; the passage quoted here remains unchanged in the final version, and can be found in the first part of the novel. The *Torpille* or "torpedo" of the title is the nickname given to the prostitute Esther Van Gobseck (referring in this case to the electric ray fish rather than the underwater projectile) due to her reputation for bringing misfortune down upon her many lovers.

Map of the Former
Arrondissements of Paris
c.1795-1859

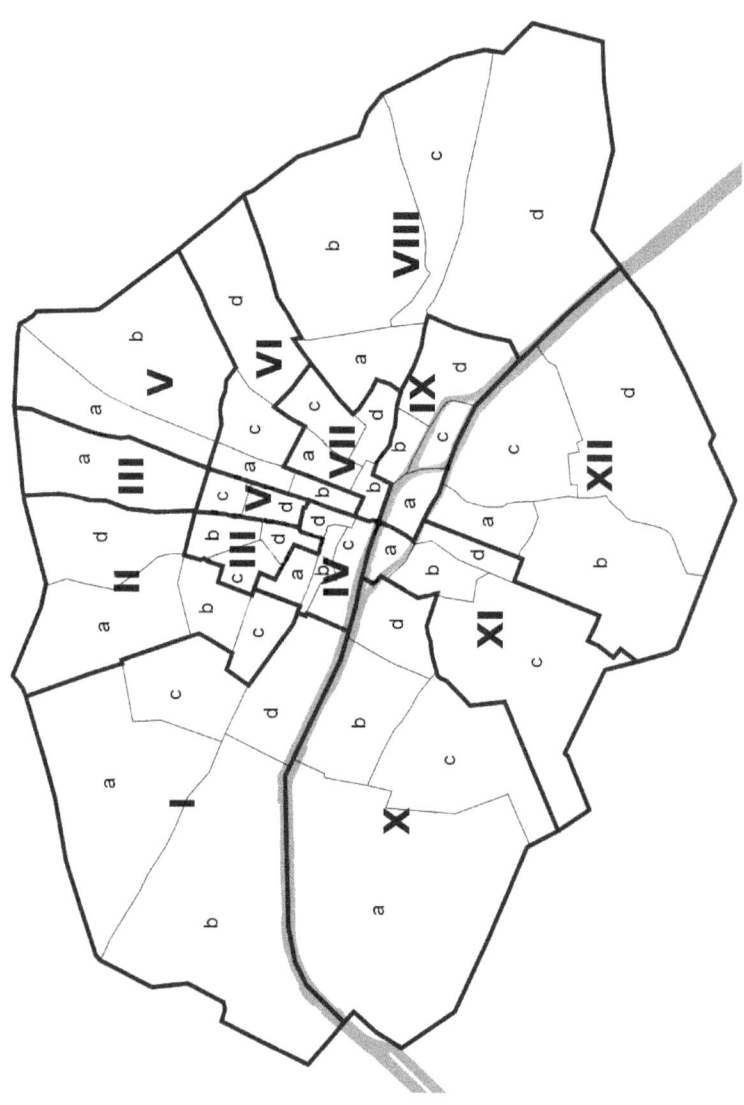

Source: Wikipedia
fr.wikipedia.org/wiki/Anciens_arrondissements_de_Paris

Arrondissement
Quartiers

I	a. Roule	VII	a. Sainte-Avoye
	b. Champs-Élysées		b. Arcis
	c. Place-Vendôme		c. Mont-de-Piété
	d. Tuileries		d. Marché-Saint-Jean
II	a. Chaussée-d'Antin	VIII	a. Marais
	b. Feydeau		b. Popincourt
	c. Palais-Royal		c. Faubourg-Saint-Antoine
	d. Faubourg-Montmartre		d. Quinze-Vingts
II	a. Faubourg-Poissonnière	IX	a. Cité
	b. Montmartre		b. Hôtel-de-Ville
	c. Mail		c. Île-Saint-Louis
	d. Saint-Eustache		d. Arsenal
IV	a. Banque	X	a. Invalides
	b. Saint-Honoré		b. Faubourg-Saint-Germain
	c. Louvre		c. Saint-Thomas-d'Aquin
	d. Marchés		d. Monnaie
V	a. Faubourg-Saint-Denis	XI	a. Palais-de-Justice
	b. Porte-Saint-Martin		b. École-de-Médecine
	c. Bonne-Nouvelle		c. Luxembourg
	d. Bon-Conseil		d. Sorbonne
VI	a. Porte-Saint-Denis	XII	a. Saint-Jacques
	b. Lombards		b. Observatoire
	c. Saint-Martin-des-Champs		c. Jardins-du-Roi
	d. Temple		d. Saint-Marcel

Balzac's Paris no longer exists, and has not existed for more than 150 years. The city as the author knew it stood from 1795 until the 1850s, after which it was extensively renovated by Baron Haussmann at the direction of Napoléon III.

A more detailed map can be found at:
commons.wikimedia.org/wiki/File:Plan_de_la_ville_de_Paris_divisé_en_12_arrondissements,_en_48_quartiers_indiquant_tous_les_changemens_faits_et_projetés.jpg

473

Selected Bibliography
and Further Reading

The French source texts from the Corrected Furne edition of Balzac's works, the versions used by Clara Bell and George Burnham Ives, the translators of the works in this volume, can be found at the following URLs:

A Second Home (*Une Double Famille*)
archive.org/stream/oeuvrescompl01balz#page/n267/mode/2up

Domestic Peace (*La Paix du Ménage*)
archive.org/stream/oeuvrescompl01balz#page/316/mode/2up

Madame Firmiani
archive.org/stream/oeuvrescompl01balz#page/230/mode/2up

A Study of Woman (*Étude de Femme*)
archive.org/stream/oeuvrescompl01balz#page/396/mode/2up

The Imaginary Mistress (*La Fausse Maîtresse*)
archive.org/stream/oeuvrescompl01balz#page/350/mode/2up

A Daughter of Eve (*Une Fille d'Ève*)
archive.org/stream/oeuvrescomp02balz#page/n217/mode/2up

The unrevised English translations by Bell and Ives can be found at the following URLs:

A Second Home
archive.org/stream/comdiehumainee22balzuoft#page/340

Domestic Peace (translated as *Peace in the House*)
archive.org/stream/comdiehumainee16balzuoft#page/80

The Imaginary Mistress
archive.org/stream/comdiehumainee16balzuoft#page/122

Madame Firmiani
archive.org/stream/comdiehumainee20balzuoft#page/254

A Daughter of Eve
archive.org/stream/honoredebalzacn16balziala#page/192

Selected Bibliography and Further Reading

Balzac, Honoré de: *Une Fille d'Ève: Scène de la Vie Privée* (Hippolyte Souverain, 1839).

Beik, Paul H.: *Louis Philippe and the July Monarchy* (D. Van Nostrand Company, Inc., 1965).

Classe, Olive (ed.): *Encylopedia of Literary Translation into English* (Fitzroy Dearborn Publishers, 2000) ISBN-10: 1884964362.

Collingham, H.A.C. & R.S. Alexander (ed.): *The July Monarchy: A Political History of France, 1830-1848* (Longman, 1988) ISBN-10: 0582021863.

Dufresny, Charles Rivière: *Oeuvres de Monsieur Rivière Dufresny*, T4 (Briasson, 1747).

Floyd, Juanita Helm: *Women in the Life of Balzac* (Holt, Rinehart & Winston, 1921).

Fournier, Édouard: *Énigmes des Rues de Paris* (E. Dentu, 1860).

France, Peter (ed.): *The New Oxford Companion to Literature in French* (Oxford University Press, 1995) ISBN-10: 0198661258.

France, Peter (ed.): *The Oxford Guide to Literature in English Translation* (Oxford University Press, 2000) ISBN-10: 0198183593.

Gerson, Noel B.: *The Prodigal Genius: The Life and Times of Honoré de Balzac* (Doubleday, 1972).

Keim, Albert & Louis Lumet: *Honoré de Balzac* (Frederick A. Stokes Company, 1914).

Lawton, Frederick: *Balzac* (Grant Richards Ltd.; Wessels & Bissell Co., 1910).

Lazare, Félix & Louis Lazare: *Dictionnaire Administratif et Historique Des Rues de Paris et de Ses Monuments* (F. Lazare, 1844).

Maurois, André: *Prometheus: The Life of Balzac* (Harper & Row, 1965).

Newman, Edgar Leon & Robert Lawrence Simpson (eds.): *Historical Dictionary of France from the 1815 Restoration to the Second Empire* (Greenwood Press, 1987) ISBN-10: 0313227519.

Raser, George B.: *Guide to Balzac's Paris: An Analytical Subject Index* (Imprimerie de France, 1964).

—————————.: *The Heart of Balzac's Paris: A Rationale of Condition* (Imprimerie de France, 1970).

Robb, Graham: *Balzac: A Life* (W.W. Norton & Co., Inc., 1994) ISBN-10: 0393036790.

Sandars, Mary F.: *Honoré de Balzac: His Life and Writings* (Stanley Paul & Co., 1904?).

Schuerewegen, Franc: "Une fille d'Eve"
www.v1.paris.fr/commun/v2asp/musees/balzac/furne/notices/fille_deve.htm

Terrasse-Riou, Florence: "Une Double Famille"
www.v1.paris.fr/commun/v2asp/musees/balzac/furne/notices/double_famille.htm

————————: "Étude de Femme"
www.v1.paris.fr/commun/v2asp/musees/balzac/furne/notices/etude_de_femme.htm

————————: "La Fause Maîtresse"
www.v1.paris.fr/commun/v2asp/musees/balzac/furne/notices/fausse_maitresse.htm

————————: "Madame Firmiani"
www.v1.paris.fr/commun/v2asp/musees/balzac/furne/notices/madamefirmiani.htm

————————————: "La Paix du Ménage"
www.v1.paris.fr/commun/v2asp/musees/balzac/furne/
notices/paix_du_menage.htm

Wormeley, Katharine Prescott: *Balzac: A Memoir* (Little, Brown,
& Company, 1900).

Zweig, Stefan: *Balzac* (The Viking Press, 1946).